The Complete Philosophy Collection (Vol. 7)

Ecce Homo, The Antichrist, Twilight of the Idols & The Birth of Tragedy — Nietzsche's Final Polemics and Early Insights

A Modern Translation

Adapted for the Contemporary Reader

Friedrich Nietzsche

Translated by Tim Zengerink

Table of Contents

Preface - Message to the Reader

What If You Could Help Rebuild the Greatest Library in Human History?

Thousands of years ago, the Library of Alexandria stood as the crown jewel of human achievement — a sanctuary where the collected wisdom of every known civilization was gathered, preserved, and shared freely.

And then, it was lost.

Through fire, conquest, and the slow erosion of time, humanity lost not just books — but ideas, dreams, discoveries, and stories that could have changed the world forever.

Today, the Library of Alexandria lives again — and you are invited to be a part of its restoration.

Our mission is simple yet profound:

To rebuild the greatest library the world has ever known, and to translate all timeless works into every language and dialect, so that no seeker of knowledge is ever left behind again.

By joining our movement to rebuild the modern Library of Alexandria, you become part of an unprecedented mission:

- **Unlimited Access to the Greatest Audiobooks & eBooks Ever Written:**

  Instantly explore thousands of legendary works—Plato, Shakespeare, Jane Austen, Leo Tolstoy, and countless more. All instantly available to read or listen, placing a complete literary universe at your fingertips.

- **Beautiful Paperback & Deluxe Editions at Printing Cost**

  Own any title as an elegant paperback, deluxe hardcover, or stunning collectible boxset—offered to you at true printing cost, delivered straight to your door. Build your personal Library of Alexandria, crafted for beauty, built for durability, and worthy of proud display.

- **Fresh Translations for Modern Readers—in Every Language & Dialect**

  Enjoy timeless masterpieces reimagined in clear, contemporary language—no more outdated phrases or obscure references. Alongside the original versions, we're tirelessly translating these classics into every language and dialect imaginable, ensuring accessibility and understanding across cultures and generations.

- **Join a Global Renaissance of Literature & Knowledge**

  You directly support expanding our library, publishing deluxe editions at true cost, translating works into all global languages, and bringing humanity's greatest stories to people everywhere. By joining today, you're not just preserving a legacy of masterpieces; you set in motion a powerful wave of literary accessibility.

Become a Torchbearer of Knowledge.

Join us for free now at **LibraryofAlexandria.com**

Together, we will ensure that the light of human wisdom never fades again.

With gratitude and a shared love of knowledge,
The Modern Library of Alexandria Team

Visit:

www.libraryofalexandria.com

Or scan the code below:

Introduction

The Fire and the Foundation: Nietzsche's Polemics and First Vision

The Complete Philosophy Collection (Vol. 7) brings together four defining works of Friedrich Nietzsche—Ecce Homo, The Antichrist, Twilight of the Idols, and The Birth of Tragedy. Together, these texts span the arc of Nietzsche's intellectual life, from his earliest fusion of art and philosophy to his final polemics before mental collapse. They showcase the full spectrum of Nietzsche's genius: poetic, aphoristic, ironic, prophetic, and always deeply personal.

These works embody Nietzsche's mission to shatter illusions—moral, religious, philosophical, and aesthetic—and to liberate the human spirit through self-overcoming. While The Birth of Tragedy introduces his original philosophical synthesis, the later writings serve as a final reckoning. Twilight of the Idols is a concise and devastating critique of modern values. The Antichrist is a thunderous assault on Christianity. Ecce Homo is a strange, brilliant, and fiercely ironic autobiography, at once confessional and mythic.

Across these texts, Nietzsche returns to core questions: What makes life worth living? What is the value of truth? How have culture, religion, and morality shaped and distorted the human soul? And how can we create new values that affirm life instead of denying it?

This introduction offers a guide through Nietzsche's explosive prose and transformative insights. These works are not meant to be read passively—they are meant to be confronted, wrestled with, and ultimately lived.

The Early Seed: The Birth of Tragedy

The Birth of Tragedy out of the Spirit of Music (1872) was Nietzsche's first book, published when he was just twenty-eight. It is a work of aesthetic philosophy, but also of existential vision. Drawing on Greek tragedy, German music, and Schopenhauer's metaphysics, Nietzsche argues that life requires not truth, but art.

He introduces two archetypal forces: the Apollonian (order, reason, form) and the Dionysian (chaos, ecstasy, dissolution). Greek tragedy, at its height, fused these elements into a vision that did not moralize suffering but transfigured it. Through the tragic chorus and the mythic narrative, the Greeks learned to affirm life even in its darkest moments.

Nietzsche contrasts this with the later "Socratic" turn in philosophy, which valued reason and dialectic over intuition and art. He blames Socrates—and by extension, modernity—for severing thought from instinct, and culture from vitality. In his eyes, modern society has become overly Apollonian: obsessed with order, clarity, and control, but lacking depth, passion, and transcendence.

Richard Wagner, at the time Nietzsche's hero, is held up as the potential savior of culture. Nietzsche saw in Wagner's music drama a new Dionysian art form. But this enthusiasm would later turn to disappointment, as Nietzsche broke with Wagner's nationalism and religiosity.

Though later criticized for its style and speculative leaps, The Birth of Tragedy remains foundational. It introduces themes Nietzsche would return to again and again: the role of suffering, the danger of moralism, and the need to find a more primal affirmation of life.

The Hammer Speaks: Twilight of the Idols and The Antichrist

In 1888, Nietzsche wrote several works in a burst of manic brilliance. Twilight of the Idols and The Antichrist are among the most pointed and provocative. They aim to destroy what Nietzsche called "idols"—false ideals that have dominated Western thought.

Twilight of the Idols (subtitled How to Philosophize with a Hammer) is a compact summary of Nietzsche's philosophy and a demolition of conventional morality. Structured as a series of aphoristic chapters, it attacks:

- Socratic rationalism, which Nietzsche sees as the death of instinct.
- Christianity, for glorifying weakness and suffering.
- German culture, for mediocrity and moral hypocrisy.
- Philosophers like Kant and Schopenhauer, for denying life in favor of abstract ideals.

He introduces ideas such as the "revaluation of all values," the physiology of morality, and the need for psychological honesty. The "hammer" is not a sledgehammer of destruction, but a tuning fork: it taps on ideas to see which ring hollow.

The Antichrist is even more incendiary. It is not merely anti-Christian—it is a passionate critique of Christian morality, metaphysics, and psychology. Nietzsche sees Christianity as the inversion of natural values. Where noble morality celebrates strength, beauty, and vitality, Christianity celebrates meekness, guilt, and self-denial. He argues that Christianity arose from ressentiment—the revenge of the weak against the strong.

Nietzsche presents Jesus not as a moral teacher, but as a spiritual rebel whose message was distorted by Paul and institutionalized into dogma. The Church, he claims, has corrupted life by teaching people to hate the body, fear knowledge, and crave redemption instead of responsibility.

These works are intentionally provocative. Nietzsche does not aim to persuade, but to provoke awakening. His goal is to destroy the illusions that keep people passive, fearful, and self-negating—and to point toward the possibility of a new, life-affirming morality.

The Final Testament: Ecce Homo

Ecce Homo, written in late 1888 but published posthumously, is Nietzsche's most personal and enigmatic book. Its subtitle, How One Becomes What One Is, suggests a spiritual autobiography—but this is no conventional memoir. It is part confession, part parody, and part philosophical summation.

Nietzsche offers chapters such as "Why I Am So Wise," "Why I Am So Clever," "Why I Write Such Good Books," and "Why I Am a Destiny." These titles are not mere arrogance—they are rhetorical provocations. He uses them to undermine false humility, mock conventional virtue, and highlight the absurdity of his intellectual isolation.

In this book, Nietzsche looks back on his entire body of work and explains what he believes it all means. He recounts the origins of each major book and clarifies his core concepts—will to power, eternal recurrence, the Übermensch, and the critique of morality. He positions himself as the antidote to nihilism and the herald of a new type of human being.

At times lucid, at times manic, Ecce Homo foreshadows Nietzsche's impending mental collapse. It radiates intensity, irony, and a profound solitude. More than anything, it is a testament to Nietzsche's refusal to compromise. He believed his mission was not merely to interpret the world, but to upend it. In Ecce Homo, we meet not just the philosopher—but the man who gave everything to his vision.

Affirmation Against All Odds: Nietzsche's Enduring Challenge

The works collected in this volume reveal Nietzsche at his most daring, his most unrestrained, and his most illuminating. The Birth of Tragedy shows the early seeds of his project: the union of art, suffering, and affirmation. Twilight of the Idols and The Antichrist sharpen his critique of morality, religion, and modernity. Ecce Homo provides a final reckoning—a summation of what he stood for and why he mattered.

Nietzsche's core concern across all these texts is not power, as often caricatured, but health—spiritual, psychological, cultural. He believed that many of the West's most cherished beliefs were symptoms of decline. To heal, we must question our deepest assumptions, face life's tragic dimension, and create new values from strength.

This is not a philosophy of comfort. It is a philosophy of courage. It demands that we live without illusions, that we say "yes" to life with all its pain and beauty, and that we become what we are—not through obedience, but through will.

Welcome to The Complete Philosophy Collection (Vol. 7). May these final and foundational writings shake your assumptions, deepen your self-understanding, and ignite your resolve to live—not safely, but fully, in the face of the abyss.

Ecce Homo

Friedrich Nietzsche

PROLOGUE

Since I plan to present humanity with the greatest challenge they have ever faced very soon, I think it's essential to explain who I am and what I stand for. Honestly, this should already be clear, as I haven't exactly been quiet about myself. However, the gap between the magnitude of my task and the small- mindedness of my contemporaries is obvious, considering that most people have neither heard me nor understood me. I exist on my own reputation, and perhaps it's just a mistaken belief that I am alive at all. Whenever I speak to the scholars who visit Ober-Engadine in the summer, I am quickly reminded that I am, in fact, not alive.

Under these circumstances, it feels like an obligation—though it clashes with my natural tendency toward privacy and my instinctual pride—to say this: Listen! I am this particular person, and for heaven's sake, don't confuse me with someone else! For example, I am certainly not some kind of monster or immoral figure. In fact, I am the exact opposite of the kind of person traditionally celebrated as virtuous. Privately, I even think this is something I can feel proud of. I consider myself a follower of the philosopher Dionysus, and I'd rather be a satyr than a saint. But just read this book! Maybe I've managed to express this contrast in a way that's both lighthearted and relatable—perhaps that's the entire purpose of this work.

Improving humanity is the last thing I would ever promise to do. I'm not trying to create new idols; instead, I want old idols to finally realize what it means to stand on shaky foundations. Destroying idols (and by idols, I mean all ideals) is much more my style. The more people have clung to an imagined "ideal world," the more they've drained reality of its worth, meaning, and truth. The "true world" and the "apparent world"—to put it plainly, the imaginary world and the real one. So far, the lie of ideals has cursed reality, twisting human instincts into something deceitful and unnatural. Values that go against human flourishing and the promise of a great future have been idolized, while the values that truly support life have been ignored.

Anyone who understands how to breathe the air of my writings recognizes that it is the air of the heights—a sharp, invigorating breeze. To take it in, one must be equipped for the challenge; otherwise, it is likely to chill or even overwhelm. Here, the ice is ever near, the isolation is profound and daunting, but at the same time, everything rests in a serene radiance under the sun. The freedom of the atmosphere is undeniable, and one feels as though an entire world lies stretched out far below. Philosophy, as I have conceived of it up until now, is an intentional journey into the coldest and most elevated regions, a deliberate venture to the icy peaks and uncharted territories of human experience. It involves seeking out everything unfamiliar and unsettling in life— everything that, until now, morality has condemned and excluded.

Through years of wandering these forbidden domains, I gained an understanding unlike anything traditionally regarded as virtuous or acceptable. My insights into the secret history of philosophers and the psychology of their towering figures began to unfold before me. Questions like "How much truth can a mind endure?" or "How much truth can a person dare to confront?" became, for me, the ultimate measure of value. Error, which so many associate with blindness or ignorance, revealed itself instead as cowardice—a refusal to face reality. Every true advance in knowledge, every genuine triumph, stems from courage, from the willingness to be unyielding with oneself, and from maintaining inner clarity and honesty. I do not argue against ideals; I simply equip myself for their company by metaphorically pulling on gloves in their presence.

The phrase nitimur in vetitum— "we strive for the forbidden"—is the essence of my philosophy and will one day ensure its victory. For it is always the Truth, without exception, that has been most strictly forbidden throughout history. Truth alone has been the great outlaw, concealed by fear and avoided by those who choose comfort over courage.

In the grand scope of my work, Thus Spoke Zarathustra holds a unique and exalted place. With this book, I offered humanity the most profound gift ever given—a gift that transcends generations and echoes across the ages. It is not merely a book; it is the very breath of mountain air, unmatched in its loftiness. Mankind as a whole, with all its struggles and triumphs, lies an unfathomable distance beneath its peaks. Yet Zarathustra is not only the loftiest book; it is also the deepest. It springs from the boundless well of truth, a source so abundant that every attempt to draw from it yields gold and goodness, over and over again.

Here, no prophet speaks—none of those grim mixtures of frailty and hunger for power that so often serve as the founders of religions. To honor wisdom, one must take care not to conflate Zarathustra's voice with theirs. Above all, one must listen closely to the tones that resonate throughout the work—the halcyon tones, calm and clear, which carry the essence of its message.

The quietest words often carry the most profound power; they are the calm before the storm. Thoughts that arrive softly, as though on the feet of doves, have the potential to shift the world.

When figs fall from the trees, they are ripe and sweet, bursting open as they hit the ground, their red skins splitting to reveal the richness inside. I am like the north wind to those ripe figs, shaking them free from their branches. In the same way, my teachings fall to you, my friends, like figs in their season. Take in their juice and savor their sweetness, for now is the time of harvest. All around us is the clear sky of autumn, the golden light of afternoon—it is a season of fullness and clarity.

What I share with you here does not come from a fanatic, nor is it a sermon demanding belief. There is no plea for faith within these pages. Instead, my words flow slowly, gently, drop by drop, as though from an infinite reservoir of light and joy. These thoughts come to you in a measured rhythm, calm and deliberate. Only the rarest among you will truly grasp them. It is not given to everyone to hear Zarathustra's voice; it is a rare privilege to understand, a rarity even to listen.

Is Zarathustra, then, a seducer? What does he say, this man who speaks so differently from sages, saints, or saviors of the world? When he returns to his solitude, his words stand in complete opposition to theirs. He does not seek followers; he does not want disciples to cling to him or his teachings. He himself is as distinct from them as his words are.

"Now I go alone, my disciples!" Zarathustra says. "You, too, must go your way, each of you alone! That is what I desire. Truly, I ask you to leave me and to arm yourselves against me. Yes, you should even feel ashamed of me! Perhaps I have deceived you. The true knight of knowledge must be able to not only love his enemies but also hate his friends when necessary.

"A pupil who remains a pupil does no honor to his teacher. Why do you not pluck at my laurels? You show me reverence, but what if your respect crumbles one day? Beware, lest the very statue you worship crushes you beneath its weight. You say you believe in Zarathustra, but what of Zarathustra? You are my believers, but what value lies in all belief?

"You found me, but you had not yet sought yourselves. This is how all believers act, and for this reason, belief holds so little worth. Now I tell you to lose me so that you may find yourselves. Only when you have all denied me will I return to you."

It is on this perfect day, when the world ripens around me and not only the grapes turn brown in the sun, that a beam of light has touched my life. I looked back at my past, I looked forward to what lies ahead, and I saw an abundance of good things, all at once. On this day, I bury my forty-fourth year—not in regret, but with gratitude. What was alive within it, what mattered, has been saved and will endure forever.

This year has given me so much: the first book of the Transvaluation of All Values, The Songs of Zarathustra, The Twilight of the Idols, and my bold attempt to philosophize with a hammer. All of this is the gift of this year, particularly its final months. How could I not feel thankful for the entirety of my life?

And so, I now feel compelled to tell myself my own story.

CHAPTER 1
WHY I AM SO WISE

The unique happiness of my existence, if it can be called that, lies in its sense of fatefulness—its deep connection to both decline and renewal. To speak in a riddle: as my own father, I am already dead; as my own mother, I still live and grow old. This dual origin, rooted both in the highest and lowest rungs of life's ladder—at once an ending and a beginning—may explain my neutrality, my freedom from bias in considering the broader questions of existence. This perspective, perhaps, is what sets me apart. I have an unparalleled sensitivity to the first signs of life's ascent or descent, an instinct as keen as that of any creature alive.

In this realm, I am a master to the core of my being, knowing both sides because I embody both sides.

My father died at the age of thirty-six. He was fragile, gentle, and melancholic, as though he were meant only to grace the world briefly—a fleeting reminder of life rather than life itself. When his life waned, mine also entered a period of decline. At thirty-six, I reached the lowest point in my vitality. Though still alive, I could barely see three steps ahead of me. This was the year 1879. I resigned from my professorship at Basel, spent a shadowy summer in St. Moritz, and endured the darkest, most sunless winter of my life in Naumburg. That winter marked my lowest ebb, and during this time, I wrote The Wander er and His Shadow. Without question, I was well-acquainted with shadows then.

The following winter, my first in Genoa, brought a new kind of clarity and sweetness to my life, born out of extreme physical frailty and suffering. From this state emerged The Dawn of Day, a work reflecting a perfect lucidity and cheerfulness, even intellectual exuberance. Yet this brightness coincided with profound physiological weakness and unrelenting pain. During a three-day headache accompanied by violent nausea, I experienced an extraordinary clarity of thought. In those moments of agony, I worked out ideas with an icy precision that eluded me in healthier times. I was neither strong enough nor detached enough during periods of vitality to achieve this level of intellectual subtlety and coldness.

My readers might recall how I view dialectics—as a symptom of decadence, much like in the famous case of Socrates. But unlike others who descend into intellectual chaos or fevered delirium, such disturbances have remained foreign to me. Even semi- stupors caused by illness, which often cloud the mind, have been entirely unknown in my experience. When I sought to understand these states, I had to turn to scholarly accounts and medical studies to grasp their nature. My circulation is slow; no one has ever detected a fever in me. Once, a doctor who treated me for nerve-related symptoms concluded, "No, your nerves are not the problem—it's me who is nervous!"

Despite enduring profound physical exhaustion, including weakness in my digestive system, no localized degeneration or organic stomach illness has ever been identified in me. My recurring vision problems, which at times verged on blindness, were always secondary symptoms, not root causes. Whenever my overall vitality improved, my eyesight recovered alongside it.

Acknowledging all this, I must emphasize that I am deeply familiar with the questions and conditions of decadence. I know them inside and out. It was during this period of decline that I developed a heightened sensitivity—an acute ability to perceive and grasp subtle distinctions, a kind of psychological "sight" capable of seeing through barriers. This art of precise understanding, this capacity for nuanced observation, became my gift during the time when everything in me was refined to its utmost delicacy. My perception sharpened; my ability to analyze, observe, and comprehend deepened.

Through this process, I learned to see healthy concepts and values from the perspective of the sick, and, conversely, to scrutinize the covert workings of decadent instincts from the viewpoint of someone brimming with the richness of life. This dual perspective became my most enduring exercise, my primary experience, and, in many ways, my greatest achievement. If I have mastered anything, it is this. Today, I have perfected the art of reversing perspectives. This ability, more than anything else, is perhaps the foundation that made a Transvaluation of All Values possible— something only I could attempt.

While it is true that I am, in some respects, a decadent, I am also fundamentally the opposite of such a being. One of the clearest proofs of this is my instinctive ability to choose the right course of action when my spiritual or physical health falters. A true decadent, by contrast, invariably seeks remedies that worsen their condition. Though I may have had certain aspects of decadence, as a whole, I remained sound. This is evident in the way I imposed strict discipline upon myself, isolating myself completely from all the comforts and habits to which I had grown accustomed. My refusal to allow myself to be coddled, cared for, or overmedicated demonstrates the sureness of my instincts, which led me toward what I most needed at the time.

I entrusted my recovery to myself alone, taking full responsibility for restoring my health. Every physiologist will agree that the first requirement for success in such a task is a fundamentally healthy nature; an inherently diseased one cannot achieve true wellness. For a sound nature, however, illness can become a profound stimulus—

an impetus toward greater vitality and an overflow of life. This is how I now view the long period of illness I endured. It was as though I rediscovered life itself, including my own being, through that suffering. I savored everything, even the smallest pleasures, with an intensity others rarely experience. From my will to health and my will to life, I forged my philosophy.

This is something I must emphasize: during those years when my vitality was at its lowest, I abandoned pessimism altogether. My instinct for self- recovery would not permit me to hold onto a philosophy of deprivation and despair. This turning point in my thinking was not a coincidence but the result of an inner vitality that refused to be extinguished.

Now, how can we recognize those who are Nature's fortunate creations— those who thrive in their very essence? Such individuals radiate a joy that delights the senses. They are solid, carved from a single block, firm yet sweet, and imbued with an innate strength. They seek out only what is good for them, and their pleasure ceases when they reach the limits of what is beneficial. They possess an uncanny ability to heal themselves, turning even the gravest misfortunes into opportunities for growth. For them, the saying is true: "What does not kill me makes me stronger."

These individuals instinctively select what they need from all they see, hear, and experience. They are a natural filter, discarding what does not serve them. Whether in the company of books, people, or nature, they remain centered in themselves. They bestow value upon what they choose, honor, and trust. They respond to life with deliberation and caution, taking their time with every stimulus. They do not rush to meet challenges halfway; instead, they assess and test everything that approaches.

They do not believe in "bad luck" or "guilt." They digest all experiences, including their own failures and the flaws of others. They possess the strength to forget when necessary, transforming every challenge into a source of growth and power.

Look, then, at the description I have just given. It is no exaggeration to say that it is a portrait of myself. I am, in every way, the opposite of a decadent. What I have outlined here is nothing less than the essence of who I am.

This intertwining of experiences—a connection to two seemingly distant worlds—reflects every aspect of my nature. I am my own counterpart, my own complement, possessing not just a first sight but a second, and perhaps even a third. By virtue of my origins, I was granted a perspective that extended far beyond the confines of the local, the national, and the narrowly defined. It took no effort for me to become a "good European." At the same time, I might claim to be more German than the modern Germans—those mere Imperial Germans—could ever aspire to be. I consider myself the last true anti-political German.

Nevertheless, my ancestry reaches into Polish nobility. It is from them that I have inherited a deep sense of race instinct—a legacy that may even include the liber um veto. This heritage reveals itself in curious ways. During my travels, I have often been mistaken for a Pole, even by Poles themselves, while I am seldom identified as a German. It sometimes seems as though I belong only to those with a mere trace of German blood.

Still, my mother, Franziska Oehler, is thoroughly German, as was my paternal grandmother, Erdmuthe Krause. The latter spent her youth in the cultured world of Weimar, where she encountered Goethe's circle. Her brother, Professor Krause, taught theology in Königsberg and was later appointed General Superintendent in Weimar after Herder's death. It is even possible that her mother, my great-grandmother, is mentioned in Goethe's diaries under the name "Muthgen." She married twice, her second husband being Superintendent Nietzsche of Eilenburg. In 1813, the year of the great wars, she gave birth to a son while Napoleon and his general staff occupied Eilenburg on October 10th.

As a daughter of Saxony, she admired Napoleon greatly, and perhaps I have inherited this admiration.

My father, born in 1813, passed away in 1849. Before serving as pastor of the parish in Röcken, near Lützen, he lived at Altenburg Castle, where he oversaw the education of four princesses. His students included the Queen of Hanover, the Grand Duchess Constantine, the Grand Duchess of Oldenburg, and Princess Theresa of Saxe-Altenburg. He held a deep, loyal respect for Frederick William IV of Prussia, who granted him his position at Röcken, though the revolutionary events of 1848 brought him much sorrow. As fate would have it, I was born on October 15th, the birthday of this very king, and was therefore given the Hohenzollern names of Frederick William. My birthdate had the advantage of always being a day of public celebration throughout my childhood, which left a lasting impression on me.

I count it as a great privilege to have had such a father. Indeed, it seems that this is the only privilege I can truly claim—aside from life itself, the great affirmation of existence. Above all, I owe him this: I can, without deliberate effort, but with a little patience, find my way into a world of higher and more delicate things. This is where I feel at home; it is there, and only there, that my deepest passions are set free. That I had to pay for this privilege with nearly my entire life does not make it any less worthwhile—it was, in the end, an excellent bargain.

To grasp even a fragment of Thus Spoke Zarathustra, a person must be, in some measure, like me. They must stand with one foot beyond the boundaries of life itself, dwelling in a realm where the ordinary and the extraordinary converge. Only there can such a work be truly understood.

I have never mastered the art of provoking hostility against myself— something for which I owe thanks to my incomparable father. Even when it might have seemed useful or desirable to arouse ill-feeling, I have been incapable of doing so. As un- Christian as it may sound, I do not even harbor ill-feeling toward myself. Examine my life from any angle, and you will rarely— perhaps only once—find any evidence of someone showing me genuine ill-will. On the contrary, you are far more likely to find too many traces of goodwill.

Even with those whom others regard as untouchable or dangerous, my experiences have invariably been positive. I have a knack for taming even the roughest characters, for bringing out a better side in those who might otherwise resist it. During the seven years I spent teaching Greek to the sixth form at the College in Basel, I never once had to punish a student. Even the laziest among them found motivation in my classroom. I have always met the unexpected with composure; in fact, I thrive on being unprepared, as it brings out my ability to remain in control. Regardless of the "instrument" I am working with—even if it is as discordant and flawed as the human being often is—I have always been able to coax something meaningful, even beautiful, from it. Only during periods of illness have I found myself unable to achieve this.

Time and again, those very "instruments" have expressed their astonishment to me, telling me they had never heard their own voices speak so beautifully. Perhaps the most touching example of this came from Heinrich von Stein, a young man of great promise who tragically died far too early. With the eager simplicity of a young Prussian nobleman, Stein had plunged deeply into Wagnerism and the philosophies of thinkers like

Dübring. Yet, when he visited me in Sils-Maria for three days—a visit he explained was not for the sake of the Engadine—he seemed utterly transformed. It was as if a storm of freedom had swept through him, raising him to his full height and granting him wings. I repeatedly told him it was due to the splendid mountain air; everyone feels such vitality at 6,000 feet above Bayreuth. But he refused to believe me.

Whatever the cause, if I have endured slights, whether minor or significant, they have rarely been driven by malice, let alone ill- will. More often, these offenses have stemmed from goodwill—a force that has caused no small trouble in my life. My experiences have given me every reason to view so-called "unselfish" instincts and "neighborly love" with suspicion. These impulses, always eager to offer assistance or advice, often betray a deeper weakness. To me, they reflect an inability to resist a stimulus. Among decadents, this pity is even exalted as a virtue.

What I find most objectionable about pity is its lack of restraint. It forgets shame, reverence, and the delicate sense of distance that is essential in human relations. Pity reeks of the masses, of vulgarity, and it too often leads to clumsy interference in the lives of others. A pitiful hand, thrust uninvited into a great destiny, into a solitary and wounded retreat, or into the unique burdens that great guilt bestows, can cause irreparable harm. Overcoming pity, I count among the highest virtues.

In The Temptation of Zarathustr a, I depicted a moment in which a great cry of distress reaches Zarathustra's ears, and pity swoops down upon him like a final temptation. It threatens to make him betray himself, to abandon his mission for the sake of an immediate emotional response. To remain one's own master in such moments, to keep the sublimity and purity of one's purpose intact, free from the base and short-sighted impulses of so-called unselfish acts— this is the ultimate challenge. It is perhaps the final test of strength, the proof of power that a Zarathustra must face.

In yet another way, I feel myself to be an extension of my father—a continuation of his life cut short all too soon. Like anyone who has never met their equal and for whom the very concepts of "retaliation" or "equal rights" seem incomprehensible, I have refrained from employing any sort of protective or defensive measures in response to the foolishness I have encountered, whether minor or significant. I do not shield myself, nor do I justify or defend. Instead, my form of retaliation is unique: I respond to an act of stupidity by swiftly sending a bit of cleverness in its wake, hoping that it might still catch up and outpace the foolishness.

To put it metaphorically, I dispatch a pot of jam to sweeten and erase the bitterness of a bad experience. If someone gives me offense, they can rest assured—I will retaliate. But my "retaliation" often takes an unexpected form: I might find a way to express my thanks to the offender, even for the offense itself, or I might make a polite request of them. Asking for something can sometimes be more disarming, even more courteous, than giving.

It also strikes me that even the rudest word or letter is far more straightforward and good-natured than silence. Silence, to me, is often an objection in disguise. Those who keep silent are usually lacking in subtlety or refinement of heart; to swallow grievances in silence breeds bad temper and even physical discomfort—it can upset the stomach. All silent people, I suspect, are dyspeptic. For this reason, I value rudeness and would not like to see it underestimated. Rudeness is, in my view, the most humane form of contradiction and, amidst the softness and delicacy of modern life, it stands as one of our first virtues. If one is rich enough in spirit, it might even bring joy to admit being wrong. Were a god to walk the earth, he would likely take on not punishment, but guilt—this willingness to embrace guilt is the truest sign of divinity.

My freedom from resentment and my understanding of its nature—these I owe, in large part, to my long illness. Resentment is not a simple matter to unravel. To truly understand it, a person must experience both strength and weakness. Illness, and the weakness that comes with it, must be held accountable for one thing above all: they diminish the very instinct of recovery, the will to fight back and heal. When illness dominates, the ability to let go, to reconcile, or to move past experiences becomes blunted. Everything seems to wound; people and events press too close; every encounter cuts deeply. Memory itself turns into a series of open wounds. To be ill is, in its way, to be caught in a state of resentment.

The only remedy for this kind of resentment is what I call Russian fatalism. It is a fatalism devoid of revolt, the kind embodied by a Russian soldier who, when the strain of a campaign becomes unbearable, simply lies down in the snow and lets go. This approach means ceasing to resist, ceasing to react—accepting nothing further, attempting nothing further, absorbing nothing further. It is a complete cessation of response, a letting go that, in the gravest cases, can even become a means of self-preservation.

This fatalism carries an extraordinary wisdom. It does not always signify a readiness for death; instead, it can represent a deliberate reduction of life's activity—a slowing down of the vital processes, akin to a will to hibernate. Taken to its extreme, we see this principle in the fakir who can sleep for weeks in a tomb, conserving himself by refusing to react. The essence of this approach lies in the recognition that one burns out too quickly by responding to every stimulus. To preserve oneself, one must stop reacting altogether.

Nothing in life consumes a person more rapidly than the passion of resentment. It eats away at the soul and the body alike, demanding energy that could otherwise be used to sustain and enrich life. To overcome resentment is to find liberation, and perhaps even strength, in letting go entirely.

Mortification, hypersensitivity, the inability to act on one's impulses for revenge, and yet the consuming thirst for vengeance—all of these, paired with the mental labor of crafting poisons of every kind, form the most destructive reaction imaginable for individuals who are already exhausted. This state accelerates the depletion of nervous energy, leading to harmful physical effects, such as an overproduction of bile in the stomach. For someone who is ill, resentment should be more strictly avoided than any other vice—it is their most perilous danger. Tragically, it is also the tendency to which they are most naturally drawn.

The profound physiologist Buddha understood this with remarkable clarity. His "religion," which might more aptly be described as a system of hygiene to distinguish it from the impoverished creed of Christianity, rested on the elimination of resentment as a means of healing. Freeing the soul from resentment was the first and most crucial step toward recovery. "Hostility is not defeated by hostility; it is defeated by friendship"—this teaching stands at the heart of Buddha's doctrine. It is not a moral directive but a physiological truth. Resentment, when born of weakness, is more damaging to the weak man himself than to anyone else. In contrast, for a person with a fundamentally rich and robust nature, resentment becomes an unnecessary and redundant emotion. To remain above resentment is a sign of inner abundance; to master it is proof of strength.

Those familiar with the seriousness of my philosophy's battle against feelings of revenge and rancor—an opposition that even extends to the doctrine of free will—will better understand why I emphasize my stance on this matter. My opposition to Christianity is, in many ways, a specific application of this broader principle. In my moments of personal decline, I forbade myself the indulgence of resentment, recognizing it as harmful to my recovery. Later, when my vitality had returned, I continued to reject such feelings, but now because they were beneath me, an insult to my dignity and strength.

That "Russian fatalism" I mentioned earlier was another tool by which I avoided falling into the clutches of resentment. It manifested in me as a resolute acceptance of even the most unbearable circumstances—whether places, situations, habits, or people—that happened to cross my path. Rather than resist or attempt to change these conditions, I held onto them stubbornly. To revolt against them, or even to acknowledge that change was possible, seemed a far worse alternative. For years, I remained steadfast in this fatalism, enduring situations that others might have abandoned without hesitation.

Anyone who attempted to jolt me out of this state, who tried to force me to confront or change my circumstances, appeared to me as an enemy. Each such attempt carried the threat of profound disruption, even danger to my life. In such moments, my fatalism was a form of wisdom, a recognition of necessity. To see oneself as destiny, to refuse to wish oneself "different" or otherwise than one is—this, in those circumstances, was the truest and most essential kind of sagacity.

War, however, is a different matter. At my core, I am a warrior. Attacking comes naturally to me—it is part of my instincts. To have the capacity to be an enemy, to truly be an enemy, might require a strong nature; in any case, all strong natures include this ability. These kinds of natures need resistance, and so they seek out obstacles to confront. The urge to attack is as much a part of strength as feelings of revenge and bitterness are connected to weakness. Take women, for example: they are often driven by a desire for revenge because their weakness makes them prone to this emotion, just as it makes them deeply affected by the suffering of others.

The strength of someone who attacks can often be measured by the level of resistance they need. Growth and power reveal themselves in the pursuit of tougher opponents—or more challenging problems. A combative philosopher, for instance, treats even intellectual questions as adversaries to be confronted head-on. The true goal isn't to defeat just any opponent, but rather to face those who force you to use all your strength, skill, and cleverness—adversaries who are your equals. To fight a worthy battle, one must first be equal to one's enemy. Where there is disdain, war is impossible. Where one commands or views something as inferior, one should not bother to wage war.

My approach to war can be summed up in four key principles. First, I only attack things that are already triumphant. If necessary, I wait until their triumph becomes clear. Second, I only attack things against which I can stand completely alone—where I have no allies and risk only myself. I have never taken a single step into the public eye without putting myself entirely at stake. That has always been my measure of what constitutes proper action. Third, I never launch personal attacks. Instead, I use a person as a lens to magnify and expose a broader, often hidden problem. For example, when I criticized David Strauss, it wasn't him I was attacking—it was the success of an outdated book that reflected the superficiality of German culture at the time. Similarly, my criticism of Wagner was not aimed at him as a person, but at the false values and mixed instincts in our culture that confuse refinement with strength and weakness with greatness.

Fourth, I only attack things that are free of personal grievances. I exclude anything where my criticisms could be tied to bad experiences or personal resentment. On the contrary, for me, attacking is often an expression of goodwill, and sometimes even gratitude. When I attack, I show respect and give importance to the thing I challenge. Whether I associate my name with an institution or a person—whether I support or oppose them— doesn't matter to me. Both are ways of engaging with something seriously.

When I fight against Christianity, I feel justified in doing so because I have never had any deeply negative or personal struggles with it. In fact, the most sincere Christians have always treated me kindly. Even as the strongest opponent of Christianity, I do not hold individuals accountable for what is ultimately the outcome of centuries of history.

I would like to point out one final trait in my character, which has caused some difficulties in my interactions with others. I have an extraordinary sense of cleanliness, so sharp that I can perceive—almost physiologically, as if by smell— the presence, even the innermost nature, of another person's soul. This sensitivity acts like psychological antennae, allowing me to detect and understand every secret. At the same time, I can sense the hidden filth lying at the foundation of certain human characters, often a result of base origins that no amount of education can completely hide. I notice this immediately, at a single glance.

When my sense of cleanliness rejects someone, they seem to sense my cautiousness, driven by my instinctive loathing—and this only adds to their unpleasantness in my perception. According to a personal rule I've long followed, purity and honesty toward myself are fundamental to my life. I could not survive in unclean surroundings. I constantly immerse myself, as it were, in water—swimming, bathing, and splashing in whatever is perfectly clear and pure.

This is one reason why my relationships with others often test my patience. My humanity does not lie in being able to sympathize with others, but in enduring the understanding of their nature. My humanity is a continual process of mastering myself. To sustain this, I need solitude—a chance to recover, to return to myself, to breathe air that is free, crisp, and invigorating.

The entirety of Zarathustra is a hymn to solitude—or, more precisely, to purity. Thankfully, it does not celebrate "pure foolishness." Anyone with an eye for color would call it a diamond. My greatest danger has always been the loathing of humanity, the disgust I feel for the common crowd. Would you listen to Zarathustra's words about how he escaped from this loathing?

"What happened to me? How did I free myself from disgust? What made my eyes see the world freshly again? How did I rise to heights where no rabble sits crowded around the well?

"Was it my very loathing that gave me wings and the strength to sense springs of joy far away? Truly, I needed to soar to the greatest heights to rediscover the source of happiness.

"Oh, I found it, my friends! Up here, on these highest peaks, the spring of joy gushes forth for me. There is a life at this well that no rabble can share with you.

"You flow too fiercely for me, spring of joy! Too often you empty the pitcher as you try to fill it again.

"But I must learn to approach you more humbly. My heart leaps too eagerly toward you.

"My heart, which burns with the heat of my summer—this short, fiery, blessed, melancholy summer—how it longs for your coolness!

"Farewell to the lingering grief of my spring! Gone is the cruelty of snowflakes in June! I am summer now—entirely summer, with the noontime sun.

"A summer on the highest peaks, with cold springs and a sacred stillness. Come, my friends, let us gather here, so that the stillness may become even more blessed!"

"For this is where we belong, high above the world—this is our home. It is too high and too steep for the unclean and their cravings to reach.

"Look into the well of my joy, my friends! Cast your pure eyes upon it! How could it ever become muddy? It will reflect back to you with its own purity, laughing in its clarity.

"On the tree of the Future we build our nest. Eagles shall bring us nourishment in their beaks, for we are the lonely ones who dwell above.

"Truly, it is not food for the unclean. They would think they were eating fire, and it would scorch their mouths!

"Indeed, we offer no shelter here for the unclean. To their bodies, our happiness would seem like an icy cavern, and to their spirits, just as cold!

"We live like strong winds, high above, as neighbors to the eagles, companions to the snow, and playmates of the sun. This is the life of the strong wind.

"One day, like a wind, I shall sweep through their midst, stealing the very breath of their souls with my spirit. This is the will of my future.

"Truly, Zarathustra is a strong wind to all the lowlands. And this is his advice to his enemies, to all those who spit and sneer: 'Be warned—never spit against the wind!'"

CHAPTER 2
WHY I AM SO CLEVER

Why do I know more than most people? Why am I, in fact, so clever? It's because I have never wasted time on questions that aren't real questions.

I have never squandered my energy. For instance, I have no personal experience with religious difficulties. I've never known what it feels like to think of myself as "sinful." Similarly, I don't have any reliable sense of what people call a "prick of conscience." From what I've heard, it doesn't seem like something particularly admirable. Once I've done something, I wouldn't dream of abandoning it to its consequences. I'd rather completely disregard the harmful outcomes when deciding on the value of an action. Too often, people lose the right perspective when faced with unpleasant results, which clouds their judgment of the deed itself. To me, a prick of conscience feels like an "evil eye." When something fails, it should be protected and valued even more carefully because it failed—that's far closer to my sense of morality.

Concepts like "God," "the immortality of the soul," "salvation," or "an afterlife" never caught my attention, even when I was a child. I never spent any time on such ideas—perhaps I was never naive enough for them? Because of this, atheism is something I've never experienced either, not even as a moment in my life. For me, disbelief in God is instinctive and inborn. I am too curious, too skeptical, and too lively to accept such an obvious and clumsy solution to the mysteries of existence. God is, in my view, a crude explanation—one that lacks subtlety and shows little respect for thinkers like myself. At its core, the concept of God feels like a rude command: "You must not think!"

I am far more interested in another question, one that seems to matter much more to humanity's well-being than any theological curiosity. This question is about nutrition. In simpler terms, it can be asked like this: "How should you feed yourself to achieve your greatest strength and power, the kind of virtue that is free from the sourness of moral preaching, like the boldness of the Renaissance spirit?"

My experiences with this matter were as poor as they could possibly have been. I'm still surprised that I only asked this question so late in life and that it took me so long to come to reasonable conclusions based on my own experiences. The only explanation I can offer is the utter uselessness of German culture, with all its "idealism." This culture, from start to finish, encourages people to ignore practical matters and chase after abstract and so-called ideal goals—like "classical culture," for example. It is absurd to try and combine "classical" and "German" into a single idea. The very notion is a little ridiculous—imagine a "classically cultured" citizen of Leipzig!

To put it plainly, I can say that for most of my life, my diet was completely wrong. If expressed in moral terms, my eating habits were "selfless," "altruistic," and "impersonal," serving only to glorify cooks and please my fellow Christians.

It was the cooking I encountered in Leipzig, along with my first study of Schopenhauer in 1865, that made me seriously renounce my "Will to Live." Ruining one's stomach by eating poorly prepared food seemed to have been solved perfectly by the cooking there. (I've heard that some changes were made to the cuisine in 1866.) As for German cooking in general—what crimes it has committed! Soup served before the meal, still referred to as alla tedesca in

Venetian cookbooks from the 16th century; meat boiled to the point of falling apart; vegetables ruined by cooking them with fat and flour; pastries reduced to heavy, tasteless lumps! And when you add to this the ancient, nearly animalistic drinking habits—not just of old Germans but of other "ancients" as well—you start to understand where German intellect truly began: in miserable, malfunctioning intestines. German intellect is indigestion—it can absorb nothing properly.

Even English food, which compared to German and even French cooking feels almost like a "return to nature"—or rather, to cannibalism—goes entirely against my instincts. It seems to weigh down the intellect, like heavy feet, or even the clumsy feet of Englishwomen. The best cuisine, in my view, is that of Piedmont. Alcoholic drinks, on the other hand, have never suited me. Just one glass of wine or beer in a day is enough to make life feel miserable for me—a true valley of tears. In Munich, I'd find my exact opposites. I admit, though, that I only fully understood this later in life, even though the signs were there when I was a boy. As a child, I thought drinking wine and smoking tobacco were nothing but youthful vanities at first and bad habits later. Perhaps the poor wine of Naumburg influenced my low opinion of wine in general. To believe wine could bring joy, I would have had to be a Christian—in other words, I'd have had to believe in something I find completely absurd.

Oddly enough, while small amounts of alcohol diluted with plenty of water make me feel unwell, larger amounts have a completely different effect—they turn me into a boisterous sailor. I've shown this bravado even as a boy. I remember composing a long Latin essay in a single night, revising and rewriting it to match the precision and brevity of my model, Sallust, while drinking strong grogs. This habit, which I developed as a student at the venerable Pforta school, may not have aligned with the dignity of Pforta, but it certainly agreed with my physiology—and perhaps even that of Sallust.

Later in life, I grew more opposed to alcohol altogether. Although I oppose vegetarianism and have personally experienced it, I cannot stress enough how harmful alcohol is for those with more spiritual or refined natures. I strongly advise abstaining from it completely. Water serves the purpose far better. I especially prefer places where fresh, running brooks can be found in every direction—places like Nice, Turin, or Sils. The saying In vino veritas— "in wine, there is truth"—does not apply to me. Once again, I find myself at odds with the common understanding of "truth." For me, spirit moves not in wine but over the waters.

Here are some further thoughts on my view of morality. A heavy meal digests more easily than one that is insufficient. The key to good digestion is that the stomach must function as a whole, which means a person should be aware of their stomach's capacity. For this reason, I strongly discourage those long, drawn-out meals I call "interrupted sacrificial feasts," which are common at any table d'hôte. Nothing should be eaten between meals, and coffee should be avoided entirely—it makes people gloomy. Tea, on the other hand, is helpful in the morning, but it should be very strong and taken in small quantities. However, if it is made even slightly too weak, it can ruin the entire day. Each person has their own preferences with tea, often within narrow and delicate limits. In hot climates, tea is not ideal for starting the day. In such cases, an excellent option is a cup of thick cocoa made with oil about an hour beforehand.

Remaining seated for long periods should be avoided as much as possible. Do not trust any thought that is not born in the open air, accompanied by physical movement. Even the muscles should be engaged in celebration. All prejudices begin in the intestines. A sedentary lifestyle, as I've said before, is the true sin against the Holy Spirit.

The question of where and how to live—of climate and location— is closely connected to the question of nutrition. Not everyone can thrive just anywhere, and those who carry great responsibilities, who must use all their strength, have an even narrower range of choices. The influence of climate on the body is so profound— affecting how quickly or slowly it functions—that choosing the wrong location or climate can not only distract a person from their true purpose but can prevent them from ever discovering it.

Without the right conditions, a person's vitality may never reach the level of artistic freedom where their soul whispers, "Only I can do this."

Even the smallest tendency toward sluggish digestion, once it becomes a habit, is enough to turn a genius into something mediocre, something "German." The climate of Germany alone can discourage even the strongest and most determined digestive systems. The speed of the body's functions is closely linked to the sharpness or dullness of the mind, for the mind itself is a product of these bodily processes.

If you were to list the places where great minds have flourished— where wit, subtlety, and a sense of humor are sources of joy, and where genius feels at home—you would find they all share one trait: exceptionally dry air. Places like Paris, Provence, Florence, Jerusalem, and Athens demonstrate that genius thrives in dry climates with clear skies. These conditions foster quick bodily functions and the ability to gather enormous energy reserves.

I know of a particular case where a man with an extraordinary mind and independent spirit became narrow-minded, timid, and irritable simply because he failed to choose the right climate for himself. I, too, could have been an example of this, had illness not forced me to think clearly and face reality. Over time, I have learned to read how climate and weather affect me, using my body like a finely tuned instrument. I can even detect changes in atmospheric humidity during a short trip, such as the journey from Turin to Milan. When I look back, I am horrified to realize that for most of my life—until the last ten years—I lived in places that were entirely wrong for me, places that I should have avoided at all costs.

Places like Naumburg, Pforta, Thuringia, Leipzig, Basel, and even Venice were all unlucky choices for someone with my constitution. I cannot recall a single happy memory from my childhood or youth. It is nonsense to attribute this unhappiness to so-called "moral" causes, such as the fact that I lacked suitable companions, though that is undeniably true. This fact remains the same today, yet it does not stop me from feeling cheerful and courageous. The real problem was my ignorance of physiological matters. This ignorance, shaped by the misguided philosophy of "Idealism," was the true curse of my life. It was a useless and foolish aspect of my existence, something that led nowhere and for which there is no compensation.

Because of this "Idealism," I made many mistakes and strayed far from my true path. For example, I became a philologist—why not at least a doctor or something else that might have opened my eyes? My time in Basel, with its rigid intellectual routines and daily schedules, was a complete misuse of my extraordinary abilities. I wasted my strength without any thought of how to replenish it or of what I was sacrificing. I lacked a healthy self- interest and the instinct to care for myself. I was in a state where I considered myself equal to anyone else, forgetting the distance that separated me from others—a state of "selflessness" that I cannot forgive myself for.

When I reached the very limit of what I could endure—when I was nearly finished—it finally became clear to me how absurd my life had been, all because of "Idealism." It was illness that finally brought me to reason.

After choosing the right food and the right climate, the next important decision is how to restore one's strength. Here, too, the more unique a person's spirit is, the more carefully they must limit themselves to what is truly beneficial. For me personally, reading is one of the ways I recover. It helps me step away from myself, wander into unfamiliar sciences, and explore other minds. Reading allows me to escape seriousness; it is where I go to take a break from my own intensity.

When I am deeply focused on my work, however, I keep all books far away. It would never occur to me to let anyone else's thoughts intrude while I am working. Reading, in such moments, would feel like letting someone else think in my presence, which I cannot tolerate. Has anyone noticed that during periods of intense focus—what might be called spiritual pregnancy—the smallest distractions or external stimuli can feel overwhelming and cut too deeply? To protect myself during such times, I instinctively avoid anything that could disturb me. I build a sort of wall around myself. Shall I allow a strange thought to climb over that wall? That is exactly what reading would mean.

After these intense periods of work come moments of rest. During these, I welcome delightful and intelligent books. But German books? I have to think back at least six months to recall the last book I read. What was it? An excellent study by Victor Brochard on the Greek skeptics, which made good use of my Laertiana.

The skeptics are, to my mind, the only philosophers truly worthy of respect among the many who wear false or multiple faces. Otherwise, I return to the same books again and again. There are not many of them, but they suit me perfectly. It is not in my nature to read widely or indiscriminately. A library, in fact, makes me uneasy.

Neither is it in my nature to love many things. Suspicion, or even hostility, toward new books feels much more natural to me than tolerance, open- mindedness, or other forms of so-called "neighborly love." I always find myself drawn back to a small group of old French authors. I believe in French culture alone and see most other European "cultures" as misunderstandings—not even worth considering in the case of German culture. The few examples of higher culture I've encountered in Germany have always had French roots. The clearest example of this is Madame Cosima Wagner, who had the sharpest sense of taste I've ever encountered.

If I don't just read Pascalbutlove him—admiring him as theultimate example of sacrifice to Christianity, destroying himself step by step, first in body and then in spirit, with terrifying consistency— if I find something of Montaigne's playful spirit in myself, perhaps even in my physical being—if my artistic sensibility drives me to defend the names of Molière, Corneille, and Racine (and often bitterly) against the wild genius of Shakespeare—none of this stops me from enjoying the company of more modern French writers. There has never been a time in history, to my mind, when so many subtle and curious psychologists have gathered in one place as they have in contemporary Paris.

A few names, chosen at random, might illustrate my point, though the list is far from complete: Paul Bourget, Pierre Loti, Gyp, Meilhac, Anatole France, Jules Lemaître. Or to name someone with strong roots, a true Latin whom I particularly admire, Guy de Maupassant.

Between ourselves, I prefer this generation even to its masters, all of whom were corrupted by German philosophy (Taine, for instance, by Hegel, whom he has to thank for his misunderstanding of great men and great periods). Wherever Germany extends her sway, she ruins culture. It was the war which first saved the spirit of France Stendhal is one of the happiest accidents of my life—for everything that marks an epoch in it has been brought to me by accident and never by means of a recommendation. He is quite priceless, with his psychologist's eye, quick at forestalling and anticipating; with his grasp of facts, which is reminiscent of the same art in the greatest of all masters of facts (ex ungue Napoleonem); and, last but not least, as an honest atheist—a specimen which is both rare and difficult to discover in France— all honour to Prosper Mérimée!. Maybe that I am even envious of Stendhal? He robbed me of the best atheistic joke, which I of all people could have perpetrated: "God's only excuse is that He does not exist" I myself have said somewhere—What has been the greatest objection to Life hitherto?—God....

Heinrich Heine gave me the clearest and most complete idea of what a lyrical poet could be. I search in vain through the entire history of ancient and modern times for anything comparable to his sweet yet passionate music. He had that divine wickedness, without which perfection is unimaginable to me. I judge the value of people, even entire races, by their ability to conceive of a god with a touch of the satyr in him. And how masterfully he wielded his native tongue! One day, it will be said of Heine and me that we were the greatest artists of the German language to ever exist, leaving all other German efforts in this field far behind.

I have always felt a deep connection to Byron's Manfred. All of its dark abysses find their counterpart in my own soul. At the age of thirteen, I was already mature enough to understand this work fully. Words fail me when faced with those who dare to mention Faust in the same breath as Manfred. The Germans are incapable of grasping the sublime; if proof is needed, look no further than Schumann. Out of frustration with that overly sentimental Saxon, I once wrote a counter-overture to Manfred, which Hans von Bülow declared unlike anything he had ever seen on paper. Such compositions, he said, were a violation of the muse Euterpe.

When I try to define Shakespeare's highest achievement, I always return to one conclusion: he conceived the type of Cæsar. This is not something that can be guessed or imagined; one either is this kind of person or one is not. The great poet creates only from his own reality, to such an extent that, over time, he may no longer be able to endure his own work. I experience this myself. After reading even a single passage from my Zarathustra, I often find myself pacing the room for half an hour, overwhelmed by an unbearable flood of tears.

I know no more heartbreaking literature than Shakespeare's. How much a man must have suffered to feel such a need to play the clown! Is Hamlet truly understood? It is not doubt but absolute certainty that drives a person to madness. To feel this, however, one must be deeply profound—an abyss, a philosopher. We all fear the truth.

And now, a confession: I am instinctively certain that Lord Bacon was the creator and self-tormented originator of this darkest form of literature. What do I care about the babble of American scholars and simpletons? The capacity for the most vivid realism in imagination is not only compatible with but often demands the most extreme realism in deeds, even monstrous crimes. It presupposes them.

We know far too little about Lord Bacon, the first true realist in the deepest sense of the word, to be sure of everything he did, desired, and endured in his innermost soul. Let the critics howl—they can go to hell! Imagine if I had published Zarathustra under a name that was not my own—say, Richard Wagner's. The cleverness of two thousand years would still not be enough to uncover that the author of Human, All Too Human was also the visionary behind Zarathustra.

Since I am speaking of the things that have brought me joy and renewed my spirit, I feel compelled to express my deepest gratitude for the experience that refreshed me most profoundly: my close friendship with Richard Wagner. There is no doubt in my mind about this. My other relationships with people I regard lightly, but I would not trade the days I spent at Tribschen—days filled with trust, cheerfulness, sublime insights, and profound moments—for anything in the world. I cannot speak for what Wagner may have been to others, but for us, no shadow ever darkened our time together.

This reflection brings me back to France. I have no arguments to offer against the Wagnerites and their ilk, who believe they honor

Wagner by imagining him to be like themselves. For such people, I reserve only a slight curl of my lip. With a temperament like mine—so alien to all things Teutonic, to the extent that even the presence of a German slows my digestion—my first encounter with Wagner was also the first time in my life that I could breathe freely. I felt him, I respected him, as someone foreign, someone utterly opposed to and a living contradiction of all the so-called "German virtues."

We who grew up in the stagnant, swampy air of the 1850s are naturally pessimistic about the concept of "German." It is impossible for us to be anything but revolutionaries, incapable of accepting a society in which hypocritical moralists sit at the top. It makes no difference to me whether these hypocrites now wear different colors, whether they dress in scarlet robes or military uniforms. The fact remains: Wagner was a revolutionary. He fled from the Germans.

As an artist, no one can truly call Europe their home except in Paris. The refined sensitivity required for Wagner's art—the ability to detect subtle distinctions, psychological nuances, and even sickness within the soul—exists only in Paris. Nowhere else is there such passion for the art of form, such seriousness about the details of staging, which is the very essence of Parisian dedication. In Germany, there is no comprehension of the immense ambition that fuels the heart of a Parisian artist. The German, by nature, is merely a "good fellow." Wagner, however, was no "good fellow."

I have already said much about Wagner's true character (refer to Beyond Good and Evil, Aphorism 269) and those to whom he is most closely related. He was one of the late French romanticists, part of that lofty and aspiring group of artists like Delacroix and Berlioz. These artists were marked by an incurable sickness at their core, fanatics of expression, and virtuosos in every sense of the word.

Who was Wagner's first intelligent follower? It was Charles Baudelaire—the same man who first understood Delacroix. Baudelaire, the quintessential decadent, became a mirror for an entire generation of artists and may have been the last of them as well.

What have I never forgiven Wagner for? The fact that he stooped to align himself with the Germans, that he became a German Imperialist. Wherever Germany spreads, it destroys culture.

All things considered, I don't believe I could have survived my youth without Wagnerian music. I was condemned to the company of Germans, and if a man wishes to escape a sense of unbearable oppression, he must find a remedy—like hashish for some. For me, it was Wagner. Wagner was the antidote to everything quintessentially German. That he was also a poison, I won't deny.

From the moment Tristan was arranged for the piano—my thanks to you, Herr von Bülow!—I became a devoted Wagnerian. Wagner's earlier works seemed beneath me, too ordinary, too "German."

To this day, I am still searching for a work that matches Tristan in its dangerous allure, its haunting, sweet quality of infinite longing. I search in vain across all the arts. Even the strange and fascinating elements in Leonardo da Vinci's works lose their appeal the moment the first notes of Tristan are played. Without a doubt, Tristan is Wagner's ultimate masterpiece. After creating it, composing The Mastersinger s and The Ring must have been mere relaxation for him. For someone like Wagner, becoming "healthier" meant regressing.

My curiosity as a psychologist is so strong that I consider it a special privilege to have lived in Wagner's time, and specifically among Germans, so that I could fully appreciate this work. The world must indeed feel empty to anyone who has not been unhealthy enough to experience this "infernal voluptuousness." For such a feeling, it is fitting, even necessary, to use a mystical formula. I probably understand better than anyone the incredible feats Wagner achieved—the fifty unique worlds of ecstasy he conjured, worlds no one else could reach. And now, as someone who is alive and strong enough to turn even the most suspicious and dangerous experiences to my advantage, I can say that Wagner was the greatest benefactor of my life.

The bond that ties us together is our shared suffering, a kind of pain, even inflicted upon each other, that few today could endure. This bond will always keep our names intertwined in the minds of others. Just as Wagner is a profound misunderstanding among Germans, so am I, and so I always will be. My dear countrymen, you lack two centuries of psychological and artistic refinement to understand either of us—and that lost time can never be regained.

To my most exceptional readers, I would like to say a word about what I truly demand from music. It must be cheerful yet profound, like an October afternoon. It must be original, overflowing with life, tender, and playful, like a soft, graceful woman with a mischievous charm. I can never accept the idea that a German could truly understand what music is. The greatest and most famous musicians labeled as German were, in fact, foreigners: Slavs, Croats, Italians, Dutch, or Jews. And those who were truly German, such as Heinrich Schütz, Bach, and Händel, belonged to a strong race that no longer exists.

For my part, I still have enough of the Pole in me to let go of all other music, as long as I can keep Chopin. I would make a few exceptions, however: Wagner's Siegfried Idyll, perhaps one or two works by Liszt, who excelled in the noble tone of orchestration, and everything created south of the Alps. I could never part with Rossini, and even less so with the Southern soul of music, embodied by my Venetian maestro, Pietro Gasti.

And when I speak of the world beyond the Alps, what I truly mean is Venice. For me, if I had to find another word for music, it would always be Venice. I cannot separate music from tears, nor can I think of joy or the south without trembling with both fear and longing.

I stood upon the bridge,

In the deep and somber night.
A distant song came drifting,
Golden drops falling softly,
Rolling over the sparkling edge.
Music, gondolas, lights—
Drunkenly they floated,
Far into the shadowy darkness.
Like a stringed instrument, my soul
Sang quietly, barely stirred,
A secret gondola song,
Glowing with vivid, dazzling joy.
—Did anyone listen?

In all these matters—choosing food, a place to live, the right climate, and recreation—the instinct to protect oneself is what drives us, and this instinct is clearest when it acts as a form of defense. Closing one's eyes to many things, shutting one's ears to what doesn't belong, and keeping certain things at a distance are the first rules of caution and the best proof that a person is not just a random accident, but someone who belongs in the world. The common word for this instinct of defense is taste.

A person's guiding rule must be to say "no" not just when saying "yes" would be a sign of indifference but also to say "no" as rarely as possible. One must avoid everything that forces frequent "no's" from them. The reason is simple: every act of defending oneself, no matter how small, becomes a waste of energy when repeated too often. These constant little efforts to keep things at bay drain our strength more than we realize. Even the act of holding things off, of keeping them away, is a use of energy—it is not neutral, and it is not free of cost.

If someone is constantly forced to defend themselves, they can become so weakened that they lose the ability to protect themselves at all. Imagine I left my house and, instead of walking into the peaceful and aristocratic city of Turin, I found myself in a dull German provincial town. My instincts would have to work overtime to block out the oppressive, timid atmosphere of that world. Or imagine I ended up in a big German city, one of those crowded, vice-filled places where nothing grows naturally, and everything, whether good or bad, is imported and crammed into its limits. Would I not feel forced to curl up like a hedgehog? But having prickles, being constantly defensive, wastes energy. It is an unnecessary burden, especially when one could instead relax, open one's hands, and live without such defenses.

Another way to protect oneself is to react as little as possible and avoid situations that trap you into always reacting. These situations force you to give up your freedom and initiative, turning you into a mere tool that responds automatically. A perfect example of this is our relationship with books. A scholar who spends most of their time handling books—someone who, like the average philologist, might go through two hundred a day—eventually loses the ability to think for themselves. If they don't have a book in hand, they cannot think at all. When they do think, they only react to ideas they've read. Over time, all they can do is respond to stimuli, endlessly saying "yes" or "no" to ideas that are already formed. They critique, but they cannot create.

This kind of scholar has lost the instinct to defend themselves, or else they would protect themselves from books. The scholar is, in a way, a kind of failure. I have seen brilliant, talented, and free-spirited people completely ruined by reading too much by the time they turned thirty. They become like spent matches, only able to give off sparks if they are struck hard enough—thoughts don't come naturally to them anymore.

Starting the day, full of fresh energy and strength, by immediately diving into a book—I consider this a terrible mistake. It is a harmful habit that squanders the best part of the day when one should instead be thinking for themselves, creating, and engaging with the world directly.

At this point, I can no longer avoid answering the question of how one becomes what one is. To answer it, I must discuss the art of self-preservation, which can be considered a kind of selfishness. If someone's life-task—their purpose and the destiny tied to it—is far greater than the ordinary, nothing could be more dangerous than coming face-to-face with oneself alongside that task. Becoming what one truly is requires not having the faintest idea of what that is in advance. From this perspective, even the mistakes in one's life gain meaning and value—temporary missteps, hesitations, moments of humility, or time spent on duties that don't belong to the actual life-task all serve a purpose.

In such situations, great wisdom—perhaps the highest wisdom— comes into play. When knowing oneself (nosce teipsum) would lead directly to ruin, forgetting oneself, misunderstanding oneself, underestimating oneself, narrowing oneself, and even becoming mediocre can be the most rational choices. Morally speaking, loving one's neighbor and living for others might actually serve as a protective strategy for maintaining the most difficult kind of self-centeredness. This is one rare case where, against my usual principles, I can side with altruistic instincts because they can ultimately serve the discipline of selfishness.

The entire surface of one's consciousness—since consciousness is indeed just a surface—must remain free from any overwhelming imperative. Beware of powerful words or dramatic gestures; they pose the risk of making your instincts understand themselves too soon. Meanwhile, the organizing "idea," the one destined to take command, grows deeper and deeper within. It begins to direct you gradually, guiding you back from your detours and mistakes. It quietly prepares individual abilities and traits, which will one day become essential to your overall purpose. Step by step, it refines all the skills that will eventually serve your ultimate task. All this happens long before it whispers anything about the task itself—the "goal," the "object," or the "meaning" of your life.

From this perspective, my life is extraordinary. To undertake the task of tr ansvaluing values, a person needs a wider range of abilities than might seem possible for one individual. Moreover, these abilities must often be in conflict with one another, yet coexist without destroying each other. This requires a careful hierarchy of capacities, a sense of distance, and the ability to separate without creating hostility. It involves resisting the urge to blur distinctions or reconcile opposing forces. To possess great diversity while remaining the opposite of chaotic—this was the first condition for my life's work. It was a long, secret process, guided by an instinctive mastery that I barely noticed at the time.

This instinct was so strong that I never once dreamed of what was developing within me. Then, suddenly, all my abilities matured, and one day they emerged in their fullest bloom. I cannot recall ever exerting myself. My life shows no trace of struggle. I am the opposite of a heroic nature. To "will" something, to "strive" toward a goal, or to have a fixed desire in mind—these are things I have never experienced. Even now, when I look toward my future—a vast and open future—it feels like gazing out at a calm sea. No sigh of longing stirs its surface. I have no wish for anything to be different than it is. I have no desire to be different than I am.

This has always been true of me. I have never had a desire. Imagine a man who, by his forty-fourth year, has never concerned himself with honors, women, or wealth—not because they didn't come his way, but because they simply didn't interest him. This is how I ended up as a University Professor one day, entirely by accident, at the age of twenty-four. I had never once imagined such a thing. Similarly, two years earlier, I became a philologist almost by chance. My first philological work, which marked the beginning of my career, was published in Rheinisches Museum at the insistence of my teacher Ritschl.

Ritschl, I say with deep respect, was the only truly brilliant scholar I ever met. He had that delightful kind of mischief that distinguishes us Thuringians, something that even makes a German seem likable. Even in the pursuit of truth, we prefer indirect paths. In saying this, I do not mean to diminish my fellow Thuringian, the insightful Leopold von Ranke.

You may wonder why I've chosen to share all these seemingly trivial and, according to conventional thinking, insignificant details with you. After all, doing so might seem to diminish me, especially if I am destined to play a role in great causes. My answer is simple: these so-called trivial matters—diet, environment, climate, recreation, and the entire art of self-care—are far more important than anything humanity has traditionally valued. It is here, in these overlooked aspects of life, that we must begin anew.

All the things humanity has exalted with such seriousness in the past are not even real. They are nothing more than illusions or, more precisely, lies born of the corrupted instincts of sick and harmful natures. Concepts like "God," "soul," "virtue," "sin," "the Beyond," "truth," and "eternal life"—all of these were created to glorify what humanity imagined as its greatness, its "divinity." And yet, every question of politics, social order, and education has been fundamentally distorted because of these falsehoods. The most harmful people have been regarded as great men, while the simple, foundational aspects of life have been dismissed and despised.

If I compare myself to those figures who have been honored as humanity's "greatest," the difference is clear. I do not even consider those so-called "first" men to be truly human. To me, they are the waste products of humanity— creatures born of disease and revengeful instincts. They are monsters filled with decay, incurable beings who take their revenge on life itself. I aim to be their opposite.

It is my privilege to possess the sharpest instinct for recognizing signs of health and vitality. There is nothing sickly in me; even in times of serious illness, I have never become morbid. And you will not find a trace of fanaticism in my nature.

No one can point to a moment in my life when I assumed an arrogant or overly emotional attitude. Greatness does not need theatrical displays—those who rely on them are false. Beware of men who seem overly picturesque or dramatic! Life has always come easily to me, even when it demanded the most from me. In those periods when I took on the heaviest responsibilities, I felt the greatest ease and joy. Anyone who saw me during the seventy days this autumn, when I accomplished an extraordinary amount of work—things no one else today could dream of doing—would have noticed my condition was one of overflowing energy and good cheer. My meals were more satisfying than ever, and my sleep was never more restful.

I know no other way to approach great tasks than as if they were play. This sense of playfulness is essential to greatness. The slightest sign of strain, a stern expression, or a harsh tone—all these are marks against a man, and even more so against his work. One must have no nerves for such things. Even suffering from solitude is a flaw; the only thing I've ever suffered from is the multitude.

From an absurdly young age—when I was just seven years old—I already knew that no human speech would ever truly reach me. But did anyone ever see me sad about it? Even now, I remain approachable and considerate toward everyone, including the lowest among people. There is no arrogance or hidden contempt in this. Anyone I despise quickly realizes it—my mere existence is enough to provoke outrage in those with corrupted blood in their veins.

My formula for human greatness is amor fati—the love of fate. This means wanting nothing to be different, neither in the past nor the future, and accepting everything for all eternity. The necessary must not only be endured but embraced, and never hidden. All idealism is a lie in the face of necessity. It is not enough to accept necessity—you must love it.

CHAPTER 3
WHY I WRITE SUCH EXCELLENT BOOKS

I am one thing, and my creations are another. Before discussing my books themselves, I want to briefly address the understanding—and, more often, the misunderstanding—that they have encountered. I will do this only in passing, as the time for a full discussion has not yet arrived. My time, too, has not yet come; some people are born to be recognized only after their time. One day, there will need to be institutions where people live and teach as I understand living and teaching. Perhaps by then, there will even be endowed positions for interpreting Zarathustra.

But it would contradict everything I stand for if I expected my truths to be understood today. That no one listens to me now, that no one knows how to receive what I offer, is not only understandable— it seems entirely appropriate. I do not wish to be confused with anyone else, and to avoid that, I must not confuse myself. As I've said before, I have experienced very few instances of ill- will in my life, and in terms of literary ill-will, I can scarcely think of any examples. Instead, what I have encountered is far too much pure foolishness.

To me, picking up one of my books is among the rarest honors a person can grant themselves. It requires a sense of reverence—like taking off one's shoes before entering sacred ground. Once, Dr. Heinrich von Stein admitted to me that he could not understand a single word of Zarathustra. I told him that this was exactly as it should be: understanding even six sentences from that book— truly living them—elevates a person to a level far beyond what modern men are capable of reaching. With this sense of distance, how could I even wish to be read by the "moderns" I am so familiar with? My triumph is the opposite of Schopenhauer's—I say, Non legor , non legar ("I am not read, nor will I be read").

That said, I do not underestimate the strange pleasure I have felt when my works have been contradicted in ways that reveal an innocence of understanding. As recently as last summer, while I was perhaps trying to use the weight of my writing to tip the balance of all literature, a Berlin University professor informed me that I ought to use a different style. According to him, no one could possibly read "such stuff" as I wrote.

It was not Germany, however, but Switzerland that gave me the two most extreme reactions to my work. In the Swiss newspaper Bund, Dr. V. Widmann published an essay on Beyond Good and Evil under the title "Nietzsche's Dangerous Book," while Herr Karl Spitteler offered a general review of all my works. These two pieces stand as milestones in my life—though I won't say what kind of milestones.

Spitteler described my Zarathustra as "advanced exercises in style" and expressed the hope that, later on, I might turn my attention to substance. Meanwhile, Dr. Widmann graciously praised my courage for attempting to abolish all notions of decency. By some ironic twist of fate, nearly every sentence in these critiques was the exact opposite of the truth—a consistency I could only admire. In fact, it was remarkable to see how simply "transvaluing all values" could transform their critiques into perfect truths about me, as though they had accidentally struck the nail on the head by aiming for the wrong target.

This leaves me eager to find an explanation. After all, no one can draw more from books—or from anything else—than they already know.

A man cannot hear what his experience has not prepared him to understand. Take an extreme example: suppose a book describes events and ideas completely beyond common experience—even beyond rare experience—and uses a language entirely new to express a unique series of insights. In such a case, the reader hears nothing at all. Worse still, because of an illusion of perception, they convince themselves that where nothing is heard, there must be nothing to hear. This has been my frequent experience, and it serves as evidence, if you will, of the originality of my insights.

Those who think they have understood my work often do so by projecting their own ideas onto it—often ideas that are entirely opposite to mine. For instance, they might interpret me as an "idealist." On the other hand, those who understand nothing dismiss me outright, denying I am worth considering at all.

Take the word "Superman" as an example. It refers to a type of man who would be among nature's rarest and most extraordinary achievements, standing in stark contrast to "modern" men, "good" men, Christians, and other nihilists. In Zarathustra, a figure who rejects morality entirely, this word carries profound meaning. Yet, almost everywhere, it is misunderstood in complete innocence as referring to an idealized figure—a higher kind of man, half-saint and half-genius. Even worse, some scholars have accused me of Darwinism based on this term, or of promoting the hero-worship championed by Carlyle, a man whose unconscious deceitfulness I once mocked with biting sarcasm.

Once, I quietly suggested to someone that he would do better to look for the Superman in a figure like Cæsar Borgia than in Parsifal. He could not believe his ears. This inability to grasp my meaning is why I have so little interest in hearing critiques of my books, especially those found in newspapers. I hope you can forgive me for this indifference. My friends and publishers know me well enough never to mention such things to me.

In one instance, however, I took note of the many misinterpretations that plagued a single book of mine, Beyond Good and Evil. I could tell you an entertaining story about it. For example, imagine the National- Zeitung, a Prussian newspaper (for my foreign readers, I note this distinction; as for me, I only read Le

Journal des Débats) treating the book as a "sign of the times" or as a piece of Tory philosophy, something even the Kreuz- Zeitung wouldn't have dared to publish.

This misinterpretation speaks to my German audience, but outside of Germany, I have been recognized by readers of extraordinary intellect and character. These are people who have proven themselves in high positions and demanding roles, and some are even true geniuses. I have been discovered in Vienna, St. Petersburg, Stockholm, Copenhagen, Paris, and New York. Yet in the flatlands of Europe—Germany—I remain largely unnoticed.

To confess, I find myself much more pleased by those who do not read me, those who have never heard my name or the word "philosophy." But wherever I go—here in Turin, for instance—faces light up at the sight of me. A small but deeply flattering pleasure comes from the old market-women who insist on selecting the sweetest grapes for me. That, I think, is what it means to truly be a philosopher.

The Poles are often called the French among the Slavs, and for good reason. A charming Russian woman would recognize my origins instantly. I cannot even pretend to be pompous; at best, I might appear slightly awkward. I can think in German, feel in German—I can manage most things—but pompousness is beyond my abilities.

My old mentor Ritschl once claimed that even my philological works read like the novels of a Parisian storyteller, absurdly gripping and full of intrigue. In Paris, people are surprised by my "audacity and subtlety"—the words of Monsieur Taine. Even in my highest and most passionate writing, there is a certain wit that keeps my work from becoming heavy or, worse, German. Wit, after all, is what I do best—it is inseparable from me. God help me. Amen.

We all know what it means to be a "long-ears," someone obtuse and unable to grasp subtlety. I dare say, however, that I have the smallest ears ever known. This is no trivial matter; it seems women sense that I understand them better because of it. I am, in essence, the anti-ass. For this reason alone, I am a kind of monster in the history of the world. In Greek, and not just in Greek, I am the Antichrist.

I am keenly aware of the privileges I enjoy as a writer. On several occasions, it has even been pointed out to me how deeply the regular reading of my works can "spoil" a person's taste. Other books, especially philosophical ones, become nearly unbearable after mine. To enter the refined and elevated world of my writing is an incomparable privilege—one that certainly cannot belong to a typical German. It is, in short, a distinction that must be earned.

For those who share my lofty will and perspective, reading my books brings true exhilaration. Such readers experience moments of pure understanding, as I descend from heights no bird has ever soared to and peer into depths no foot has ever dared to tread. Some have told me that it is impossible to set down one of my books, that even their nights are disturbed by it. My works are both proud and subtle, often reaching the pinnacle of human endeavor—cynicism. To grasp their ideas requires hands capable of both tenderness and fearlessness. Weakness of spirit, whether physical or psychological, completely excludes someone from truly engaging with them. This includes not just spiritual frailty but also cowardice, impurity, and a lurking, vindictive nature. A single word from me can flush out the hidden colors of someone's worst instincts.

Among my acquaintances, I observe a range of reactions to my writings. These serve as fascinating and instructive experiments. Those who want nothing to do with the content of my books—often my so-called friends—adopt a detached, "impersonal" tone. They offer me congratulations for producing yet another book and wish me luck. They comment that my writing seems more cheerful or shows signs of "progress." The truly corrupt—the "beautiful souls," whose falsity is absolute—cannot make sense of my works at all. With the consistency of all such "beautiful souls," they decide my work is beneath them. Then there are the more common types, the "cattle" among my acquaintances, many of them Germans. They hint, in their clumsy way, that they don't always agree with me, though they might concede a point or two. I've even heard such lukewarm remarks about Zarathustra.

A feminist mindset—whether in women or men—also bars entry into the fearless labyrinth of my knowledge. To appreciate my works, one must be unsparing with oneself and disciplined in one's habits. Only through this hardness can one remain lighthearted and merry in the face of unrelenting truths. When I imagine the ideal reader of my works, I see a being of monstrous courage and insatiable curiosity, someone with agility, cleverness, and wisdom—a natural adventurer and explorer.

In truth, no one has described my intended audience better than Zarathustra himself. His words capture perfectly the kind of person to whom I address my works, and the only kind of person capable of understanding their riddles:

"To you, bold adventurers and experimenters, and to all who have ever sailed under cunning sails on treacherous seas;

To you who delight in enigmas and twilight, whose souls are drawn by flutes into every dangerous abyss;

For you do not creep along timidly, clinging to a thread with trembling fingers; and where you can guess, you despise the need to argue."

I will now pass just one or two general remarks Let me now delve deeply into my art of style. Style, in essence, is the means of conveying a state of being, an inner tension, or a profound emotion through signs. This includes the rhythm and tempo of those signs. Style is not merely a decorative or superficial endeavor; it is the communication of life itself. Given the enormous variety of inner states within me, I possess a corresponding variety of styles—

perhaps the most diverse range of styles ever available to one individual.

A good style is one that truthfully expresses an internal condition. It must not falter over its signs, misjudge their tempo, or fail to capture the shifting moods it represents. All the laws of phrasing, rhythm, and structure emerge from the artistic depiction of moods. But the concept of "good style," standing alone, is foolishness—a mere abstraction, like "beauty in itself" or "goodness in itself." Style is only meaningful when it achieves communication, and that communication requires ears that can hear it and individuals who are capable of receiving and understanding it. Without these, style is no more than an echo in an empty hall.

For example, Zarathustra is still searching for its readers, and I suspect it will search for a long time. A man must be worthy of listening to it. Until such people emerge, the art poured into that book will remain unrecognized. No one before me had dared to create such new, strange, and deliberately crafted artistic forms, only to release them like seeds to the wind. That such a thing was possible in the German language had yet to be proven; indeed, I would have denied it myself before I achieved it. Before my time, no one knew what the German language—or any language—was truly capable of.

I was the first to discover the art of grand rhythm and elevated style in prose, capable of expressing the vast oscillations of sublime and superhuman passion. With the dithyramb The Seven Seals, the final discourse of the third part of Zarathustra, I soared miles beyond anything that had ever been called poetry. The art there reached heights that surpass what anyone had thought possible.

The voice that speaks in my works belongs to a psychologist without equal. A discerning reader—a reader of the kind I deserve—might recognize this immediately. Such a reader would approach my works with the same care and reverence with which the old philologists read their Horace. Yet, what the world widely accepts as truth often seems to me to be nothing more than naive errors. For instance, the belief that "altruism" and "egoism" are opposites is an elementary mistake. The "ego" itself is nothing but an illusion, an idealized fabrication. There are no truly altruistic or egoistic actions; both ideas are psychological nonsense.

Similarly, the notion that "man pursues happiness," or that "happiness is the reward of virtue," is nothing but hollow rhetoric. The belief that "pleasure and pain" are opposites is another such fallacy. Morality—the great corrupter of humanity—has distorted every psychological truth, down to the absurdity of labeling love as "unselfish." A man cannot love unless he is firmly rooted in himself. This is something women understand instinctively; they care little for men who are "unselfish" or without strong individuality.

May I claim, incidentally, that I understand women? This knowledge forms part of my Dionysian legacy. Perhaps I am the first true psychologist of the "eternally feminine." Women like me—it has always been so, except for those unfortunate ones, the emancipated types, who lack the essence of motherhood. I refuse to let myself be torn apart by them! A perfect woman will tear you apart when she loves you. I know these enchanting Maenads all too well. What a dangerous, sly, and predatory creature she is—and yet how irresistible!

A vengeful woman would storm the gates of Fate itself. Women are more wicked and clever than men, and their goodness often signals degeneration. Cases of "beautiful souls" among women almost always arise from some physiological defect, but I will go no further, lest I stray too far into medical analysis. The fight for "equal rights" is, in itself, a symptom of illness. Truly womanly women instinctively resist rights and equality because they understand the natural order—the eternal war between the sexes—that places them in the highest rank.

Have people understood my definition of love? It is the only definition worthy of a philosopher. Love, in its essence, is war; at its foundation, it is the mortal enmity between the sexes. And how does one save or cure a woman? Give her a child! A woman needs children; a man is only ever a means to that end. As Zarathustra says, "Man is a means, not the goal."

The emancipation of women stems from the hatred of barren women toward their fertile counterparts. Their fight against men is nothing more than a strategy to lower the status of womanhood itself. By striving to become the "Ideal Woman," these individuals aim to undermine the natural hierarchy. Their weapons are university education, trousers, and political rights. These "emancipated" ones are the anarchists of the feminine world, driven by a deeply rooted instinct for revenge.

To clarify my view, which is both honest and uncompromising, I will reveal one clause of my moral code against vice. By "vice," I mean every opposition to nature, every form of idealism. The clause states: "The preaching of chastity is a public incitement to unnatural acts. All denigration of sexual life, all attempts to sully it by calling it 'impure,' constitute the essential crime against life itself— the essential crime against the Holy Spirit of Life."

To provide an example of my psychological insight, I offer this analysis from Beyond Good and Evil. I forbid any guessing as to whom I describe in the following passage:

"The genius of the heart, as possessed by the great hermit, the divine tempter, and the natural Pied Piper of souls. His voice reaches into the deepest parts of every conscience; his words and gestures carry an irresistible pull, compelling others closer, ever closer. The genius of the heart silences arrogance and vanity, polishing rough souls and awakening in them a longing to reflect the heavens as a placid mirror does. He teaches the clumsy and the hurried hand to pause, to grasp more delicately, to uncover hidden treasures of kindness and sweetness buried under thick ice. This genius leaves every person richer, not crushed or overwhelmed by the gifts of another, but revitalized within themselves—more fragile, perhaps, but filled with new hopes, new desires, and new aspirations."

CHAPTER 4
THE BIRTH OF TRAGEDY

To fully appreciate The Birth of Tragedy (1872), one must set aside certain preconceptions. This work created a stir and even captivated readers despite its errors—especially through its alignment with Wagnerism, which it treated as if it were a herald of cultural ascent. This alone made the treatise significant in Wagner's career, surrounding his name with great expectations. To this day, I am occasionally reminded, even during a performance of Parsifal, that I bear some responsibility for fostering the belief that Wagner's movement represented a cultural renaissance. The book has often been cited with an exaggerated title: The Second Birth of Tragedy from the Spirit of Music. Many read it merely as a collection of new formulations to justify Wagner's art, purpose, and mission, and in doing so, entirely missed its deeper significance.

A more accurate title for the book might have been Hellenism and Pessimism. The real value of the work lies in its first attempt to show how the Greeks managed to overcome pessimism, how they wrestled with it and triumphed. Tragedy itself stands as proof that the Greeks were not pessimists. Schopenhauer, as with so many other things, misunderstood this entirely. He failed to see that Greek tragedy was a counterbalance to despair, a creation of strength rather than weakness.

When viewed objectively, The Birth of Tragedy is a work profoundly out of step with its time. No one would guess it was conceived during the thunderous battles of Wörth. The ideas took shape on chilly September nights under the walls of Metz, amidst my duties caring for the wounded. It feels more like a work written fifty years earlier, steeped in an indifference to politics that might today be dismissed as "un-German." In places, the influence of Hegel wafts through its pages, and the occasional turn of phrase still carries the morbid stench of Schopenhauer's philosophical cadaver.

At its core, the book presents an idea: the duality of the Dionysian and the Apollonian. This concept is translated into metaphysics, with history portrayed as the evolution of this tension. Tragedy represents the resolution of this duality into unity. From this vantage point, disparate elements that had never before been connected are suddenly juxtaposed, illuminating one another. Opera and revolution, for instance, are shown in an entirely new light.

The book's two most groundbreaking contributions are, first, its psychological understanding of the Dionysian phenomenon among the Greeks. It offers the first true analysis of this aspect of their culture, recognizing it as the singular root of all Greek art. Secondly, it addresses Socraticism in an entirely new way. Socrates is revealed as the instrument of Greek decline, a typical decadent. For the first time, "Reason" is presented as opposed to instinct— reason at any cost, exposed as a destructive, life- draining force.

The book is strikingly and deliberately silent about Christianity. Christianity is neither Apollonian nor Dionysian. It denies all aesthetic values, which are the only values The Birth of Tragedy acknowledges. Christianity, in its essence, is profoundly nihilistic, whereas the Dionysian symbol represents the ultimate affirmation of life, embracing it in its fullest extremes. At one point, however, the Christian priesthood is mentioned in the book as a "treacherous order of goblins" or as "subterraneans," reflecting their opposition to the aesthetic and life-affirming values celebrated in the text.

The book's attitude toward Christianity underscores its broader philosophical stance: it embraces life, even its darkest aspects, in direct opposition to the denial inherent in Christianity. The Dionysian, for all its chaos and danger, embodies the ultimate "yes" to existence. Christianity, by contrast, represents the ultimate "no," a retreat from the richness and fullness of life into a shadowy world of negation and abstraction. This contrast, though not stated overtly, permeates the work, shaping its every insight.

Thus, The Birth of Tragedy stands as a bold and original attempt to rethink the foundations of art, culture, and human existence itself. It challenges deeply held assumptions and reveals new possibilities for understanding life's complexities. That its true value has often been overshadowed by its association with Wagner is, perhaps, an irony befitting the book's own tragic themes.

The beginning of my philosophical journey was extraordinary beyond words. It was as if my deepest personal insights had found their perfect historical counterpart—the only example of its kind in existence. This realization allowed me to be the first to truly understand the astonishing phenomenon of the Dionysian. Simultaneously, by recognizing Socrates as a decadent, I demonstrated the unassailable precision of my psychological insights, entirely unaffected by any kind of moral prejudice. To perceive morality itself as a symptom of decline—this was an innovation of the highest order, a landmark event in the history of knowledge.

With my two foundational doctrines, I soared far above the simplistic chatter about Optimism and Pessimism. I was the first to see the real contrast at work: on one side, the degenerate instinct that turns against life with a hidden vengeance, as embodied in Christianity, Schopenhauer's philosophy, and to some extent even Plato's. This is the essence of idealism in all its forms—a turning away from life. On the other side stands a formula for the ultimate affirmation of life, a profound "yes" born from an overwhelming and overflowing abundance of vitality. This "yes" embraces all of existence, even its suffering, guilt, strangeness, and questions. It is not a conditional affirmation; it is an unreserved exultation of life as it is.

This final and most joyful affirmation of life is not only the highest ideal but also the deepest and most scientifically grounded truth. It declares that nothing in existence must be suppressed or discarded. Everything has its place and its necessity. What

Christianity and other nihilistic philosophies reject—what they condemn and fear—belongs to a far higher order in the hierarchy of values than what the instincts of degeneration call "good" or acceptable.

To grasp this truth requires a certain courage, and courage itself requires an excess of strength. Only a man who is overflowing with life's energy can approach the truth, for the proximity to reality depends entirely on the measure of his strength. For the strong, knowledge and affirmation of reality are necessities. Just as essential for the weak, who are driven by fear, are flight, denial, and the construction of ideals—those elaborate lies meant to shield them from life. The weak cannot afford the luxury of truth. Lies are their tools of survival, their indispensable refuge.

He who truly understands the word "Dionysian" and, more importantly, understands himself through that term, has no need to argue against Plato, Christianity, or Schopenhauer. His very being rejects their decay. His senses, his instincts, his very breath can detect the stench of decomposition that emanates from their doctrines. For such a person, refutation is unnecessary—his existence itself is the counterargument.

In these doctrines, I had discovered the essence of tragedy—the ultimate psychological explanation of what tragedy truly is. I explored this concept fully in The Twilight of the Idols (Aph. 5, part 10): "To say 'yes' to life, even to its strangest and most challenging aspects; to rejoice in life's infinite vitality, even when it demands the sacrifice of its highest forms—this is what I called the Dionysian. It is the gateway to understanding the psychology of the tragic poet. It is not about purging terror and pity, or expelling dangerous passions through catharsis, as Aristotle misunderstood it. Instead, it is about moving far beyond terror and pity, to become the eternal desire for Becoming itself—a desire that finds joy even in destruction."

In this sense, I claim the title of the first tragic philosopher—a direct and absolute contrast to any pessimistic philosopher. Before me, there was no philosophical translation of the Dionysian experience into something emotional and profound. Tragic wisdom was entirely absent. Even among the greatest Greek philosophers of the two centuries before Socrates, I found no evidence of it. The closest exception, and the one figure who gave me some sense of warmth and resonance, was Heraclitus.

The affirmation of impermanence, of destruction, and of the ceaseless flow of Becoming over the static concept of Being— this is the defining feature of a Dionysian philosophy. It is an enthusiastic embrace of contradiction and conflict, of the endless cycle of creation and annihilation. In all of these elements, I must recognize Heraclitus as the thinker who has come closest to my own ideas so far.

Heraclitus's insights resonate deeply with my own. The doctrine of "Eternal Recurrence"—the idea that all things repeat themselves endlessly in a cyclical pattern—finds a kindred spirit in Heraclitus. While it is most fully articulated in Zarathustra, one might trace its origins, or at least its echoes, to earlier thinkers. The Stoics, who borrowed many of their core ideas from Heraclitus, hint at this concept in their works. Whether or not it was explicitly taught before my time, the doctrine of Eternal

Recurrence remains integral to my philosophy, as it captures the ceaseless, unending rhythm of existence in its eternal dance of creation and destruction.

This work expresses a profound and extraordinary hope. Even now, I see no reason to abandon the dream of a Dionysian future for music. Let us look a hundred years into the future and imagine that my efforts to dismantle two thousand years of hostility toward nature and humanity—two thousand years of desecration and suppression—have finally succeeded. If this hope is fulfilled, a new movement will rise, a party of life-advocates dedicated to the most monumental of tasks: the elevation and perfection of mankind, coupled with the uncompromising eradication of all that is degenerate and parasitical. Out of this abundance of life, flourishing once again on earth, the Dionysian state will inevitably reemerge. I promise the arrival of a tragic age, an age of the highest art that affirms life in its entirety. Tragedy will be reborn, but only after humanity has faced and understood the hardest and most necessary struggles—wars waged not in despair, but with the wisdom and strength to endure their knowledge without being overcome by it.

A psychologist might observe that what I heard in Wagnerian music during my youth and early adulthood was not truly Wagner. Instead, it was the music of my own spirit, something I instinctively transformed and reinterpreted in light of the new life-force that surged within me. My essay, Wagner in Bayreuth, serves as proof of this transformation. In all its pivotal psychological moments, I am the central figure, the one being described. Wherever Wagner's name appears in the text, you may confidently substitute it with my own or with "Zarathustra." The entire vision of the dithyrambic artist in that essay is a portrait of the author of Zarathustra, already fully formed. It delves into profound depths that never intersect with the real Wagner. Indeed, Wagner himself sensed this. He could not recognize his own reflection in my essay.

Thus, "the idea of Bayreuth" was transfigured into something far beyond Wagner or his time—into a vision comprehensible only to those familiar with my Zarathustra. It became a vision of the Great Noon, a future moment when the highest individuals will dedicate themselves to humanity's greatest tasks. Perhaps this is even the vision of a festival that I might live to witness. The passionate tone of the essay's opening pages reflects nothing less than universal history. The gaze discussed on page 105 of the book is unmistakably the gaze of Zarathustra. Wagner, Bayreuth, and the pitiable smallness of German mediocrity become mere clouds on which an infinite mirage of the future is projected.

Psychologically, my essay attributes many of my own defining characteristics to Wagner's nature: the juxtaposition of the brightest and most destructive forces, a Will to Power unparalleled in history, spiritual courage without compromise, and a boundless capacity for intellectual growth unhampered by a lack of practical action. The essay brims with prophecy. It speaks of the imminent resurrection of the Greek spirit, of the urgent need for men who will serve as counter-Alexanders, retying the severed Gordian knot of Greek culture.

Listen closely to the weighty tone with which the idea of a "sense for the tragic" is introduced on page 180—it carries the resonance of world history. In truth, this essay contains little else but world-historic accents. Its objectivity is unlike anything that has ever existed: an absolute certainty about who I am, projected onto random realities. The truths it reveals about me spring from unfathomable depths. On pages 174 and 175, the style of Zarathustra is foretold with unerring precision. And the description on pages 144 to 147 of the event for which Zarathustra stands—the monumental act of purifying and consecrating humanity—is unparalleled in its grandeur. No more magnificent expression will ever be written for such a vision.

CHAPTER 5
THOUGHTS OUT OF SEASON

The four essays that make up Thoughts out of Season are openly combative in tone, leaving no doubt that I was no idle dreamer. These essays reveal a penchant for wielding a metaphorical sword and, perhaps, a dangerously deft hand in doing so. The first of these assaults (1873) targeted German culture, which I regarded with unrelenting contempt even then. I saw it as utterly hollow—devoid of meaning, direction, or purpose. It was nothing more than "public opinion" masquerading as culture. To assume that Germany's military victories were a testament to its cultural superiority—or worse, proof of its culture triumphing over that of France—was, to my mind, a perilously misguided notion.

The second essay (1874) turned its attention to the corrosive effects of modern scientific study on life itself. It exposed the mechanized, dehumanized nature of this pursuit, which, in its obsession with impersonal "efficiency" and the so-called "division of labor," had led to a diseased way of life. The true purpose of science—its potential to serve culture—was forgotten entirely. Instead, modern scientific endeavor had become a factory for producing barbarism. In this essay, I was the first to identify the celebrated "historical sense" of the century not as an intellectual achievement but as a sickness—a glaring symptom of decay.

In the third and fourth essays, I erected a signpost pointing toward a higher ideal of culture, one that sought to restore the original and noble meaning of the term. Within these essays, I presented two examples of extraordinary self-love and self-discipline—figures who embodied the utmost disdain for everything that surrounded them: the Empire, so-called culture, Christianity, Bismarck, and even the notion of "success." These figures were Schopenhauer and Wagner—or, to put it plainly, Nietzsche himself.

Of the four essays, the first sparked an extraordinary reaction. Its impact was spectacular. I had touched upon the raw nerve of a nation basking in triumph and dared to declare that its victory was not a milestone for culture but perhaps the opposite. Responses poured in from every corner, particularly from admirers of David Strauss, whom I had lampooned as the epitome of the German "Philistine of Culture." I portrayed him as smugly self-satisfied, the author of a provincial creed dressed up as profound philosophy in The Old and the New Faith. Following the publication of my essay, the term "Philistine of Culture" entered common usage in Germany.

Strauss's supporters—whose vanity I had wounded as loyal Württembergians and Swabians—responded with the naïve and clumsy outrage I had anticipated. Their indignation was so transparent that it bordered on the comical. The Prussian critics, on the other hand, were sharper and carried an air of military precision—one might say their responses had a touch of

"Prussian blue." Among the most disgraceful reactions was that of the Leipzig newspaper Grenzboten, whose editorial conduct enraged my friends in Bâle. It took considerable effort on my part to dissuade them from pursuing legal action against the paper.

Despite the torrent of opposition, a few older intellectuals sided with me for reasons that were sometimes mysterious but nevertheless gratifying. Among these was Ewald of Göttingen, who publicly acknowledged the devastating precision of my critique of Strauss. Another was the Hegelian philosopher Bruno Bauer, who from that point onward became one of my most attentive readers. These voices, though few, confirmed to me the depth of the wounds I had inflicted on the complacent façade of German culture.

In his later years, he often mentioned me in significant contexts, particularly when directing figures like Herr von Treitschke, the Prussian Historian, toward a proper understanding of "Culture." Treitschke had completely lost sight of this concept, and it was suggested that my works could provide the necessary clarity. The most thorough and detailed commentary on my book came from Würzburg, written by Professor Hoffmann, a former student of the philosopher von Baader. Hoffmann foresaw a monumental future for me, predicting that I would bring about a decisive moment in the discourse surrounding atheism. He identified me as its most instinctive and radical advocate, recognizing that atheism had drawn me to Schopenhauer in the first place.

The review that garnered the most attention and provoked the greatest reaction was Carl Hillebrand's bold and incisive appraisal of my work, published in the Augsburg Gazette. Hillebrand, known for his mild temperament, was the last truly humane German writer with the skill to wield a pen effectively. His critique, later included in his collected essays in a slightly more cautious tone, treated my book as an event—a pivotal moment signaling an awakening. He described it as a revival of German earnestness and passion in spiritual matters. Hillebrand spoke with the utmost respect about the form of my work, praising its refined taste and perfect tact in distinguishing between individuals and ideas. He called it the finest piece of polemical writing in the German language, a masterclass in an art that Germans typically find both perilous and undesirable.

Hillebrand's review went beyond merely agreeing with my perspective. He emphasized my daring critique of the deterioration of German language and writing, noting that contemporary authors, posing as purists, could no longer construct proper sentences. Sharing my disdain for the literary idols of the time, he ended his review with admiration for my courage—especially the audacity to put the nation's most beloved figures on trial in the court of reason. He recognized this as the "greatest courage of all," a trait seldom found in an era of complacency.

The repercussions of this essay were invaluable to me. It secured my reputation in a way that rendered others hesitant to challenge me directly. Since then, there has been a noticeable silence regarding my work. In Germany, I have been treated with a brooding caution, and I have enjoyed a freedom of speech that few, especially in the "Empire," could claim. My paradise lies in "the shadow of my sword." Fundamentally, all I had done was to implement one of Stendhal's maxims: he suggested that one should make an entrance into society by engaging in a duel. My choice of opponent could not have been more fitting—the foremost free-thinker of Germany.

In this confrontation, a new kind of free thought emerged, one distinct from the European and American breed of libres penseurs. These self-proclaimed "free thinkers," with their modern ideas, are nothing more than stubborn fools and jesters. I find myself in greater opposition to them than to any of their adversaries. Like their opponents, they aim to "improve" humanity—but always in their own image. If they could comprehend the essence of what I stand for, they would undoubtedly wage war against it. Yet their belief in an "ideal" remains unshaken. In stark contrast, I stand as the first Immoralist.

I should not claim that the last two essays in Thoughts out of Season, dedicated to Schopenhauer and Wagner, respectively, were primarily aimed at thoroughly analyzing these two figures or solving their psychological mysteries. This isn't to say that there aren't moments of insight. For example, in the second essay, with an instinctive certainty, I identified the core of Wagner's nature as rooted in theatrical talent—a force that relentlessly pursued its ultimate conclusions. Yet, my true aim in writing this essay was something altogether different. What I sought to address was not psychology but an unprecedented challenge in education: the formation of a new understanding of self-discipline and self-defense, carried to a point of resolute hardness—a path toward greatness and monumental historic duties.

Broadly speaking, I took hold of two prominent, yet previously undefined, archetypes—grasping them by the forelock as one seizes fleeting opportunities—not to define them, but to express my thoughts on entirely different matters. I sought to expand the range of concepts, formulas, and tools at my disposal. I even hinted at this explicitly, with what now strikes me as uncanny foresight, on page 183 of Schopenhauer as Educator. Plato used Socrates in much the same way: as a cipher for his own ideas. Looking back now, with greater clarity and distance, I cannot deny that these essays ultimately point back to me.

The essay Wagner in Bayreuth is, in many ways, a prophecy of my own future. Meanwhile, Schopenhauer as Educator reveals my most intimate, secret history, chronicling the evolution of my thought. Above all, these works contain the vow I made to myself—a promise that resonates with the position I hold today, from a height where I no longer speak with mere words but with thunderbolts! In those days, I was far from the place I now occupy, but I saw it clearly, even then. I was never under any illusions about the path I had to take, the vast sea I had to navigate, the dangers I would face—and, ultimately, the triumph I envisioned.

What stands out in this book is the calm certainty with which it promises— a serene confidence in a future that could not remain merely a promise. Every word was lived deeply, painfully, and intimately. There are moments in its pages that bleed with suffering, yet a wind of immense freedom sweeps through the entire work. Even its wounds are not presented as objections.

This essay also illuminates my understanding of what it means to be a philosopher: a figure who is a living, dangerous force, a catalyst that threatens to shake everything to its core. My concept of the philosopher diverges by miles from the image of even someone like Kant, let alone the academic "ruminators" or professors who pretend to the title. For those willing to see, this essay offers invaluable insights into that understanding. And yet, at its heart, it is not truly "Schopenhauer as Educator" speaking— it is "Nietzsche as Educator," offering my own vision.

Given that my occupation at the time was that of a scholar—and perhaps because I understood my craft well—the essay also provides a sharp portrayal of scholarly psychology. It reveals my sense of distance from academia and my unwavering conviction about my true purpose. What was my genuine life-task, and what were merely tools, interludes, and secondary pursuits? My wisdom lies in having been many things, in many places, so that I could ultimately become one thing—so that I could reach a singular goal. It was part of my fate to be a scholar for a time, even though it was only a step along the way.

CHAPTER 6

HUMAN, ALL-TOO-HUMAN

Human, All- Too- Human, along with its two sequels, stands as a monument to a profound personal crisis. The book, subtitled A

Book for Free Spirits, is, in nearly every sentence, a testament to triumph. Through it, I cleansed myself of all that was alien to my nature. Idealism, for instance, is utterly foreign to me. The title itself declares: "Where you see ideal things, I see human things—oh, all-too-human!" It reflects a hard-won clarity. I know men better now. The term "free spirit" as used in this book should be understood not as some lofty ideal, but as a spirit that has reclaimed its freedom, one that has taken itself back.

The tone throughout the work is a marked departure from my earlier writings. My voice is now sharper, cooler, and at times unflinchingly hard and scornful. There is an air of refined spirituality, a noble taste, that strives to master a turbulent and passionate undercurrent. This change is no coincidence. It is fitting that the book appeared in 1878, coinciding with the centenary of Voltaire's death. Voltaire, an intellectual aristocrat and a man of the sharpest wit, was the very antithesis of the writers who followed him—and in that sense, I consider him a kindred spirit. Associating my work with his name marked a decisive step forward in my journey.

Delving deeper into the pages of this book, one encounters a relentless and pitiless spirit that leaves no stone unturned. I shine a steady, unblinking light into the hidden lairs of ideals, exposing the places where they retreat, where they fester and linger as last refuges. With a torch that cuts through the shadows like a blade, I illuminate the dark corners where these illusions thrive. This is warfare, but not the kind accompanied by smoke, gunpowder, or the postures of combat. All of that would still be "idealism." Instead, this is a cold, clinical dismantling. One by one, errors are methodically placed on ice. The ideal is not attacked—it is left to freeze. Genius freezes here, as does sainthood, heroism, faith, conviction, and even pity. Under my relentless scrutiny, even the sacred "thing in itself" succumbs to the frost.

The context of the book's creation is revealing. It was born during the first musical festival at Bayreuth, and my feelings of profound alienation there played a significant role. Anyone familiar with the visions that had guided me up to that point might guess how disoriented I felt when I "woke up" in Bayreuth. It was as though I had been dreaming. Nothing was familiar. I recognized neither the surroundings nor even Wagner himself. My memories of Tribschen—the secluded haven of bliss where we had shared incomparable moments—found no reflection here. Those exquisite days when we laid the first stone and celebrated among a small circle of discerning souls—those days were gone.

What had happened? Wagner had been translated into something entirely German. The Wagnerite had claimed dominion over Wagner. What we saw now was "German art," a "German master," and, worst of all, German beer. For those of us who understood the refined, cosmopolitan nature of Wagner's art, this vulgar transformation was unbearable. I have encountered three generations of Wagnerites, from Brendel—who absurdly equated Wagner with Hegel—to the "idealists" of the Bayreuth Gazette, who confuse Wagner with themselves. I have been subjected to every variety of confession about Wagner from these so- called "beautiful souls." But amidst this cacophony, not one intelligent word has ever reached my ears.

What a grotesque assembly they were! The likes of Nohl, Pohl, and Kohl, and an endless parade of their kind. No type of monstrosity was absent—not even the anti-Semite. Poor Wagner! Into whose hands had he fallen? If only he had been consigned to a herd of swine! But no, he was left to the Germans. For posterity's amusement, someone ought to preserve a genuine Bayreuthian in a jar of spirits—not for their "spirit," mind you, for that was precisely what they lacked—with the inscription: "A specimen of the spirit upon which the German Empire was founded."

Enough! In the middle of the festivities, I could endure no more. I packed my bags and departed for a few weeks, leaving behind even the charms of a delightful Parisian woman who sought to console me. I sent Wagner a brief, fatalistic telegram to excuse my absence. I retreated to Klingenbrunn, a remote village buried deep in the Böhmerwald, carrying my melancholy and my scorn for Germans as though they were an illness.

There, under the title The Ploughshare, I began jotting down a series of stern psychological observations. These fragments—each one severe and incisive—may have eventually found their way into Human, All- Too- Human. They reflect the depths of my contempt for the debasement I had witnessed and my determination to chart a new path. This book, with its cool precision and unrelenting dissection of ideals, became the vessel for that determination. It stands as both a monument to that moment of estrangement and a weapon forged to clear the way for free spirits yet to come.

What had occurred within me during that period was not merely a severance from Wagner—it was a broader crisis, a misalignment of my instincts so profound that neither Wagner nor my professorship at Basel could be viewed as anything more than symptoms. A surge of frustration overtook me, a sharp impatience with myself. I recognized, with stark and overwhelming clarity, that it was long overdue for me to confront my own existence and redirect my efforts toward my true purpose. The realization of how much precious time I had wasted struck me like a blow. My life as a philologist appeared futile and absurd when weighed against the demands of my life's actual task. I felt a deep sense of shame over my false modesty, my willingness to settle for something far below my potential.

For ten long years, my intellectual nourishment had stagnated. In that time, I had not added a single meaningful fragment to my knowledge, and much of what I had once known had faded amidst the monotony of a dry and trivial scholastic routine. Crawling with meticulous care through the minutiae of ancient Greek metrics—that was what my work had devolved into. I saw myself clearly, as if from the outside: thin, emaciated, bereft of realities, and with "ideals" that were worthless, known only to the devil. A searing thirst for something more overcame me, and from that moment onward, I devoted myself entirely to the study of physiology, medicine, and the natural sciences. I only returned to history when the demands of my life's task made it absolutely necessary.

It was also then that I first discerned a connection between an instinctively repulsive vocation—one of those so-called "callings" that are, in truth, the furthest thing from what one is truly called to do—and the craving to numb the resulting emptiness through narcotic-like art, such as Wagner's. Upon observing the world around me, I noticed that many young men were trapped in the same plight. An unnatural way of life inevitably breeds further unnatural practices. In Germany—or rather, to clarify, in the Empire—far too many are forced into premature decisions about their futures, choices that soon weigh so heavily upon them that they cannot be cast off. These individuals, craving an escape from their burdens, turn to Wagner as they would to an opiate. For a fleeting moment—or five or six hours—they are able to forget themselves, to escape from their own existence.

At this point, my instincts rebelled against any further compliance, any further self-betrayal. I resolved to reject all that was false within me, even if it meant embracing the harshest conditions of life. Illness, poverty, adversity— anything seemed preferable to the indignity of the selfishness I had fallen into. This selfishness, born of my youthful ignorance and perpetuated by laziness disguised as a "sense of duty," now seemed utterly intolerable. At that critical juncture, I found an unlikely ally in my inherited physical fragility, a predisposition to early death passed down from my father's side. This weakness proved a gift in disguise. Illness gradually loosened the bonds that held me captive, sparing me the need for any abrupt or violent break. I alienated no one; instead, I gained the goodwill of those around me.

Illness also granted me the permission—indeed, the mandate—to completely overhaul my way of life. It compelled me to forget the past, to rest, to embrace leisure, and to cultivate patience. But above all, it required me to think. My failing eyesight was the final stroke that severed my ties with bookish pursuits—plainly put, with philology. Delivered from the tyranny of books, I ceased reading altogether for years. This was, without a doubt, the greatest gift I ever gave myself. The deepest part of me, long buried and silenced by the constant chatter of other voices (for that is what reading truly is), began to stir and awaken. At first timid and uncertain, it eventually found its voice again.

I have never felt greater joy than during the sickest and most painful moments of my life. These periods of suffering marked a profound return to myself. This "return" was nothing less than the highest form of recovery, and from it, my eventual cure emerged naturally. To understand the depth of this transformation, one need only examine The Dawn of Day or The Wanderer and His Shadow. These works bear witness to the rebirth of my truest self—a self that illness, in all its cruelty, had paradoxically made possible.

Human, All- Too- Human, a testament to my rigorous self-discipline, represents the decisive end of all the "Superior Bunkum," "Idealism," "Beautiful Feelings," and other indulgent sentimentalities that had once infiltrated my being. This work was primarily conceived and drafted in Sorrento, where its environment lent itself to clarity and resolution. However, the final shaping and completion of the book occurred during a winter in Basel under far less accommodating conditions. The process was, in fact, quite peculiar. Peter Gast, then a student at the University of Basel and a close and loyal friend of mine, played a pivotal role. My head was often wrapped in painful bandages, and I found myself dictating passages while Gast not only wrote them down but actively refined and corrected them as we went along. To be entirely truthful, while I may have been the author, he was very much the composer of the work.

When the book was finally finished and sent to me, it arrived as a surprising gift to the deeply ailing person I was at the time. In my enthusiasm, I dispatched two copies to Bayreuth, and it was then that fate decided to add its own dramatic touch. By sheer coincidence, a copy of the Parsifal text arrived at the same time, accompanied by a personal inscription from Wagner himself: "To his dear friend Friedrich Nietzsche, from Richard Wagner, Ecclesiastical Councillor." The timing of this crossing of books struck me with a peculiar resonance. It was as though the clash of two swords echoed in the air. Both Wagner and I sensed this moment deeply, for we met it with silence. Shortly after, the first Bayreuth pamphlets emerged, revealing a shift in Wagner's path that I now saw had been long overdue for me to confront. Astonishingly, Wagner had turned to piety.

The clarity with which I grasped my life-task during that period (1876), and the profound certainty of its historical significance, resonates throughout the pages of Human, All- Too- Human. One particular passage captures this certainty, despite my instinctive cunning in avoiding the use of the word "I." This time, however, the omission was not intended to bestow historical grandeur on Schopenhauer or Wagner, but rather on another friend of mine, Dr. Paul Rée. Paul, a sharp and discerning thinker, was far too astute to be misled by this subtle maneuver—though others were not so perceptive. Among my readers, there are hopeless cases, the quintessential German professors, whose telltale response to this passage reveals their misunderstanding of the book as a form of "superior realism." These minds, stuck in their small, provincial interpretations, fail to grasp the radical undercurrents within the work. For proof, one need only compare this passage to the introduction of The Genealogy of Mor als, which directly counters these limited views.

The passage in question reads: "What, after all, is the principal axiom reached by the boldest and coldest thinker, the author of On the Or ig in of Mor al Sensations (read: Nietzsche, the first

Immoralist), through his incisive and decisive analysis of human actions? 'The moral man,' he asserts, 'is no closer to the intelligible (metaphysical) world than the physical man, for there is no intelligible world.' This theory, hardened and sharpened under the hammer- blows of historical knowledge (read: The Transvaluation of All Values), may, at some point in the future—perhaps around 1890—serve as the axe laid to the root of humanity's 'metaphysical need.' Whether this will ultimately be more of a blessing or a curse to humanity's welfare is hard to determine, but it will certainly be a theory of immense consequence, fruitful yet terrifying, bearing the Janus-face that all profound knowledge possesses."

This excerpt alone signals the revolutionary potential of Human, All- Too- Human. It is not merely a book but a turning point, a tool that challenges humanity's deepest metaphysical assumptions. It strikes at the very roots of what had been taken for granted for millennia, offering a perspective at once liberating and unsettling. Such ideas require immense courage to confront, for they demand not just intellectual understanding but an emotional readiness to let go of comforting illusions. This book, therefore, stands as both a personal triumph and a herald of the intellectual storms to come.

CHAPTER 7
THE DAWN OF DAY: THOUGHTS ABOUT MORALITY AS A PREJUDICE

With this book, I begin my campaign against morality. But do not expect the acrid scent of gunpowder—it carries far more pleasant fragrances, provided you have the sensitivity to detect them. There is neither heavy nor light artillery in its pages. If the ultimate goal is a negative one, the means of achieving it are entirely different—they lead naturally to the conclusion, not as a cannon- shot but as a gentle unfolding of logic. Should the reader close this book feeling a cautious hesitancy toward everything once revered under the name of morality, it remains true that not a single sentence here is openly negative. Not a single attack, no sharp malice, resides within these pages. Instead, the book rests like a serene marine creature basking in the sunlight between two rocks, exuding calmness and happiness.

For indeed, at that time, I was that marine creature. Nearly every line in this work was either thought out or caught, like a fisherman pulling treasures from the sea, amidst the rugged rocks along the Genoan coastline. There I lived in solitude, communing with the ocean, exchanging its boundless secrets for the clarity of my thoughts. Even now, when I chance to leaf through its pages, I feel as though each sentence is a hook drawing forth something incomparable from the depths. The book's very surface seems to tremble with subtle shivers of memory, alive with the thrill of discoveries long past.

The art of this book lies in its delicate grasp of fleeting things—those quick and silent moments I liken to "godlike lizards." But unlike the young Greek god who cruelly skewered his quarry, I captured these ephemeral moments with something far gentler—my pen. Above the doorway of this book is written the Indian maxim: "There are so many dawns which have not yet shed their light." This is the guiding spirit of the work. Where does the author search for this new morning, this undiscovered light that promises not just a single day, but a whole world of days to come? In the Transvaluation of all Values, in breaking free from all moral constraints, in the bold affirmation of everything previously condemned, shunned, or damned.

This is a book of affirmation, suffused with light, love, and tenderness. Its glow extends over what has been called evil, restoring to it its soul, its untroubled conscience, and even its rightful claim to existence on this earth. Morality is not attacked here—it simply ceases to be relevant. This book ends not with finality but with an open question. Its final word is "or?"—a fitting closure for a work that seeks not to resolve, but to open doors to possibilities yet unimagined. This is the only book I know of that dares to close with a question, and one that invites the reader into uncharted realms of thought and existence.

My life's mission is to prepare humanity for one supreme moment—a Great Noon—when it can finally awaken to its full consciousness. This moment will be when humanity casts its gaze both backward and forward, stepping out from under the oppressive weight of chance and the manipulations of priests. For the first time, humanity will pose the ultimate question: Why and for what purpose does it exist as a whole? This task arises from my firm conviction that humanity does not naturally find the right path, nor is it guided by some divine hand. On the contrary, it is precisely under the guise of its most sacred values that the instincts of negation, decay, and degeneration have gained their most seductive and destructive influence.

The question of the origin of moral values is, therefore, of utmost importance to me. It determines the very future of humanity. We are commanded to believe that everything is in the best possible hands, that the Bible assures us of a Providence that wisely governs human destiny. Yet when this belief is translated into reality, it amounts to nothing more than a deliberate effort to suppress the truth. That truth is the exact opposite: humanity has, until now, been in the worst hands. It has been ruled by the physiologically flawed, the cunning, the vengeful, and the so-called "saints"— those who slander the world and degrade humanity. These men, cloaked in virtue, have been the architects of corruption.

The clearest evidence of this is that priests—and their disguised counterparts, the philosophers—have established dominion not only within religious communities but across all facets of life. The morality of decay, the will to nonexistence, has been elevated to the status of universal morality. This is revealed in the exaltation of altruism as an absolute value and the widespread hostility toward egoism. To me, anyone who denies this point is already infected. Yet, I stand against the whole world on this matter.

For a physiologist, such opposition in values is undeniable. If even the smallest organ in the body ceases to assert its self-preserving powers, to claim its right to exist and flourish, the entire organism begins to degenerate. The physiologist has no hesitation in removing the diseased parts; there is no room for pity in this work. But the priest desires precisely the opposite: the degeneration of all humanity. His goal is to preserve and even sanctify that which is weak and decayed, and the cost of this preservation is the vitality of humankind itself.

What are we to make of the deceitful concepts that serve morality— concepts like "soul," "spirit," "free will," and "God"? Their sole purpose is the physiological ruin of humanity. When earnest energy is diverted from the instincts of self-preservation and the enhancement of life, when anemia and the contempt for the body are enshrined as ideals and called "salvation," what is this but a recipe for decline? Such morality, which glorifies the rejection of natural instincts and selflessness, has been nothing less than a doctrine of decadence.

It is in this context that I wrote The Dawn of Day. This work marked my first direct confrontation with the morality of self-renunciation. It was here that I began my battle against the age- old glorification of self-sacrifice, a battle to dismantle the moral framework that demands humanity's submission to weakness and decay. In this, I seek not only to critique but to reclaim life itself—its vigor, its instincts, its unapologetic will to thrive.

CHAPTER 8

JOYFUL WISDOM: LA GAYA SCIENZA

Dawn of Day is a book that says yes to life, filled with depth, clarity, and kindness. This same spirit is found even more strongly in The

Gay Science. Nearly every line of this book blends deep thought with lighthearted playfulness. One verse, written as a tribute to the most beautiful January I have ever experienced, reflects the profound joy and gratitude that inspired the entire work. The whole book feels like a gift. These lines capture the spirit of wisdom transformed into joy:

"Thou who with cleaving fiery lances

The stream of my soul from its ice dost free,

Till with a rush and a roar it advances

To enter with glorious hoping the sea:

Brighter to see and purer ever,

Free in the bonds of thy sweet constraint,—

So it praises thy wondrous endeavour,

January, thou beauteous saint!"

Anyone who understands what "glorious hoping" means here cannot miss its connection to the shining beauty of the opening words of Zarathustra, as they appear in radiant light at the end of the fourth book. Or, they may recognize it in the weighty and timeless sentences at the close of the third book, where a destiny for all ages is first given its form. The songs of Prince Free- as- a- Bird, most of which were written in Sicily, vividly recall the Provençal idea of the Gaya Scienza—the joyful science—that celebrated the union of poet, knight, and free spirit. This early Provençal culture stands apart from all others with its clarity and refinement.

The last poem, "To the Mistral," is a vibrant, exuberant dance song. In it, the new spirit dances freely and joyfully over the grave of morality. It is the perfect embodiment of the Provençal spirit—a celebration of life and freedom expressed through art.

CHAPTER 9
THUS SPAKE ZARATHUSTRA: A BOOK FOR ALL AND NONE

I now want to recount the story behind Zarathustra. The central idea of the work—the Eternal Recurrence, the most profound affirmation of life ever conceived—first came to me in August 1881. I noted the idea on a piece of paper and added the words: "Six thousand feet beyond man and time." On that day, I was wandering through the woods near the Lake of Silvaplana, and I stopped by a towering pyramid-shaped rock close to Surlei. It was in that moment the thought struck me.

Looking back, I realize that two months before this inspiration, I experienced a clear premonition of it in the form of a sudden and dramatic shift in my tastes, particularly in music. The entire work of Zarathustra could almost be categorized under the label of music. Its creation was made possible by what felt like a rebirth in my ability to listen deeply. In Recoaro, a small mountain village near Vicenza where I spent the spring of 1881, my friend and maestro Peter Gast, who had also experienced his own kind of rebirth, and I discovered that a new kind of music, lighter and brighter than anything before, seemed to hover around us like a phoenix with luminous plumage.

If I calculate the time from this awakening to the completion of Zarathustra, I arrive at a period of about eighteen months. The book was produced under the most unlikely circumstances, with the final section—quoted in part in my preface—being written in February 1883 during the sacred hour in which Richard Wagner passed away in Venice. The exact eighteen- month gestation period might, to Buddhists, suggest the cycle of rebirth attributed to a female elephant.

During this time, I was occupied with The Gay Science. That book contains hundreds of signs foreshadowing something unprecedented, for it marks the beginnings of Zarathustra. In fact, the fundamental idea of Zarathustra is expressed in the second-to-last aphorism of the fourth book of The Gay Science. This same period also saw the creation of the Hymn to Life, composed for mixed choir and orchestra. The score was published in Leipzig two years later by E. W. Fritsch and provides a glimpse into my spiritual state during this period—a state consumed by what I call "tragic pathos," the profound affirmation of life that fills both the heart and body. One day, this hymn will surely be sung in my memory.

It is important to clarify something regarding the Hymn to Life. The text is not mine, though this is a common misunderstanding. Instead, it was written by Miss Lou von Salomé, a brilliant young Russian woman with whom I was then on friendly terms. Anyone capable of understanding the final lines of the poem will grasp why I admired and preferred it. There is true greatness in those words, for they do not see suffering as a rejection of existence. Instead, they proclaim:

"And if thou hast no bliss now left to crown me— Lead on! Thou hast thy Sor row still."

During the following winter, I found myself on the serene and peaceful Gulf of Rapallo, a small inlet near Genoa nestled between Chiavari and Cape Porto Fino. The conditions were far from ideal—my health was frail, the weather was cold and unusually rainy, and the little albergo where I stayed sat so close to the water that the rough sea often disrupted my sleep. Despite these unfavorable circumstances—or perhaps because of them, as if to prove that pivotal creations often arise in defiance of adversity— this is where Thus Spoke Zarathustra was born. Each morning, I would set out on a southerly walk along the breathtaking road to Zoagli, which winds through a pine forest and offers expansive views of the sea. In the afternoons, when my health allowed, I would traverse the bay from Santa Margherita to the far side of Porto Fino. This landscape had a profound effect on me, not least because it was deeply cherished by Emperor Frederick III. In the autumn of 1886, I returned to this idyllic place and learned that he had visited here once more, seeking solace and joy in its beauty.

It was on these paths, both literal and metaphorical, that the essence of Zarathustra came to me. The character himself seemed to leap from the shadows and waylay me. To truly understand this figure, one must first grasp the core physiological foundation of his existence: what I call great healthiness. I have explained this concept most personally and clearly in one of the final aphorisms of the fifth book of The Gay Science (No. 382). There, I wrote:

"We new, nameless, unfathomable creatures—firstlings of a future still unproved—we who seek a new purpose require new tools, including a healthiness that is stronger, sharper, tougher, and more joyful than any the world has yet known. Whoever wishes to feel, within his soul, the entire spectrum of values and ideals that have shaped humanity until now—who desires to sail the full expanse of this conceptual Mediterranean—must be willing to sacrifice something: he must possess, and constantly acquire, great healthiness. This is not a gift but a continual achievement, requiring endless effort and, often, the sacrifice of that very health itself."

As I walked those roads, I felt myself one of these "Argonauts of the ideal," voyaging through uncharted seas, bruised and shipwrecked, yet always recovering, dangerously healthy, and propelled ever forward. Before us lies an undiscovered land, a horizon no one has yet seen, a world teeming with beauty, terror, strangeness, and divinity. Such a vision ignites a wild, uncontainable curiosity and a desperate lust to claim it. Confronted with such vistas, how could anyone be content with the man of today? How could we not, at the very least, view his loftiest aspirations with thinly veiled amusement—or perhaps ignore them altogether?

A different ideal compels us now. It is dangerous, enchanting, and extraordinary, an ideal not meant for everyone. Indeed, few could claim the right to pursue it. This ideal belongs to a spirit that plays, naturally and without effort, with everything humanity has called sacred, moral, or divine. To this spirit, even the highest values of humanity appear as threats, symptoms of decay, or temporary lapses in self-awareness. Its ideal is one of overwhelming vitality and benevolence—so immense it often appears inhuman. This ideal stands beside all the solemnity and gravitas of human history, turning them into something unintentionally humorous, a parody of seriousness itself. Yet, paradoxically, it is with this spirit that true seriousness begins. It raises the first profound question, shifts the axis of the soul, and heralds the arrival of tragedy.

Thus Spoke Zarathustra was born out of this spirit and these walks, a testament to an ideal of life so vast that it seems to mock everything smaller than itself. It was conceived amidst the crashing waves and pine-laden paths, embodying not just a rejection of the old but a resounding "yes" to something entirely new.

Has anyone in the late nineteenth century truly grasped what poets of stronger, earlier times meant by inspiration? If not, let me attempt to explain. Inspiration is a force so profound that, were one even slightly superstitious, it would be nearly impossible not to think of oneself as merely an instrument—a vessel, a mouthpiece, or even a medium for an immense and overwhelming power. The idea of revelation comes closest to describing the experience. Something strikes with such sudden clarity, something so deep and transformative, that it feels undeniably real and unshakably certain. You don't seek it; you hear it. You don't ask for it; it comes unbidden. A thought ignites like a bolt of lightning, arriving with such force and necessity that there is no room for doubt. For me, inspiration is never a matter of choice—it seizes me entirely.

The ecstasy that accompanies it is almost unbearable at times. There are moments when the intensity of it breaks, releasing a torrent of tears. During these episodes, my movements often follow the rhythm of my thoughts—one moment rushing forward as if propelled by an unseen force, the next slowing to a halt, unable to bear the weight of the experience. I feel entirely beyond my own control, yet with an acute awareness of countless subtle sensations coursing through me, as if every nerve is alive, from the crown of my head to the tips of my toes. In this state, even pain and darkness do not oppose the overwhelming happiness but become essential elements within it, like shadows that define the brilliance of light.

This state of being is also marked by an instinctive sense of rhythm, an innate harmony between the internal and the external. The larger the inspiration, the greater the need for sweeping, expansive rhythms to carry it, almost as if the scale of the rhythm mirrors the tension of the creative force. Everything happens as if in a storm—spontaneous, absolute, and filled with a sense of power and freedom. Figures, metaphors, and similes emerge involuntarily, as though the universe itself conspires to provide them. There is no distinction between imagery and reality; each expression feels entirely natural and true. It feels, as Zarathustra once put it, that all things rush to offer themselves as symbols and allies:

"Here do all things come caressingly to thy discourse and flatter thee, for they would fain ride upon thy back. On every simile thou ridest here unto every truth. Here fly open unto thee all the speech and word shrines of the world, here would all existence become speech, here would all Becoming learn of thee how to speak."

This, for me, is the essence of inspiration. I cannot doubt its authenticity, but I also know how rare it is. To find another who might truly say, "This is my experience too," I suspect I would need to search thousands of years into the past.

After such intense moments, the aftermath is often fraught with difficulty. For weeks after such creative peaks, I was ill in Genoa. The spring that followed was bleak; I spent it in Rome, struggling to endure an environment utterly unsuitable for the poet of Zarathustra. Rome, a city I did not choose for myself, only deepened my despondency. I sought refuge elsewhere and considered moving to Aquila—a town founded in defiance of Rome and embodying everything the Eternal City did not. In some ways, Aquila mirrored my own antagonism toward the established order. Like Frederick II, the great atheist and opponent of the Church to whom I feel so closely connected, I dreamed of founding my own city as a symbol of resistance. Yet fate led me back to Rome, despite my efforts to avoid it. I ended up in Piazza Barberini, after failing to find a more anti-Christian corner of the city. At one point, desperate to escape the stench of the streets, I even inquired at the Palazzo del Quirinale for a quiet room suitable for a philosopher.

In a small chamber overlooking the Piazza, with the soothing sound of fountains below, I composed The Night- Song—perhaps the loneliest song I have ever written. During this time, I was haunted by a melancholic refrain, the echo of which resided in the words "dead through immortality."

When summer arrived, I returned to the sacred place where the idea of Zarathustra had first struck me. There, in just ten days, I wrote the second part. Remarkably, neither the first, second, nor third parts required more than ten days each. By the following winter, beneath the radiant skies of Nice—light that seemed to infuse my very being—I completed the third part, bringing my monumental task to a close in under a year. The landscapes around Nice, with their hidden trails and lofty heights, are forever hallowed in my memory. These were the settings for moments of unparalleled creativity, including the arduous climb to Eza, a Moorish village perched high among the rocks, where I conceived the decisive chapter, Old and New Tables.

At the height of my creative energy, my physical vitality also surged. My body seemed as inspired as my mind, and I moved with a boundless energy that felt almost divine. In those days, it was not unusual for me to dance spontaneously or to walk for hours—sometimes seven or eight at a stretch—over the hills without a hint of fatigue. My sleep was deep and restorative, my laughter frequent and unrestrained. I was, in every sense, robust and alive, brimming with a patience that allowed the currents of creativity to flow freely through me.

In this state of union between body and mind, I found myself not merely creating but living Zarathustra. It was as though the spirit of the work had possessed me entirely, driving me forward with a force as inexorable as it was exhilarating.

Aside from the brief bursts of intense creativity, lasting only ten days at a time, the years I spent creating Zarathustra and the time that followed were marked by unparalleled suffering. To create something immortal comes at a great cost; a man must be prepared to die many times over during his life to achieve it. I have come to understand something I call "the rancor of greatness." Everything great—a monumental work or a transformative deed—inevitably turns against its creator as soon as it is complete. The mere fact of being its author makes one vulnerable in ways that are hard to describe. In its completion, it becomes something alien, something almost unbearable to confront. It stands apart, as though the weight of human fate is tied to it, and the creator must now shoulder this burden, staggering under its enormity. This rancor of greatness feels as if one's own achievement seeks to crush its creator.

Equally harrowing is the oppressive silence that surrounds such creation. Solitude, in this context, is not a gentle reprieve but a suffocating isolation, wrapped in layers impenetrable to the outside world. I have often felt as though solitude possesses seven layers of armor through which nothing can break. One ventures out among people, greets old friends, tries to rejoin the rhythm of the world, but it is all in vain. Instead of connection, one finds only new deserts.

Even the faces of friends seem to withhold their warmth, their greetings become perfunctory or hesitant. At best, there is a quiet rebellion in their eyes, as though my presence disrupts their peace. Nothing seems to wound so deeply as the palpable sense of distance I inadvertently create in others simply by being who I am. Few are those rare souls who can exist without the need to revere or who are not unsettled by the sudden realization of a profound gap between themselves and another.

This gulf, this tension, manifests in various ways. I came to sense a strange hypersensitivity to the smallest of disturbances, as though the finer threads of my being had been stretched too thin. The immense energy spent in creating from the deepest, most secret parts of oneself leaves little reserve for the ordinary defenses required in daily life. The smallest pricks—a sharp word, a trivial slight—can sting disproportionately, not because they are significant in themselves, but because there is no strength left to endure even the slightest discomfort. During such times, even digestion feels sluggish, movement becomes a laborious task, and the chill of suspicion creeps into the mind. It is as if the body's energy has been entirely redirected, leaving other faculties neglected, open to weariness, cold, and doubt.

Suspicion, I have often thought, is frequently a misinterpretation of the signals our body sends us—a mistake in the understanding of cause and effect. Once, when I found myself in this fragile state, hypersensitive and withdrawn, I became aware of a herd of cows before I could even see them. Their presence, though distant, conveyed a sense of warmth that softened my mood. It was a moment of strange comfort, an unspoken connection to something simple and unthreatening, a reminder of life's gentler, more humane sensations. That warmth reached me in a way no human interaction could at the time. It soothed the rawness of my condition, however briefly, offering a fleeting reprieve from the relentless demands of greatness and the wounds it leaves behind.

This work stands entirely apart from anything else ever created. To mention poets in its context seems almost inappropriate; nothing born of such an overflowing abundance of strength can be compared to it. The concept of the "Dionysian" reached its peak in this creation, becoming the ultimate act of affirmation. Everything other men have achieved pales in comparison—it appears narrow, confined, and timid. Imagine that Goethe or Shakespeare, for all their genius, would have been unable to draw a single breath in this atmosphere of relentless passion and towering heights. Imagine that, alongside Zarathustra, even Dante becomes merely a believer, a follower of truth, not its creator—a soul inspired but not one who defines fate or rules worlds. The poets of the Vedas, though revered as priests, could not have been worthy even to loosen the sandals of Zarathustra. Yet these comparisons barely begin to illustrate the gulf, the soaring expanse, the endless azure solitude in which this work resides.

Zarathustra stands alone, with an eternal claim to say: "I draw around me circles and holy boundaries. Ever fewer are they that climb with me to ever loftier heights. I build me a mountain range of ever holier mountains." Gather all the wisdom, strength, and goodness from every great soul that ever lived—it still would not be enough to create a single one of Zarathustra's discourses. The ladder upon which he ascends and descends stretches infinitely. He has seen further, willed further, and ventured further than any human has dared to dream. Each of his words brims with contradiction, and yet he is the ultimate affirming spirit, binding all contradictions together into a harmonious unity. The highest and the lowest aspects of human nature, the sweetest joys and the most terrifying truths, flow from a single source with unerring certainty. Before Zarathustra, no one truly grasped what it meant to experience height, depth, or truth. His coming marks the dawn of a new comprehension—of wisdom, of the probing of the soul, of the very art of language itself.

In Zarathustra, even the most mundane and common subjects are imbued with words that have never before been spoken. Every sentence trembles with profound passion. Eloquence transforms into music, and words leap forth like bolts of lightning, illuminating futures no one has yet imagined. The most masterful parables humanity had ever known seem clumsy and childlike next to the way Zarathustra's language transforms into vivid imagery, returning to the primal essence of metaphor and meaning. Witness how Zarathustra descends from the mountain, speaking the gentlest, kindest words to everyone he encounters. Watch how he touches even his opponents—the priests—with delicate compassion, sharing in their suffering, their pain at being themselves. At every moment, he transcends mere humanity, and the concept of the "Superman" becomes a living reality. Beneath him lies all that humanity once considered great, now dwarfed, distant, and almost forgotten.

The essence of Zarathustra's greatness radiates through his halcyonic brightness, his nimble steps, the flashes of mischief and exuberance that define his being. Such qualities, once thought incompatible with true greatness, are now revealed as its prerequisites. In embracing opposites, in encompassing both the darkest depths and the most radiant heights, Zarathustra embodies the pinnacle of life. It is in this extraordinary breadth, this infinite accessibility to contradiction, that he feels himself to be the highest of all living things. And when he defines what it means to be the highest, one cannot help but abandon the search for his equal.

"The soul with the longest ladder, able to descend into the deepest depths, "The vastest soul, wandering furthest through its own domain,

"The most necessary soul, hurling itself into chance from sheer desire, "The steadfast soul, plunging headfirst into Becoming,

"The possessing soul, compelled to savor the longing and the will,

"The soul that flees from itself, only to overtake itself in the widest of circles, "The wisest soul, sweetly seduced by folly,

"The most self-loving soul, in which all things find their origin, their ebb, and their flow."

But this is the very essence of the idea of Dionysus. Another perspective leads us to this same idea. The psychological problem embodied by the figure of Zarathustra is this: how can someone who, in an utterly unprecedented way, says "no" and acts "no" to all that has been affirmed until now, still remain a spirit of affirmation? How can he, who shoulders the heaviest destiny and whose very existence is bound to the weight of fatality, still be the brightest and most transcendental of spirits—how can Zarathustra, who is a dancer, embody this paradox? How can someone who perceives reality with the hardest and most piercing clarity, who has thought the most "profound and abysmal thoughts," refrain from interpreting these things as objections to life itself, or even to the eternal recurrence of existence? How, instead, does he become the very affirmation of all things, embodying "the tremendous and unlimited saying of Yes and Amen"? ... "Into every abyss do I carry the blessing of my affirmation to Life." This, yet again, is the very idea of Dionysus.

What language would such a spirit use when speaking to his own soul? It would be the language of the dithyramb. I am the inventor of the dithyramb. Listen to the way Zarathustra speaks to his soul in Before Sunrise (iii. 48). Before my time, such radiant joys and divine tenderness had no voice. Even the deepest melancholy of such a Dionysian spirit takes form as a dithyramb. Consider, for instance, "The Night-Song"—the eternal lament of a being condemned to never love, precisely because of his superabundance of light and power, the inexhaustible sun burning within him.

"It is night: now all gushing springs raise their voices. And my soul too is a gushing spring.

"It is night: now do all lovers sing. And my soul too is the song of a lover.

"Something unquenched and unquenchable is within me, yearning to speak. A longing for love courses through me, and it speaks only the language of love.

"Light am I: would that I were night! But this is my solitude, that I am surrounded by light.

"Alas, why am I not dark and deep like the night! How joyfully would I drink from the breasts of light!

"And even you, twinkling stars and glowing fireflies on high, would I bless— and be blessed in the gifts of your light.

"But in my own light do I dwell, ever drinking back into myself the flames I send forth.

"I do not know the joy of the hand that reaches to grasp, and often I have dreamed that stealing must be sweeter than taking.

"Wretched am I that my hand may never rest from giving; an envious fate is mine, to see eyes full of expectation and nights made bright with longing.

"Oh, the sorrow of all who give! Oh, the clouds that shroud my sun! This longing for desire! This burning hunger at the very end of the feast!"

This is the song of one who, overflowing with light, is doomed to forever pour out without being replenished. It is the lament of someone who lives so close to the sun of existence that its brightness denies him the darkness of love. Even this sorrow, however, is transformed by Zarathustra into something transcendent. It is not a complaint, but a testament to the Dionysian spirit that finds meaning, beauty, and affirmation even in the unbearable.

"They take what I give them; but do I truly touch their soul? There is a gulf between giving and receiving, and the smallest gulf is often the hardest to bridge. My gifts illuminate, yet a void remains between my light and their hearts.

"An appetite is born from my beauty: would that I could harm those whom I fill with my light; would that I could rob them of the gifts I have bestowed upon them! In this yearning, I feel a thirst for wickedness.

"To pull back my hand just as theirs stretches out to meet it—like the wavering waterfall hesitating in its descent—such is my longing for vengeance born of my fulness.

"My solitude conspires to create such cravings, and my overabundance gives birth to these dark desires. The joy I found in giving has withered with each deed; my virtue, overwhelmed by its own abundance, has grown weary of itself.

"He who gives risks losing the delicate shame that makes the act meaningful; he who always shares grows numb in hand and heart. I no longer see the trembling humility of those who receive; my hands have grown too callous to feel their quivering.

"Where have you gone, the tears from my eyes, the bloom of my heart? Oh, the desolation that all givers know! Oh, the silence that surrounds every beacon of light!

"Countless suns wander the empty spaces of the cosmos; their light speaks to all that is dark, yet they are silent toward me. This is the cruel truth of light: it despises that which also shines. Pitiless, it follows its path, and in its innermost heart, it resents its peers.

"Every sun follows its own unwavering course, driven by an unyielding will. This is their coldness, their nature—to blaze forward, indifferent to others who shine. And yet, it is only the spirits of the night, the creatures of darkness, that find solace in light. Only they draw their warmth, their sustenance, from its glow.

"Alas, there is ice all around me. My hand burns itself against the frost. Within me is a thirst, an aching desire for those who thirst in return.

"It is night: woe is me, that I must shine even now! I thirst for darkness, for the solace of shadow and the comfort of companionship. It is night, and my longing spills forth like a spring. I yearn to speak; my soul demands release.

"It is night: now all gushing springs raise their voices, and my soul, too, becomes a gushing spring. It is night: only now do lovers lift their songs, and my soul becomes the song of a lover."

These words express something beyond what any mortal has ever dared to write, feel, or endure. This lament, this yearning, belongs not to man but to a god—only Dionysus could suffer in this way. The only fitting reply to such a dithyramb on the solitude of light is Ariadne. And who knows Ariadne better than I? Only I understand her. Such riddles—did anyone before even know they were riddles? I doubt it.

One day, Zarathustra defines his life's task with piercing clarity— and it is also mine. Let no one mistake its meaning: it is a yea- saying so profound that it justifies, redeems, and embraces even all that has passed. It is the ultimate affirmation, the boundless acceptance of life, even in its pain, its loss, and its solitude.

"I walk among men as though they are fragments of the future—pieces of the vision I see within me. And all my work, all my effort, is devoted to one thing: shaping these fragments, riddles, and seemingly meaningless accidents into a unified whole.

"And how could I endure being a man, if man were not also a poet, a solver of riddles, and a redeemer of chance! To redeem the past, to transform every 'it was' into 'thus I willed it'—this alone could save me!"

In another passage, Zarathustra defines with utmost precision what "man" can mean to him. Man is neither an object of love nor of pity. Zarathustra, having mastered even his loathing for humanity, sees man as an unfinished thing—a raw material, an unshaped and ugly stone awaiting the sculptor's chisel.

"Never to cease willing, never to cease valuing, never to cease creating! Oh, may I never fall into that great weariness!

"Even in my hunger for knowledge, I find joy only in the will to create and to grow. If there is innocence in my knowledge, it is because the will to create pulses within it.

"It was this creative will that drew me away from God and gods. For what would remain to create if gods already existed? But this same will drives me back to man, my burning, creative will forever urging me forward. Thus it compels the hammer to strike the stone.

"Alas, you men, within this stone sleeps an image—the image of all my dreams! Alas, that it must sleep in the hardest and ugliest of stones!

"Now my hammer rages without mercy against this prison. Fragments of stone fly everywhere—but what is that to me?

"I will finish what I began, for a shadow once came to me—the stillest, the lightest thing on earth approached me!

"It was the beauty of the Superman that came to me as a shadow. Alas, my brethren, what are the gods to me now?"

Let me draw attention to one final perspective, inspired by the italicized line. A Dionysian life-task demands not just vision and creation, but the unyielding hardness of the hammer. It requires, as one of its essential qualities, the capacity to take joy in destruction. The command "Harden yourselves!" and the profound belief that all creators must be hard—these are the true hallmarks of a Dionysian nature.

CHAPTER 10
BEYOND GOOD AND EVIL: THE PRELUDE TO A PHILOSOPHY OF THE FUTURE

my work for the years that followed was laid out as clearly as one could imagine. With the yea-saying portion of my life's task completed, it was now time to undertake the negative half— both in word and deed. This was the work of the transvaluation of all values that had existed up until then, the great war—the summoning of the day when the decisive outcome of this struggle would be unveiled. Meanwhile, I had to gradually seek out my peers— those who, from a position of strength, could extend a hand in aiding my project of destruction. From this point forward, all my writings became forms of bait: perhaps I understand the art of fishing as well as anyone else? If nothing was caught, the fault was not mine. The waters simply held no fish.

In all its significant aspects, this book (1886) stands as a critique of modernity—a critique that spans modern science, art, and politics, while also offering glimpses of a type of person who would be the complete antithesis of the modern man. This noble, affirmative type was as different from the contemporary human as one could imagine. In this regard, the book serves as a school for gentlemen—a term I employ here in a more profound and transformative sense than it has ever been used before. All the things that modernity boasts about—such as the much-praised "objectivity," the sentimentality of "sympathy with all that suffers," the "historical sense" with its slavish subservience to foreign tastes, its groveling before petits faits, and its insatiable hunger for science—are exposed as oppositional to the noble type I endorse. They are, in fact, almost uncouth.

If you bear in mind that this book follows Zarathustra, you might begin to sense what kind of sustenance and discipline gave rise to it. The vision that, under tremendous pressure, had learned to gaze far into the distance— Zarathustra, after all, sees further than even the Tsar—is here directed with deliberate sharpness toward what lies immediately before it: the present, the nearby, the contemporary. The aphorisms, as well as the book's form, embody a conscious redirection from the instincts that made Zarathustra possible. Its refinement in style, aspiration, and the art of deliberate silence are among its more apparent qualities. Psychology is wielded here with a deliberate hardness, even cruelty. Not a single word in the book could be described as good- natured. Every page carries the severity of an unflinching gaze at the truth.

Yet, curiously enough, this rigor serves as a kind of rejuvenation. Who can fathom the type of recreation one might need after expending so much goodness in writing Zarathustra? From a theological perspective—and mark this well, for I seldom speak as a theologian—it was God Himself who, at the end of His great work, reclined in the form of a serpent at the base of the tree of knowledge. This was His way of recovering from being God.

After all, He had made everything far too beautiful. The devil, in this interpretation, is simply God's moment of idleness on the seventh day.

CHAPTER 11
THE GENEALOGY OF MORALS: A POLEMIC

The three essays that make up this genealogy are, in terms of style, ambition, and the mastery of surprise, some of the most extraordinary things ever written. Dionysus, as you may recall, is also the god of shadows and mystery, and this spirit pervades every part of the work. Each essay begins in a way designed to perplex the reader: the tone is cool, detached, almost scientific, with an air of deliberate irony. This composure is not accidental but carefully calculated—it stands at the forefront like a mask, concealing what lies beneath. Slowly, however, this calm gives way; flashes of insight like distant lightning streak across the intellectual horizon. From the depths, unsettling truths emerge, faint at first, like rumblings in the distance, but growing louder and closer with every moment.

Before long, the essays gain a ferocious momentum, their tempo building toward a fever pitch. Each ends in a crescendo of thunder and revelation, where new and terrifying truths blaze forth amidst the storm. In the first essay, the truth revealed is the psychology of Christianity: its origin not in the "Spirit" but in resentment.

Christianity, at its core, is unmasked as a counter-movement, a rebellion against the reign of noble values—a great uprising from the depths of the weak against the strong.

The second essay delves into the psychology of conscience. Here, conscience is shown to be far from the divine voice in man, as it is commonly regarded. Instead, it is the instinct for cruelty turned inward once it can no longer be expressed outwardly. For the first time, cruelty is laid bare as one of the most ancient and indispensable building blocks of culture. Without this inward cruelty, civilization itself could not have taken root. The essay uncovers the brutal truth that the foundation of our highest ideals rests upon violence redirected against the self.

The third essay confronts the origin of the immense power wielded by the ascetic ideal—the ideal of the priest. This ideal, despite being fundamentally harmful—a will to nothingness and decay— has exerted incredible influence throughout human history. Why? Not because of divine endorsement or activity behind the priest, as is often believed, but because it has thrived in the absence of alternatives. It has survived as a faute de mieux, a last resort, because until Zarathustra, no competing ideal existed. Humanity, it seems, would rather strive toward nothingness than not strive at all.

This final essay answers a crucial question: why has mankind embraced an ideal that negates life itself? It reveals that the ascetic ideal flourished because it was the only game in town. Until the dawn of Zarathustra, man had no counter-ideal, no vision of life affirming itself with equal intensity. Thus, these essays serve as three groundbreaking preludes, decisive first steps from the perspective of a psychologist, toward the Transvaluation of all Values.

Through this work, for the first time, the psychology of the priest is laid bare, exposing the underpinnings of an ideal that has dominated and corrupted human aspirations for millennia. Each essay is an essential piece of the puzzle, uncovering not only the origins but also the consequences of the values humanity has lived by—and pointing toward the path beyond them. This is a book that challenges, confronts, and compels. It is no mere analysis; it is a manifesto for transformation.

CHAPTER 12

THE TWILIGHT OF THE IDOLS: HOW TO PHILOSOPHISE WITH THE HAMMER

This work—scarcely more than one hundred and fifty pages in length— stands out as a true anomaly among books. With its bright yet ominous tone, like a mischievous demon laughing through the ruins of tradition, it is unlike anything else. Its creation occupied so few days that I hesitate to admit the number, though its impact feels timeless. There is no work richer in content, more audacious, more revolutionary—or more wicked. Anyone wishing for a swift overview of how everything before my time was fundamentally inverted should begin with this book. That which I call "Idols" in the title refers to the old truths humanity has clung to until now. Put simply, The Twilight of the Idols declares that these so-called truths are approaching their inevitable end.

No reality, no ideal, escapes unscathed in this book. The word "touched" barely suffices to describe what is done here; it is more accurate to say that everything is overturned, challenged, and dissected. Not only do I address the eternal idols of humanity but also the most recent, those "modern ideas" that are already showing signs of decay. A powerful wind blows through the pages, shaking the trees and scattering fruit—truths—everywhere. There is a certain extravagance, the overabundance of a rich autumn, in this work: truths spill forth in such quantities that one trips over them, even crushes them underfoot. Yet those truths that remain in hand are undeniable and absolute. These are not fleeting insights; they are decrees, final and irrevocable. I alone possess the true standard of "truth." I alone decide.

It feels as though a second consciousness has awakened within me, as though the very will to life has illuminated for me the downward path humanity has followed for ages. This path, previously celebrated as the way to "Truth," I reveal as a descent into decay and disillusionment. The obscure impulses that guided humanity—the darkness, the fear—are no longer veiled. The "good man," so celebrated in the past, was precisely the one most blind to the true path. Speaking seriously, no one before me knew this path. Only after my time can humanity find hope again, discover its purpose, and follow roads leading toward a genuine culture. I am the herald of this new culture, and because of that, I am also a harbinger of fate.

Immediately after completing this book, I plunged headlong into the daunting task of the Transvaluation of All Values, with an unshakable sense of pride and certainty in my immortality. Each moment felt steeped in a timeless grandeur, and I engraved sign after sign on the tablets of brass with the confidence of a force of destiny. The Preface was born on the morning of September 3, 1888. After finishing it, I stepped outside to be greeted by one of the most breathtaking days I have ever seen in the Upper

Engadine—a day so radiant, so rich in contrast, with colors ranging from glacial whites to the warm hues of the southern light, that it seemed a reflection of the work I had just completed.

I remained in Sils-Maria until September 20, delayed by flooding that left me as one of the last visitors in this extraordinary place. My gratitude for it knows no bounds, and I have bestowed upon it the gift of an immortal name. My departure was not without its perils; the journey was fraught with challenges, including a dramatic arrival in a flooded Como in the dead of night. Yet, on the afternoon of September 21, I reached Turin, the city that has become my chosen home. I returned to my spring lodgings at 6 Via Carlo Alberto, overlooking the magnificent Palazzo Carignano, the birthplace of Vittorio Emanuele. From my window, I could see the Piazza Carlo Alberto and beyond it, the hills. Without pause or distraction, I resumed my work. Only the final quarter of the Transvaluation remained to be written.

On September 30, I experienced a triumph unlike any other: the seventh day, a moment of divine leisure by the banks of the Po. On this same day, I penned the Preface to The Twilight of the Idols, a task that offered me a kind of joyful recreation amid the intensity of September's labor. Never in my life had I known such an autumn, a season so extraordinary that it exceeded my wildest imaginings of what earthly beauty could be. It was as if a Claude Lorrain painting had come to life and stretched into infinity. Each day rivaled the last in wild, unearthly perfection, an unbroken chain of luminous hours that seemed to herald the dawning of something eternal.

CHAPTER 13
THE CASE OF WAGNER: A MUSICIAN'S PROBLEM

To truly understand this essay, a person must feel the loss of music's greatness as deeply as they would feel an open wound. What do I mean when I say I suffer from the fate of music? I mean that music has lost its power to transform the world and to say "yes" to life. It has become music in decline— no longer the joyful flute of Dionysus. But if someone loves music as much as their own life, if their joy and sorrow are tied to it, they may find this essay gentle and even full of restraint. To remain cheerful under such circumstances, to laugh kindly at oneself while speaking critically—ridendodicere severum, as the saying goes—is to embody humanity. Who would doubt that I, an old artilleryman at heart, could bring out my heavy guns against Wagner if I wanted to? Yet I held back. I have loved Wagner.

There is something meaningful in attacking a figure who is more subtle and unknown than most would guess. It is part of my life's work. Oh, there are still many other "unknowns" I must unmask, and not just this Cagliostro of music! Above all, my critique must include the German people themselves. They are becoming lazier in matters of the spirit, weaker in instincts, but more honest.

Their appetite for contradictions is something to behold! They can accept "faith" alongside science, Christian love alongside anti-Semitism, and the desire for power (for the Empire) served alongside the gospel of humility, all without showing the slightest sign of mental indigestion. Imagine having no discomfort in the face of such opposites! Imagine this neutrality, this lack of bias! See the German sense of fairness, which gives equal weight to all things—finding everything appealing. Without question, the Germans are idealists.

When I was last in Germany, I witnessed firsthand the strange way German taste seemed determined to give equal admiration to Wagner and The Trumpeter of Säckingen. Even in Leipzig, where one might have expected a celebration of Heinrich Schütz—one of the truest German musicians, in the older and more noble sense of "German"—their energy went instead into founding a Liszt Society. The society aimed to promote elaborate, intricate, and even cunning church music. This was their choice, instead of honoring a master like Schütz, whose legacy transcended narrow nationalism. Without question, the Germans are idealists.

Yet, I will not hold back from saying what needs to be said about the Germans. I refuse to mince words, for who else will speak the unpleasant truths if I do not? The Germans are culpable for their shocking laxity in historical understanding. They have entirely lost the breadth of vision required to grasp the flow and values of culture. Instead of this expansive view, they have narrowed their perspectives to politics or religion, becoming mere puppets of those institutions. Worse still, they actively reject this broader understanding. A man in Germany must first be "German," must first belong to "the race," before he is permitted to pass judgment on historical values or lack thereof. To them, being "German" is an argument in itself. "Germany above all" becomes not just a national slogan but a principle. Germans see themselves as the custodians of the "moral order of the universe" throughout history. They set themselves in opposition to the Roman Empire, claiming to represent freedom. They set themselves against the Enlightenment, claiming to restore morality with their so-called "Categorical Imperative."

This arrogance manifests even in their history writing. There is a history molded by the ideals of the German Empire, a history warped by anti-Semitism, and a history shaped to flatter the Court. Herr von Treitschke exemplifies this, unashamedly producing a historical narrative that serves ideological ends. Recently, an idiotic opinion—one ascribed to Vischer, a Swabian aesthete now deceased—circulated in German newspapers as a "truth" every German must accept. He proclaimed, "The Renaissance and the Reformation together constitute a whole—the aesthetic rebirth and the moral rebirth." When I hear such absurdities, I lose all patience. I feel it my duty to confront the Germans with the enormity of what they have done.

For the past four centuries, every major crime against culture weighs on their conscience. Their failures stem from an endless cowardice in facing reality, a cowardice that also keeps them from confronting truth. This cowardice is paired with an instinctive love of falsehood, which the Germans dignify with the name "idealism." It was the Germans who cost Europe the full fruits of its last great age—the Renaissance. Just when a higher order of values had emerged—values affirming life, nobility, and the future, triumphing over the degenerative values of the Church—Luther, that cursed monk, restored Christianity. And not only Christianity but the very values that deny life and glorify self-denial. At a moment when Christianity lay defeated, when even its core had begun to shift, Luther breathed new life into it. Christianity, that denial of the will to live, was raised once more to the status of a religion. Luther, a monk driven by his own impossibilities, lashed out at the Church, and yet, in doing so, inadvertently saved it. The Catholic Church should celebrate Luther; he was their unlikely savior. They should honor him with festivals and plays, for he revived their waning dominance.

And then there is the German inclination to compromise truth with idealism, a tendency that has repeatedly undercut the integrity of intellectual progress. Twice in history, when a courageous and scientific outlook had been achieved, the Germans undermined it. Leibniz and Kant are the two great examples of this betrayal of intellectual honesty. They paved the way back to the old ideals, to compromises that allowed falsehood to persist under the guise of truth. Leibniz and Kant remain two significant obstacles to Europe's intellectual maturity.

Finally, consider Napoleon. At a pivotal moment when a unifying force appeared on the European stage, a man of genius and will capable of consolidating Europe into a political and economic unity, the Germans intervened. With their Wars of Independence, they derailed the profound significance of Napoleon's work. By doing so, they condemned Europe to its current state— fragmented, irrational, and sickly. Nationalism, that most anti- cultural and divisive force, took root, and Europe remains shackled by it. Instead of unity, Europe is now a patchwork of small states, obsessed with petty, municipal politics. The Germans robbed Europe of its higher purpose and her chance at becoming something greater. They plunged her into a dead end.

Who else but me can see the way out of this dead end? Who else has the vision for an aspiration grand enough to bind Europe together again?

And after all, why should I hold back my suspicions? I suspect that the Germans will try to reduce a great fate—my fate—to something trivial, a mere squeak, the birth of a mouse. So far, they've done nothing but disappoint me, and I have little hope that the future will bring any improvement. Yet, how I wish I could be proven wrong! It would delight me to find myself a false prophet in this regard. My natural readers and listeners are already found among Russians, Scandinavians, and the French—will it always be this way? Can the Germans never rise to meet me?

In the history of knowledge, Germans have offered little beyond doubtful contributions. Their intellectual legacy consists largely of "unconscious" deceivers. This description fits figures like Fichte, Schelling, Schopenhauer, Hegel, and Schleiermacher just as aptly as it does Kant or Leibniz. They were all, in essence, Schleier macher s— "veil-makers," concealing rather than revealing truth. The Germans must not be allowed the honor of claiming the first truly honest intellect in their history, the one in whom truth finally triumphed over four thousand years of self-deception. To equate my intellect with what is called the "German intellect" would be an insult. That label— "German intellect"—is like foul air to me. I can barely breathe in its presence, for it reeks of psychological uncleanliness. This uncleanliness has become instinctive among Germans; it seeps into every word they speak and every thought they express.

The Germans have never undergone a rigorous century of self-examination, like the French did in the seventeenth century. A La Rochefoucauld or a Descartes—these men were upright, a thousand times more so than even the greatest of Germans. Germany has yet to produce even a single true psychologist. And psychology, as I see it, is a standard by which we measure the cleanliness— or uncleanliness—of a people. How can someone be truly deep if they are not even clean, not honest with themselves? The Germans are like women, in the sense that their so-called "depth" is an illusion—

there's simply nothing to fathom. You cannot call them shallow because there is no depth to measure against.

What Germans call "deep" is nothing more than a refusal to be clear about themselves. This unclean self-obscurity, this instinctive refusal to examine one's own nature, is what they mistake for depth. Perhaps we should begin using the word "German" as an international epithet for this sort of psychological depravity. Take, for example, the German Emperor, who at this very moment is proclaiming it his Christian duty to liberate the slaves in Africa. Among Europeans, this kind of behavior would simply be called "German."

Have the Germans ever produced a truly deep book? They lack even the idea of what a book should be. I've encountered scholars who believe Kant is deep. At the Prussian Court, Herr von Treitschke is likely considered deep. And when I praise Stendhal as a profound psychologist, I often find myself forced to spell out his name, especially when speaking to German university professors. It seems they can't even recognize depth when it is right before them.

And why shouldn't I see this through to the end? I take pleasure in clearing the air, and it's even part of my ambition to be recognized as someone who fundamentally despises the Germans. I expressed my doubts about the German character as early as the age of twenty-six (see Thoughts out of Season, vol. ii. pp. 164, 165)—to me, the Germans are simply intolerable. Whenever I try to imagine the type of person who opposes me in every instinct, the image that comes to mind is always that of a German. The first question I ask myself when analyzing a man is whether he has a sense of distance—whether he perceives rank, order, and hierarchy between people. Does he discern gradations in all things? This, to me, is the hallmark of a true gentleman. Without it, one belongs hopelessly to that open-hearted, open-minded, overly good-natured species known as la canaille.

But the Germans? They are canaille through and through—so irredeemably good-natured! A man lowers himself simply by associating with them. The German places everyone on the same level, with no sense of distinction. Except for my interactions with a handful of artists—and above all, with Richard Wagner—I cannot recall spending a single pleasant hour in German company. Imagine, for a moment, that the most profound spirit of all ages were to appear among the Germans. Surely one of their pompous saviors of the Capitol would declare his own crude soul to be just as great. I cannot endure this race, which drags everyone into bad company, lacks any understanding of nuance (and I, being a nuance, suffer for it!), and has no esprit in its feet. They don't even know how to walk—they have legs but no feet.

The Germans are so utterly lacking in self-awareness that they don't even realize how vulgar they are. Worse, they feel no shame in merely being German. They insist on having their say in everything, imagining themselves fit to judge every question. I fear they have even presumed to judge me. My entire life stands as proof of this claim. I've searched in vain among them for a shred of tact or delicacy toward me. Among the Jews, I have found such qualities, but among the Germans—never.

I am naturally inclined to be kind and gentle to everyone; I don't believe in making distinctions lightly. But that doesn't mean I don't see things clearly. I hold no exceptions, not even for my friends. I can only hope this has not harmed my reputation for fairness among them. There are, however, five or six points of honor I have always upheld, and the truth is that, for many years, I've regarded nearly every letter I've received as a form of cynicism. There's more cynicism in goodwill shown toward me than in outright hatred. I've often told my friends directly that they've never taken the time to study any of my writings. From the faintest hints, it's obvious they don't even grasp what lies buried in my books.

Take my Zarathustra, for example. Which of my friends has seen it as anything more than an audacious and, thankfully, harmless display of arrogance? A full decade has passed, and not one person has felt a moral obligation to defend my name against the absurd silence in which it has been buried. It was a foreigner—a Dane—who first demonstrated the instinct and courage to protest against my so-called friends. Where in today's German universities would lectures on my philosophy, like those Dr. Brandes delivered last spring in Copenhagen, even be possible? Dr. Brandes, a true psychologist, has more than earned that title.

For my part, these slights don't hurt me. What must be, does not offend me. Amorfati—love of fate—is the very core of who I am. Still, this doesn't mean I lack a taste for irony, even world- historic irony. And so, about two years before unleashing the shattering thunderbolt of the Transvaluation, which will send all of civilization into convulsions, I sent The Case of Wagner into the world. I gave the Germans yet another opportunity to blunder and immortalize their stupidity at my expense. They still have time to rise to the occasion—and have they done so? Magnificently! My dear Germans, let me extend my heartfelt congratulations.

CHAPTER 14
WHY I AM A FATALITY

I know my destiny. A day will come when my name will evoke the memory of something immense and earth-shattering—a crisis unlike any other in history.

It will be remembered as the most profound conflict of consciences and the judgment day for all that has previously been held sacred, demanded, or believed. I am not merely a man—I am dynamite. Yet, let there be no confusion: I am not the founder of a religion. Religions are for the masses, for the easily led. Every encounter with a religious person leaves me with the urge to wash my hands. I have no need for "believers"; in fact, I distrust belief itself—I am too skeptical, too filled with malice, even to believe in myself. I never speak to the masses; I avoid them.

The thought that one day I might be declared "holy" terrifies me. This is why I am publishing this book in advance—to defend myself from being misunderstood, from being turned into something I am not. I refuse to be a saint. I would much rather be a clown, and perhaps I am one. Still, despite this— or rather because of it—I am the voice of truth. For no figure has ever been more inflated with falsehood than the so-called saint. My truth is horrifying, for it reveals that what humanity has called "truth" until now has been nothing but lies. The Transvaluation of All Values—this is my formula for humanity's greatest awakening, for its most profound step toward clarity. In me, this awakening became reality and genius.

It is my destiny to stand as the first truly honest human being, to position myself against the deceptions of millennia. I was the first to uncover truth because I was the first to recognize falsehood for what it truly is—I could smell it, detect its essence. My genius lies in my sense of smell. I contradict as no one has ever contradicted before, yet I am anything but a mere negation. I am a herald of joy, of a kind so unprecedented that it has never even been imagined. I have uncovered tasks so vast and significant that they redefine what humanity can hope for. Only now, after my existence, can humanity begin to dream anew.

Thus, I am, unavoidably, a man of destiny. When Truth rises against the falsehoods of the ages, the result is upheaval—shocks, earthquakes, a reconfiguration of mountains and valleys. These are not mere metaphors but the natural consequences of such a confrontation. Politics, too, will be transformed, elevated into the realm of spiritual warfare. The ancient foundations of society, built on falsehoods, will be obliterated, sent scattering into the void. Wars will erupt—wars unlike any the world has ever known. Only after me will the earth see politics on a scale that matches the magnitude of this transformation.

If you need a formula for such a destiny made flesh, you will find it in my Zarathustra:

"And he who would be a creator in good and evil—verily, he must first be a destroyer, and break values into pieces.

"Thus the greatest evil belongeth unto the greatest good: but this is the creative good."

I am, by far, the most terrifying man to have ever existed. Yet this does not diminish the fact that I will also become the most beneficent. I understand the profound joy of annihilation—this joy matches the extent of my power to destroy. In both destruction and affirmation, I follow the nature of Dionysus, who cannot separate the act of negation from the exultation of saying yes. I am the first immoralist, and in this, I am fundamentally the annihilator.

People have never asked me, as they should have, what the name Zarathustra signifies in my hands, especially as I call myself the first immoralist. It is worth noting that this Persian figure, above all others, was the antithesis of what an immoralist might be. Zarathustra was the first to perceive the struggle between good and evil as the fundamental engine of existence itself. He was the one who transformed morality into a metaphysical framework, presenting it as force, cause, and ultimate purpose. But this very fact makes the answer obvious: Zarathustra created the most monumental error of all—morality. Therefore, it falls to him to be the first to reveal its flaws. Not merely because his experience with this error surpasses that of any other thinker, though all of history itself has already served as the experiment proving the failure of the so-called "moral order of things," but because Zarathustra stands as the most truthful thinker. In his teachings, truthfulness becomes the supreme virtue—the complete antithesis of the cowardly retreat of the idealist, who shies away from reality. Zarathustra has more courage in his body than all other thinkers combined. To tell the truth and aim directly—that is the first and highest Persian virtue. Have I made myself understood? The overcoming of morality through truthfulness—the moralist transcending himself into his own opposite—is what Zarathustra's name means in my mouth.

The title "Immoralist" involves two layers of denial. First, I reject the type of human being that has traditionally been exalted as the highest—the good, the kind, and the compassionate. Second, I reject the dominant moral framework that has been accepted as morality itself, namely, the morality of decay—what is commonly referred to as Christian morality. Of these two negations, the latter is the more critical, for the overvaluation of goodness and kindness is, in my view, already a result of decadence, a symptom of weakness incompatible with an affirmative and ascending life. Affirmation of life cannot exist without simultaneously negating and annihilating those elements that oppose it.

Let us pause for a moment to examine the psychology of the "good man." To assess the worth of any type of person, we must calculate the cost of sustaining them and understand the conditions required for their existence. For the good man, the condition of his existence is falsehood. Put differently, he must refuse to see reality as it truly is, regardless of the cost. This refusal stems from an insistence that reality ought always to align with his benevolent instincts and be receptive to the meddling of ignorant yet well-meaning hands. To treat suffering as a problem to be eradicated, as though it were inherently unjust, is one of the most foolish ideas ever conceived—a folly so disastrous it rivals the idea of eliminating bad weather out of pity for those caught in the rain.

In the grand economy of the universe, the harsh realities of existence— manifested in passions, desires, and the will to power—are infinitely more essential than the trivial comforts associated with "goodness." Goodness is a delicate luxury, requiring tolerance just to permit it a small place, as it is based on a distortion of our natural instincts. I will take the opportunity to reveal the catastrophic historical consequences brought about by this optimism, this monstrous offspring of the so-called "good men." Zarathustra, the first to recognize that the optimist is as degenerate as the pessimist—and perhaps even more destructive— declared:

"Good men never speak the truth. False shores and false harbors were ye taught by the good. In the lies of the good were ye born and bred. Through the good, everything hath become false and crooked from the roots."

Thankfully, the world is not built solely on the instincts that create the shallow happiness of the gregarious herd animal. To aspire for all humanity to become "good," to turn every person into a benevolent, altruistic, blue-eyed soul—or, as Herbert Spencer desired, into a creature of altruism—would strip existence of its nobility and grandeur. It would emasculate humanity, reducing it to a pitiful state akin to the uniformity and stagnation of ancient Chinadom. And yet, this is precisely what some have tried to achieve, calling it morality.

In this light, Zarathustra identifies "the good" alternately as "the last men" and "the beginning of the end." Above all, he sees them as the most harmful type of human being, for they secure their survival at the expense of truth and the future.

"The good—they cannot create; they are always the heralds of the end. They destroy him who carves new values onto new tablets; they sacrifice the future at their own altar. In doing so, they crucify not only the creator but the entire future of humanity! The good—they are always the beginning of the end. And while slanderers of the world do much harm, the harm inflicted by the good is the most disastrous of all."

Zarathustra, as the first psychologist of the "good man," is necessarily a friend to the so-called "evil man." When a weakened, declining type of humanity achieves the highest status, it must have risen to this position at the expense of its opposite—the strong, life-affirming individual who embodies certainty and vitality. When the gregarious, herd-like man basks in the glory of what is deemed the purest virtue, the exceptional man—one who stands apart—must necessarily be cast down and labeled as "evil." If deceit claims the name of "truth" for itself, the truly honest man will be found among those who are despised.

Zarathustra is unequivocal on this point. He declares that it was precisely his knowledge of the "good," of those considered the "best," that instilled in him a profound horror of humanity. It was this repulsion that gave him wings, enabling him to soar into distant and unimaginable futures. He openly admits that his ideal man—his envisioned type—is something beyond human, especially in opposition to the "good man." To the good and the just, Zarathustra's superman appears as a devil.

"Ye higher men, on whom my gaze now falls, this is the doubt that ye awaken in my heart, and this is the source of my secret laughter: methinks ye would call my Superman—the devil! So alien are your souls to all that is great, that the Superman would seem monstrous to you for his goodness."

From this passage, and only from this passage, can one grasp the ultimate aim of Zarathustra—the kind of man he envisions. This man faces reality as it truly is; he is strong enough to endure and embrace it. He is not estranged from the essence of existence; rather, he embodies it. In his nature resides all the terrible, awe- inspiring, and ambiguous aspects of reality itself. Only through such a connection to the core of existence can humanity achieve greatness.

I have adopted the title of "Immoralist" not only as a surname but as a badge of distinction and honor. I take immense pride in this name, which sets me apart from all of humanity. No one before me has placed Christian morality beneath them; such an act requires an elevated perspective, a distance from convention, and an unparalleled psychological depth—a depth not even imagined before my time. Until now, Christian morality has been the enchantress Circe for every thinker; all served her cause. Who before me dared to venture into the dark caves from which the toxic vapors of this ideal—this condemnation of the world— spewed forth? Who even suspected that such caves existed?

Had any philosopher before me ever truly been a psychologist, rather than the opposite—a masterful deceiver, an "idealist"? Before my time, psychology simply did not exist. To be the first in this unexplored realm is not without its cost; indeed, it is a fateful role, for it comes with the burden of being the first to despise. My danger lies in the profound loathing I feel for mankind.

Have you understood me? What defines me, what sets me apart from all of humanity, is that I unmasked Christian morality. For this reason, I needed a word that would serve as a direct challenge to everyone. The fact that this unmasking had not been accomplished before seemed to me the gravest uncleanliness humanity carries on its conscience—self-deception elevated to instinct. It represented the fundamental will to blindness regarding every phenomenon, every causality, and all reality. In essence, it was an almost criminal fraud in matters of psychology. Blindness to Christianity is the essence of criminality, for it is the ultimate crime against life itself. Ages and peoples, the first and the last, philosophers and old women alike—except for perhaps five or six moments in history, and myself as the seventh—are all guilty of this blindness.

Until now, the Christian has been the "moral being," a peculiar anomaly whose absurdity, vanity, and self-destructiveness surpass what even the fiercest despiser of humanity could have imagined. Christian morality is the most venomous of all lies; it is humanity's ultimate corrupter. It is not the error itself that enrages me when I behold this spectacle, nor the millennia of a lack of "goodwill," discipline, decency, or bravery in intellectual matters that Christianity's triumph reveals. Rather, it is the war against nature that horrifies me—a grotesque elevation of anti-nature to the pinnacle of morality and law, hanging over humanity as the oppressive weight of the Categorical Imperative.

Imagine such a colossal failure—not merely as an individual or a people but as a species, as humanity itself! To teach contempt for the very instincts that sustain life, to fabricate the concepts of "soul" and "spirit" solely to defy the body, to implant the idea that life's most essential prerequisite—sexuality—is inherently impure, and to label self-love as evil because it represents the natural need for growth and self-expansion: this is the legacy of Christian morality. Even the term "self-love" is a malicious slander. Conversely, the signs of decline— conflict within instincts, selflessness, loss of stability, suppression of individuality, and the fetishization of "love for one's neighbor"—are exalted as the ultimate moral values. What nonsense! What perversity!

Is humanity itself degenerating? Or has it always been in this state? One thing is certain: you have been taught the values of decay as though they were the highest virtues. The morality of self-renunciation, the kind that has been preached without exception, is fundamentally the morality of decline. The fact, " I am falling apart ," is sanctified and universalized into the imperative, " You all must fall apart." This self-denying morality does more than deny the self—it denies life itself at its roots.

Yet, there remains the possibility that it is not all of humanity that is in decline but only a parasitic subset: the priests. These priests, using morality and deception as their tools, ascended to their positions as arbiters of value. They found in Christian morality the perfect means to power. And, truth be told, this is my belief. Humanity's so-called leaders—its theologians, teachers, and moral philosophers—have, without exception, been decadents. Their reinterpretation of values into a form of hostility toward life—this is morality itself.

Let me offer my definition: Morality is the idiosyncrasy of decadents who seek to take their revenge upon life—and succeed. I place tremendous importance on this definition.

Have you understood me? Everything I have said here, I already proclaimed five years ago through my voice in Zarathustra. The unmasking of Christian morality is an event unparalleled in history—a true catastrophe. The one who exposes it is a force majeure, a destiny, a disruption so vast that it splits human history in two. Time will be measured as before him and after him. The lightning strike of truth has obliterated what was once held highest; and anyone who grasps what this flash has annihilated should examine their hands to see whether they hold anything of substance anymore. Everything once revered as truth has been unveiled as the most harmful, spiteful, and insidious expression of life—a holy ruse, a pretext, aimed at draining vitality, at leeching the blood from life itself. Morality, revealed in its true form, is nothing less than vampirism.

The man who unmasks morality simultaneously unveils the hollowness of the values in which humanity has believed. He sees nothing worthy of reverence even in the figures once deemed most sacred. To him, the "holy" are the most fatal of miscarriages— fatal because they enthrall and ensnare. The concept of "God" was invented as the very antithesis of life. Everything harmful, poisonous, and hostile to life was bound together and given form in Him. The notions of "beyond" and "true world" were fabricated to devalue the only world that exists. Their purpose was to strip earthly reality of its meaning, its goal, its task, and leave it aimless. The inventions of "soul," "spirit," and finally "immortal soul" were tools to disparage the body, to weaken it, to make it "holy"—to cultivate a terrifying frivolity toward the aspects of life that truly matter: nutrition, habitation, intellectual nourishment, care for the sick, hygiene, and the environment.

In place of health, humanity was offered the "salvation of the soul"—a cyclical madness swinging between convulsions of guilt and the hysterical ecstasy of redemption. The concept of "sin," along with its cruel companion "free will," was crafted to confuse and distort our instincts, turning mistrust of them into second nature. The concepts of "selflessness" and "self-denial" embody the marks of decay. The lure of what is harmful, the inability to discern one's own benefit, and even self-destruction have been transformed into virtues: into man's "duty," his "holiness," his "divinity."

And now, to reveal the ultimate atrocity: the notion of the "good" man. Everything weak, diseased, flawed, and inherently decaying is upheld and celebrated—when, in truth, it should be eradicated. The natural law of selection is denied. Worse, opposition to the proud, healthy, life-affirming individual—the one certain of the future and who guarantees it—is turned into an ideal. Such a person is labeled the "evil one." And all of this has been believed in under the guise of morality! Écrasez l'infâme! Crush the infamous!

Have you understood me? This is the battle: Dionysus versus Christ.

SONGS, EPIGRAMS, ETC.

SONGS

TO MELANCHOLY

O Melancholy, do not be angry with me

For pointing this pen to sing your praises alone.

And in your honor, with my head bent low,

I crouch like a hermit on a lonely tree stump.

So often have you seen me thus—at least you did yesterday—

Sitting still in the blazing morning sun,

While, scanning for his feast,

The hungry vulture screamed as it soared down into the valley.

Yet you were mistaken, foul bird, though I,

Leaning against my log, seemed lifeless as a mummy.
You could not see these eyes, burning with ecstasy,
Darting here and there, bold and full of pride.
Though they did not rise to the heights where you flew,
Nor reached those distant cliffs among the clouds,
Instead, they dove even deeper,
Seeking to light up the abysses of Destiny within.
So often, in defiance and strange freedom,
Crouched like a savage at his altar,
I held thoughts of you, Melancholy,
A young penitent reciting from his prayer book.
There I sat, immersed in the vulture's flight,
In the thunderous fall of the avalanche's path.
You spoke to me—not with the falsehood of man—
You spoke, though with a face both stern and dreadful.
You are the harsh goddess of wild and untamed nature,
A mistress who comes with threats to overpower and test me,
To show me the vulture's sweeping arc
And the laughing avalanches, daring to dismay me.
Around us, life breathes in panting violence,
The torment of survival raging in every change.
High on some steep, cold cliff,
A flower tempts the roaming butterfly.
I am all of this—I feel it shivering through me—
The butterfly tricked, the lonely flower,

The vulture and the frozen waterfall,
The storm's moan—all these are symbols of your power.
O grim goddess, before you I bow deeply,
With my head on my knee, my lips bursting with songs of praise.
I cry out in a terrible hymn,
For Life, for Life, always thirsting for Life!
O vengeful goddess, do not be angry, I beg,
That I have tried to capture you in my rhymes.
He trembles who sees your terrible face;
He falters who receives your fearsome touch.
With trembling, I chant song upon song,
Revealing my thoughts in halting rhythms.
The black ink flows, the sharp quill scratches,
O goddess, goddess—let me scold you in peace!

AFTER A NIGHT STORM

Today, you linger dimly in misty veils,
Gloomy goddess, over my windowpane.
The pale snowflakes whirl grimly,
And the swollen brook roars down to the plain.
By the jagged light of lightning's glare,
Under the untamed rumble of thunder's roll,
In the valley's shadowed depths, you were brewing—
Sorceress!—your damp and poisoned chalice.
Through the midnight I shuddered, hearing

The ecstasy of your voice—and cries of torment.
I saw your bright eyes glimmering,
Your right hand trembling as it wielded
The mace of thunder you hurled with fury.
Near my desolate bed, I heard the crashes
Of your armored steps, the clash of weapons,
Your brazen chain striking against the sashes,
And your voice commanding: "Come! Hear who I am!
They call me the immortal Amazon.
I shun all that is weak or womanly;
Manly scorn and hatred in war enthrall me.
I am both the tigress and the victor!
Wherever I tread, corpses fall before me;
Torches of fury blaze from my eyes,
And my mind is a forge of poisons. Bow before me!
Crawl, you worm of Earth, you flickering wisp—or perish!"

HYMNS TO FRIENDSHIP

(Two Fragments)

1

Goddess of Friendship, hear our song,
A hymn we offer to your grace!

Where friendship's joyful gaze shines bright, Its warmth and kindness bring delight.

Come close and lend your guiding hand, With rosy dawn upon your face,

And in your grasp the faithful pledge, Of youth eternal, time embraced.

2

The morning fades; the noonday sun
Beats down its heat upon our heads.
Beneath the arbour's shade we rest,
Singing of friendship's endless thread.
Friendship was our life's first light,
Its glow shall linger through the night.

THE WANDERER

All through the night, a wanderer goes,
With sturdy strides and steady pace.
By winding valleys, hills that rise,
He travels onward, no set place.
Fair is the night, yet on he moves,
Uncertain where the path shall lead,
With neither rest nor slowing speed.
A bird's sweet song breaks through the air,
"Ah, bird, what hast thou done to me?
You grip my senses, hold my feet,
And pour this vexing melody.
It stirs my heart, I cannot leave,
To listen is my only choice—
Why draw me near with such a voice?"
The good bird answers, breaking song:

"I do not call you; you are wrong.
With every trill, my mate I seek,
From hills afar, through night so bleak.
I sing for her, not for your plight.
To me alone the night's unfair—
But that's no matter; onward fare.
Why stand you still?
What has my music done to you,
O wanderer lost?"
The bird grew quiet, deep in thought,
And pondered why his song had caught
The roamer's will—
"What power lies in tunes I weave,
To make him pause and still not leave?"

TO THE GLACIER

At the hour of noon, when first
Summer steps into the mountains,
Summer, the boy with weary, burning eyes,
He begins to speak,
Yet his words are only seen, not heard.
His breath comes heavy, like the labored sigh
Of a fevered man on his sickbed.
The glacier, the fir tree, and the spring
Respond to his call—

Yet we perceive their answer only in sight.
The torrent leaps faster from the rock,
Rushing down as if to greet him,
Pausing like a white, trembling column,
Yearning in its stance.
The fir tree, dark and steadfast,
Looks truer than ever before.
And between the ice mass and cold grey stone,
A sudden light emerges—
A sign once seen, remembered still.
Even the dead man's eye
Surely finds light again,
When sorrowfully embraced
By his child's kiss.
Surely, for one fleeting moment,
A flame glows back into life,
And the lifeless eye speaks,
"My child!
Ah, child, you know I love you true!"
So all things glow and speak—the glacier speaks,
The brook, the fir tree,
All with their glance share the same words:
"We love you true,
Ah, child, you know we love you, love you true!"
And he,

Summer, the boy with weary, burning eyes,
Filled with woe,
Gives kisses ever more fervent,
And will not leave.
Like veils, his words
Flow from his lips,
Cruel and piercing:
"My greeting is parting,
My coming, my going,
In youth, I fade away."
All around they listen,
Holding their breath
(No bird dares sing),
Shuddering, they flee
Like gleaming rays
Across the mountain;
All around they ponder—
But no one speaks.
It was at noon,
At the noontide hour, when first
Summer steps into the mountains,
Summer, the boy with weary, burning eyes.

AUTUMN

It is Autumn—Autumn shall surely break your heart!

Translated by Tim Zengerink

Fly away! Fly away!—

The sun creeps slowly up the hill,

Step by step it climbs,

Pausing to rest at every turn.

How pale the world has grown!

The wind, on weary and slackened strings,

Plays his mournful tune.

Fair Hope has fled afar—

He cries out in longing.

It is Autumn—Autumn shall surely break your heart!

Fly away! Fly away!

O fruit of the tree,

Do you tremble, do you fall?

What secret did the Night whisper to you,

That icy shivers adorn your purple cheek?

You are silent, you do not answer—

Who still speaks in your place?

It is Autumn—Autumn shall surely break your heart!

Fly away! Fly away!

"I am not beautiful,"—

So whispers the lone star-flower,—

"Yet I love mankind

And bring them comfort.

Many flowers will they see,

Yet they will stoop to me,

And break me, alas!
So that, for a fleeting moment,
Their eyes might shine
With memories of far lovelier things than I
I see it—I see it—and so, I fade."
It is Autumn—Autumn shall surely break your heart!
Fly away! Fly away!

CAMPO SANTO DI STAGLIENO

Maiden, with gentle hands
You stroke your lamb's soft fleece,
Yet from your eyes, bright and burning,
Light and flame never cease.
Creature of merry laughter,
Beloved both near and far,
Blessed with kindness and grace,
Amorosissima!
What broke your joy so soon?
What grief does your heart endure?
Who would not gladly worship,
If they had your love, so pure?—
You are silent, yet your eyes
Hold tears that are not far.
You are silent: will you yearn and die,
Amorosissima?

Translated by Tim Zengerink

THE LITTLE BRIG NAMED "LITTLE ANGEL"

They call me "Little Angel"—
Now I am a ship, but I was once a girl,
Ah, and still too much of a girl!
My steering wheel shines so bright,
But it spins only for the sake of love.
They call me "Little Angel,"
Adorned with a hundred flags,
With a captain at the helm, proud and vain,
Guiding me, full of grandeur and flair
(He himself is like an ornament).
They call me "Little Angel,"
And wherever a small spark glows,
I rush towards it like a lamb,
Eager to follow my path—
I have always been such a lamb!
They call me "Little Angel"—
Do you think I can bark and howl
Like a dog, with my mouth spewing
Flames and smoke?
Ah, my mouth is like the devil's own.
They call me "Little Angel."
Once I spoke a harsh word,
So sharp that when my lover heard,
He fled far away, swiftly and fast.

Yes, I killed him with that word!
They call me "Little Angel."
One day I leapt so quickly from a cliff,
I broke a rib when I hit the ground—
And my soul slipped free of my body,
Yes, it escaped me through that rib.
They call me "Little Angel."
But my soul, like a frightened cat,
Landed on this ship in one swift leap,
Bounding quickly—one, two, three!
Its claws are sharp, ready to strike.
They call me "Little Angel"—
Now I am a ship, but I was once a girl,
Ah, and still too much of a girl!
My steering wheel, so bright and clear,
Spins only for the sake of love.

MAIDEN'S SONG

Just yesterday, at seventeen years,
I gained wisdom, a maiden so fair.
Now I seem grey-haired and wise in all things,
Except for the youth still in my hair.
Yesterday, a thought crossed my mind—
Was it a thought? You mock and sneer!
Have you ever truly had a thought,

Or was it just a feeling near?
Can a woman dare to think at all?
Wisdom once declared with might:
"A woman must follow, not lead the way,
For if she thinks, she loses her right."
So speaks old wisdom, aged and grim,
Yet I trust it not, no matter how vast.
Its words hop and sting like a biting flea:
"A woman who thinks won't be good at last."
To such wisdom, honored and old,
I bow my head in careful thought.
But let me share my own insight now,
A truth from life that wisdom brought.
Yesterday, a voice spoke within,
Its message clear, listen if you can:
"A woman may always be more beautiful,
But far more interesting—is man!"

"PIA, CARITATEVOLE, AMOROSISSIMA"

Cave where the silent dead now sleep,
O marble falsehood, cold and white,
Strangely, your quiet lies I keep,
For they set my heavy soul alight.
But today, yes, only today,
My soul is moved, and tears arise,

At you, the stone with words to say,

At you, the carvings beneath the skies.

This image here (none need to know)

I kissed not long ago in haste.

When there's so much in life to love,

Why did I kiss cold stone in waste?

Who can say why I felt the need?

"A fool for a grave!" you jeer, you scoff.

Yet I kissed the tombstone's creed—

Even the long inscription carved aloft.

TO FRIENDSHIP

Cave where the silent ones now lie,

O marble mask of cold disguise,

Strangely, I love your quiet sigh,

For in your stillness, freedom lies.

But today, yes, just for today,

My heart is moved, and tears will fall,

At you, the stone etched with decay,

At you, the carvings that say it all.

This image here (I'll keep it low),

Not long ago, I bent and kissed.

With so much life to love and know,

Why did I seek what death had missed?

Who understands the heart's strange way?

"A fool of tombs!" you mock, you chide.

Yet still I kissed that stone's display—

Even its long, cold words of pride.

PINE TREE AND LIGHTNING

Above man and beast, I've grown so tall, I speak, but none will hear my call.

Too high, too lone, my crest ascends, I wait—but for what, to what end?

The clouds draw near, pressing the sky,

I await the first bolt from on high.

TREE IN AUTUMN

Why did you fools disturb my dream

When I stood blind in blissful gleam?

Never before did fear so seize,

My golden peace replaced by unease.

Great beasts with trunks so rough and rude,

Why knock? Where are your manners crude?

I hurled in haste, though fear held sway,

My ripe fruit at your heads that day.

AMONG FOES (OR AGAINST CRITICS)

(After a Gypsy Proverb)

Here's the gallows, there's the cord,

And the hangman's beard, red as fire.

Around me swarm the venomous horde—
Nothing new, I've faced this ire.
I've seen this sight so many times,
Now, laughing, boldly I defy,
"You'll fail to end me with your crimes:
To die? No, no—I cannot die!"
You beggars envy what I've gained,
The prizes you have never won.
True, I suffer—but you've been drained;
Your life is spent, your race is run.
Many times I've faced near death,
Yet still I burn, I breathe, I fly.
Your noose will fail to steal my breath:
To die? No, no—I cannot die!

THE NEW COLUMBUS

"Dearest," Columbus said, "beware,
Never trust a Genoese again.
They always gaze at skies laid bare,
Forever chained by distant plains.
Strange lands call me; they pull, they bind—
Genoa fades into the past.
Stay cool, my heart! My hand must guide.
The sea ahead—land at last?
We'll stand firm and play this game,

No turning back, no space for retreat.
What greets us there? One fate, one name:
A single death, one joy complete."

IN LONESOMENESS

The crows are calling,
Their wings whirr as they fly toward town.
Soon the snow will fall,
Blessed are those who have a home to settle down.
Rooted firm, you stare behind—
How far back do your thoughts now roam?
Fool, what folly made you blind
To wander this harsh world alone?
This world—a gate
To endless deserts, silent and bare.
Whoever fate has stripped of solace,
Shall find no rest, no refuge there.
Now you stand pale,
Your journey frozen, cold as stone,
Like smoke whose trail
Is lost to skies more chilled, more lone.
Fly, bird, and scream
Your song apart, like fowl of the wastes.
Hide your broken, bleeding heart,
A fool encased in frozen haste.

The crows are calling,
Their wings whirr as they fly toward town.
Soon the snow will fall,
Woe to those with no home of their own.
My Answer
The man assumes,
Good heavens, that I'd return
To those warm rooms,
Where German ovens quietly burn.
My friend, you see—
It is your folly driving me away,
My pity for thee
And for all German fools today!

VENICE

ON the bridge I stood,
Mellow was the night,
Music came from far—
Drops of gold outpoured
On the shimmering waves.
Song, gondolas, light,
Floated a-twinkling out into the dusk.
The chords of my soul, moved
By unseen impulse, throbbed
Secretly into a gondola song,

With thrills of bright-hued ecstasy.

Had I a listener there?

EPIGRAMS

CAUTION: POISON!

If you cannot laugh at what's here, then don't start reading;

For if you read and do not laugh, some medicine you'll be needing!

HOW TO FIND ONE'S COMPANY

It's best to jest with those who jest:

Those who love to tickle, are tickled best.

THE WORD

I love the living word so much,

That flies to you with a merry touch,

Ready to greet with a cheerful nod,

Sweet in misfortune, a kind-hearted prod.

Yet it has blood, it can breathe so deep,

It whispers to doves or makes bold leaps.

It curls, it flies, it plays its role—

Whatever it does, it delights the soul.

But tender, the word must always stay,

Ill and well within a single day.

If you'd preserve its little life,

Hold it lightly, avoid all strife.

Don't press too hard, don't look unkind,
A harsh glance can end it, leave it maligned.
Then it lies there lifeless, a pitiful sight,
Cold, formless, battered, devoid of light.
A dead word is a hateful thing,
A hollow sound, a rattling ring.
Curses on trades that deal in decay,
Turning bright words into lifeless clay!

THE WANDERER AND HIS SHADOW

A Book

You'll neither move on nor turn around?
Even for chamois, no path is found?
So here I stand, I wait, I hold,
What eye and hand can grasp and mold.
A narrow ledge, morning's red light,
Below—world, man, and death in sight!

JOYFUL WISDOM

This isn't a book—who says it's so?
Books are coffins where dead things go!
They prey on what's gone, what's buried deep,
But in my book, the present leaps.
This isn't a book—who says it's so?
Who cares for coffins and ghosts that glow?

This is a promise, an act of might,
A bridge burned behind, for dark or light.
A wind from the sea, a lightened chain,
The hum of wheels, a ship in reign.
Cannons roar, their smoke soars high,
The sea—a monster—laughs and spies.

DEDICATION

The one with much to say will hold
A wealth of thoughts, untold.
The one who strikes like a lightning flash
Must first stay hidden in the clouds' vast sash.

THE NEW TESTAMENT

Is this your sacred, holy book,
For blessings, curses, or what you look?
Come now, truly—is this fair?
God tempts a wife at the very stair?

THE "TRUE GERMAN"

"O people of the best pretenders,
To you I'm loyal," he said, a defender.
Yet into the swiftest boat did he shift,
And off he sailed to Cosmopolis, adrift.

TO THE DARWINIANS

This honest Brit, no fool was he,
But call him Philosopher? Really?
Would you put Darwin by Goethe's side?
To majesty this seems a sly deride:
Genii majestatem—must you chide?

TO HAFIZ

(Toast Question of a Water-Drinker)

The inn you've built stands tall and grand,
It towers over every house in the land.
The brew you made inside, so fine,
The world could drink it, yet not decline.
The bird once known as the phoenix rare,
Now finds its place as your guest there.
The mouse that birthed a mountain wide,
Reflects your spirit, nothing to hide.
You are all and none, the wine, the inn,
The phoenix, the mouse, the mountain within.
You long to return to your own embrace,
Yet yearn to flee from your very place.
You've fallen from every towering height,
But even in depths, your soul shines bright.
The drunkenness that fills every drinker's mind—
Why, Hafiz, do you still seek wine?

TO SPINOZA

A lover of "All is One" so devout,
With love of God, your reason held stout.
Shoes off! This ground must be sacred, you'd say,
But beneath your love a torch would lay.
A hidden flame of vengeance burned,
The God of your people by hate was spurned.
Hermit, have I read your thoughts too plain?
Or misread the truth in your hidden disdain?

ARTHUR SCHOPENHAUER

What he taught has seen its day,
But what he lived shall stay and stay.
Look at him, no slave was he,
He never bowed to mortal decree!

TO RICHARD WAGNER

O restless soul who chafes at chains,
Never free, but bound by pains.
Though victorious, still confined,
More disgusted as the years unwind.
Each balm you drink turns into poison,
Each victory feels like loss, forlorn.
At last, upon the Cross, you fall,

Helpless beneath its weight and thrall.
I watched this play with dread and doubt,
Its air of prison wrapped about,
The incense heavy, the church's fume—
I found it strange, a haunted gloom.
But now I throw my fool's cap high,
For I escaped that dreadful sky!

MUSIC OF THE SOUTH

Everything my eagle once saw so clearly,
I now feel deep within me today.
Though my hope was faint and gray,
Your song struck my ear like an arrow,
A soothing touch, a healing sound,
Descending from the heavens on its way.
Now I long for lands of southern warmth,
For happy isles where Greek nymphs play!
There, my heart turns the ship's desire—
No ship ever sailed to a sweeter bay.
Here's a riddle—can you guess?
"When man discovers, woman must invent."

TO FALSE FRIENDS

You stole—your eyes betray you still.
What, just a thought you took?

How shrill! Why show such rudeness, modest now?
Take more—my thoughts, my words—here, bow!
Take all I have, you greedy beast,
Feast until your filth's released.

FRIEND YORICK

Cheer up, Yorick! If this thought brings pain,
And now I fear it's troubling again,
Is it not "God"? Though it might be wrong,
It's your own child, where you belong.
Your flesh, your blood, your wayward kin,
That brings the ache, that pokes within.
Your little rogue with tricks to play—
Will the rod change their path today?
So, Yorick, leave that gloomy road,
And let me whisper, soft and clear,
One little word, a healing code,
My own remedy for this tear:
"Who loves his God will chide him too,
For love will show what's strong and true."

RESOLUTION

It's wise to live as fits my mind,
Not by what others have designed.
If God made the world as dull as He could,
Then I'll praise it still, as anyone should.

And if my path won't follow straight,
If it curves and bends as I create,
That's the way the wise man starts,
While the fool's way ends, despite his arts.
The world keeps moving, never still,
Night craves the day's bright light.
Sweet sounds the voice of "I will,"
Sweeter yet, the song of "I might."

THE HALCYONIAN

Today a woman shyly spoke,
As though her words might be a joke:
"What would you be like in ecstasy,
If sober, you feel such bliss as we see?"

FINALE

Laughter is a serious art.
Each day I wish to play it better.
Did I succeed today or not?
Did the spark spring from the heart?
It matters little if the head laughs loud,
If the heart inside wears no glowing shroud.

DIONYSUS-DITHYRAMBS OF THE POVERTY OF THE RICHEST

Ten years have passed—

Translated by Tim Zengerink

Not a drop has touched me,
No rain-filled breeze, no dew of love—
A dry, barren land.
Now I beg my wisdom,
Do not hold back in this drought;
Overflow yourself, let your dew trickle down,
Be the rain for this thirsty wilderness!
Once, I commanded the clouds
To leave my mountains;
Once, I said to them,
"More light, you dark ones!"
Today, I call them back:
Cover me with your full skies;
—I want to milk you,
You lofty cows!
Wisdom warm as milk,
sweet love's dew,
I pour over the land.
Away, away, you gloomy truths!
I will not have bitter, impatient truths
On my mountains.
Let truth approach me today,
Gilded with smiles,
Sweetened by the sun, kissed by love—
I long to pluck a ripe truth from the tree.

Today, I stretch out my hands
To grasp the threads of chance,
Wise enough to guide them,
To outwit chance like a playful child.
Today, I will welcome even
The unwelcome,
I will not bristle against destiny....
—Zarathustra is no hedgehog.
My soul,
Insatiable in its thirst,
Has tasted all that is good and evil,
Dived into every depth.
Yet like a cork,
It always rises to the surface again,
Floating like oil on dark seas.
Because of this, they call me fortunate.
Who are my father and mother?
Isn't my father Prince Plenty?
And my mother Silent Laughter?
Didn't their union create me,
The enigmatic beast—
Me, the monster of light—
Me, Zarathustra, who squanders all wisdom?
Today I am sick with tenderness,
A soft, dewy wind,

Zarathustra waits, waits on his mountains—
Sweet and simmering
In his own essence,
Beneath his peak,
Beneath his ice,
Tired and happy,
A Creator on his seventh day.
—Silence!
A truth passes over me Like a drifting cloud—
With invisible lightning, it strikes me.
On broad, slow stairs,
Its happiness ascends to me:
Come, come, beloved truth!
—Silence!
This truth is mine!
From shy eyes,
From velvet shivers,
Her gaze meets mine,
Sweet and mischievous,
like a maiden's glance.
She has guessed the cause of my joy,
She has understood me—ha! what is she thinking?
A purple dragon
Lurks in the depths of her maiden's eyes.
—Silence! My truth speaks!—

"Woe to you, Zarathustra!
You look like someone
Who has swallowed gold:
They will cut open your belly one day!
You are too rich,
You, the corrupter of many!
You make too many envious,
Leave too many poor.
Even your light casts a shadow on me—
I feel a chill: leave, you rich one,
Leave, Zarathustra,
step away from your sun."

BETWEEN BIRDS OF PREY

Whoever dares to descend here
Is quickly swallowed by the depths!
But you, Zarathustra,
You still love the abysses,
You love them as the fir tree does.
The fir sends its roots deep down
Where even the rocks themselves
Gaze in fear at the depths.
The fir pauses before the chasm,
Where everything else
Wishes to plunge.

Amid the wild rushing
And leaping torrents, It stands patient, Silent, stern,
And alone.
Alone!
Who would dare
To be a guest here—
To be your guest?
Perhaps a bird of prey,
Delighting in others' misfortunes,
Will cling stubbornly
To the hair of the steadfast watcher,
Laughing wildly,
A vulture's mocking laugh.
Why so steadfast?
It mocks you so cruelly:
One must have wings to love the abyss.
One must not cling to the cliffs
Like you, hanging there!
O Zarathustra,
Cruel Nimrod!
Once a hunter of gods,
You wove a spider's web to catch virtue,
You were an arrow of evil!
And now,
You are hunted by yourself,

Your own prey,
Trapped within your own soul.
Now
Alone to me and to yourself,
Divided by your own knowledge,
Among a hundred mirrors
False to yourself,
Surrounded by countless memories,
Uncertain,
Weary from every wound,
Shivering in the cold,
Strangled by your own noose,
Self-knower!
Self-executioner!
Why did you tie yourself
With the rope of your wisdom?
Why did you lure yourself
Into the old serpent's paradise?
Why did you sneak
Into yourself, your own depths?
Now you are sick,
Poisoned by the serpent's venom,
A captive,
Carrying the heaviest burden.
In your own tunnel,

Bent as you dig,
In your own cavern,
You dig into yourself,
Helpless, stiff,
A cold corpse,
Crushed under a hundred weights,
Overburdened by your own self.
A knower!
A self-knower!
The wise Zarathustra!
You sought the heaviest weight,
And in doing so, you found yourself.
Now you cannot escape yourself.
Watching,
Chewing,
Unable to stand tall anymore!
Even in your grave,
You will grow crooked—
A deformed spirit.
Not long ago, you were so proud,
Standing tall on the stilts of your pride!
Not long ago, the godless hermit,
The hermit with one companion—the devil,
The crimson prince of every wickedness!
But now—

Between two nothings,

You crouch,

A question mark,

A tired riddle,

A puzzle for vultures.

They will "solve" you.

They already hunger for your "answer."

They circle above their "riddle,"

Above you, the condemned one!

O Zarathustra,

Self-knower!

Self-hangman!

THE SUN SINKS

Not much longer will you thirst,

O parched heart!

A promise is in the air;

From unknown voices, I feel a breeze—

The great coolness is coming.

My sun burned hot above me at midday:

Greetings to you who arrive,

You sudden winds,

You cool spirits of the afternoon!

The air feels strange and pure.

See how the night

Translated by Tim Zengerink

Glances at me sideways,
Like a seducer...
Be strong, my brave heart,
And ask no questions of "Why?"
Day of my life!
The sun sets,
And the calm waters
Are already gilded.
The rock breathes warmth—
Did happiness at midday
Find its rest upon it?
In green light,
Happiness still glimmers up from the brown depths.
Day of my life!
Evening draws near.
Your gaze already
Glows faint and dim,
Your dew now spills Its quiet tears.
Across the white seas,
The purple of your love spreads,
Your last tender holiness hesitates.
Golden joy, come forth!
You, the sweetest foretaste—
A foretaste of death!
Did I rush my path too swiftly?

Now, as my step grows weary,

Your gaze still finds me,

Your happiness still embraces me.

Around me, only waves and play.

All that was hard

Has sunk into the blue oblivion.

My boat now drifts idly.

The storm, the motion—how have they been forgotten!

Desire and hope are drowned,

The sea and soul are calm.

Seventh Solitude!

Never before felt!

Sweet certainty draws closer,

And the sun's warmth touches me deeper.

Doesn't the ice on my summit glow yet?

Silvery, light, a fish—

Now my vessel swims freely...

THE LAST DESIRE

This is how I want to die,

Just as I saw him die—

My friend, who, like a god,

Brought fire and lightning to my shadowed youth.

He was buoyant yet profound,

Deep even in the heat of battle,

With a dancer's light heart.

Among warriors,

His heart was the lightest.

Among victors,

His brow bore the weight of thought—

A man of destiny, standing firm,

Casting his gaze back and forward,

Always grounded, always aware.

Victory weighed heavy on him,

Yet he sang as both triumph and death

Approached him, hand in hand.

Even in death, he commanded,

And his command demanded destruction.

This is how I want to die,

Just as I saw him die—

Victorious and unyielding.

THE BEACON

Here, where the island rises from the seas,

A towering altar of rock stands tall.

Beneath dark skies,

Zarathustra lights his mountain flames,

A guiding signal for lost ships,

A call for answers to wanderers.

The flames, their gray-white glow,

Stretch eagerly toward the heavens,
Reaching for ever-purer heights—
A serpent coiled in restless anticipation.
This signal is my creation.
These flames are my soul,
Unquenchable in its hunger for the unknown,
Rising higher and higher in silent heat.
Why did Zarathustra flee from beasts and men?
Why did he leave behind all lands?
He has wandered through six solitudes,
Yet even the sea was not lonely enough for him.
On this island, he climbed higher,
On the mountain, he became fire.
In his seventh solitude,
He casts his line into the abyss.
Storm-beaten sailors!
Broken remnants of ancient stars!
Oceans of the future, boundless skies!
To all who are alone, I cast my line.
Answer the fire's call!
Let me, a fisherman on these high peaks,
Catch my seventh and final solitude!

FAME AND ETERNITY

Tell me, how long will you dwell

In this dark despair of yours?
Beware, lest your gloom
Shadows your face so deeply
That others see in it
A bitterness sharper than the sea
Why does Zarathustra climb
The steep and lonely mountains?
Suspicious, hardened, and sour,
He keeps his home far from human eyes.
Suddenly, a flash of lightning splits the sky,
Thunder roars in the deep valley below,
The mountains tremble and crack apart.
Born of hatred and lightning's embrace,
The storm of Zarathustra's wrath
Looms above like a menacing cloud.
You who live safely under roofs,
Hide! Seek shelter!
For storms ride the wind with triumph,
Shaking walls and breaking barriers.
Lightning scars the night's face,
And eerie truths gleam like phantoms,
Mocking the ordinary.
In the storm, the curse of Zarathustra's fury ignites.
This fame, loved by the world,
I touch only with gloves. I scorn it

And trample it beneath my feet.
Who longs to earn it?
Who casts themselves in its path?
These merchants of gold,
Greedy hands reaching for fame.
They clasp it with slick palms,
While its hollow echo
Wins the world's applause.
Do you want to buy it?
No skill is needed.
They're all for sale.
Just dig deep into your purse,
Let their hands take freely,
And they'll sell it to you.
But if your offer isn't enough,
They'll parade their "virtue"
To hide their bitterness.
They all claim to be virtuous.
For them, virtue and fame walk hand in hand.
The louder they talk of virtue,
The closer they are to fame.
Virtue has always been fame's accomplice.
Among these so-called virtuous,
I'd rather be guilty of every vile act.
When I see fame's shamelessness,

Its boldness displayed for all to see,
I feel no ambition, only disdain.
Among such company,
I would choose the lowest place.
This fame, loved by the world,
I touch only with gloves. I scorn it
And trample it beneath my feet.
Hush! I sense something vast.
Should such greatness remain unspoken?
Then speak, heart,
And let your words carry their power.
I look up at the starry sky,
O night, silent and deep,
Voiceless cries of the stars.
And there! A sign—
A constellation falls toward me.
O highest crown of existence,
O eternal tablets,
You come to me!
Your beauty is hidden to all,
But you reveal yourself to me.
O shield of destiny!
O carved truths of eternity!
You know what the world despises,
And what I alone cherish.

You stand untouched by time,

Beyond the reach of change.

Only you, O necessity,

Can awaken eternal love in me.

O highest crown of life!

O shield of fate!

Unreachable, untouchable,

You are the eternal "Yes" to life.

And I, forever, am your "Yes."

For I love you, eternity!

FRAGMENTS OF DIONYSUS-DITHYRAMBS

3

My home is in the highlands,

Yet I do not yearn for them.

I lift my eyes not to the peaks—

I am one who looks down,

One who must offer blessings—

And all who bless look downward.

11

This is how I began,

By unlearning all self-pity.

13

Your courage lay not in smashing idols,

But in destroying the idol-worshipper within you.

14

Look there, standing firm,
Those heavy cats carved from granite,
Those old, ancient values.
Woe to me! How can they be overthrown?
Scratching cats,
With paws bound in chains,
They sit still,
Their glances dripping with poison.

17

A lightning strike gave me wisdom:
Its sword of unbreakable steel
Split apart every shadow of darkness.

19

A thought burns within me,
Flowing as hot as lava—
Yet all streams of lava
Eventually build walls around themselves.
And every thought, in the end,
Becomes trapped by its own rules.
This is my will:
Because it is my will,
All happens as I desire.
That is my greatest wisdom:
I willed what I must,

And turned every "must" into my choice.

Since then, "must" has ceased to exist for me.

23

Deception

Is the heart of warfare. The fox's cunning

Is my hidden armor.

25

We of the new underworld

Dig deep for undiscovered treasures.

To the ancients, disturbing the earth

Was seen as godless.

Now, that same godlessness is reborn.

Do you not hear the earth's depths rumble?

28

Seeking love, only to find masks—

Uncovering cursed masks,

And breaking them apart!

29

Do I love you?

Yes, like a rider loves the steed

That carries him toward his goal.

30

His pity is harsh,

His caring touch bruises.

Do not offer your hand to a giant!

31

Do you fear me?

Do you fear the tightly drawn bow?

Do you fear that someone might notch an arrow and let it fly?

33

I am only a maker of words. What do words matter?

What do I matter?

34

Ah, my friends,

Where has all that is called "good" gone? Where are all the good people?

Where is the innocence of these falsehoods? I call all that is good:

Leaves, grass, happiness, blessings, and rain.

35

It wasn't through sins or great mistakes—

It was through their perfection that I suffered, For I suffered most because of men.

Songs, Epigrams, Etc.

36

"Man is evil."

The wisest once spoke these words To console me.

37

And only when I become a burden to myself Do you weigh heavy upon me!

38

Too soon, too quickly, I laugh again:

It's easy for a foe

To make amends with me.

39

I am gentle with man and chance; Gentle with all, even the grass:

Like a patch of sunshine on winter curtains, Damp with tenderness,

A thawing wind for snowbound souls. But proud am I toward petty gains, Where I see the merchant's long finger. It's always my preference

To be deceived—

Such is the command of my delicate taste.

Ecce Homo

40

A strange breath spits at me,

Am I a mirror that becomes clouded at once?

41

Little people,

Trusting, open-hearted, But with low, narrow doors

That only the smallest can enter.

How can I pass through the city gates,

When I have forgotten how to live among dwarfs?

42

My wisdom was like the sun— I wanted to give them light, But I only misled them.

The sun of my wisdom Blinded the eyes

Of these poor bats.

43

You have seen darker, more evil things than any seer ever could. No sage has walked through the wild revelry of Hell as you have.

Songs, Epigrams, Etc.

44

Back off! You follow too closely on my heels!

Step away, or my wisdom will trample you and crush you!

45

"They say your path leads straight to Hell!" So be it! If Hell is my destination,

I will pave my way there with my own well-crafted truths.

46

You say your God Is a God of love?

Is the sting of conscience A sting from God?

A sting of love?

48

They chew on gravel,

They grovel on their bellies Before little round objects.

They worship anything that refuses to fall—

These final servants of God,

These supposed believers!

Ecce Homo

50

They made their God from nothing;

Is it any surprise He has become nothing?

51

You loftier men! There have been times,

More reflective and thoughtful than

Our today and tomorrow.

52

Our time is like a sick woman— Let her scream, rage, and scold,

Breaking tables and dishes as she goes!

54

You claim to climb?

Is it true that you ascend, You loftier men?

Are you not like a ball, Launched to great heights

By the lowest part of yourselves?

Do you not flee from who you truly are,

O climbers?

Songs, Epigrams, Etc.

55

What you thought You had to despise— You only abandoned.

56

All men join the chorus! "No, no, and no again!"

What's this endless talk of heaven?

We do not wish to enter the kingdom of heaven; The kingdom of earth is ours to claim!

57

It is the will that redeems. But he who has nothing to do

Will find even nothingness a source of torment.

58

You can't bear it anymore, Your cruel destiny.

Love it—you have no other choice!

59

Only these free us from suffering. (Choose now:)

A sudden death,

Ecce Homo

Or a long, drawn-out love.

60

Death is certain,

So why not find joy while we live?

61

The worst excuse

I kept hidden from you—that life had grown dull! Let it go, so you can enjoy it once again!

62

Lonely days,

You must tread with brave feet!

63

Loneliness

Does not plant seeds, it ripens them.

And even then, the sun must be your ally.

64

You must plunge back into the crowd—

Among the throng, you grow tough and polished. Solitude weakens,

And eventually destroys.

Songs, Epigrams, Etc.

65

When the hermit feels overwhelming fear, When he runs and runs,

Not knowing where,

When storms rage behind him,

And lightning seems to accuse him, When his cavern spawns phantoms That fill him with terror.

67

Throw your pain into the depths, Forget it, man! Forget!

Forgetting is divine!

Do you want to fly?

Do you want to feel at home in the heights? Cast your heaviest burden into the sea!

Here is the sea—throw yourself into it! Forgetting is divine!

69

Look ahead, never look back! We sink to the depths

When we keep gazing into them.

Ecce Homo

70

Beware, beware

Of warning the reckless!

Your warning will only drive them To leap into every abyss!

71

Why did he throw himself from the heights? What led him astray?

His pity for all that is lowly misled him,

And now he lies there—broken, useless, and cold.

72

Where did he go? Who knows? We only know he sank.

A star vanished into the empty void, And the void was left even lonelier.

73

What we lack But truly need, We must take.

And so, I took for myself a clear conscience.

74

Who could ever grant you your right? So take it yourself!

Songs, Epigrams, Etc.

75

O waves,

Magnificent waves, are you angry with me?

Do you raise your crests in fury? With my rudder, I strike Squarely at your folly.

This little boat,

You will carry it to eternal life.

77

When no new voices were heard, You turned old words

Into laws.

When life grows rigid, laws arise.

78

Do you think that

What no one can disprove Must therefore be true?

Oh, how innocent you are!

79

Are you strong?

Strong like a beast of burden? Strong like a god? Are you proud?

So proud you show off

Ecce Homo

Your vanity without shame?

80

Beware,

Never beat the drum Of your destiny!

Step aside

From the noise of fame! Do not be known too soon!

Be one who hoards their renown.

81

Do you reach for thorns?

Your fingers will pay the price.

Better reach for a dagger.

85

Be like a golden tablet,

And they will engrave upon you In letters of gold.

86

He stands tall,

With more "justice"

In the smallest part of his toe Than I have in my whole head.

Songs, Epigrams, Etc.

A creature of virtue, Draped in spotless white.

87

Already, he imitates himself, Already, he grows tired, Already, he retraces old paths—

Though not long ago, he loved exploring the unknown. Secretly burned—

Not for his beliefs,

But because he lost the courage

To find new ones.

88

He spent too much time in the cage, That runaway!

Too long, he feared The sight of a jailer.

Now, timidly, he goes on his way, But stumbles over everything— Even the shadow of a stick trips him.

89

You smoky, musty rooms,

You cramped cages and narrow hearts, How could your spirits ever be free?

Ecce Homo

90

Narrow-minded souls! Souls of merchants!

When the coin drops into the box, Their soul follows right after!

92

Are you like women,

That you desire to suffer

From the very thing you love?

99

They are so cold, these learned men!

If only a lightning bolt could strike their meals,

And their mouths could learn to consume fire!

101

Your false love For the past,

Your love for graves and the dead, Steals from life,

It robs the future. An antiquarian

Is but a craftsman of dead things,

Living among coffins and bones.

Songs, Epigrams, Etc.

103

Only a poet Who can lie

Willfully and skillfully, Can truly tell the truth.

104

Is our hunt for truth

Nothing more than a hunt for happiness?

105

Truth

Is a woman—no different—

Clever in her modesty.

She denies what she desires most, Hiding her face.

What does she yield to If not force?

Force is her need.

Be firm, you sages! You must compel her, That bashful Truth.

For her joy,

She craves constraint—

Yes, she is a woman, no better.

Ecce Homo

106

We once thought ill of each other, Kept apart by distance.

But now, in this small hut, Bound by the same fate, How could we still be foes? We must love those

Whom we cannot escape.

107

Love your enemy, Let the thief rob you.

The woman hears—and obeys.

110

A proud gaze,

Veiled by silken curtains, Rarely clear,

Honors those

Who manage to see it revealed.

111

Lazy eyes, Slow to love—

But when they do, their lightning strikes

Like golden flashes

Songs, Epigrams, Etc.

Guarded by a dagger over the treasure of love.

117

I have no sympathy for crabs. Grab them, and they pinch you;

Leave them alone, and they crawl backward.

119

Rivers and men both move crookedly, Twisting, yet reaching their goal.

That is their highest courage— To fear not the winding path.

121

Would you catch them? Then speak to them

As you would to lost sheep: "Your path, your path— You've lost it!"

They follow anyone

Who flatters them so:

"What? Did we have a path?" They whisper to one another, "It seems we did have a path."

The End

The Antichrist

Friedrich Nietzsche

Prologue

This book is meant for the rarest kind of people. Perhaps none of them are alive today. Maybe they are among those who will one day understand my Zarathustra. How could I mistake myself for those who are just now beginning to listen? My time is not now; it will come the day after tomorrow. Some men are born only to be understood after their death.

I know all too well what it takes to understand me, and why one must. To endure the weight of my seriousness and my passion, a person must have intellectual integrity, a strength so sharp it borders on hardness. He must be used to living at great heights, looking down on the petty chatter of politics and nationalism as something far beneath him. He must be indifferent, never questioning whether the truth benefits him or brings him misfortune. He must have a strength that draws him toward questions no one else dares to ask—the courage to confront what is forbidden and a destiny tied to navigating life's labyrinth. He must know the solitude of seven lifetimes. He must have new ears to hear unheard music, new eyes to see what lies furthest away, and a conscience open to truths no one has dared to discover before. He must also possess the ability to conserve his energy with great discipline, to channel his passion and strength wisely. Above all, he must have a deep reverence for himself, a love for himself, and absolute freedom over himself.

Such are my readers—my real readers, my destined readers. What value do the rest have? The rest are simply humanity. To understand me, one must rise above humanity in power, in greatness of soul—and in scorn.

The Antichrist

Let us look at each other directly. We are Hyperboreans—we know just how far removed we are from the rest. "Neither by land nor by water can you reach the Hyperboreans," said Pindar long ago. We live beyond the North, beyond the ice, even beyond death—our life, our happiness lies there. We have found that happiness; we know the way to it. It came from thousands of years wandering in the labyrinth. Who else has found it? The modern man? "I don't know the way in or out; I am whatever doesn't know either the way in or out," says the modern man with a sigh.

This modern age made us sick—sick with its lazy peace, its cowardly compromises, and the self-righteous dirtiness of its constant "Yes" and "No." This tolerance, this wide-open heart that "forgives" because it "understands," feels like a hot, stifling wind to us. We would rather live in the cold ice than among these modern virtues and soft southern breezes. We were brave; we spared neither ourselves nor others, but it took us a long time to figure out where to direct that courage. We became somber, and they called us fatalists. Our fate was one of fullness, tension, and stored-up strength. We longed for lightning and great deeds, not for the weakling's happiness or resignation. The air around us was heavy with thunder, and as we embodied nature, even the skies seemed dark—because we had not yet found our path. Our formula for happiness: a Yes, a No, a straight line, a goal.

What is good? Whatever increases the feeling of strength, the will to power, and power itself in a person.

What is evil? Whatever comes from weakness.

What is happiness? The feeling that strength grows, that resistance is overcome.

Not satisfaction, but more power. Not peace at any cost, but struggle. Not virtue in the moral sense, but effectiveness—virtue in the Renaissance sense, free from moral constraints.

The weak and the flawed should perish: this is the first principle of our kindness. And one should even help them perish.

What is more damaging than any vice? Active compassion for the weak and flawed—Christianity.

The problem I am setting here is not what will replace mankind in the chain of life—man is an end—but what kind of man should be created, should be desired, as the most valuable, the one most worthy of life, the one who can secure the future.

This higher type of man has appeared many times in history, but always as a rare accident, an exception, never something deliberately created. Often, this type has been the most feared; in fact, it has been seen as the ultimate terror. Out of this fear, the opposite type has been nurtured and achieved: the tame animal, the herd animal, the sickly human—the Christian.

Humanity does not represent progress toward something better, stronger, or higher as people think today. This idea of progress is modern—and false. The European today is far beneath the European of the Renaissance in terms of worth. Evolution does not automatically mean improvement, growth, or strength.

True, in isolated cases and different parts of the world, a higher type of person can and does emerge. Compared to the masses, this person may appear as a kind of superhuman. These rare, fortunate occurrences have always been possible and will likely remain so. Entire races, tribes, or nations may occasionally represent such strokes of luck.

We must not dress up or beautify Christianity: it has waged a relentless war against the higher type of man. It has suppressed the deepest instincts of this type, turning these instincts into the very definition of evil. Christianity created its concept of "the Evil One" from the traits of the strong man, labeling him as the ultimate outcast. It has sided with the weak, the lowly, and the flawed, elevating opposition to life's natural instincts of self- preservation into an ideal.

Even the brightest minds have been corrupted by it, as Christianity painted the highest intellectual values as sinful, misleading, and full of temptation. The most tragic example of this is Pascal, who believed his brilliant mind had been ruined by original sin, when in truth, it was Christianity that destroyed it.

What a tragic and painful picture I see: I have pulled back the curtain to reveal humanity's decay. When I use the word "decay," it carries no moral judgment—it is free from that suspicion. I emphasize this again: I mean decay in the sense of decline, of décadence. Strangely, I find this decay most evident in those who have aimed highest at "virtue" and "godliness." What I argue is that the values humanity holds in the highest regard today are décadence values.

I call an animal, a species, or an individual corrupt when it loses its instincts—when it chooses what harms it. A history of humanity's "higher feelings" and "ideals" (a task I may yet undertake) would likely explain why man has degenerated. To me, life is an instinct for growth, survival, accumulating strength, and achieving power. When the will to power is absent, disaster follows. My claim is that the highest values of humanity have been emptied of this will, and that the values of décadence and nihilism now dominate under the guise of sacred names.

Christianity calls itself the religion of pity. Pity, however, opposes all the invigorating passions that enhance the energy of life; it weakens and drains power. When a man pities, he loses strength. Pity amplifies the suffering that already exists, spreading it like a contagion. In extreme cases, pity can demand total sacrifice, an enormous cost for an often trivial cause—as in the death of the Nazarene. That's one way to see it. But there's a deeper issue: the reactions pity provokes reveal its true danger to life. Pity goes against the very law of evolution, the principle of natural selection. It preserves what is ready to perish; it sides with the weak, the disinherited, and the condemned. By supporting the flawed and the suffering, pity makes life appear bleak and uncertain.

Humanity dared to call pity a virtue. In fact, in some moral systems, pity was hailed as the ultimate virtue, the foundation of all others. But this view came from a nihilistic philosophy, one that essentially denied life. Schopenhauer recognized this: pity denies life and makes it seem unworthy of living. Pity is the tool of nihilism. Let me stress this again: this weakening, contagious instinct undermines all the instincts that sustain and enhance life. Pity, as a protector of the miserable, becomes an agent of décadence. It encourages extinction—not openly, of course, but under the guise of "the other world," "God," "true life,"

Nirvana, salvation, or blessedness. This seemingly innocent language from religious and ethical teachings hides its true aim: the destruction of life.

Schopenhauer hated life, which is why pity seemed virtuous to him. Aristotle, on the other hand, recognized pity as a sick and dangerous state of mind. His remedy was tragedy, a kind of purging. The instinct for life demands that we find ways to puncture and release the dangerous build-up of pity, like the one we see in Schopenhauer's work or in modern culture, from Tolstoy to Wagner. This accumulation of pity must be burst, its poison discharged.

Nothing in our modern age is more harmful than Christian pity. To heal this sickness, we must be unmerciful, wield the knife without hesitation. This is our task, our responsibility as philosophers. This is what it means to be Hyperboreans.

We need to be clear about who we see as our opponents: theologians and anyone with theological influence in their blood—that sums up our entire philosophy. To truly understand the danger they pose, one must have confronted it up close, or better yet, experienced it personally and almost succumbed to it. Only then can one realize it's no small matter. The so-called free- thinking of many naturalists and scientists strikes me as a joke— they lack real passion about these issues; they haven't suffered. This poison spreads much further than most people imagine. I see the arrogant attitude of theologians in all who call themselves "idealists." These are people who claim a higher perspective, allowing them to look down on reality with suspicion.

The idealist, like the priest, holds onto lofty concepts and uses them with a kind of benevolent disdain against reason, the senses, honor, enjoyment, and science. To them, these things are inferior, corrupting forces. They imagine the soul as a pure thing that rises above it all. As if humility, chastity, poverty—in short, so-called holiness—haven't caused far more harm to life than any imaginable vice or horror. The idea of the "pure soul" is a complete lie. As long as priests—these professional deniers, slanderers, and poisoners of life—are seen as a higher kind of human being, there can be no answer to the question, "What is truth?" The truth has already been turned upside down when the advocate of emptiness is mistaken for its representative.

I wage war against this theological instinct because I see its traces everywhere. Anyone with theological blood in their veins is dishonest and untrustworthy in everything. The pitiful product of this condition is called faith. Faith means closing one's eyes to oneself forever, to avoid seeing the lies that cannot be undone. On this false foundation, people build their ideas of morality, virtue, and holiness. They make their flawed perspective sacred by calling it "God," "salvation," or "eternity." They declare that no other way of seeing the world has value.

I uncover this theological instinct wherever I look—it is the most widespread and deeply rooted falsehood on earth. Whatever a theologian declares as true is almost certainly false. This can serve as a reliable guide to truth. Their instinct for self-preservation is so strong that they resist truth in every form, ensuring it can never be honored or even spoken. Wherever theologians hold influence, they reverse values, forcing the meanings of "true" and "false" to switch places. Whatever harms life is called "true," while whatever uplifts, strengthens, and celebrates life is labeled "false."

When theologians, through the "conscience" of rulers or the masses, seize power, there is no doubt about their ultimate goal: they aim to bring everything to an end. Their nihilistic will to destruction is always at the heart of their actions.

Among Germans, I am immediately understood when I say that theological blood is the downfall of philosophy. The Protestant pastor is the grandfather of German philosophy, and Protestantism itself is its original sin. Protestantism can be defined as a half-paralyzed form of both Christianity and reason. Simply mentioning the "Tübingen School" makes it clear what German philosophy essentially is—a refined form of theology. The Suabians are known as the most skilled liars in Germany; they lie without malice, almost innocently.

Why was there such celebration among German scholars—most of whom are the sons of pastors and teachers—when Kant appeared? Why does the echo of their conviction that Kant marked a new beginning still resonate? The theological instinct in German academia immediately recognized what Kant's work made possible once again. A secret path back to the old ideals was reopened. The concept of the "true world" and morality as the foundation of existence—the two most harmful errors ever conceived—were, thanks to Kant's crafty skepticism, made less vulnerable. They might not have been proven, but they were no longer easily refuted. Reason no longer claimed the right to demolish these ideas. Reality was reduced to mere "appearance," while an entirely false notion of existence was elevated as reality. Kant's success was a theological success, not a philosophical one. Like Luther and Leibniz before him, Kant became another obstacle to German integrity, which was already fragile.

Now, a word against Kant as a moralist. True virtue must be something we create for ourselves; it must emerge from our personal needs and as a defense of our life. In every other case, it is a threat. Virtue that does not belong to one's own life endangers it. A virtue rooted in mere reverence for the abstract idea of "virtue," as Kant proposed, is destructive. Ideas such as "virtue," "duty," or "the good for its own sake"—virtues grounded in impersonality or universal validity—are mere illusions. They reflect the decay and ultimate breakdown of life, embodying the stagnant spirit of Königsberg.

In contrast, the deepest laws of survival and growth demand that each individual discover their own virtue, their own unique imperative. A nation collapses when it confuses its specific duty with some general, abstract concept of duty. Nothing leads to a more complete disaster than impersonal duties or sacrifices made to serve lifeless abstractions. Yet, no one seems to have recognized Kant's categorical imperative as a danger to life. It was only protected because of the theological instinct. A life- driven action proves itself right through the joy it brings. And yet, that nihilist, Kant, with his deeply Christian instincts, treated joy as an objection.

What destroys a person faster than working, thinking, and feeling without inner necessity, without personal desire, and without pleasure? To act as a mere machine of duty is a recipe for decline and even for madness. Kant himself became a victim of this—a true descent into idiocy. And this man lived in the same era as Goethe! This spinner of lifeless abstractions was celebrated as the German philosopher and is still held in high regard today.

I hesitate to even speak about what I think of the Germans. Didn't Kant see the French Revolution as a transformation of the state from something inorganic to something organic? Didn't he ask if there was any event that could be explained without assuming some moral faculty within humanity? And, according to Kant, this faculty demonstrated "mankind's tendency toward the good," once and for all. His answer to this was "revolution." Instinct gone wrong in every possible way, instinct rebelling against nature— that is German decay transformed into philosophy. That is Kant!

I exclude a few skeptics, those rare examples of decency in the history of philosophy; the rest lack even the slightest idea of intellectual honesty. These so- called great minds and prodigies behave like women—they consider "beautiful feelings" as valid arguments, believe that an emotional outburst is proof of divine inspiration, and treat conviction as the mark of truth. In the end, Kant— with his "German" innocence—tried to give this kind of intellectual corruption a scientific spin by naming it "practical reason." He intentionally created a version of reasoning meant for moments when actual reasoning was inconvenient, especially when the moral command "thou shalt" needed to take center stage.

If we recall that philosophers originally evolved from the priestly type, then this inherited self-deception ceases to surprise. When a man feels he has a divine mission—perhaps to uplift, save, or free humanity—when he senses a divine spark within and believes himself a voice for supernatural commands, it's only natural that he considers himself above mere logical standards of judgment. He feels sanctified by his mission, a figure of a higher order. What does such a priest have to do with philosophy? He sees himself as far above it. And throughout history, the priest has held authority, defining what is "true" and "false."

We shouldn't underestimate the importance of this: we free spirits are already a "revaluation of all values." We stand as a visible rebellion and triumph over the old concepts of "truth" and "untruth." The most valuable insights are the last to be achieved, and the greatest of these insights are about the methods we use. For thousands of years, the methods and principles of the scientific spirit—so commonplace today—were despised. Anyone who leaned toward them was cast out from "decent" society, labeled an "enemy of God," a mocker of truth, or even "possessed." A man of science was treated as untouchable, like a member of an outcast class.

For centuries, we faced humanity's overwhelming foolishness and their shallow ideas of what truth should be. Their expectations of what serving the truth meant, along with all their moral commands, were hurled at us. Our goals, methods, and careful, skeptical approaches were viewed as shameful and contemptible. Looking back, we might even wonder if people's blindness wasn't tied to an aesthetic preference. They demanded truth to be dramatic, something that thrilled their senses. From scholars, they expected spectacle and strong emotional appeal. It was likely our modesty, our quiet approach, that clashed with their tastes.

How accurately they sensed it—these self-important defenders of God!

We have forgotten certain ideas and grown more humble in every way. We no longer see humans as descended from the "spirit" or the "divine"; instead, we place them back among the animals. Humans are the strongest of animals because they are the cleverest, and their intelligence is a result of this. However, we are cautious not to let this lead to arrogance, such as thinking humans are the pinnacle of evolution. In truth, humans are far from being the crown of creation; many animals exist at similar levels of development. Even saying this might be overstating it, for humans are, relatively speaking, the most flawed and unhealthy of all animals. They have strayed the farthest from their instincts, yet they remain the most fascinating.

As for the lower animals, Descartes had the daring to describe them as machines. Modern physiology supports this view. However, Descartes' mistake was setting humans apart. Today, we know humans only to the extent that we see them as machines too. Previously, humans were said to possess "free will" as a gift from higher beings, but now this idea no longer makes sense. What we once called "will" is now understood as a result of various conflicting and harmonious stimuli—a reaction, not an independent force. The will does not "act" or "move" as we once thought.

In the past, people believed that human consciousness, or "spirit," was proof of divine origin. To perfect themselves, people were told to withdraw from earthly experiences and shed their physical selves, leaving only the "pure spirit." We now see consciousness as a sign of imperfection—a trial, an experiment, or even a misunderstanding. It consumes energy needlessly and cannot achieve anything perfectly. The idea of a "pure spirit" is sheer foolishness; remove the body, the senses, and the nervous system, and all that remains is error.

Christianity disconnects morality and religion from reality entirely. It offers imaginary causes like "God," "soul," "spirit," and "free will" (or "unfree will"), and imaginary effects like "sin," "salvation," "grace," and "forgiveness." Its stories involve imaginary beings—God, spirits, and souls—and its version of natural history is centered on humans while denying natural causes. Its psychology misinterprets feelings and bodily states, labeling them with terms like "repentance," "temptation," or "the presence of God." Its teleology imagines destinations like "the kingdom of God" or "eternal life." Unlike dreams, which reflect reality in some way, this fictional world distorts, cheapens, and denies it.

When "nature" was set against "God," the natural became synonymous with the "bad." This entire fabricated world stems from a hatred of nature, or reality, and reveals a deep discomfort with the real. Who feels compelled to escape reality? Those who suffer in it. To suffer from reality is to be a flawed reality. The imbalance of pain over pleasure drives this false morality and religion. That imbalance, in turn, is the very definition of decay.

A closer look at the Christian concept of God inevitably leads to one conclusion—a criticism that must be faced. A nation that still has confidence in itself clings to its own god as a representation of its strength and identity. Through this god, the people honor the values and conditions that ensure their survival and celebrate their virtues. The god becomes a projection of their pride and their sense of power, a figure to whom they can give thanks. A wealthy people will naturally offer from their abundance; a proud people will need a god to whom they can make sacrifices as an expression of their vitality. Religion, in this sense, becomes a form of gratitude—a way to acknowledge the miracle of their own existence, for which they feel compelled to create a god to thank.

Such a god must have the capacity to do both good and harm, to be a friend or a foe, and to inspire awe through acts of both kindness and wrath. To strip a god of these dual traits, reducing him to a god of pure goodness, would go against human nature itself. People need a god who reflects their full range of experiences and emotions—good and evil alike. A god who cannot express anger, revenge, envy, scorn, cunning, or the exhilaration of victory and destruction is a god no one could understand, let alone revere. Why would anyone desire a god so one-dimensional?

However, when a nation begins to lose its belief in its own future—when hope for freedom fades, and submission seems like the only path to survival— its concept of god also begins to change. This god, once a representation of collective strength and the thirst for power, transforms into a figure of meekness, humility, and peace. He preaches "peace of soul," forbids hatred, and promotes universal love, extending even to one's enemies. Such a god becomes moralistic, personal, and all-encompassing. No longer the god of a strong people, he turns into the god of private lives and cosmopolitan ideals.

Once, this god embodied the might of a nation, the strength and ambition that fueled its people. But now, this god is no longer aggressive or commanding. Instead, he is reshaped to align with weakness, embodying the virtues of those who lack power. When gods are stripped of strength, passion, and masculine virtues, they become the gods of those in physical or moral decline. These people do not see themselves as weak; they call themselves "the good."

The dualistic idea of a good god versus an evil god emerges from this decline. Those who feel oppressed reimagine their god as pure goodness, while stripping the gods of their oppressors of any redeeming qualities, turning them into devils. This transformation of gods into either purely good or purely evil figures is a byproduct of societal and moral decay. Both the overly good god and the concept of the devil are the products of decadence.

How, then, can anyone seriously regard the evolution of the Christian god—from the god of Israel, a national deity, to the Christian god, a universal embodiment of goodness—as progress?

Even intellectuals like Renan fall into this naïve interpretation. Yet the opposite is true. When everything essential to life's ascension—strength, courage, pride, and mastery—is removed from the concept of god, he becomes nothing more than a crutch for the weak, a comfort for sinners, and a refuge for the sick. He is reduced to a savior, a redeemer, the last vestige of divinity's purpose.

This transformation represents the decline of the godhead itself. Once the god of a chosen people, rooted in a specific nation and its power, he becomes a wanderer, like the people who created him. No longer tied to one place or people, he spreads across the world, becoming a universal god. As his following grows, so does his detachment from his original identity. He becomes the god of the masses, of the weak, and his once-proud attributes are lost.

This universal god does not grow into a majestic figure like the gods of proud, ancient peoples. Instead, he remains a shadow of his former self—still marked by his origins in a small, oppressed nation. His earthly kingdom is not one of grandeur but of the underworld, hidden in the shadows and ghettos of the world. He is pale, weak, and a reflection of human frailty.

Even the intellectuals—those pale thinkers who analyze reality through abstraction—have taken over this god. They spun their webs of metaphysics around him until he was subdued and transformed into one of them. He began spinning his own abstract theories, embodying the ideals of philosophers like Spinoza. Over time, he grew thinner and more abstract, becoming the "pure spirit," the "absolute," the "thing-in-itself." This final stage marks the collapse of a once-great god, reduced to an idea, a shadow of his former strength.

The Christian concept of God—a god who is the champion of the weak, a spinner of metaphysical webs, a being reduced to pure spirit—stands as one of the most corrupted and degenerate ideas of divinity ever conceived. It marks a dramatic low point in the evolution of what gods have historically represented. This god, rather than celebrating life, vitality, and existence, becomes a direct contradiction to these very forces. Instead of affirming life and glorifying its essence with a resounding "Yes!" he becomes the eternal "No!"—a declaration of war against life, nature, and the will to live. This god transforms into a symbol for rejecting the here and now, denying the world as it is, and replacing it with fabrications of an imagined "beyond." In him, emptiness itself is worshipped, and the will to embrace nothingness is sanctified.

The failure of the robust northern European races to discard this frail, lifeless god reflects poorly on their spiritual insight and their capacity to distinguish true vitality in religion. These people, whose physical and cultural strength could have driven them to dismiss such a decayed and worn-out relic of human weakness, instead absorbed this god into their instincts. In doing so, they allowed disease, resignation, and contradiction to infiltrate the core of their values. The consequences of this failure still reverberate through their culture, evident in the inability to create new gods or fresh expressions of divine power. Two millennia have passed, and yet no new gods have emerged. Instead, the world continues to cling to this pitiful deity of Christian monotony—a bland, uncreative projection of human decay. This god is a grotesque hybrid of emptiness and contradiction, a hollow image conjured from the collective weariness of the soul. He embodies the instincts of decadence, giving legitimacy to cowardice, resignation, and spiritual exhaustion.

In condemning Christianity, I do not wish to neglect its distant relative, Buddhism, a faith with an even larger number of followers. Both religions fall into the category of nihilistic systems, born from similar physiological and psychological conditions. However, there is a profound difference between them. For this insight, critics of Christianity owe a debt to Indian scholars who have illuminated the nuances of Buddhism. Unlike Christianity, Buddhism is grounded in realism—a hundredfold more so. It reflects a tradition of profound philosophical inquiry and retains an ability to confront reality objectively and without illusion. By the time Buddhism emerged, it had already discarded the concept of "god."

In fact, Buddhism is perhaps the only historical religion that can be described as genuinely positive, even in its approach to knowledge and truth. Its epistemology aligns with strict phenomenalism, focusing solely on observable phenomena and experiences. Buddhism does not frame life as a struggle against "sin"; rather, it addresses the reality of human suffering directly. This acknowledgment of suffering replaces the moral self- deceptions that Christianity clings to, transcending simplistic notions of good and evil. In this way, Buddhism situates itself, in my terms, "beyond good and evil."

The foundation of Buddhism lies in two significant physiological realities: first, an extreme sensitivity to sensory experience, which manifests as an acute susceptibility to pain; and second, an extraordinary intellectualism, characterized by prolonged engagement with concepts and logical processes. These traits lead to a state where the sense of individuality is overtaken by an ideal of the "impersonal." For those who have lived as objectivists or possess a heightened capacity for detached observation, these conditions are all too familiar.

These physiological and intellectual traits often culminate in a state of depression, which Buddha sought to alleviate with specific, pragmatic solutions. His teachings prescribed living outdoors and embracing a life of travel to maintain balance. Moderation in eating and careful dietary choices were emphasized, as well as caution in the use of intoxicants. Similarly, Buddha warned against stirring up passions, as they can disrupt emotional equilibrium and intensify physical agitation. Above all, he advised against excessive worry—whether about oneself or others.

Buddha's approach was methodical and focused on fostering a state of quiet contentment and cheerful tranquility. He encouraged the cultivation of thoughts that support well-being while discouraging those that lead to distress. For him, "goodness" was synonymous with health and vitality—a condition where the body and mind flourish in harmony. His vision of goodness and health stands in stark contrast to Christianity's idealization of suffering and self- denial, making Buddhism a practical, life-affirming system rather than a nihilistic rejection of existence.

Prayer is absent in Buddhism, as is asceticism. There is no rigid system of categorical imperatives or disciplinary practices, even within the walls of monasteries—leaving is always an option.

These methods would only serve to amplify the already heightened sensitivity that Buddhism aims to address. For the same reason, Buddha does not advocate for conflict with unbelievers. His teachings oppose revenge, hostility, and resentment, with their refrain echoing through Buddhist texts: "Enmity never ends enmity." He understood that these emotions are unhealthy for those striving to follow his path. Buddha observed mental exhaustion as a result of excessive "objectivity"—a condition where individuals lose focus on themselves and their inner balance, leading to a weakening of self-interest or egoism. To counteract this, his teachings emphasize returning all spiritual interests to the self. In Buddhism, taking care of oneself is a moral responsibility. The central question, "How can one escape suffering?" becomes the axis around which the entire spiritual practice revolves. It's worth noting the parallel to Socrates, who similarly waged war against empty intellectualism and elevated self-interest to the status of morality.

Buddhism thrives in conditions marked by mild climates, societies of gentleness and openness, and the absence of militarism. It takes root among well- educated and culturally refined individuals. Cheerfulness, calm, and freedom from desire are its principal goals—and they are fully attainable. Unlike other faiths, Buddhism does not merely aspire to perfection; it achieves it as the norm.

Christianity, on the other hand, reflects the instincts of the downtrodden and oppressed. It is a faith embraced by those at the bottom, seeking salvation from their suffering. Its central practices revolve around examining sin, engaging in self-criticism, and constantly interrogating one's conscience. Emotional connection to a perceived power—called "God"—is heightened through prayer, while salvation is portrayed as a gift, an unattainable ideal, something granted by "grace." Christianity operates in secrecy and shadow; it despises openness. Hygiene and care for the body are scorned, labeled as indulgent or sensual, and the church has historically opposed cleanliness—such as when Christian rulers in medieval Spain closed Cordova's 270 public baths after driving out the Moors.

Cruelty is another hallmark of Christianity, both toward oneself and others. Hatred of unbelievers, a willingness to persecute, and an embrace of somber, troubling thoughts are central to its ethos. Christianity values epileptoid mental states—emotional extremes glorified as religious experience. Its dietary practices encourage poor health and overstimulate the nerves. It promotes disdain for earthly rulers and the aristocratic class while fostering a secret competition with them. Christians surrender their physical selves to rulers but claim their souls as their own. This attitude reflects Christianity's fundamental hatred for intellect, pride, courage, and freedom. It opposes the joy of the senses and resents joy in general.

When Christianity expanded beyond its original roots among the impoverished and marginalized of the ancient world, it faced a new challenge: gaining power among barbarian peoples. These were not weary or defeated individuals, but raw, untamed men, strong yet maladjusted. Their dissatisfaction with themselves and the world stemmed not from over- sensitivity, as in Buddhism, but from an intense drive to inflict harm and achieve satisfaction through acts of hostility. To conquer these barbaric societies, Christianity absorbed their concepts and values, adopting practices such as the sacrifice of firstborn children, the drinking of blood as a sacrament, and a general contempt for intellect and culture. It embraced physical and psychological torture, as well as the ostentatious rituals of a dramatic cult.

Buddhism, by contrast, is suited for societies that have advanced in their moral and cultural development—those that have grown gentle, refined, and overly spiritualized. Its call is one of return: to peace, to balance, to cheerfulness, and to temperance in both spirit and body. Europe, in its current state, is not ready for Buddhism. Christianity, however, appears at a much earlier stage of societal evolution, where it seeks to tame beasts of prey by making them ill. Weakness is Christianity's strategy for taming and "civilizing" its followers.

Buddhism offers guidance for civilizations nearing their peak, weary from centuries of progress. Christianity, by contrast, arises in uncivilized conditions, sometimes serving as the very foundation upon which societies begin to build. Its purpose is not to elevate or refine but to subdue, to weaken, and to control.

Buddhism and Christianity are not just different; they are complete opposites in many ways. Buddhism does not rely on prayer or ascetic practices. It avoids imposing strict disciplines or rules that would heighten sensitivity and stress. Monastic life, while organized, is flexible—leaving is always an option. Buddha's teaching discourages conflict and enmity, rejecting revenge, hostility, or resentment. The Buddhist refrain, "Enmity never ends enmity," captures its essence. These passions, harmful to health and peace, stand opposed to the purpose of his teachings.

Buddha observed that mental fatigue often arose from over-objectivity, where individuals lost connection with themselves and their personal interests. This imbalance weakened the instinct of self-preservation. His solution was to direct spiritual focus back toward the self. In Buddhism, self-care is not just encouraged—it is a moral imperative. The core question of his philosophy, "How can one escape suffering?" shapes every practice and teaching. This emphasis on personal well-being recalls Socrates' focus on self-knowledge and morality rooted in individual needs.

For Buddhism to flourish, specific conditions are necessary: a mild climate, a culture of gentleness, and a lack of militarism. Its teachings appeal to educated and spiritually advanced societies. It seeks calm, cheerfulness, and the absence of harmful desires— not as unreachable ideals but as realities. In Buddhism, perfection is not something to strive for; it is something achievable here and now.

Christianity, in stark contrast, is the religion of the downtrodden, rooted in the instincts of the oppressed. It appeals to those who suffer and struggle with their own existence. At its core, Christianity revolves around sin, self-criticism, and guilt. It glorifies suffering as a path to salvation, urging believers to seek divine grace rather than personal empowerment. God, as conceived by Christianity, is an emotionally charged being whose favor must be sought through prayer and submission. Salvation is painted as unattainable without divine intervention. Christianity thrives in secrecy, fostering a culture of shame, concealment, and self-denial.

The body, in Christian teachings, is despised as corrupt, and bodily care is seen as indulgent. Cleanliness and hygiene are often condemned as vain or sinful. Historically, this disdain for the physical led to actions like the closure of public baths after the Christian conquest of Cordova. Cruelty—toward oneself and others—has also been deeply rooted in Christian practice. This includes a hatred of unbelievers and a willingness to persecute those with differing views. Somberness and self-denial are prized, while joy and celebration are discouraged. Christian dietary laws, often restrictive, aim to produce a state of nervous tension that mirrors the inner turmoil celebrated in religious devotion.

As Christianity spread from the underprivileged classes of the ancient world to barbarian tribes, it encountered strong but undeveloped individuals—those more inclined to aggression than introspection. Unlike Buddhism, which aims to heal spiritual exhaustion, Christianity seeks to subdue raw and untamed energy. To appeal to barbaric societies, it adopted elements of their culture: blood sacrifices, disdain for intellectual pursuits, and rituals rooted in violence and fear. Christianity's aim was not refinement but control—weakening the strong to civilize them.

Buddhism speaks to societies that have grown weary from their own refinement, offering a return to peace and balance. It fosters a moderate spirit and a strong body, appealing to those who are spiritually advanced but tired. Europe, with its lingering aggression and lack of spiritual maturity, remains unprepared for Buddhism. Christianity, by contrast, thrives in societies still in their early stages of development. It lays foundations where none exist, but it does so by taming, weakening, and controlling.

Buddhism seeks to restore strength and serenity in the later stages of civilization. Christianity, however, rises at the start, shaping cultures through domination and suppression rather than elevation or enlightenment. One is a call to peace for the weary; the other, a strategy to subdue the wild and untamed. Both religions, in their own ways, leave profound marks on the societies they touch.— [4]

The psychological type represented by the Galilean figure is still recognizable, but it was only in its most distorted and degraded form—altered and burdened by foreign elements—that it could serve the purpose for which it has been used: as the model of a savior for humanity.

The Jews are arguably the most remarkable people in history. When faced with the existential question of whether to continue or perish, they chose, with extraordinary determination, to exist at any cost. This decision came at the price of fundamentally altering all aspects of nature and reality, both internally and externally. They opposed the very conditions that had traditionally allowed civilizations to thrive, rejecting natural laws and creating an idea that defied them. Religion, culture, morality, history, and psychology—one by one, these were reshaped by the Jews into their opposites, their natural meanings overturned.

This phenomenon appeared later on, magnified and imitated to a vast degree, in the form of the Christian Church. Compared to the "people of God," Christianity offers no originality. It is a mere imitation. In this way, the Jews became the most influential people in world history. Their legacy has so deeply distorted human reasoning that a modern Christian can hold anti-Semitic views without realizing that such views are the natural conclusion of Judaism's influence.

In my Genealogy of Morals, I provide the first psychological analysis of the fundamental ideas behind two opposing moral systems: noble morality and ressentiment morality. The latter is born from a denial of the former. The moral framework of Judaism and Christianity falls entirely into this second category. To reject everything associated with the elevation of life—such as strength, beauty, power, and self-approval—required an extraordinary instinct for ressentiment. This instinct, sharpened to the point of genius, invented an "other world," where affirming life itself became the greatest sin.

Psychologically, the Jews display extraordinary vitality. Faced with conditions that seemed insurmountable, they consciously chose to ally themselves with the instincts of decadence—not because they were overtaken by those instincts, but because they saw them as tools for defying the world. Far from being decadent themselves, the Jews mastered the art of appearing so. With unparalleled theatrical skill, they took control of all decadent movements (such as Paul's version of Christianity) and transformed them into forces more powerful than any philosophy or movement that affirmed life directly.

For those who sought power through Judaism and Christianity— primarily the priestly class—decadence became a tool rather than an affliction. These figures had a vested interest in making humanity sick, in corrupting its understanding of "good" and "evil," "truth" and "falsehood." This manipulation not only endangered life but also slandered it. By redefining values in a way that served their aims, they weaponized decadence to achieve influence and control.

The history of Israel serves as a critical example of how natural values can be distorted and denatured. Five key observations highlight this process. Initially, during the period of the monarchy, Israel maintained a natural relationship with its world, grounded in strength and self-assurance. Jahveh, their god, embodied their sense of power, pride, and aspirations. He symbolized their hope for victory, their connection to nature, and their reliance on life's necessities—like rain for their crops. Jahveh was the god of justice because he represented the confidence and authority of a people who held power and wielded it with a clear conscience. This was a typical belief system for any nation that felt secure and dominant.

The religious practices of the time reflected this natural outlook. The people expressed gratitude for their triumphs, for their prosperous herds, for the fruitful seasons. Their god was intertwined with their sense of destiny and their pride in their achievements. Even when adversity struck—internal strife and the looming threat of the Assyrian empire—this perspective lingered as an ideal. They longed for a leader who would be both a valiant warrior and a fair judge, a vision upheld by the prophets like Isaiah, who critiqued and satirized the shortcomings of their times.

However, reality failed to meet these hopes. Jahveh, once the embodiment of their might and promise, no longer seemed capable of fulfilling their needs. Instead of abandoning him, his followers redefined him. This reinterpretation came at a cost: Jahveh's character was denatured to fit a new narrative. No longer a god who reflected Israel's pride and power, he became a god of conditions and obedience—a god wielded by religious leaders to enforce their moral and social agendas.

The clerics used Jahveh's name to create a new framework of understanding: happiness became a reward, and suffering was rebranded as punishment for sin. This moral manipulation introduced the fraudulent concept of a "moral order of the world," which replaced the natural understanding of cause and effect with artificial, moralized causation. Nature itself was undermined by this reinterpretation, leading to an entire system of thought that denied the natural world and its laws.

Jahveh was no longer the god who inspired courage and self-reliance or offered help and wisdom. Instead, he became a god who demanded submission and compliance—a tool for control. Morality, which should have been a reflection of the conditions necessary for a healthy, thriving community, was now twisted into something abstract and life-denying. It became a perversion of human imagination, casting a shadow of suspicion and guilt over existence.

Jewish and Christian morality thus represent a profound corruption. They transformed chance and misfortune into guilt, labeling unhappiness as sin and prosperity as temptation. The result was a profound physiological distortion— a sickness of the soul wrought by the burdens of conscience. This morality doesn't reflect the instincts that nurture life and vitality; instead, it opposes them, poisoning natural joy and freedom with fabricated guilt and fear.

The idea of God was distorted; the concept of morality was twisted—and yet the Jewish priests didn't stop there. They erased the entire history of Israel, discarding it as if it were worthless. These priests achieved a complete falsification of history, a process that much of the Bible clearly shows. With unparalleled arrogance and in defiance of tradition and historical facts, they reinterpreted their people's past in religious terms. In doing so, they turned it into a ridiculous system of salvation, where every offense against Yahweh was punished and every act of devotion to Him was rewarded. This manipulation of history would seem far more disgraceful to us if thousands of years of church- led historical distortions hadn't already dulled our sense of truth in historical matters.

Philosophers supported the church in this deception: the falsehood about a "moral order of the world" runs through the entire history of philosophy, including even the most recent ideas. What does a "moral order of the world" mean? It claims that there is a "will of God" that permanently defines what people should and shouldn't do. According to this view, the value of a nation or an individual is measured by how well they obey this divine will. It also suggests that the fate of a nation or individual is determined by this will, which rewards obedience and punishes disobedience. But reality shows us something completely different: the priest—a parasitic type of person who can only exist by undermining healthy views of life—misuses the name of God. He labels the social order, in which he has the authority to determine all values, as "the kingdom of God." He refers to the methods for creating this order as "the will of God." With cold and calculated cynicism, he judges entire nations, eras, and individuals by how much they submit to or oppose priestly power.

Watch how they operate: under the influence of the Jewish priesthood, the great era of Israel became an age of decline. The Exile, with its long sequence of disasters, was rewritten as punishment for that earlier great age—when priests had not yet taken control. They turned the powerful and completely free heroes of Israel's history into either miserable zealots and hypocrites or entirely "godless" figures, depending on their current agenda. They reduced every significant event to a senseless formula: "obedient or disobedient to God."

They went even further: the "will of God" (which essentially means the tools needed to maintain the priests' power) had to be clarified, and for that, they needed a "revelation." In simple terms, they committed a massive literary fraud by fabricating "holy scriptures." With elaborate ceremonies, days of penance, and loud mourning over the supposed sins of the past, these scriptures were officially presented. They declared that the "will of God" had always existed as an unchanging truth, but humanity had neglected the "holy scriptures."

However, they also claimed that the "will of God" had already been revealed to Moses.

What actually happened? The priest had, once and for all, clearly outlined what he wanted—down to the tiniest detail. He specified the tithes he was entitled to, from the largest offerings to the smallest (not forgetting the tastiest portions of meat, as priests were big fans of steaks). In short, he explained exactly what "the will of God" required. From that point on, life was organized so that the priest became essential at every major life event—birth, marriage, illness, death, and even meals (or "sacrifices"). The priest was always there, interfering with natural life and calling it "sanctification."

Here's the key point: every natural habit, every institution that arose from human instincts—such as the state, justice, marriage, care for the sick and poor, and all the essentials of life—was devalued and even reversed in its purpose by the parasitism of priests. Through their actions, all these things, which once had genuine value, were reduced to nothing or even turned into their opposites, thanks to what they called the "moral order of the world."

The idea requires authority—a force that can assign values is necessary, and the only way this authority can generate such values is by rejecting and condemning nature. The priest achieves this by devaluing and defiling nature; this is the only way he can sustain his existence. What is labeled as disobedience to God—though it truly means disobedience to the priest and "the law"—is now called "sin." The path to "reconciliation with God" is, unsurprisingly, precisely the one that most tightly binds individuals to the power of the priest. He alone holds the keys to salvation, or so he claims. From a psychological perspective, the concept of "sin" is vital to every society built on an ecclesiastical foundation. Sin becomes the most reliable weapon of power, the core tool for the priest's survival. He thrives on sin; without the concept of "sinning," his role would collapse entirely. The fundamental rule is clear: "God forgives those who repent," which, in plain language, means "those who submit to the priest's authority."

Christianity emerged from a foundation so decayed that every natural value, every aspect of life that was real and uncorrupted, faced direct opposition from the ruling class's deepest instincts. It developed as a relentless war against reality itself, a war so intense and unyielding that no subsequent movement has surpassed it in its hostility toward life. The so-called "holy people," who embraced priestly values and redefined all aspects of life through priestly labels, consistently condemned the natural world as "unholy," "worldly," and "sinful." This mindset reached its ultimate expression in Christianity, where even the last remnants of reality—the concept of a "holy people" or the "chosen people" of Jewish tradition—were rejected. Christianity went so far as to deny Jewish identity itself, pushing this rejection of reality to an extreme that bordered on self-destruction.

This phenomenon is of extraordinary importance: the small, rebellious movement associated with Jesus of Nazareth represents a reawakening of the Jewish instinct, though in an altered form. It is, in essence, the priestly instinct taken to such an extreme that it could no longer tolerate the priesthood itself as a reality. It sought an even more fantastical state of existence, a vision of life more disconnected from reality than any ecclesiastical system before it. Christianity, in its essence, denies the church as much as it claims to uphold it. I find it impossible to identify the true target of the rebellion attributed to Jesus, whether accurately or not, if it was not the Jewish church. And by "church," I mean it in the exact sense we use the word today.

This was a revolt against the established order of things: the "good and just," the "prophets of Israel," and the entire hierarchical structure of Jewish society. It was not a rebellion against corruption but against the systems of caste, privilege, and formalized tradition. It rejected the notion of "superior men" and cast aside everything the priests and theologians represented. Yet, the hierarchy under attack by this movement, however briefly, was the very structure that ensured the Jewish people's survival. This social and religious framework was their lifeline, their last vestige of independent political existence. To challenge it was to challenge the most deeply rooted national instinct and the strongest will to survive that humanity has ever witnessed.

Jesus, the saintly anarchist, rallied the marginalized—the outcasts, the "sinners," and the despised—against the established order. He appealed to those who had been excluded from society, encouraging them to rise up against the institutions that defined their lives. If we are to trust the accounts in the Gospels, his words were so radical that they would earn him exile or imprisonment in any modern society. This man, who stirred up the downtrodden and defied the foundations of his community, was undoubtedly a political criminal, at least insofar as it was possible to be one in a society so lacking in political structure. His challenge to the status quo sealed his fate. The inscription on the cross— declaring him "King of the Jews"—is proof enough. He did not die for the sins of others, as is so often claimed, but for his own rebellion against the order of his time. There is no credible reason to believe otherwise, no matter how frequently this narrative is repeated.

Whether Jesus himself was aware of this contradiction—or whether it was the only contradiction he recognized—is an entirely different question. Here, I am led to the profound psychological mystery of the figure we call the Savior. To begin, I must admit that few texts challenge me as much as the Gospels. My difficulties, however, differ entirely from those that spurred the scholarly curiosity of the German intellect to one of its most remarkable achievements. Many years ago, like all other young academics, I immersed myself with the meticulous passion of a philologist in the work of the incomparable David Strauss. At that time, I was twenty years old, and the intellectual exercise was a delight. Now, however, I find myself too serious for such endeavors. What interest do I have in resolving the contradictions of "tradition"? How can one seriously refer to pious legends as "traditions"?

The hagiographies of saints form one of the most dubious literary genres that exist. To scrutinize them with the tools of scientific inquiry, when no corroborative historical documents exist, seems to me to doom the entire endeavor from the start. It is no more than a sophisticated form of idle scholarship. What genuinely matters to me is not the historical accuracy of these accounts but the psychological type that emerges from them—the character of the Savior. This type may be discernible in the Gospels, however distorted or burdened it may be with later additions. It appears in the same way that the figure of Francis of Assisi emerges in his legends—not because of them, but in spite of them.

The focus here is not on whether the accounts in the Gospels truthfully record what Jesus did, said, or how he met his end. The real question is whether his type remains conceivable to us—whether it has been faithfully transmitted across time. All the attempts I have encountered to interpret the "soul" of Jesus through the Gospels strike me as marked by a shocking superficiality. For instance, M. Renan, that performer of psychological tricks, introduced two thoroughly inappropriate notions to explain the nature of Jesus: the concept of the genius and that of the hero. These are deeply flawed interpretations, for there is nothing more fundamentally opposed to the essence of the Gospels than the concept of a hero.

The Gospels present a perspective that is the complete antithesis of heroism or the taste for struggle. They embody a rejection of resistance, transforming even the inability to oppose into a moral virtue. Consider the phrase "resist not evil!"—arguably the most profound sentence in the Gospels and perhaps their central theme. It encapsulates a state of being in which blessedness arises from peace, gentleness, and an incapacity to harbor enmity. This is the core of the "glad tidings": the revelation of the true life, the eternal life, as something already discovered and present—not as a distant promise, but as a reality within. This life is rooted in a love that knows no barriers, no exclusions, no distances. Jesus claims nothing uniquely for himself. In his view, every person is a child of God, and as such, all are equal. To frame Jesus as a hero is to commit a profound misinterpretation.

Equally flawed is the application of the term "genius" to Jesus. Our modern understanding of "spirituality" and intellectual sophistication has no relevance to the context in which Jesus lived. His world operated on entirely different premises. From a physiological standpoint, a completely different term would be more appropriate. We know, for instance, of a condition involving an extreme sensitivity of the tactile nerves, where sufferers recoil from physical contact and avoid any solid grasp.

Taken to its logical extreme, such a disposition could manifest as an instinctive aversion to reality—a retreat into the intangible, the incomprehensible. It might express itself as a distaste for anything fixed or concrete, whether customs, institutions, or temporal structures like time and space. Such a mindset feels at home only in a realm devoid of tangible reality— a purely internal world, an imagined "true" or "eternal" realm.

This perspective finds its perfect expression in the idea: "The Kingdom of God is within you." Here lies the ultimate psychological retreat: a turning away from all external realities, a flight into the inner sanctum of the self, where the external world is not merely rejected but The instinctive rejection of reality, the profound aversion to the world as it is, stems from an acute sensitivity to pain and irritation—a sensitivity so extreme that even the slightest "touch" becomes unbearable. Every sensation cuts too deeply, leaving no space for even the smallest confrontation with discomfort. This kind of deep susceptibility alters the way a person interacts with the world, leading to an instinctive exclusion of all hostility, all boundaries, all aversions. This avoidance arises not out of a moral stance, but from the overwhelming experience of suffering that even the smallest resistance or compulsion to resist causes. Such resistance feels not only intolerable but harmful—something prohibited by the basic instinct for survival. In this state, peace and joy become conceivable only when all forms of resistance are eliminated, even toward the most harmful or dangerous forces. Love, then, becomes the sole possible response, the last conceivable avenue for life to continue.

These two physiological realities—this extreme sensitivity to pain and the absolute rejection of resistance—are the fertile ground upon which the doctrine of salvation has grown. I see this as a remarkable and elevated form of hedonism, one that paradoxically emerged on the most unhealthy of foundations. It is worth comparing this to the salvation doctrine of paganism, particularly Epicureanism, which bears similarities to this phenomenon but with a vital difference: Epicureanism is infused with Greek vigor and energy. Yet Epicurus himself was a quintessential example of decadence. I was the first to recognize him as such. His philosophy, too, revolves around the avoidance of pain, even of the most minor discomforts. Ultimately, such avoidance leads naturally and inevitably to a religion of love, which can be seen as the endpoint of this trajectory.

I have already shared my perspective on this issue. It begins with the assumption that the type of the Savior has come down to us only in a distorted and highly altered form. Such distortion is not only likely but almost certain, given the many factors that could have influenced the preservation of this figure. The environment in which this enigmatic person lived undoubtedly left its mark on him. Furthermore, the early Christian communities, shaped by their own struggles and history, must have added layers of meaning and character to the figure of the Savior. These additions were often tailored to serve their own needs, whether for propaganda or for rallying believers during times of crisis. The milieu of the Gospels is itself peculiar—a strange, unsettling world reminiscent of the scenes from a Russian novel, filled with societal outcasts, nervous disorders, and what might now be called "childish simplicity." Such a setting would have inevitably coarsened and simplified the type of the Savior.

The earliest disciples, in particular, likely struggled to comprehend such an extraordinary figure. To make sense of him, they had to reshape and recast him into forms they could understand. This meant translating a life full of symbols and mysteries into something more concrete and familiar. In their hands, the figure of the Savior took on attributes they could relate to: the prophet, the messiah, the moral teacher, the miracle worker, and even the fiery judge. Each of these roles represented opportunities to misunderstand his essence. Over time, these layers of interpretation became inseparable from the original type.

One cannot overlook the tendency of all veneration, especially within sects, to erase the unique and often unsettling traits of the figure they revere. What is strange, individual, or challenging is smoothed over, replaced with more palatable, conventional qualities. It is deeply regrettable that no Dostoevsky lived during the time of this fascinating figure. Dostoevsky, with his ability to capture the sublime mingled with the morbid and the childlike, might have portrayed this Savior with the depth and complexity he deserved. As it stands, the Savior, as a type of decadence, may indeed have been a profoundly contradictory figure, combining the sublime with the fragile. Such a possibility cannot be ignored. Yet the historical record works against this idea, for such contradictions, if present, would likely have been preserved with greater accuracy and objectivity. Instead, what we find suggests a systematic reshaping of the figure to suit the needs of early Christian propaganda.

This reshaping has created an apparent contradiction between two vastly different images of Jesus. On the one hand, we see the peaceful preacher of the Sermon on the Mount, a figure reminiscent of a new Buddha, bringing a message of inner peace and harmony to a land far removed from India. On the other hand, we have the fiery, combative figure—a bitter adversary of theologians and ecclesiastics—whom Renan, with his characteristic malice, exalted as "the great master of irony." I have no doubt that much of this venom, and just as much of this supposed brilliance, was injected into the concept of Jesus by the heated rhetoric of early Christian propaganda.

It is well known how unscrupulous sectarians can be when shaping the image of their leader to suit their own needs. When the early Christians found themselves in need of a cunning, argumentative, and sharp-witted theologian to challenge rival theologians, they fashioned such a figure out of their Savior. They placed ideas into his mouth with little hesitation, ideas that were essential to their mission but utterly foreign to the Gospels themselves. Concepts like "the second coming," "the last judgment," and a host of promises and expectations common in that era were attributed to Jesus, despite their clear divergence from his original teachings. In doing so, they created a figure that served their purposes but moved further away from the reality of the man who had once lived.

I must emphasize again that I oppose any attempts to portray the Savior as a fanatic. Even the word impér ieux used by Renan is enough to dismantle the entire idea of the type. The message of the "glad tidings" is simple: contradictions no longer exist. The kingdom of heaven belongs to the innocent, to those who approach life with the openness of children. The faith expressed here is not a militant faith. It does not battle against anything, for it has always been present, from the beginning. It represents a sort of spiritual regression to a childlike state. Physiologists would recognize this as a delayed or incomplete maturity in the organism, a result of degeneration rather than development.

This faith does not rage, it does not condemn, and it does not seek to defend itself. It carries no sword, and it has no awareness of the divisions it might one day cause, setting man against man. It does not rely on miracles, rewards, promises, or scriptures to prove its validity. It is entirely self-contained, its own miracle, its own reward, its own promise, its own "kingdom of God." This faith does not express itself through doctrines or formulas; it simply exists and protects itself by avoiding such constructs. Certainly, the cultural and educational influences of the time shaped its language and symbols. In early Christianity, one finds a distinctly Judaeo-Semitic flavor, such as the idea of eating and drinking at the Last Supper, which reflects this context. This idea, like so many other Jewish concepts, was later misinterpreted and altered by the church. But even this must be understood as symbolic language, a mode of parable, rather than literal belief.

Indeed, this anti-realist perspective is grounded in an understanding that the world itself is symbolic. The figure of Jesus would have spoken differently depending on his cultural context. Among Hindus, he might have used the language of the Sankhya philosophy; among the Chinese, he might have spoken in the terms of Lao-tse. The underlying message, however, would remain unchanged, for the symbols themselves are secondary to the truth they aim to convey. In this sense, Jesus could even be described, with some interpretive freedom, as a "free spirit." He cared nothing for established norms, for institutions, or for rigid rules. For him, the "letter kills," and all that is established stifles the true essence of life.

To Jesus, life was an inner experience, an unfolding truth that could not be confined to words, laws, or doctrines. His concepts of "life," "truth," and "light" referred to the innermost realities of existence. Everything else—the natural world, the material reality, and even language—served merely as signs and allegories pointing to these inner truths. It is crucial to avoid being misled by ecclesiastical prejudices when interpreting this symbolism. The wisdom of Jesus was not bound to religion, worship, history, science, politics, psychology, art, or any worldly knowledge. His "wisdom" was, paradoxically, a profound ignorance of these things. He did not engage with culture because he had no need to resist or oppose it—he simply did not acknowledge it.

The same applies to his relationship with the state, social structures, labor, war, or even the concept of the world as understood by ecclesiastical authorities. He did not deny the world, for he was completely unfamiliar with the ecclesiastical notion of "the world." Denial itself was foreign to him; it was not something he was capable of. Likewise, Jesus lacked any inclination to argue or to defend his beliefs through logical proofs. His "proofs" were entirely internal— flashes of insight, feelings of bliss and self-assurance, simple manifestations of what he called "power." His doctrine did not contradict others, because it did not recognize that any other doctrines existed. It could not even conceive of opposition. When confronted with differing views, it responded not with arguments but with a heartfelt lamentation for the "blindness" of others, a genuine sympathy for those without "light."

The psychology of the Gospels contains no trace of guilt, punishment, or reward. The concept of "sin" as something that creates a barrier between God and man is entirely absent. The essence of the "glad tidings" is precisely the abolition of this distance. Eternal bliss is not something promised for the future, nor is it conditional on specific actions. It is understood as the only true reality, with all else serving merely as symbols to help describe it.

This perspective on life gives rise to a completely new way of living—a distinctly evangelical way of being. A Christian is not defined by belief but by action, by a way of living that reflects this inner reality. He does not resist those who oppose him, neither outwardly nor in his heart. He does not distinguish between people based on nationality, religion, or ethnicity; he sees no difference between neighbors and strangers, Jews and Gentiles. His love and forgiveness extend to everyone. He harbors no anger and despises no one. He neither appeals to courts of justice nor abides by their rules; he refuses to swear oaths or divorce his wife, even in the face of infidelity.

Beneath all these actions lies a single guiding principle, a singular instinct from which all else flows. This instinct is the foundation of the evangelical life, shaping every aspect of how the Christian exists in the world.

The life of the Savior was the living embodiment of this way of being, carried out with such purity that even his death was a continuation of it. He required no formulas, no rituals, no intermediaries in his relationship with God—not even prayer. He had moved beyond the entirety of the Jewish framework of repentance and atonement. For him, the only path to feeling "divine," "blessed," "evangelical," or a "child of God" was through a way of life. It was not through "repentance," not through "prayer and forgiveness" that one reached God. The Gospel way itself was the pathway to God; it was God.

The Gospels effectively abolished the Jewish concepts of "sin," "forgiveness of sin," "faith," and "salvation through faith." They denied the entire structure of Jewish religious dogma, offering instead the "glad tidings" as a radical alternative. What the Gospels introduced was not another doctrine but a profound reorientation of life—a rejection of all external rules and beliefs in favor of a direct and lived experience of the divine.

The deep instinct of the Christian, the internal guide that shows how to live in a way that feels like being "in heaven" or "immortal," even amid the ordinary struggles of existence, is the sole psychological reality of what is called "salvation." It does not depend on adopting a new faith but on living a new way of life. This distinction is fundamental to understanding the essence of the Gospel message.

If I have grasped anything about this extraordinary symbolist, it is that he recognized subjective realities as the only true realities. For him, "truths" were internal experiences, deeply felt, while everything else—nature, history, time, and space—was secondary.

These external realities existed only as symbols, materials for parables to illustrate inner truths. The concept of "the Son of God," for instance, does not represent a specific historical figure, a concrete individual tied to a particular moment in time. Instead, it signifies an eternal fact, a psychological symbol that transcends time entirely.

This same symbolic understanding applies to the God of this symbolist, the "kingdom of God," and the "sonship of God." These are not crude, literal notions but profound metaphors for experiences and realities beyond ordinary comprehension. Nothing could be further from the true spirit of the Gospels than the institutionalized, ecclesiastical interpretations of God as a person, of the "kingdom of God" as a future event, or of the "kingdom of heaven" as a distant paradise. The idea of the "Son of God" as a literal second person of the Trinity is equally alien to the original message of the Gospels.

Such interpretations—if I may use a strong metaphor—are like thrusting a fist into the eye of the Gospels. They demonstrate a profound disrespect for the symbolic language of these texts, a kind of historical cynicism that reduces profound spiritual metaphors to clumsy dogma. Yet, for those who look carefully, the meaning of symbols like "Father" and "Son" remains clear—at least to those capable of understanding them. The "Son" symbolizes the experience of entering into a state of universal transformation and beatitude, while the "Father" represents the sensation of eternity and perfection itself. Together, these symbols articulate the spiritual experience of profound unity and fulfillment.

It is almost embarrassing to compare this elegant symbolism with what the church has made of it. The ecclesiastical interpretation, with its rigid and literal stories, often seems closer to mythological tales like those of Amphitryon than to the profound psychological and spiritual truths that the Gospels intended to convey. The reduction of such sublime metaphors into crude literalism is not only a misunderstanding but a distortion that has shaped history in ways that obscured the original depth of these symbols[13] at the very threshold of Christian "faith," we find the introduction of a dogma—a belief in the "immaculate conception." And what has this dogma achieved? By insisting on a so-called purity in conception, it has ironically stripped conception itself of its natural purity. In elevating it to the status of a miraculous event, it has sullied the simple, inherent beauty and sacredness of natural processes. This is not a celebration of life but a rejection of its reality, a denial of the very essence that makes existence profound. The concept, meant to sanctify, instead diminishes. By defining "immaculateness" through exclusion, it casts a shadow over what should be whole, complete, and untouchably pure in its natural state.The "kingdom of heaven" is not a distant promise, not something to be anticipated beyond this world or after death. It is not a place, nor an event to be awaited. Instead, it is a state of the heart, a condition of being. The idea of natural death, as it is commonly understood, is entirely absent from the Gospels. Death is not a transition, not a passage to something greater; it belongs to a different realm altogether—a realm that is merely symbolic, useful only as an allegory. For the bearer of "glad tidings," concepts like the "hour of death" or the crises of physical life hold no meaning. Time, measured in hours and days, is irrelevant to his message. The "kingdom of God" is not something to come in the future, not something to wait for. It does not belong to yesterday, today, or tomorrow, and it is not tied to the hope of a millennium. It is a living experience, something felt within. It is everywhere and yet nowhere at the same time.

The bearer of "glad tidings" lived and died in alignment with the way of life he taught—not to "save mankind" in the sense of erasing their sins, but to reveal a new way of living. His life was his message, and his death was its culmination. He faced his accusers, the judges, and even the executioners with a demeanor that reflected his teachings. He resisted nothing, did not defend his rights, and did not attempt to escape his fate. On the contrary, he accepted the ultimate penalty, even invited it, as an extension of his message. On the cross, he prayed, suffered, and loved— even for those who inflicted harm upon him. His way was one of submission, not defiance; love, not condemnation. To defend oneself, to show anger, or to assign blame—these were actions entirely foreign to his nature. Instead, he embraced even the Evil One, responding with love rather than resistance.

We, the free spirits, are perhaps the first to grasp the profound integrity of this way of life—something misunderstood for nineteen centuries. Only now are we beginning to comprehend the instinct and passion for truth that characterized this figure. He waged a quiet war against the "holy lie," a lie more insidious and dangerous than all others. His integrity stood in opposition not only to falsehoods but also to the structure that emerged in the aftermath of his teachings: the church. Mankind, motivated by selfishness and a desire for advantage, created the church out of a denial of the very principles the Gospels embodied.

For those who look for signs of irony in the great drama of existence, Christianity offers one of the most staggering examples. That humanity would kneel before something that directly opposes the essence of the Gospels—their origin, meaning, and guiding law—is a profound paradox. The concept of the "church" sanctifies precisely what the bearer of "glad tidings" rejected and left behind. This contradiction stands as a monumental example of world-historical irony, unmatched in its magnitude.

Our age prides itself on its historical awareness, yet it continues to delude itself into believing that Christianity began with the crude tale of a miracle worker and savior, with the spiritual and symbolic elements added later. In reality, the reverse is true. The history of Christianity, from the moment of the crucifixion onward, is the story of an ever-deepening misunderstanding of an original symbolism. As Christianity spread to larger, less sophisticated populations, it became necessary to simplify and vulgarize its teachings to suit the limited understanding of these masses. The result was a progressive coarsening of its message.

To meet the demands of a growing and increasingly unrefined audience, Christianity absorbed the rituals and beliefs of various underground cults of the Roman Empire. Over time, it became entangled with the superstitions and irrationalities of countless sickly ideologies. It was Christianity's fate to adapt itself to the needs of the most base and degraded, resulting in a faith that became as distorted and corrupt as the needs it served. From this degeneration emerged the church—a manifestation of barbarism masquerading as spiritual authority. The church became the embodiment of hostility to truth, to nobility of spirit, to intellectual discipline, and to spontaneous human kindness.

Christian values, which were meant to be noble and transformative, were replaced by a system that served only to perpetuate dishonesty and power. It is only now, through the perspective of free spirits, that we have re-established the true dichotomy between the values of the church and the noble values of the Gospels. This recognition restores the greatest of all contrasts in values—a contrast that had been obscured by centuries of misunderstanding and distortion.

I cannot help but sigh here. There are days when I am gripped by a despair deeper than any melancholy—an overwhelming contempt for humanity. Let me be clear about what I despise and whom I despise: it is the modern man, the man of today, the one I am forced to call my contemporary. This man of today suffocates me with the stench of his decay, his moral rot, his empty words, and his hollow convictions.

Toward the past, I feel no such disdain. Like anyone who seeks to understand, I approach history with tolerance—a kind of restrained generosity. With grim patience, I walk through the millennia of human madness, whether it is called "Christianity," "Christian faith," or the "Christian church." I do not hold humanity accountable for its historical delusions; those times were shaped by ignorance and circumstances beyond the understanding of those who lived them. But when I turn to the present—when I confront the modern age—my restraint crumbles. A new level of revulsion overtakes me. This age knows better. It has no excuse. What was once mere sickness has now become something grotesque and indecent. Today, it is indecent to call oneself a Christian. And that is where my disgust begins.

I look around me, and I see that not a shred of what was once called "truth" remains intact. The word itself—truth—has become unbearable. Even the sound of a priest speaking it is intolerable. Any person with even the slightest sense of honesty must know that when a theologian, priest, or pope speaks today, he does not merely err—he lies. And he knows he lies. Gone are the days when such falsehoods could be excused as innocent or born of ignorance. No, the priest knows full well that there is no "God," no "sinner," no "Savior." He knows that "free will" is a fabrication, that the "moral order of the world" is a sham. The deeper reflection and self-mastery required to face these truths leave no room for pretense. No honest man can claim ignorance of these facts anymore.

The ideas of the church are now exposed for what they are: the most vile counterfeits ever conceived. These notions were created to corrupt nature, to undermine natural values, and to poison human vitality. The priest is no longer a figure of mystery or reverence; he is revealed as the ultimate parasite, the venomous spider spinning his web of deception to ensnare and subjugate. We now see the true purpose behind the sinister inventions of priestly doctrine: their concepts—"the other world," "the last judgment," "the immortality of the soul," and even the very notion of the "soul"—were never anything more than tools of domination, instruments of cruelty. Through them, the priest secured his power, holding humanity in a grip of fear and self-loathing.

We know this now. Our collective conscience has awakened to the truth. We understand the grotesque legacy of these lies, the profound degradation they have wrought upon humanity. They reduced people to a state of self-abasement so pitiful that it inspires only disgust. The very sight of the human soul, corrupted by these lies, is enough to provoke revulsion. Yet, despite this awareness, the world continues as before. Nothing changes. The last remnants of decency and self-respect seem to have vanished entirely.

What are we to make of modern statesmen, men who are otherwise bold, pragmatic, and openly anti-Christian in their actions, still calling themselves Christians and taking communion? What could be more hypocritical? A prince, commanding armies, embodying the egoism and pride of his people—yet without a hint of shame, he declares himself a Christian. And whom does Christianity deny? What does it call "the world"? To be a soldier, to be a judge, to be a patriot; to defend oneself; to act with honor; to pursue one's advantage; to feel pride—all these basic human instincts and values are now labeled anti- Christian.

What does this mean for the modern man who still calls himself a Christian? It means he is a walking contradiction, a monstrosity of falsehood. Every action he takes, every instinct he follows, every value he demonstrates in his daily life stands in direct opposition to the creed he professes. And yet, without a trace of shame, he continues to cling to this identity, declaring himself a Christian as though the word still held meaning. This is the height of hypocrisy, the final degradation of honesty, integrity, and authenticity in the modern age.

Let me take a step back and recount the true story of Christianity. The very word "Christianity" itself is a profound misunderstanding. At its core, there was only ever one Christian, and he died on the cross. The "Gospels" died with him. From the moment of his death onward, what came to be called the "Gospels" became the complete opposite of what he had lived and taught. They became "bad tidings," or what might more aptly be termed a Dysangelium. It is a fundamental error—indeed, a nonsensical one—to view "faith," particularly faith in salvation through Christ, as the defining characteristic of the Christian. True Christianity lies solely in the way of life lived by the one who died on the cross. His way of being, his life, and his actions were the essence of what it means to be Christian.

This way of life remains possible, even now, and for certain people, it may even be necessary. Authentic, primitive Christianity—the original way of being embodied by Christ—can still exist in any age. It is not about faith, but about action—or, more accurately, a deliberate avoidance of certain actions. It is not about a belief system but about a fundamentally different state of being.

Psychologists understand that states of consciousness, or the acceptance of something as true, are of negligible importance compared to the instincts that drive human behavior. The entire notion of reducing Christianity to an intellectual acceptance of "truth" is a profound error. It negates the very essence of Christianity. To equate being Christian with mere belief is to misunderstand it completely. In reality, there are no Christians. The person who, for two thousand years, has been called a "Christian" is nothing more than a psychological self-deception. When examined closely, this so-called Christian, despite all his "faith," is governed entirely by his instincts—and what base instincts they are!

Throughout history, faith has served as little more than a disguise, a mask that conceals the true forces at work: instincts. Consider the case of Luther, for instance. His "faith" was merely a front, a justification that veiled the instinctual drives operating behind it. Faith, in this context, is the quintessential Christian form of cunning. People proclaim their faith loudly, but their actions invariably follow the dictates of their instincts. This has been the pattern in every age.

The ideas within the Christian worldview have no contact with reality. Instead, they are driven by an instinctive hatred of reality itself, a rejection of the world as it is. This hostility to reality is the primary force underlying Christianity—the one true motive power of its existence. And what does this imply? That the entire structure of Christianity is built on a foundational error, a misconception that conditions everything about it. Replace any one of its erroneous ideas with a genuine reality, and Christianity collapses entirely. It cannot survive without its errors.

When viewed dispassionately, Christianity stands out as one of the strangest phenomena in human history—a religion not only built upon falsehoods but actively creative and ingenious in inventing falsehoods that harm life and poison the human spirit. It is a spectacle that might well amuse the gods, particularly those who are also philosophers. These gods, like the ones I encountered in the famed dialogues at Naxos, might find themselves momentarily entertained by this peculiar drama. Once their disgust—and ours—subsides, they might even feel a glimmer of gratitude for the absurdity of it all. Perhaps this strange exhibition is the only reason our small, wretched planet deserves even a passing glance from omnipotence—a brief flicker of divine interest.

Let us, then, not underestimate the Christians. The Christian, though false to the point of innocence, is still far above the ape. In fact, applying a well- known theory of descent to Christians is nothing short of polite. In their case, such a theory becomes a courtesy, a small concession to civility in the face of the endless spectacle they provide.

The fate of the Gospels was sealed by death—by the death on the cross. Everything turned on that event, that unexpected and shameful end. The cross, a symbol of degradation reserved for the lowest strata of society, carried an appalling paradox that confronted the disciples with a profound and inescapable question: "Who was he? What was he?" The shocking nature of his death shook them to their core, filling them with dismay, a sense of profound insult, and even a suspicion that such an end might refute the very cause they had believed in.

The haunting question, "Why this way?" loomed over them, demanding an explanation.

In their minds, everything had to be accounted for; everything had to have a reason, not just any reason, but the highest and most divine. The love of a disciple does not tolerate chance. For them, there could be no accidents in the life of their Master. It was this desperate search for meaning that opened the chasm of doubt. And then came the inevitable question, striking like lightning: "Who put him to death? Who was his true enemy?" The answer, clear and immediate, was the dominant powers of Judaism, its ruling class.

From that moment on, the disciples found themselves in opposition to the established order. Jesus was suddenly reimagined as a figure in revolt against authority, against the structures of power that had condemned him. Until then, the militant, defiant side of his character had been absent from their understanding. They had seen him as embodying the opposite: a message of peace and reconciliation. The very essence of his life and teachings— the way he lived and the way he died—had been misunderstood by his closest followers. They failed to grasp the central point of his death: the example he set, his total freedom from and transcendence of ressentiment. His death, far from being a defeat, was meant to demonstrate his teachings in the most profound and public way imaginable.

Yet his disciples could not forgive his death. They did not respond with the serene calmness of heart that his teachings demanded, nor were they willing to follow his example by embracing a similar fate. Instead, they were overtaken by the most unevangelical of emotions: revenge. They could not accept that the cause might end with his death. To them, there had to be recompense, a settling of accounts, a divine judgment. But nothing could be further from the Gospel spirit than the concepts of "recompense," "punishment," and "judgment."

With this shift, the popular Jewish expectation of a messiah surged back to the forefront of their thinking. They refocused their hopes on a future event, an apocalyptic moment when the "kingdom of God" would arrive with vengeance upon Jesus' enemies. They transformed his teachings, which had been a living realization of the kingdom of God, into a promise of something yet to come. This was a profound misunderstanding. The Gospels had proclaimed the kingdom of God as something already present, as a reality embodied in Jesus' life and teachings. To relegate it to a future event was to undo its fulfillment and misrepresent its essence.

At the same time, their grief and rage twisted their understanding of Jesus himself. Suddenly, all the contempt and bitterness they harbored against the Pharisees and theologians became projected onto the character of their Master. In this, they remade him in their own image, turning him into a figure who opposed the Pharisees and theologians by embodying their very characteristics—he was now a Pharisee and theologian in his own right, wielding the same tools of denunciation and judgment that he had once transcended.

Their veneration of Jesus also took a distorted and extravagant form. They could no longer accept his message of equality—that all men are children of God. This teaching, so central to his Gospel, was abandoned in their need for revenge and superiority. They elevated Jesus far above themselves, turning him into something entirely separate and inaccessible. In doing so, they mirrored the actions of the Jews in earlier times, who had distanced themselves from their God by elevating him to an unattainable height as a way of asserting dominance over their enemies.

Thus arose the constructs of the One God and the Only Son of God— born not out of the teachings of Jesus, but out of the disciples' inability to reconcile his death with their own instincts for vengeance, superiority, and power. What had once been a message of profound equality and present fulfillment became distorted into a doctrine of separation, hierarchy, and deferred hope. The faith that emerged from this distortion bore little resemblance to the life or teachings of the man who died on the cross.

From this distortion sprang an absurd and tragic question: "How could God allow such a death?" The bewildered and desperate reasoning of the early Christian community answered this riddle with a terrifying absurdity: God had sacrificed his son for the forgiveness of sins. And in that moment, the spirit of the Gospels was extinguished. The central message of Jesus—the abolition of guilt, the denial of any separation between God and man, the living embodiment of unity with the divine—was replaced with the abhorrent idea of sacrifice for sin. And not just any sacrifice, but the most barbaric form imaginable: the sacrifice of the innocent for the guilty. This was not salvation; it was a regression to the worst kind of paganism, dressed in the language of holiness.

Jesus himself had eradicated the concept of "guilt." He denied the existence of a chasm between God and humanity, and his life was the demonstration of this denial. His "glad tidings" were the announcement of this unity, not as a privilege for the few but as a reality for all. Yet, with this new doctrine of sacrifice, his message was corrupted. Bit by bit, the figure of the Savior was transformed by doctrines entirely foreign to his life and teachings: the doctrine of divine judgment, the second coming, the resurrection, and the idea of death as a necessary atonement. These alterations shifted the meaning of the Gospels away from the here and now, away from the realization of blessedness in this life, and toward the promise of a state of existence after death.

The worst of these distortions came at the hands of St. Paul. With the audacity of a rabbinical logician, Paul cemented the indecent idea of the resurrection with his infamous claim: "If Christ did not rise from the dead, then our faith is in vain." This single declaration reduced the essence of the Gospels to a doctrine of personal immortality—the most contemptible and unfulfillable promise imaginable. Paul did not stop there; he preached this immortality as a reward, entrenching the idea that faith was transactional, something done for the sake of a future payoff.

What, then, truly ended with the death of Jesus on the cross? It was a new, original attempt to establish peace and happiness on earth—a movement akin to Buddhism, but distinct in that it promised nothing and sought to fulfill everything here and now. Buddhism fulfills through its teachings and practices; Christianity, corrupted from its outset, promised everything and fulfilled nothing. And what followed the "glad tidings" of the Gospels? The most disastrous possible news: the doctrines of Paul.

In Paul, we find the complete antithesis of the "bearer of glad tidings." He was not the messenger of peace but the architect of hatred, the embodiment of its relentless logic and vision. Everything in Paul's work was sacrificed to this hatred: above all, the figure of the Savior himself. Paul nailed Jesus to the cross a second time—not with nails, but with his words and doctrines. The life, example, teachings, and even the death of Jesus were repurposed and twisted to serve Paul's own agenda. The essence of the Gospels—their meaning, their law—was obliterated under the weight of Paul's theological contrivances.

What Paul left in place of historical truth was a fabrication. He erased the actual history of Jesus' life and death, inventing a narrative that suited his needs. The yesterday and the day before yesterday of Christianity were wiped clean, rewritten to align with Paul's vision. The history of Israel itself was recast to serve as a prelude to Paul's version of the Savior. In his narrative, all the prophets were reinterpreted as having foreshadowed his "Christ," and the entire religious history of humanity was manipulated to appear as though it culminated in Paul's theology.

The figure of Jesus, his teachings, his way of life, his death, and even the meaning of that death—nothing escaped this falsification. The concept of the "risen" Jesus became the focal point, and Paul shifted the entire weight of Jesus' life to this fabricated event. The real life and teachings of the Savior no longer mattered. For Paul, what was important was the death on the cross, and more than that, what could be built upon it.

To see Paul as sincere or honest, as someone who genuinely believed in the hallucination he claimed as proof of the resurrection, would be an absurdity for any psychologist. Paul was a man who willed the end and therefore willed the means. He knew what he needed to achieve his goals and was unbothered by the untruths he propagated. The fools to whom he preached were quick to accept these fabrications, swallowing his claims without question. For Paul, what mattered was power, and he used Christianity as a vehicle for priestly dominance.

The concepts, teachings, and symbols he introduced all served one purpose: to subjugate the masses and organize them into obedient mobs. His doctrine of immortality, and with it the promise of judgment, became his most potent tool for establishing priestly control. This invention, this mechanism of power, was so effective that even Islam later adopted it wholesale. Mohammed borrowed Paul's central device—the belief in the immortality of the soul and the judgment to come—as the cornerstone of his own religious structure. In Paul, the priesthood found its most cunning architect, and Christianity became a religion of domination rather than liberation, a faith of control rather than fulfillment.

When the center of gravity in life is shifted away from life itself and placed in a "beyond"—into nothingness—then life is robbed of its very essence, its meaning, and its balance. The grand falsehood of personal immortality undermines all reason and natural instincts, dismantling the very foundation upon which life thrives. Once this lie takes hold, everything in the human instinct that supports life, fosters its flourishing, and secures its future is cast under suspicion. The instincts that once guided humanity to thrive now become threats to the salvation of the soul. To live in such a way that life loses all meaning—this becomes the new "meaning" of life.

Why cultivate a sense of civic responsibility? Why take pride in one's lineage or honor one's forebears? Why work together, trust one another, or concern oneself with the common good? Why strive to contribute to the betterment of society? Under the Christian doctrine, all these are mere distractions, temptations leading one astray from the "straight and narrow path." Life becomes reduced to a single, all-encompassing command: "One thing only is necessary."

The poisonous idea that every man, by virtue of possessing an "immortal soul," is equal to every other man, regardless of his character, accomplishments, or contribution, leads to an absurd inflation of the self. In this distorted vision, the "salvation" of each insignificant individual is elevated to a matter of infinite importance, as though the laws of the universe should bend and nature itself should be suspended for the sake of the petty concerns of small-minded bigots and those teetering on the edge of madness. This grotesque exaltation of selfishness—this transformation of vanity into cosmic significance—is contemptible beyond measure. And yet, it is precisely this appeal to personal vanity, this flattery of the weak and the downtrodden, that Christianity owes its success. By magnifying the self-worth of the "botched," the dissatisfied, the downtrodden, and the refuse of humanity, it gathered to itself the disgruntled masses, those who found life too harsh and unforgiving.

The "salvation of the soul" is, in plain terms, the proclamation that "the world revolves around me." This doctrine of poisonous self- importance, masquerading as equality, became the cornerstone of Christianity. Under its influence, the principle of "equal rights for all" was introduced as a sacred truth, and from the dark recesses of human envy and bad instincts, Christianity launched its most insidious attack. It declared war on every instinct of reverence and respect for distinction between individuals, undermining the essential prerequisites for any upward movement, for any progress in civilization.

From the ressentiment of the masses, Christianity forged its most potent weapon—an unrelenting assault on all that is noble, joyous, and elevated in life. It turned its sights against the very happiness and vitality of the earth, dragging everything down to its level. To grant "immortality" to every Peter and Paul, to proclaim that every soul is of equal worth regardless of its merit, was the greatest and most vicious affront ever inflicted upon noble humanity. It flattened the peaks of human greatness, extinguishing the spark of aspiration and excellence that drives civilization forward.

And let us not overlook the corrosive influence that Christianity has exerted upon politics. Today, no one dares to stand for special rights or the right to rule. The courage to take pride in oneself and one's equals, the honor of noble distinction, and the "pathos of distance" that separates the exceptional from the ordinary—all of these have been eroded by the Christian lie of the equality of souls.

Our politics is gravely ill with this lack of courage. The aristocratic ethos, the belief in the refinement and elevation of a select few, has been shattered by the falsehood of equality. This same lie now fuels the belief in the "rights of the majority," which continues to ignite revolutions. But every revolution, guided by

Christian values, inevitably devolves into a grotesque carnival of blood and crime. Let us not be deceived—Christianity is the root cause. Its teachings have inverted the natural order, turning every uprising into a revolt against what is noble, strong, and elevated in life.

Christianity is, at its heart, the revolt of all that creeps upon the ground against all that soars to great heights. It is the gospel of the "lowly," designed to drag down what is lofty and magnificent. Rather than uplifting the weak, it lowers the strong, reducing the sublime to the mediocre and the extraordinary to the common.

In its obsessive glorification of the downtrodden, it has made a virtue of smallness and a sin of greatness, leaving humanity poorer, weaker, and further from its highest potential.

The Gospels stand as a profound testament to the corruption that had already taken root within the earliest Christian community. What Paul later developed into a fully articulated system, with the unrelenting logic of a rabbi, was in fact merely the culmination of a decay that began with the death of the Savior. These texts must be read with the utmost care, for behind every word lies a complexity that challenges even the most discerning reader. I must admit—though I hope it will not be held against me—that it is precisely this complexity that offers unparalleled joy to a psychologist. The Gospels are a masterpiece of psychological refinement, not naive in their corruption but deliberate, an artful triumph in the realm of spiritual and moral manipulation.

In this sense, the Gospels stand alone. They are unlike any other part of the Bible. Here, we are unmistakably among Jews, and this fact is key to understanding their nature. The genius displayed in the Gospels is the genius of creating a profound delusion of personal "holiness," a skill unmatched in any other book or by any other people. This elevation of fraud—both in language and in posture—to the level of an art form is not a random occurrence or the product of individual talent. It is, rather, the result of centuries of Jewish tradition and practice, honed to perfection.

Judaism, with its relentless focus on "holiness," appears in Christianity as the ultimate refinement of this art: the fabrication of holy lies. After long centuries of training and discipline, this practice reached a level of mastery in the Christian tradition. The

Christian, in this sense, is the perfected Jew, not merely inheriting this talent but multiplying it. He is, in a way, threefold the Jew. The instinct to adopt only those concepts, symbols, and attitudes that align with priestly practice—while instinctively rejecting all other forms of thought and value—is not just tradition. It is inheritance. It operates with the force of nature, passed down and deeply ingrained.

The entire world, even the greatest minds of its most enlightened eras, has allowed itself to be deceived by this artifice. The Gospels have been read as books of innocence, which in itself is a testament to the extraordinary skill with which the deception was executed. The naïveté of their readers is astonishing. If these sanctimonious frauds and self-appointed saints could be seen in their true form, even for an instant, the farce would collapse. It is precisely because I cannot read a single word of theirs without picturing their theatrical piety—their rolling eyes, their false humility—that I have had enough of them. Their hypocrisy is intolerable.

For most people, however, books are just literature, and they fail to see beyond the surface. Let us not be deceived by the words "judge not," for these same figures condemn to hell anyone who stands in their way. In exalting God, they glorify themselves. In demanding virtues that suit their own needs, they present themselves as warriors for goodness, truth, and light. "We live, we die, we sacrifice ourselves for the good," they proclaim— though in reality, they simply act as they are compelled to by their base instincts. Forced by their hypocrisy to slink in shadows and conceal their true motives, they convert this necessity into a virtue. Their lives of humility are not a choice but a defense mechanism, rebranded as proof of their piety.

This brand of humble, chaste, and charitable fraud is a morality designed to manipulate. The Gospels are, at their core, texts of moral seduction. These people understood the utility of morality as a tool for control. Morality became their ultimate device for leading humanity by the nose. The conscious conceit of being "chosen" hides behind a veil of modesty, but this modesty is a mask for arrogance. They, the "community," the "good and just," claim a monopoly on truth and virtue, while relegating the rest of humanity—"the world"—to the status of outsiders.

This is the most dangerous form of megalomania the earth has ever seen. These small-minded bigots and liars claimed exclusive rights to concepts such as "God," "truth," "light," "spirit," "love," "wisdom," and "life," as though these ideas were synonymous with themselves. They sought to set themselves apart from the rest of humanity, to elevate their pettiness to the level of universal truth. They turned values on their heads, declaring that the Christian was the ultimate measure of all things—the salt of the earth, the standard of humanity, and even the arbiter of the final judgment.

This disaster was made possible only because it found fertile ground in the pre-existing megalomania of Judaism. The Judaeo-Christians, once they found themselves in conflict with mainstream Judaism, had no choice but to adopt the same tactics of self-preservation that Jewish instincts had long employed— only now, they used them even against the Jews themselves.

Christianity became, in essence, a "reformed" Judaism, a mirror image of its parent tradition, wielding the same tools of exclusion and self-glorification.

Let me offer a clear example of what these petty minds have projected onto the figure of their Master—the unfiltered creed of "beautiful souls":

" And whosoever shall not receive you, nor hear you, when ye depart thence, shake off the dust under your feet for a testimony against them. Verily I say unto you, it shall be more tolerable for Sodom and Gomorrha in the day of judgment, than for that city" (Mark 6:11).

How evangelical indeed! This is the language not of humility or grace but of vengeance and condemnation. It reveals the deep corruption that pervades the very foundations of the Gospels, transforming what could have been a message of peace into one of division, arrogance, and self-righteousness.

"And whosoever shall offend one of these little ones that believe in me, it is better for him that a millstone were hanged about his neck, and he were cast into the sea" (Mark 9 :42).

How very evangelical indeed! A message of love and humility expressed through threats of punishment so severe they border on the grotesque. What a curious way to inspire goodness—by invoking images of drowning with millstones.

"And if thine eye offend thee, pluck it out: it is better for thee to enter into the kingdom of God with one eye, than having two eyes to be cast into hell fir e; W her e the worm dieth not, and the fir e is not quenched" (Mark 9:47).

Ah, but it is not truly the eye that is meant here. This is not about the literal removal of body parts but about severing ties with anything deemed "sinful"— and yet, the language is unmistakably barbaric. How perfectly these words reflect the Christian preoccupation with violence as a means to sanctity, a moral calculus that prefers mutilation to perceived impurity.

"Verily I say unto you, That there be some of them that stand her e, which shall not taste of death, t ill they have seen the kingdom of God come with power " (Mark 9 :1).

Well lied, lion! A bold proclamation, indeed, yet how many centuries have passed since these words were spoken, and where is this "kingdom of God"? How prophetic, how divine—until one recalls that such declarations of imminent glory were never meant to be verifiable. A clever evasion of accountability.

"Whosoever will come after me, let him deny himself, and take up his cross, and follow me" (Mark 8 :34).

Here we see the core of Christian morality, built not on affirmation but on denial—of the self, of life, of joy. For... what? A promise, a vague reward in the beyond. As a psychologist might note, the very logic of these "fors"—the reasons behind the self-denial—undermine the morality they seek to uphold. And that, of course, is what makes it quintessentially Christian.

"Judge not, that ye be not judged. With what measure ye mete, it shall be measured to you again" (Matthew 7 :1).

What an astounding notion of justice—justice as a mirror of one's own actions, as if the universe were a tit-for-tat mechanism. This "just judge," it seems, operates less on principles and more on the whims of reciprocity.

"For if ye love them which love you, what reward have ye? do not even the publicans the same? And if ye salute your brethren only, what do ye mor e than others? do not even the publicans so?" (Matthew 5:46).

Here lies the principle of "Christian love": a love that demands distinction, that insists upon being extraordinary, and most of all, that expects payment in the form of eternal reward. Selfless, indeed!

"But if ye forgive not men their trespasses, neither will your Father forgive your trespasses" (Matthew 6 :15).

Quite compromising for this "Father" figure, who seems less like an embodiment of divine mercy and more like a scorekeeper, eager to withhold forgiveness if his terms are not met. A deity of conditional grace, at best.

"But seek ye first the kingdom of God, and his righteousness; and all these things shall be added unto you" (Matthew 6 :33).

"All these things"—the necessities of life, food, clothing, shelter—will apparently be provided. A promise that, to put it mildly, is far from accurate. Earlier, this God even dabbled as a tailor, fashioning garments for his chosen ones. How practical!

"Rejoice ye in that day, and leap for joy: for , behold, your reward is great in heaven: for in the lik e manner did their father s unto the prophets" (Luke 6 :23).

The audacity of such a statement! The "rabble," with their self-glorifying comparisons, dare to liken themselves to prophets. What impudence, what megalomania, to align their grievances with the legacies of those who truly shaped history.

"Know ye not that ye are the temple of God, and that the spirit of God dwelleth in you? If any man defile the temple of God, him shall God destroy; for the temple of God is holy, which temple ye are" (1 Corinthians 3:16).

What sanctimonious arrogance! To equate oneself with a "holy temple," to assume divine indwelling, and then to invoke destruction for those who fail to uphold this illusion of sanctity—one cannot heap enough contempt upon such pretension.

"Do ye not know that the saints shall judge the world? and if the world shall be judged by you, are ye unworthy to judge the smallest matters?" (1 Corinthians 6 :2).

Not merely the ravings of a lunatic, unfortunately, but the calculated rhetoric of one seeking dominance. And yet, Paul does not stop here.

"Know ye not that we shall judge angels? how much more things that pertain to this life?"

The delusion expands further. Saints judging the world was not grandiose enough—now they will judge angels as well! This is no longer mere arrogance but a flight into the absurd, a theology built on unbridled megalomania and the elevation of mediocrity to cosmic significance. Such impostures reveal the true spirit of early Christianity: not a doctrine of humility but a machinery of control and self-aggrandizement.

"Hath not God made foolish the wisdom of this world? For after that in the wisdom of God the world by wisdom knew not God, it pleased God by the foolishness of preaching to save them that believe. Not many wise men after the flesh, not many mighty, not many noble are called: But God hath chosen the foolish things of the world to confound the wise; and God hath chosen the weak things of the world to confound the things which are mighty; And base things of the world, and things which are despised, hath God chosen, yea, and things which are not, to bring to nought things that are: That no flesh should g lory in his presence." (1 Corinthians 1:20ff)

To truly grasp the psychological depth of this passage—arguably one of the clearest expressions of the moral framework underlying a Chandala morality— one must revisit the first part of my Genealogy of Morals. There, the stark opposition between noble morality and the morality born from ressentiment and impotent vengefulness is laid bare. Paul, above all others, stands as the supreme apostle of vengeance. His vision is one of turning every instinct of the downtrodden into a weapon against the powerful, of exalting weakness as virtue while condemning strength as sin.

What is the natural consequence of such a framework? It is that one would do well to handle the New Testament with gloves. The filth contained within it practically demands such precaution. To linger among the early Christians, even through the medium of their texts, is as unpleasant as mingling with Polish Jews— not because of any particular grievance against them, but simply because neither leaves behind a pleasant aroma.

In all my examination of the New Testament, I have not found a single instance of genuine humanity—nothing free-spirited, kind, open-hearted, or upright. The instincts for vitality and elevation, the first steps toward greatness, are entirely absent. What remains are the lowest instincts—vindictive, envious, cowardly—and even these lack courage. The text reeks of a shutting of the eyes, of a pervasive self-deception, of a cowardice that cloaks itself in virtue. Compared to this, every other book feels clean, invigorating, even joyful.

After reading Paul, I turned with relief and delight to the immortal Petronius. How different his tone—so wanton, so charming, so alive! Petronius possesses that enduring health and cheerfulness that breathes life into his words. Of him, one might echo Boccaccio's description of Cesare Borgia: "è tutto festo"—completely festive, completely sound.

In stark contrast, the early Christians made a critical miscalculation. Their attacks on others served only to highlight the worth of their adversaries. Anyone denounced by an early Christian emerges unscathed, if not elevated, by the association. Indeed, to be the target of such hatred becomes a badge of honor. The New Testament unwittingly inspires admiration for everything it condemns. Even the Pharisees and scribes—regular objects of its venom—gain a certain dignity. To be so hated, one must have had qualities worth despising. Hypocrisy? As if early Christians could level such a charge without irony! Their hatred of privilege required no justification other than its existence. Privilege alone was enough to provoke their wrath.

The early Christian—and, I fear, the last Christian as well—is driven by an instinctive rebellion against privilege in all its forms. His war for "equal rights" is eternal, born from an unrelenting need to elevate his weakness by tearing down the strength of others. For such a man, every standard—be it intellectual, moral, or aesthetic—becomes "worldly" and therefore evil. The Christian moral code transforms nobility, beauty, freedom, and pride into vices, while raising mediocrity, timidity, and submission to divine virtues.

It is impossible to ignore the dishonesty inherent in every word uttered by such a figure. His values are corrosive, his actions destructive, and his instincts toxic. Yet, paradoxically, his hatred serves as a reliable measure of value.

Whatever the Christian priest condemns, we may be certain is worth preserving. In this way, the Christian, especially the priest, becomes an inverted criterion of worth.

And what of the figures within the New Testament? Only one stands out as worthy of honor: Pilate, the Roman viceroy. His noble Roman disdain for the Jewish quagmire in which he found himself is unmatched. One Jew more or less—what difference did it make to him? His scorn for the petty drama before him added a touch of Roman dignity to a text otherwise devoid of it. Pilate enriched the New Testament with its only statement of enduring value—a single question that is both its critique and its undoing: " W hat is truth?"

With this question, Pilate dismissed the sham seriousness of those who surrounded him. He stood apart from their lies and self-delusions, embodying the clarity and strength of a world that saw beyond petty moralistic games. In this moment, the Roman viceroy became the unintentional savior of the text— a beacon of realism in a sea of falsity.

What sets us apart is not that we fail to find God—in history, in nature, or even beyond nature—but that we reject what has been honored as God. We do not see such a figure as "divine" but as pitiable, absurd, and ultimately harmful. We regard this so- called God not merely as an error but as a profound crime against life itself. We do not merely deny the Christian God; we deny that such a God could be God. Were someone to present us with proof of the Christian God's existence, it would make us believe in him even less. In simple terms: deus, qualem Paulus creavit, dei negatio—the God as Paul created him is the negation of God.

A religion like Christianity, which fails to engage with reality on any level and crumbles the moment reality asserts itself, must inevitably set itself against the "wisdom of this world." Christianity cannot coexist with science, clarity, or intellectual integrity. It thrives only by poisoning, defaming, and vilifying all disciplines that demand lucidity and rigor, all qualities that embody the freedom and nobility of the mind. Faith, as Christianity defines it, is not merely separate from reason—it is a direct veto against reason. In practice, faith requires falsehood at any cost.

Paul understood this necessity. He knew that the lie, packaged as "faith," was indispensable. The church later inherited and institutionalized this insight from Paul. The God that Paul invented for himself—a God who "made foolish the wisdom of this world"—is not divine revelation but a reflection of Paul's own will to power. This God is the expression of a Jewish instinct to impose one's will upon others by declaring it divine law (thora). Paul's war was not only theological but also deeply practical: he sought to eradicate the "wisdom of this world," which he identified as his greatest threat. His specific enemies were the philologists and physicians of the Alexandrian school. These practitioners of knowledge represented everything that stood in opposition to Paul's invention.

No one can be a philologist or a physician without, in essence, being an Antichrist. A philologist sees through the veil of the "holy books," exposing their fraudulence. A physician discerns the physiological degeneration of the Christian ideal, diagnosing it as incurable. To the philologist, Christianity is a literary deception; to the physician, it is a symptom of sickness.

Has anyone ever truly understood the famous story at the beginning of the Bible? The narrative of God's mortal fear of knowledge? It has gone unnoticed by most, yet it reveals the fundamental anxiety of the priestly mind. This priest- book par excellence begins with the acknowledgment of the priest's only real danger: knowledge. Ergo, "God" faces the same peril. The story of Eden is not about humanity's fall but about the priest's struggle to maintain control.

The old God, entirely spirit, entirely priestly, entirely "perfect," strolls through his garden in boredom, seeking diversion. Even gods cannot escape the tedium of eternity. In his idleness, he creates man—a creature to entertain him. But man, too, grows bored. God, moved by pity, creates animals to distract man, but they fail to suffice. Man seeks dominion over them, rejecting the role of mere animal himself. So God creates woman, ending boredom—but also beginning a cascade of unintended consequences. Woman, the second mistake of God, introduces chaos. Priests have always known that "woman is a serpent" and that "from woman comes all evil in the world." And what was her ultimate crime? She introduced man to knowledge.

Through woman, man tasted the forbidden fruit of the tree of knowledge. And God, realizing his mistake, was seized by terror. Man, his greatest blunder, had become a rival. Knowledge threatened to make man godlike, spelling the end for both gods and priests. Thus, the moral of the story becomes clear: science, as the pursuit of knowledge, is the ultimate sin, the origin of all other sins. This is the essence of priestly morality: "Thou shalt not know." Everything else follows from this foundational command.

But God's terror did not make him less cunning. How could he defend himself against knowledge? The answer came in stages. First, he expelled man from paradise. Happiness and leisure foster thought, and thought is dangerous. Man must be made to suffer—only suffering can keep him from thinking. So the priest invented distress, death, childbirth's agonies, old age, decrepitude, and above all, sickness. These miseries served as tools of control, preventing man from indulging in dangerous curiosity.

And yet, despite these efforts, knowledge continued to grow. The edifice of human understanding rose higher and higher, casting a shadow over the gods. Desperate, God took another step: he invented war. By dividing peoples and setting them against one another, he ensured that they would be too consumed by conflict to pursue knowledge. War, among other things, is the greatest disruptor of science. And yet, even war could not fully halt humanity's progress. Knowledge flourished in defiance of all obstacles.

Finally, God resolved to end it all. "Man has become scientific—there is no help for it," he concluded. And so, his ultimate solution was the flood: to drown mankind, to erase his greatest mistake. Yet even this failed to extinguish humanity's thirst for knowledge. The legacy of science and reason persists, growing ever stronger, while the gods and their priestly servants continue to weaken under its light.

The opening of the Bible lays bare the entire psychology of the priest. The priest's singular and greatest fear is science—the clear and systematic understanding of cause and effect. This fear is not accidental; it is foundational. Science, the pursuit of knowledge, thrives only under favorable conditions. To seek knowledge, a man must have time, intellectual abundance, and the freedom to explore. But this is precisely what the priest cannot allow. For the priest, the solution has always been simple and consistent: "Man must be made unhappy."

From this logic emerged the concept of "sin." Sin is the priest's weapon, the first invention deployed to stifle the human mind. Guilt, punishment, and the so-called "moral order of the world" were all crafted to stand against science, against liberation, and against humanity's progress toward self-empowerment. These ideas redirected man's gaze inward, away from the external world and its truths. Instead of looking at the world with reason and curiosity, man was taught to close his eyes and suffer. Suffering became his condition—his justification for needing the priest. The physician, who sought to heal suffering and restore strength, was replaced by the "Savior," whose role was to deepen man's dependence on the priestly class.

This invention of guilt and punishment—along with doctrines of "grace," "salvation," and "forgiveness"—constitutes a lie of the highest order. These concepts are utterly without psychological reality; they exist solely to undermine man's sense of causality. They deny the natural consequences of actions and replace them with supernatural fabrications. Cause and effect are transformed into the whims of invisible forces: "God," "spirits," and "souls." These fabrications reduce natural outcomes to "moral" consequences, cloaked in rewards and punishments. In doing so, they destroy the foundation of knowledge itself, perpetrating the greatest crime against humanity—the deliberate obliteration of understanding.

Sin, this act of man desecrating himself, was invented for one purpose: to make science, culture, and human elevation impossible. The priest's power depends entirely on the perpetuation of sin. Through it, the priest rules.

At this point, I cannot refrain from offering a psychology of "belief" and the "believer"—for the benefit of those who still claim to believe. If anyone still fails to recognize how indecent it is to be "believing," or how much belief signifies a decline, a broken will to live, they will soon enough. My words are clear even to the deaf.

Among Christians, there exists a peculiar criterion of truth often referred to as "proof by power." It follows a simple formula: "Faith makes one blessed; therefore, it is true." This argument, if we may call it that, is entirely circular. One might immediately object that the blessedness faith promises is not a demonstration of truth—it is merely a promise, suspended upon the condition of belief. "One shall be blessed because one believes." But even this promise, rooted as it is in a wholly transcendental "beyond," remains undemonstrated and un-demonstrable. How can such a claim serve as a proof?

The so-called "proof by power" reduces to a mere belief that the effects promised by faith will eventually manifest. Translated into a formula: "I believe that faith makes me blessed; therefore, it is true." But this reasoning is absurd as a criterion of truth. Let us assume for the sake of politeness that faith's promise of blessedness can be demonstrated—not merely hoped for or whispered by the suspicious lips of priests. Even then, could the sensation of blessedness—pleasure, in technical terms—ever serve as a proof of truth?

The answer is unequivocal: no. If anything, pleasure often serves as a proof against truth. When sensations of pleasure influence the judgment of what is true, they render such judgments deeply suspect. Pleasure proves nothing beyond itself. Why, then, should one assume that truth must be accompanied by agreeable feelings? Why should truth be easier, more comfortable, or more pleasurable than falsehood? Experience, particularly the experience of disciplined and profound minds, teaches the opposite. Every small victory for truth has come at an enormous cost—sacrificing the comforts of the heart, the bonds of love, and the securities of human trust.

The pursuit of truth demands greatness of soul. It is the hardest of all services, requiring courage, sacrifice, and an unrelenting commitment to intellectual integrity. And what is this integrity? It is the refusal to yield to the seductions of comfort, pleasure, or convenience in matters of understanding. It is the relentless demand that we face the world as it is, not as we wish it to be. This is the true meaning of intellectual honesty, the cornerstone of any genuine elevation of humanity.

It means that a person must be strict with their own heart, reject the appeal of "beautiful feelings," and treat every "yes" and "no" as a matter of conscience. Faith may make people feel blessed, but that does not make it true—it is, instead, a lie. The fact that faith, in certain situations, can create a sense of happiness does not prove that the ideas behind it are real. The happiness caused by being fixated on one belief does not validate that belief. In truth, faith does not move mountains; it creates mountains where none existed before. This becomes clear enough with a simple walk through a lunatic asylum. Of course, this would never be obvious to a priest, whose instincts compel him to deny reality, insisting that illness is not illness and asylums are not asylums.

Christianity depends on sickness in the same way that the Greek spirit thrived on a superabundance of health. The true purpose behind the entire system of salvation offered by the church is to make people ill. Even the church itself, when viewed honestly, seems to aim toward turning the world into one enormous madhouse, a kind of universal Catholic asylum. The ideal type of religious person that the church desires is, in fact, a typical décadent. Whenever a religious crisis overtakes a society, it is marked by epidemics of nervous disorders. The "inner world" of the religious person is indistinguishable from that of someone who is overstressed and worn out. The so-called "highest" states of mind celebrated by Christianity as supremely valuable are often epileptic in nature. The church has only ever regarded the insane or outright frauds as holy, all under the pretense of honoring God.

At one point, I even described the entire Christian method of penance and salvation as a deliberate way of cultivating madness on ground already prepared for it, ground weakened and unhealthy. Not everyone can be a Christian; one cannot simply "convert" to Christianity. Instead, a person must already be sick enough to be drawn into it.

We, on the other hand, who have the courage to embrace health and even contempt, have every reason to despise a religion that teaches people to misunderstand their own bodies. Christianity clings to the superstitions surrounding the "soul" and makes a "virtue" out of inadequate nourishment. It views health itself as an enemy, a form of temptation, or even as the devil. Christianity convinces itself that a "perfect soul" can live in a broken and decaying body, and to justify this, it creates a twisted concept of "perfection." This so-called perfection is nothing more than a pale, sickly, and irrational state of mind, which it calls "holiness." This holiness is not a sign of strength or vitality but instead a series of symptoms—signs of a body that is impoverished, weakened, and permanently disordered.

As a movement within Europe, Christianity has always been an uprising of all the rejected and discarded elements of society— those who, under the banner of Christianity, now sought power. It was not the decline of an ancient, noble civilization that gave rise to Christianity, as some claim. This idea, which is still widely believed today, is entirely false and deserves to be challenged. Christianity did not emerge from the decay of classical antiquity. On the contrary, when the weak and marginalized classes of the Roman Empire were drawn into Christianity, the noble classes of the time were at their strongest and most refined. Christianity's triumph was the victory of the majority, the rise of democracy with its instincts for resentment and revenge.

Christianity was never tied to any one nation or race; it was a universal call to all those who felt disinherited by life. Its allies were found among the oppressed, the outcasts, and the sick. At its core, Christianity harbors a deep resentment against health and vitality. It despises everything that is strong, proud, and beautiful. Consider again the infamous words of Paul: "And God hath chosen the weak things of the world, the foolish things of the world, the base things of the world, and things which are despised." This sums up Christianity's entire approach: through this mindset, décadence triumphed.

The symbol of God on the cross encapsulates this victory, yet its deeper meaning is often missed. Christianity elevates suffering to the divine. Anything that suffers or hangs on the cross is declared sacred. This extends to humanity itself: because we all suffer, we are all divine. From this logic, Christianity proclaims that only it is divine.

Thus, Christianity achieved its victory by destroying a nobler way of thinking. It remains, to this day, the greatest misfortune to have befallen humanity.

Christianity opposes all forms of intellectual well-being— it can only use a form of reasoning that is flawed and sickly, which it presents as "Christian reasoning." It aligns itself with everything irrational and curses the "intellect" as though it were a sin, condemning the pride of a healthy, functioning mind. Since Christianity inherently thrives on sickness, the Christian concept of "faith" must also be considered a form of sickness. The church, therefore, bans all direct, honest, and scientific paths to understanding as dangerous and forbidden. From the very beginning, doubt itself is treated as a sin.

The complete lack of psychological clarity in priests is immediately apparent just by observing them—it is a direct symptom of their state of décadence. Similar traits can be seen in hysterical women and in children suffering from physical and emotional weakness: a distorted instinct, a delight in lying simply for the sake of lying, and an inability to see or move straightforwardly. Faith, in this sense, represents a willful refusal to acknowledge the truth. The pietist or priest, whether male or female, is fundamentally dishonest because they are ill; their instincts demand that truth must never be allowed to win. For the believer, anything that leads to sickness is considered good, while everything that stems from vitality, strength, and abundance is deemed evil. This instinct to lie is what marks someone destined to become a theologian.

Another sign of the theologian is their complete unsuitability for philology. By philology, I mean the art of reading carefully and thoughtfully—the ability to understand facts without twisting their meaning or abandoning caution, patience, and subtlety in interpretation. Philology, in this sense, is the practice of restraint in understanding. This applies whether one is reading books, interpreting news, analyzing major historical events, or even examining weather statistics—let alone the so-called "salvation of the soul."

The way theologians, whether in Berlin or in Rome, explain a passage of scripture, a personal experience, or even a military victory by calling upon the lofty imagery of the Psalms of David is so absurdly bold that it could drive a philologist mad. And what can one say when pietists and other such simple- minded folks claim that the "finger of God" is responsible for turning their mundane, insignificant lives into miracles of "grace," "providence," and "salvation"? Even the smallest amount of intellectual effort—or common decency—should be enough to expose the childishness and unworthiness of such claims.

Imagine encountering a god who always cured your cold at just the right time or arranged for you to step into a carriage precisely as it started to rain. Such a god would appear so ridiculous that he would have to be abolished, even if he truly existed. A god reduced to the role of a household servant, a mailman, or a walking almanac—at his core, he would be nothing more than a name for the most foolish kind of chance.

The idea of "Divine Providence," which is still believed by a significant portion of educated Germans, is itself one of the strongest arguments against the existence of God. It is so absurd that no stronger argument against God could be imagined. And if nothing else, it is a powerful argument against the Germans themselves.

It is far from true that martyrs prove the truth of a cause; in fact, I would argue that martyrs have nothing to do with truth at all. The way a martyr loudly proclaims what he believes to be true, throwing it in the face of the world, shows such a low level of intellectual honesty and such an inability to engage with the problem of "truth" that there is no need to refute him. Truth is not something one person possesses while another lacks; this kind of thinking is the mark of peasants or peasant-like apostles such as Luther. The more intellectually honest a person is, the more modest and careful they will be about claiming knowledge. To truly know even a few things and to gracefully admit ignorance about everything else—that is the hallmark of someone with intellectual discipline.

The way prophets, sectarians, free-thinkers, Socialists, and church leaders understand "truth" is nothing more than proof that they have failed to begin even the smallest intellectual discipline or self-control required to discover real truth. The deaths of martyrs, we should note, have been unfortunate events in history. They have led people astray. The simple-minded conclusion that many idiots, women, and common folk draw—that there must be value in a cause for which someone dies, or for which, as in early Christianity, people willingly seek death—has done immense harm to the pursuit of facts and the spirit of investigation. Martyrs have not helped truth; they have harmed it. Even today, the mere fact of persecution gives unwarranted respect to the most baseless sects and beliefs.

But why should this be? Does the value of a cause increase simply because someone has died for it? An error made honorable through martyrdom is still an error—it has merely gained a dangerous charm. Do you theologians imagine we will grant you the privilege of being martyred for your lies? The best way to deal with a cause is to respectfully put it aside and let it fade. That is also the best way to deal with theologians. This was the great, world-shaping mistake of every persecutor: they gave undue respect to the causes they opposed, gifting them the seductive appeal of martyrdom. Even now, women kneel before an error because they have been told that someone died on a cross for it. But is the cross an argument?

There is only one figure who has said what has needed to be said about this for thousands of years—Zarathustra. They left bloody marks along their paths and convinced themselves that blood proved the truth of their beliefs. But blood is the worst evidence for truth. It corrupts even the purest teachings, filling hearts with madness and hatred. What does it prove when someone walks through fire for their beliefs? Far more meaningful is when a teaching emerges from within one's own fire.

Do not be deceived: great intellects are always skeptical. Zarathustra himself is a skeptic. The strength and freedom that come from intellectual power— especially an overflowing abundance of it—express themselves as skepticism. People with rigid convictions are not the ones who shape what is truly fundamental in values or lack of values. Those who cling to convictions are like prisoners; they cannot see far enough ahead, nor can they see what lies beneath them. By contrast, someone who wishes to speak meaningfully about value and non-value must be able to view hundreds of convictions below and behind them, understanding their place from a great height.

A mind that strives for greatness and seeks the means to achieve it must necessarily be skeptical. True strength and independence of thought require freedom from all forms of rigid belief. This grand passion, which serves as both the foundation and the driving force of a skeptic's existence, is more enlightened and more commanding than the skeptic himself. It enlists every part of his intellect into its service, makes him unsparing, and gives him the courage to use methods others might call unholy. At times, it may even permit him to adopt convictions, but only as tools. Conviction becomes a means to an end, a device that can accomplish much when wielded wisely. However, a grand passion never submits to conviction—it rules over it as a sovereign.

On the other hand, the need for faith, for something absolute that demands unwavering belief, reveals a weakness. The "man of faith," no matter what he believes in, is fundamentally dependent. Such a person cannot set himself as his own goal, nor can he find purpose within himself. The believer does not belong to himself; he is merely a means to someone else's end, waiting to be used. His instincts lead him to exalt an ethic of self-denial above all else. He embraces it willingly, driven by prudence, experience, and even vanity. Every kind of faith is, at its core, a symptom of self-denial and self-alienation.

When one considers how vital it is for the majority of people to have external rules and restraints to guide them, it becomes clear why belief and conviction are so necessary. For the weak- willed—and especially for women—order, control, or even a higher form of slavery is the only condition under which they can thrive. Convictions provide these individuals with structure and support; they are, in a sense, their backbone. To maintain this rigid framework, such people must avoid seeing many things and remain entirely partial. They become completely absorbed in their chosen cause, judging all values with unshakable certainty. But these very traits place them in opposition to the truthful person, who values openness and inquiry.

The believer is not free to ask whether something is "true" or "not true" based on his own conscience. To do so would be to undermine his entire foundation. His pathological narrowness of vision turns him into a fanatic— examples include Savonarola, Luther, Rousseau, Robespierre, and Saint-Simon. These figures stand as stark contrasts to the strong and liberated spirit. Yet the grandiose postures of such sickly minds, these intellectual epileptics, often captivate the masses. Fanatics are dramatic, and humanity is more inclined to admire a striking pose than to listen to well-reasoned arguments.

Let us take another step into the psychology of conviction and "faith." Some time ago, I raised the question of whether convictions might actually be more dangerous enemies of truth than lies. Today, I want to state this question more directly: is there any real difference between a lie and a conviction? Most people believe there is—but then, most people believe many things that are questionable. Every conviction has a history. It begins in primitive forms, passes through stages of doubt and error, and only later becomes a firm belief. What if falsehood itself is simply one of these early stages of conviction?

Sometimes, all it takes is a change of people: what the father believed to be a lie becomes a conviction for the son.

I call it lying when someone refuses to see what is right in front of them or refuses to acknowledge it for what it truly is. It doesn't matter whether this lie is spoken aloud or kept within—it remains a lie. The most common lie is the one a person tells themselves; deceiving others is comparatively rare. This deliberate blindness, this refusal to see the world as it is, is often the first requirement for belonging to any group or party. To be a partisan is to be a liar. Consider, for example, the German historians who are convinced that Rome represented tyranny, while the Germanic peoples brought liberty to the world. What is the difference between this conviction and a lie?

Is it any surprise that all partisans—like those German historians— instinctively cling to moral platitudes? Morality survives largely because party members of every kind feel they need it constantly. "This is our conviction: we proclaim it to the world; we are willing to live and die for it. Let us respect everyone who holds strong convictions!" I have actually heard this argument from anti-Semites. But the opposite is true! An anti-Semite does not become more respectable simply because he lies out of principle.

Priests, who are more cunning in these matters, recognize the problem with convictions—that is, with lies elevated to principles because they serve a purpose. To avoid this issue, they have borrowed a clever tactic from the Jews: they introduce concepts like "God," "the will of God," and "revelation." Kant, with his categorical imperative, took a similar approach. According to this reasoning, there are questions about truth or falsehood that humans cannot answer. The most important questions, the ultimate problems of value, lie beyond human comprehension. To know the limits of reason—this, they claim, is true philosophy.

Why, then, did God reveal his will to humanity? Surely, God would not do something unnecessary. The argument goes that humans could not figure out for themselves what is good or evil, so God had to teach them his will. From this perspective, the priest does not lie. The questions of "true" or "false" do not apply to the matters the priest discusses. After all, how can one lie about something if it is impossible to know the truth of it? Thus, the priest becomes merely the voice of God.

This kind of priestly reasoning is not unique to Judaism or Christianity. It is a hallmark of the priestly mindset throughout history, whether among ancient pagans or the priests of later décadence. (Pagans, by the way, are those who say "yes" to life and use "God" as a term to affirm all things.) Terms like "law," "the will of God," "holy books," and "inspiration" are nothing more than tools by which priests gain and maintain power. These concepts are the foundation of all priestly institutions and of every priestly or priestly-philosophical form of government.

The "holy lie" is not exclusive to one religion. It appears in the teachings of Confucius, the Code of Manu, the Quran, and the Christian church—and even Plato was not free of it. Whenever you hear the phrase "Truth is here," you can be certain of one thing: the priest is lying.

In the end, the question becomes: what is the purpose of lying? My main objection to Christianity lies in the fact that its so- called "holy" ends are nowhere to be seen. Instead, it leads only to destructive outcomes: poisoning minds, spreading slander, denying life, despising the body, and degrading humanity with the concept of sin. Because its ends are harmful, its methods are equally harmful.

In contrast, I have an entirely different reaction when reading the Code of Manu. This work is incomparably more intellectual and refined; it would be an insult to intelligence to even mention it in the same breath as the Bible. The reason is clear: the Code of Manu is rooted in true philosophy, not the foul mix of rabbinical legalism and superstition that pervades the Bible. It offers even the most discerning psychologist something of substance to explore. Most importantly, it stands fundamentally apart from any kind of Bible. In the Code of Manu, the nobles, philosophers, and warriors maintain their rightful authority over the masses. The text is filled with noble values, a sense of completeness, and an affirmation of life. It reflects a triumphant, self-assured embrace of existence—the entire work seems to glow with sunlight.

In the Code of Manu, the topics that Christianity treats with crude vulgarity—such as procreation, women, and marriage—are addressed with earnestness, respect, and a deep sense of love and trust. How can anyone seriously give children and women a book like the Bible, which contains repulsive teachings such as: "To avoid fornication, let every man have his own wife, and let ever y woman have her own husband; ... it is better to marry than to burn"? Is it possible to call oneself a Christian while accepting a worldview that corrupts the origin of humanity with the doctrine of the immaculata conceptio, reducing it to something base and shameful?

I know of no text that speaks with more delicacy and respect about women than the Code of Manu. These ancient sages and elders have a gallantry toward women that is nearly impossible to match. Consider this passage: "The mouth of a woman, the breasts of a maiden, the prayer of a child, and the smoke of sacrifice are always pure." Or this one: "There is nothing purer than the light of the sun, the shadow cast by a cow, air , water , fir e, and the breath of a maiden." And finally, this striking statement— perhaps another holy lie, but a charming one nonetheless: "All the openings of the body above the navel are pure, and all below are impure. Only in the maiden is the You can clearly see the unholiness of Christianity's methods by comparing its goals with those of the Code of Manu. When you place these two entirely opposite sets of goals side by side and examine them closely, the contrast becomes undeniable. Any serious critique of Christianity must expose its means and ends as contemptible. A book of laws like the Code of Manu originates from the same source as any truly good legal code—it represents the accumulated wisdom, insight, and ethical experimentation of many centuries. It brings long processes of trial and error to a conclusion; it codifies rather than creates.

Such codification relies on an essential principle: the methods used to establish the authority of a hard-won truth must differ completely from those used to prove or explain it. A lawbook does not include arguments for its laws, nor does it recount their utility or origins. To do so would undermine the imperative tone, the commanding "thou shall" on which obedience depends. This is where the issue lies. At a certain point in a people's development, the wisest among them—those with the most hindsight and foresight—declare that the period of experimentation in determining how life should be lived has ended. Their task then becomes to gather as much as possible from the lessons learned through these hard and often painful experiences. The priority shifts to ensuring stability and avoiding further experimentation, preventing values from remaining in constant flux, endlessly questioned and redefined.

Two strategies support this goal. First, revelation: the claim that the laws are not of human origin but were given by divine power. This suggests the laws were not discovered through trial and error but were instead perfect, eternal, and miraculous from the start. Second, tradition: the belief that the laws have stood unchanged since the dawn of time and that questioning them dishonors one's ancestors. By grounding the authority of law in the idea that it was both given by God and upheld by the forefathers, a powerful double layer of legitimacy is created.

The higher purpose of these strategies is to slowly shift people's focus away from thinking consciously about right and wrong and instead instill instincts that operate automatically. Such automatism is essential for achieving mastery and perfection in the art of living. Writing a lawbook like the Code of Manu is an effort to provide a society with the tools to achieve future greatness and aspire to mastery in life. For this to happen, adherence to the law must become unconscious—this is the purpose of every so- called holy lie.

The caste system, the highest and most central law of the Code of Manu, does not represent arbitrary invention. It reflects a natural law of the highest order, one that no modern ideas or human whims can alter. In every healthy society, three fundamental types of people naturally emerge, each distinct yet interdependent. These groups differ in their physical and intellectual characteristics, their roles in society, and their sense of fulfillment. Nature, not Manu, determines who belongs to these castes: those with superior intellect, those with physical strength and temperament, and the majority who display mediocrity. The first two groups are the chosen few, while the last represents the larger mass.

The highest caste—the smallest and most exceptional group—embodies perfection and possesses privileges unavailable to the rest. This caste represents happiness, beauty, and all that is truly good in life. Only the most intellectually gifted have the right to beauty and nobility; only they can transform goodness into a strength rather than a weakness. Pulchrum est paucorum hominum—beauty belongs to the few. For these superior individuals, vulgarity, pessimism, or indignation at the imperfections of the world are unworthy traits. Indignation and pessimism are the attitudes of the Chandala. For the most intellectual among us, the world appears perfect. They understand that even what is beneath them, what is distant, what is flawed— even the Chandala—is part of that perfection.

The most intelligent and strongest individuals find joy where others would only see hardship. They thrive in challenges, embrace self-discipline, and transform asceticism into a natural instinct. For them, difficult tasks are privileges, and they find pleasure in carrying burdens that would crush anyone else. Even the pursuit of knowledge becomes a form of asceticism for them. These individuals are the most honorable of all, but they are also the most cheerful and charming. They rule not because they desire power but because they embody it; it is impossible for them to occupy a subordinate position.

The second caste consists of those who uphold the law and maintain order—noble warriors, protectors, and judges, with the king as their highest expression. This caste serves as the practical arm of the intellectual elite, taking on the more arduous tasks of governance and carrying out their directives. They are the followers and loyal enforcers of the highest caste's vision.

Nothing in this system is arbitrary. To suggest otherwise is to dishonor nature. The caste system reflects life's fundamental principles, ensuring societal stability and allowing for the development of higher types. Inequality of rights is not a flaw—it is a necessity for the existence of rights at all. A right is always a privilege, aligned with one's place in the natural order. Even mediocrity has its privileges.

Life becomes more demanding as one ascends to higher ranks. The air grows colder, and the weight of responsibility increases. A high civilization is like a pyramid—it can only stand on a broad base of mediocrity. This foundation is crucial, as most professions—craftsmanship, commerce, agriculture, science, and much of art—require mediocre abilities and aspirations. Exceptional individuals would find such roles unsuitable. Mediocrity is a form of happiness for the majority, as they are naturally inclined toward specialization and mastery of a single task. To despise mediocrity is unworthy of a deep thinker; it is the necessary condition for the emergence of the exceptional.

When exceptional individuals treat those of average ability with greater care and consideration than they do their equals, it is not merely out of kindness but a recognition of duty.

Who do I despise most among today's crowds? The rabble of Socialists, those preachers to the Chandala who corrupt the instincts of the working man. They make him resentful, envious, and dissatisfied with his simple, contented life. They teach him revenge and poison his natural sense of joy. The true injustice is not in unequal rights but in the lie of "equal" rights. What do I call bad? I have already answered: anything born of weakness, envy, or revenge. The anarchist and the Christian share the same origin.

In the end, the purpose behind a lie makes all the difference. Does it serve to preserve or to destroy? Christianity and anarchism are alike in their ultimate goal: both aim for destruction. History provides overwhelming evidence of this. Compare Christianity with the Code of Manu, which sought to turn the conditions for life's flourishing into an enduring social order. Christianity, in contrast, defined its mission as destroying such an order—precisely because life thrived under it. The Code of Manu represents the careful application of wisdom gathered over centuries, a means of harvesting the fullest possible benefits from life's long and difficult experiments. Christianity, on the other hand, destroyed that harvest in a single night.

Consider the imperium Romanum, the Roman Empire—a monumental achievement of organization under the most challenging conditions. It was unparalleled in history, a masterpiece of order and strength, standing as a model against which everything before and after seems crude and clumsy. Yet the so-called "holy" anarchists of Christianity turned the destruction of this empire into a sacred duty. They sought to dismantle "the world"—their term for the Roman Empire—until nothing remained. Even crude conquerors like the Germans and their ilk were able to take control of the ruins.

The Christian and the anarchist are both décadents. Neither is capable of contributing anything constructive; instead, they act only to dissolve, poison, and weaken. Their hatred is directed at everything strong, enduring, and life- affirming. Christianity was the vampire that drained the lifeblood of the Roman Empire. Overnight, it wiped out the vast achievements of the Romans, who had cultivated the soil for a great culture that could endure and develop over centuries. This simple fact is still not fully understood.

The Roman Empire, as we know it from history and from the increasing understanding of its provinces, was only the beginning of something even greater. It was a work of grand-scale artistry, destined to prove its worth over millennia. To this day, nothing comparable has been built—or even imagined— on such a scale, with such an eternal vision. This Roman organization was so robust that it could survive even poor leadership. The personalities of individual emperors mattered little—this is the hallmark of truly great architecture. But not even this structure could withstand the most corrupting force of all: Christianity.

These stealthy Christians, creeping through society under the cover of night and secrecy, drained people of their interest in real, tangible things and their instincts for reality. This cowardly, soft, and deceptive group gradually alienated every noble and virtuous soul that had once aligned its purpose with Rome. Concepts like hypocrisy, secrecy, and dark ideas about the sacrifice of the innocent and mystical union through blood-drinking became dominant. At the heart of it all was the slow-burning revenge of the Chandala—the lowest, most resentful instincts turned into power. Rome succumbed to the very type of religion that Epicurus had fought against.

To understand what Epicurus battled, one need only read Lucretius. Epicurus did not oppose paganism; he fought against what we now recognize as Christianity—the corruption of human souls through ideas of guilt, punishment, and immortality. He stood against the cults of the underground, the hidden Christianity that was already taking root. Denying the concept of immortality was, for Epicurus, a genuine act of salvation. His victory was clear: in Rome, every respectable mind was Epicurean—until Paul arrived.

Paul embodied the Chandala hatred of Rome and the world, wielding it with a genius for destruction. As the quintessential Jew,

Paul recognized how the small Christian sect could ignite a "world fire." With the symbol of "God on the cross," he unified the subversive elements and anarchist movements across the empire, forging them into an immense force. "Salvation is of the Jews"—this became the Christian formula.

Christianity was the culmination of all underground cults, including those of Osiris, the Great Mother, and Mithras. Paul's genius lay in recognizing this and exploiting it. With ruthless disregard for truth, he attributed to the "Saviour" ideas that would resonate with adherents of every Chandala religion. He reshaped Christ into something even a priest of Mithras could accept. This was Paul's "revelation" at Damascus: he realized that belief in immortality was essential to devalue life on earth, that the concept of "hell" could conquer Rome, and that the notion of an otherworldly "beyond" would spell the death of this world.

Nihilist and Christian—they rhyme in German, and they do much more than rhyme.

The entire labor of the ancient world was wasted. I can hardly find words to describe the outrage this inspires in me. When we consider that all this effort was only the foundation for a project meant to last thousands of years, the entire purpose of antiquity seems to vanish! Why did we have the Greeks? Why did we have the Romans? All the essential tools for a scholarly culture were already in place. The methods of science were developed, humanity had mastered the unmatched art of reading with purpose—a vital skill for maintaining a cultural tradition and uniting the sciences. The natural sciences had already aligned with mathematics and mechanics, progressing steadily. The sense of fact, that most valuable sense of all, had established its schools, and its traditions had lasted for centuries.

Do we fully grasp this? Every critical element necessary to begin great work was ready—and the most essential part, methods, was already there. These methods are the hardest to develop and the most fiercely resisted by laziness and habit. What we have painstakingly reclaimed today, through relentless discipline and effort—despite lingering bad instincts and remnants of Christian tendencies within us—was already present two thousand years ago. Keen observation, a steady hand, patience, attention to detail, and a commitment to truth—all these existed long before. Beyond that, there was a refined sense of tact and taste, not as mere mental exercises or the awkward pretensions of "German" culture, but as something deeply embodied, instinctive, and real. All of it—lost! Overnight, it was reduced to a memory.

The Greeks! The Romans! Their instinctive nobility, their refined taste, their disciplined inquiry, their genius for organization, their dedication to securing humanity's future, and their resounding affirmation of life—all embodied in the Roman Empire, a reality that transcended art, becoming truth and life itself. All of it swept away in a single night—not by a natural disaster, nor by the crushing feet of barbaric invaders like the Teutons. No, it was undone by cunning, sneaky, bloodless parasites. It wasn't conquered; it was drained dry. Hidden resentment and petty envy took control. Everything wretched, sickly, and filled with malice—the entire ghetto of the soul—rose to power.

If you read any Christian agitator, like St. Augustine, you can clearly sense the kind of vile characters that rose to prominence. Yet, it would be a mistake to think these leaders of Christianity lacked intelligence. On the contrary, they were incredibly clever— so clever that their cunning seemed almost saintly. What they lacked, however, were respectable, honest, and clean instincts. Between us, they were not even men in the truest sense. If Islam holds Christianity in contempt, it has every right to do so. At least Islam assumes it is dealing with men.

Christianity destroyed the entire harvest of ancient civilization for us. Later, it also wiped out the entire cultural legacy of the Muslim world. The magnificent Moorish culture in Spain, which was closer to our senses and taste than ancient Greece and Rome, was crushed. I won't say by whom. Why? Because its origins lay in noble and manly instincts. It affirmed life, even the rare, refined luxury of Moorish life. Yet the Crusaders waged war against something that deserved their reverence, something so advanced that even the culture of the nineteenth century pales in comparison. What did they seek? Booty. The Orient was wealthy. Let us be clear: the Crusades were no more than organized piracy. The German nobility, with its Viking roots, fit naturally into this role. The Church knew precisely how to manipulate them.

The German noble was always the Church's loyal guard, always in service to its worst instincts—and well-paid for his loyalty. It was through the strength of German swords, the sacrifice of

German blood, and the courage of German warriors that the Church succeeded in waging its relentless war against everything noble on Earth. This raises painful questions. The German nobility stands outside the history of higher culture. The reasons are obvious. Christianity and alcohol—the two great forces of corruption.

In essence, there is no meaningful choice between Islam and Christianity, just as there is none between an Arab and a Jew. The decision has already been made; no one can pretend otherwise. Either a person is a Chandala, or they are not. "War to the knife with Rome! Peace and friendship with Islam!" This was the sentiment and action of Frederick II, that great free spirit, that genius among German emperors. What does it say that a German must first be a genius, a free spirit, before they can even feel decently? I cannot fathom how a German could ever truly feel Christian.

The entire labor of the Renaissance, the last great harvest of civilization in Europe, was destroyed—and the Germans were responsible for it. Do we truly understand, or will we ever understand, what the Renaissance was? It was the reversal of Christian values, an attempt, using every available instinct, resource, and genius, to bring forth the triumph of nobler, higher values. This was the greatest war in history, the most crucial question ever posed—it is my question too. The Renaissance was a direct and fundamental attack on Christianity, aimed at its very core. It sought to replace its values with those that affirmed life, embedding these ideals into the instincts and desires of those at the center of power.

I imagine what could have been—a vision so enchanting, so luminous with beauty and art, that it seems otherworldly. It was a spectacle of significance and paradox, rich enough to make the gods of Olympus erupt in eternal laughter: imagine Cæsar Borgia as pope! Do you understand now? That would have been the triumph I long for even today. It would have swept Christianity away forever.

But what happened? A German monk named Luther came to Rome. With all the bitterness of a failed priest, he rebelled against the Renaissance. Instead of appreciating the miracle unfolding before him—the conquest of Christianity in its very heart—his hatred grew. Religious men think only of themselves. Luther saw only the corruption of the papacy, failing to see that the old sin, the original corruption that was Christianity itself, was no longer sitting on the papal throne. In its place was life, vitality, a triumphant yes to all that is bold, beautiful, and exalted.

Luther attacked this miracle and restored the church. He crushed the Renaissance, rendering it meaningless—a grand, wasted effort. Oh, what the Germans have cost us! Their work has always been futility. The Reformation, Leibniz, Kant, so-called German philosophy, the wars of "liberation," the empire—all of it substitutes for what was once possible, for what is now irretrievable. These Germans, I confess, are my enemies. I despise their unclean thinking, their cowardice before an honest yes or no. For a thousand years, everything they have touched has been tangled and corrupted. They are responsible for Europe's half-measures and compromises, for its sickness—and for Protestantism, the filthiest and most incurable form of Christianity.

If humanity can never rid itself of Christianity, it will be the Germans' fault.

And now I come to my final judgment. I condemn Christianity. I accuse the Christian church of the most profound corruption imaginable. It seeks to bring about the worst kind of decay. It has corrupted everything it has touched, turning every value into worthlessness, every truth into a lie, every act of integrity into spiritual depravity. And let no one speak to me of the "humanitarian blessings" of Christianity! The church's very existence depends on suffering. It creates suffering to sustain itself, to ensure its survival.

Consider the "worm of sin." This misery was a gift from the church to humanity. Or the idea of "equality of souls before God," which served as a tool for the resentment of the base-minded. This explosive idea has led to revolutions, to the modern drive to overthrow entire social structures. Christian dynamite!

Christianity's so-called "humanitarianism" is nothing but a mockery. It has turned humanity into a contradiction, a self-destructive force, driven by lies at any cost. It has cultivated contempt for all that is good, honest, and natural. Its ideals—anemic and "holy"—have drained life of its vitality, love, and hope. The notion of an afterlife denies reality itself. The cross has become the symbol of the most insidious conspiracy ever devised—against health, beauty, intelligence, kindness, and life itself.

This is my eternal accusation against Christianity. I will write it on every wall, in letters so large that even the blind can see. I call Christianity the greatest curse, the deepest corruption, the most insidious revenge. It spares no means— however poisonous, hidden, or small—in its war against life. I call it the one immortal stain on the human race.

And yet humanity marks time from the dies nefastus, the day this calamity began—the first day of Christianity. Why not from its end? Why not start today, with the reversal of all values?

Twilight of the Idols

Friedrich Nietzsche

Translated by Tim Zengerink

Prologue

To stay cheerful while dealing with a grim and extremely serious task is no small artistic skill. Yet, what could be more essential than cheerfulness? Nothing is ever truly successful unless vibrant energy has helped create it. Only extra strength proves real power. A rethinking of all values—a question so dark and massive that it even casts a shadow over the one who raises it—is a task so heavy with consequence that anyone who takes it on must occasionally step into the sunlight to shake off a seriousness that becomes overwhelming, unbearably so. This goal justifies any method, and every event along the way becomes an unexpected benefit. Above all, war. War has always been the ultimate strategy for those who have delved too deeply into their own thoughts or grown too profound; a wound provokes the strength to heal.

For many years, I've lived by a saying, though I'll keep its origin a secret from curious scholars: "The spirit grows, virtue flourishes through a wound."

At other times, another way to recover, one I prefer even more, is to question idols. There are more idols than truths in the world, and this is why I have such a "sharp eye" for this world. It is also why I have such a "sharp ear." To ask questions of these idols with a hammer, and maybe hear that familiar hollow sound that comes from something empty—what joy this brings to someone who listens carefully, even with a mind attuned to what isn't spoken. For an old psychologist and Pied Piper like me, even the things that wish to remain silent cannot help but reveal themselves.

This book, as its title suggests, is mainly a kind of relaxation, a flash of light, a playful escape for a psychologist in his free time. But could it also be a new kind of battle? Are we once again questioning new idols? This small work is a bold declaration of war. As for questioning idols, this time, it isn't just the idols of the present day but the eternal ones that are struck with a hammer, as though they were tuning forks. These idols are certainly the oldest, the most self-assured, and the most puffed-up. None are more hollow. Yet this doesn't change the fact that they are believed in more than any others. They are never even called idols—at least, not the most revered ones among them.

Chapter 1
Maxims – And Missiles

Idleness is the root of all psychology. What? Does that mean psychology is a kind of vice? Even the bravest among us rarely has the courage to face what they truly know. Aristotle said that to live alone, a person must be either an animal or a god. But there's a third option missing: one must be both—a philosopher.

"All truth is simple."—Isn't that a double lie? Sometimes, I choose to remain blind to certain things. Wisdom places limits even on knowledge. A person recovers best from their extraordinary nature—from their intellect—by letting their instincts take over for a while.

So which is it? Is humanity just a mistake made by God? Or is God simply a mistake made by humanity?

From life's school of war: That which doesn't kill me makes me stronger.

Help yourself, and others will help you too. This is the true meaning of loving your neighbor.

A person should never be ashamed of their actions. Once a deed is done, they shouldn't disown it. Feelings of guilt are indecent.

Can a donkey be tragic? To be crushed under a burden it can neither carry nor throw off—isn't this the fate of a philosopher?

If someone knows why they exist, they can figure out how to live. Happiness isn't the goal of life; only the English make that their aim.

Man created woman—out of what? Out of a rib taken from his god, from his "ideal."

What are you searching for? Do you wish to multiply yourself tenfold, a hundredfold? Are you seeking followers? Look for zeros, not people!

Those of us who belong to the future, like myself, are harder to understand than those who mirror their time, but we're treated with more respect. Simply put: we are never fully understood— that's why we have authority.

On women: "Truth? Oh, you don't understand truth! Isn't it an insult to all our sense of modesty?"

There is an artist after my own heart, humble in his needs. He only desires two things: his bread and his art—panem et Circem.

Those who cannot impose their will onto the world at least give it some meaning. They believe there's already a will within it. (This is the essence of faith.)

What? You chose virtue and a heart full of passion, yet you still glance enviously at the rewards of the shameless? But by choosing virtue, you've renounced all "advantages"... (this belongs nailed to the door of an anti-Semite).

The perfect woman writes literature as if it were a minor vice, a passing experiment, all the while looking around to see if anyone is noticing—and hoping that someone does.

One should only choose situations where fake virtues are unnecessary, where, like a tightrope walker on their rope, one must either fall, stand firm, or find a way out.

"Evil men have no songs."—How, then, do the Russians have songs?

"German intellect"—for eighteen years this phrase has been a contradiction in terms.

When a man tries to find the origins of everything, he becomes like a crab. The historian always looks backward; eventually, he even starts believing backward.

Feeling content keeps a person from catching a cold. Has a woman who knew she was well-dressed ever gotten sick?—No, not even if she was barely covered by rags.

I distrust anyone who builds elaborate systems and avoid them. The desire to create a system shows a lack of honesty.

Man thinks women are profound—why? Because he can never fully understand them. Women are not even shallow.

When a woman has masculine virtues, she can make you want to run away.

When she doesn't have any masculine virtues, she runs away herself.

"How often conscience used to sting in the past! It must have had strong teeth back then! But today, what's gone wrong?"—A question for the dentist.

Mistakes made in haste rarely come alone. The first time, a person always overdoes things. Because of that, they make a second mistake, where they end up doing too little.

When a worm is stepped on, it curls up. This shows its caution—it lowers the chances of being stepped on again. In moral terms, this is called humility.

There is a kind of hatred for lies and deceit that comes from a sharp sense of humor. There is also the same hatred, but born from cowardice—the fear of lying because it's forbidden by divine law. Too cowardly to lie...

What tiny things bring happiness! The sound of bagpipes. Life without music would be a mistake. The German even imagines God as a singer.

"One can only think and write while sitting" (G. Flaubert). Now I've got you, you nihilist! Living a sedentary life is the true sin against the Holy Spirit. Only the thoughts that come to you while walking have any real worth.

Sometimes, we psychologists are like restless horses, growing uneasy as we see our own shadow rise and fall before us. A psychologist must look away from himself if he wants to see anything clearly.

Do we immoralists harm virtue in any way? No more than anarchists harm royalty. In fact, only after being shot at have princes returned to their thrones with greater strength. The moral of the story: morality must be tested by attack.

Are you rushing ahead?—Are you doing so as a leader or as an exception? Or perhaps you're just running away?... This is the first question of conscience.

Are you authentic, or are you just acting? Are you the real thing or merely a representative of it? Or, worse, are you just a copy of an actor?... This is the second question of conscience.

The disappointed man says: "I searched for great men, but all I found were imitators of their ideals."

Are you someone who observes from the sidelines, or someone who lends a hand? Or are you someone who looks away or even turns their back? This is the third question of conscience.

Do you want to follow, lead, or walk your own path alone? A person must know what they desire—and that they truly desire something. This is the fourth question of conscience.

They were merely rungs on my ladder, steps I used to climb higher. For that purpose, I had to move past them. But they thought I wanted to stop and rest on them.

Does it matter whether others agree that I'm right? I am far too right. And the one who laughs best today will also laugh last.

The formula for my happiness: a Yes, a No, a straight path, and a goal.

Chapter 2
The Problem of Socrates

Throughout history, the wisest minds have always agreed on one thing: life is not good. No matter the time or place, their words have been the same— filled with doubt, sadness, weariness, and even hostility toward life. Even Socrates, in his final moments, said: "To live is to be sick for a long time. I owe a cock to the god Æsculapius." Even Socrates had had enough of life. But what does that mean? What does it suggest? In the past, people would have said—and it was said loudly, especially by the Pessimists—"Surely there must be some truth in this! The agreement of the wisest proves it." Should we say the same thing today? Can we?

Instead, we now respond: "Surely there must be some sickness here." These so-called great thinkers of every age need to be examined more closely! Could it be that they all shared something physically or mentally fragile, something decadent? Is it possible that wisdom comes to earth like a crow drawn to the faint smell of decay?

This bold and disrespectful thought—that these great thinkers were actually signs of decline—first came to me in connection with a case where both scholarly and common opinions stood firmly against my own view. I came to see Socrates and Plato as symptoms of a culture in collapse, as tools of the disintegration of Greece, as fake Greeks, even anti-Greek (this was my argument in The Birth of Tragedy, 1872). The agreement of these sages— the consensus sapientium, as I increasingly realized—was not evidence that they were right about life. Instead, it suggested that they all shared some underlying physical or mental weakness that made them take the same negative stance toward life. Their judgments about life, whether positive or negative, are not true in themselves. Their value lies only in what they reveal about their creators. Such judgments are symptoms, and nothing more. In themselves, these opinions about life are meaningless.

You must grasp this critical idea: the value of life cannot be measured. A living person cannot judge it because they are too involved—they are part of the conflict, not a neutral observer. A dead person cannot judge it either, for obvious reasons. For a philosopher to see life's value as a problem suggests something is flawed in their perspective. It raises a question about their wisdom—or even their lack of wisdom.

Could it be that all these so-called great thinkers were not only signs of decline but also not wise at all? Let us now return to the case of Socrates.

Judging by his origins, Socrates came from the lowest social class—Socrates was part of the common mob. You know, and can still observe in the descriptions of him, how remarkably ugly he was. In Greek society, where beauty was highly valued, ugliness was not only an objection but often taken as evidence of deeper flaws. Was Socrates truly Greek? Ugliness often reflects a thwarted or disrupted development, or perhaps one stunted by mixed influences. In other cases, it signals a degenerative decline. Anthropologists who study criminals say that the typical criminal is often ugly: monstrum in fronte, monstrum in animo—a monster in appearance, a monster in spirit. Does that mean the criminal is a degenerate? Was Socrates, then, a typical criminal?

This idea wouldn't conflict with the infamous judgment made about Socrates by a physiognomist, which deeply upset his friends. While passing through Athens, a foreigner skilled in reading faces told Socrates directly that he was a monster and that his body harbored every kind of vice and passion. Socrates simply replied: "You know me, sir!"

Not only do Socrates' wild and chaotic instincts point to degeneracy, but so do his extreme reliance on logic and the peculiar malice that seemed tied to his disfigured features. We must also not forget his auditory hallucinations, which he religiously interpreted as "the demon of Socrates." Everything about him was excessive, exaggerated, almost comical—a caricature. His nature was also secretive, filled with hidden motives and underlying currents. I attempt to understand the strange personality behind the Socratic equation: Reason = Virtue = Happiness. This is perhaps the strangest formula ever devised, and it fundamentally contradicted the instincts of the earlier Greeks.

With Socrates, Greek taste shifted toward dialectics. What happened as a result? First, the refined and noble taste of earlier Greek culture was overthrown. Dialectics allowed the common crowd to rise to prominence. Before Socrates, the art of argument was avoided in polite society; it was considered improper and even disgraceful. Young men were warned against indulging in it. Arguing and constantly explaining oneself were seen as suspicious behaviors. Honest people, like honest things, don't need to constantly justify themselves. It was considered poor form to put everything on display. Anything that required proof was seen as having little inherent value.

In societies where authority was respected, where people gave commands rather than explanations, the dialectician was viewed as a kind of jester. People laughed at him and didn't take him seriously. Yet Socrates, a master of dialectics, managed to make people take him seriously. How did this happen? What was going on?

A person resorts to dialectics only when they have no other options available. People know that using it creates suspicion and that it's not particularly persuasive. Nothing is more easily overturned than the effect of a dialectical argument—this is clear from the experience of any debate or discussion. Dialectics can only be a last resort, the weapon of someone who has no other tools left. One must be desperate to demand their rights this way; otherwise, they wouldn't need to rely on it. This is why the Jews became skilled in dialectics. Reynard the Fox was a dialectician. But what about Socrates—was he one too?

Is Socratic irony a form of rebellion, a weapon of resentment from the common people? Did Socrates, oppressed and suffering, enjoy his inherent cruelty by inflicting sharp attacks through his arguments? Was he taking revenge on the noblemen he managed to charm? As a dialectician, a person wields a ruthless weapon; they can dominate and even humiliate their opponents. By defeating someone in debate, the dialectician undermines them; their victory is always a compromise. The dialectician forces their opponent to prove they're not a fool, which often provokes anger and renders them defenseless. A dialectician paralyzes their opponent's thinking. Could dialectics, for Socrates, have been a form of revenge?

I have explained why Socrates could repel people; now it's just as important to understand why he was so captivating. One reason is that he invented a new kind of Agon, a competitive struggle, becoming the first master of verbal combat in Athens' elite circles. He charmed others by appealing to the Greek love of competition—he transformed intellectual debate into a new kind of contest between men and youths. Socrates also had an intense and magnetic personality, one deeply rooted in eroticism.

But Socrates saw even further. He understood his noble Athenian peers better than they understood themselves. He recognized that his situation—his unusual inner conflict—was not unique. The same kind of decline was quietly spreading everywhere: ancient Athens was dying. Socrates realized that the entire world needed him—his method, his remedy, and his unique technique for self-discipline and survival. Everywhere, instincts were in chaos;

everywhere, people were teetering on the edge of excess. The monstrum in animo—the monster within—had become a widespread threat. "Instincts must be tamed," he thought. "We need to find a counterforce, a ruler stronger than they are."

When the physiognomist unmasked Socrates, calling him a volcano of evil desires, Socrates, the great Master of Irony, uttered a few revealing words that explain his nature. "That is true," he admitted, "but I overcame them all."

How did Socrates manage to master himself? His case was, at its core, simply the most extreme and visible example of a widespread crisis. It was a time when no one could control themselves, and instincts constantly clashed with one another. As the clearest example of this disorder, Socrates fascinated people. His shocking ugliness made him impossible to ignore, and his ability to present himself as a solution—a cure for this state— made him even more compelling.

When a man feels compelled, as Socrates did, to turn reason into a tyrant, it is a clear sign that something else is attempting to seize control. In Socrates' case, reason was seen as a savior. Neither Socrates nor his followers had the freedom to choose whether to be rational—they had no choice. At that time, being rational was mandatory, a last resort. The intensity with which all of Greek thought embraced reason reveals the severity of their situation: humanity was at a critical crossroads. The options were stark—either perish or cling desperately to excessive rationality.

The moral focus of Greek philosophy from Plato onward, and its reverence for dialectics, stemmed from a pathological state. The equation Reason =

Virtue = Happiness essentially meant: we must follow Socrates' example and constantly confront our dark passions with the light of reason. We must prioritize cleverness, precision, and clarity above all else. To yield to instinct or the unconscious was seen as a descent into chaos.

I have now explained why Socrates was so captivating: he appeared as a healer, a savior. But should we examine the flaws in his faith in "reason at any cost"? It was an illusion, a self- deception among philosophers and moralists, to believe they could free themselves from decline simply by fighting against it. This approach cannot lead to liberation. The tools they used, the path they chose as a solution, were themselves symptoms of the very degeneration they sought to overcome. They only altered the form of the problem—they did not eliminate it. Socrates was a misunderstanding. The entire morality of "improvement," including that of Christianity, was also a misunderstanding.

The brightest light of reason—this insistence on clarity, coldness, caution, and conscious control—opposed to instinct and detached from it, was itself a disease, simply a different kind of sickness. It was not a path back to "virtue," "health," or "happiness." To be forced to fight against one's instincts is the very definition of degeneration. As long as life is ascending, happiness is synonymous with instinct.

Did Socrates, the most intelligent of self-deceivers, understand this? Did he admit it to himself at the end, in his brave acceptance of death? Socrates wanted to die. It wasn't Athens that gave him the hemlock—it was his own hand. He pushed Athens to hand him the poisoned cup. "Socrates is not a doctor," he may have whispered to himself. "Only death can heal this. Socrates himself has simply been sick for a very long time."

Chapter 3

"Reason" In Philosophy

You ask me what defines the peculiarities of philosophers? For example, their lack of a sense of history, their disdain for the idea of change, and their obsession with preserving things like the ancient Egyptians did. They believe they honor something by removing it from its history, placing it "under the aspect of eternity"—essentially turning it into a mummy. For thousands of years, philosophers have dealt with mummified ideas; nothing alive has ever emerged from their work. These worshippers of concepts kill and preserve things when they idolize them—they endanger the life of everything they claim to revere. To them, death, change, aging, and even growth and creation are flaws, even arguments against life itself. What is, they claim, cannot change; and what changes, they insist, is not real.

All philosophers believe—desperately—in the idea of Being. But because they cannot grasp it, they search for reasons why this understanding is denied to them. "There must be some illusion, some trick, preventing us from knowing the true nature of Being," they say. "Where is this deceiver?" Then, triumphantly, they declare: "We've found it—it's sensuality!" The senses, they argue, are immoral in other ways and deceive us about the true world. The moral they draw is this: we must rid ourselves of the illusion brought by the senses, of change, of history, of lies. For them, history is nothing but belief in the senses, belief in falsehood. Their conclusion: we must reject everything the senses tell us. We must reject humanity and everything connected to it. Let us become philosophers—mummies, believers in monotony, grave-diggers! Above all, they cry, let us cast aside the body, this miserable obsession of the senses. The body, they claim, is infected with every flaw of logic and is neither real nor possible, even though it has the audacity to pretend otherwise.

With great respect, I make an exception for Heraclitus. While other philosophers dismissed the senses because they revealed variety and change, Heraclitus dismissed them because they seemed to show permanence and unity. Yet even Heraclitus was unfair to the senses. The senses do not lie, as the Eleatics thought, nor as Heraclitus believed. They don't lie at all. It is our interpretation of what the senses reveal that introduces falsehood—the lies of unity, matter, substance, and permanence. Reason is the source of these distortions. As long as the senses show us a world of change and impermanence, they are truthful. Heraclitus was entirely correct, however, in saying that the idea of Being is an empty illusion. The "apparent" world is the only world that exists; the so-called "true world" is nothing but a false add-on to it.

What delicate instruments our senses are! Take the human nose, for example—no philosopher has ever spoken of it with the reverence and gratitude it deserves. Yet, for now, it is the most finely tuned instrument we have. It can detect even the tiniest changes in motion, subtleties that even a spectroscope cannot measure. Our scientific achievements today reach as far as we have trusted our senses, sharpened them, enhanced them, and followed their evidence to its limits. What lies beyond that is incomplete and not yet science—it is metaphysics, theology, psychology, epistemology, or abstract systems like logic and mathematics. In all of these fields, reality is not even considered, not even as a problem, just as the broader value of these symbolic conventions like logic is not questioned.

Another strange trait of philosophers is just as dangerous. They confuse the last things with the first. They take what appears last—unfortunately, as it often shouldn't appear at all—"the highest concept," the most general, emptiest, and vaguest shadow of reality, and place it at the beginning, treating it as the origin. This, too, reflects their habit of reverence: the highest thing must not have arisen from anything lower, it must not have grown or developed at all. Their moral: anything of the highest rank must be causa sui—its own cause. If something derives from something else, it loses value and becomes suspect.

All the so-called higher values—like Being, the Absolute, Goodness, Truth, and Perfection—are assumed to be of the highest rank. They cannot have evolved; they must be self- caused. Moreover, these concepts must be alike, never in conflict with one another. And so they arrive at their grand concept of "God," the final, most diluted, and emptiest thing, which they declare to be the first cause, the ens r ealissimum, the ultimate reality. Imagine humanity taking the mental cobwebs spun by these diseased minds seriously! And yet, humanity has paid a high price for doing so.

Let us contrast this with how we approach the problem of error and deception in things (and notice, I politely say "we"). In the past, people saw change and evolution as proof that the world was deceptive, that something was leading us astray. Today, however, we understand that the real source of error lies in our rational thinking. Whenever we insist on unity, identity, permanence, substance, cause, materiality, or Being, we are driven into error— despite knowing from careful study that the error lies here.

This is similar to how people once believed their eyes deceived them about the sun's motion. In this case, it isn't our eyes but our language that keeps reinforcing these mistaken concepts. Language was developed in a time when human psychology was still very primitive. If we look at the origins of language metaphysics—that is, reasoning itself—we find it rooted in a kind of fetishism. Language imposes the idea of a doer behind every deed; it assumes that willpower is a cause and that the self, the "ego," is a kind of Being or substance. This faith in the ego as a substance is then projected onto the world, creating the concept of "things." From the ego alone comes the idea of Being.

At the root of all this is a grave mistake: the belief that the will is something active, a force. Now we know it's just a word. Much later, in a far more enlightened world, philosophers marveled at how certain and reliable these categories of reason seemed. They concluded that these concepts could not have come from experience since experience actually contradicts them. Where, then, do they come from? In both India and Greece, people made the same mistake: "We must have lived in a higher world once," they thought, "because we possess reason!" But the truth is, we came from a much simpler and less developed state.

Nothing has been more convincing than the error of Being, as first proposed by the Eleatics. Their concept of Being is supported by every word and sentence we speak! Even those who opposed the Eleatics fell into the trap of their idea, such as Democritus with his theory of the atom. "Reason" in language—what an old and cunning deceiver it is! I suspect we will never rid ourselves of the idea of God as long as we believe in grammar.

To make this important and novel perspective clear, I will summarize it in four points to simplify understanding and encourage discussion.

Proposition One. The arguments claiming this world is only "apparent" actually support its reality. No other kind of reality can be proven.

Proposition Two. The qualities people attribute to the "true Being" of things are actually qualities of nonexistence. The "true world" was constructed by denying the real world, and it is indeed an illusion—a moral and optical trick.

Proposition Three. Imagining another world makes no sense unless there is a deep, instinctual urge to slander, diminish, and distrust this life. In that case, this imaginary "better" world is just an act of revenge against the life we live.

Proposition Four. Dividing the world into a "true" and "apparent" world, whether in Christianity or Kant's philosophy (which is essentially Christianity in disguise), is a sign of decline and a symptom of decaying life. The fact that an artist values appearances more than reality does not contradict this. For the artist, "appearance" is reality, but in a refined, intensified, and improved form. The tragic artist is not a pessimist—they affirm even the most troubling and terrifying aspects of life. They are Dionysian.

Chapter 4

How The "True World"

Ultimately Became a Fable the History of An Error

The true world is reachable by the wise, the virtuous, and the devout. They live in it—they are it.

(This earliest version of the idea was relatively simple, clever, and convincing. It was essentially a rewording of "I, Plato, am the truth.")

The true world, though unattainable for now, is promised to the wise, the virtuous, and the devout—especially to the sinner who repents.

(The idea evolves: it becomes subtler, more deceptive, more elusive. It takes on a new form—it becomes feminine, it becomes Christian.)

The true world is beyond reach. It cannot be proven or promised, but merely thinking about it provides comfort, obligation, and direction.

(This is essentially the same old sun, but seen through a haze of doubt and skepticism. The idea becomes lofty, pale, northern—Königsbergian.)

The true world—is it unattainable? In any case, it is unattained. And because it is unattained, it is also unknown. As something unknown, it can no longer comfort, save, or command. How could the unknown demand anything of us?

(The first light of dawn. Reason begins to stir and stretch. The cockcrow of positivism.)

The "true world"—an idea that no longer has any use, that no longer demands anything—a pointless, unnecessary idea, now discarded: let us get rid of it!

(The brightness of morning; breakfast; the return of common sense and joy.

Plato blushes in shame, and all free spirits celebrate wildly.)

We have abolished the true world. What remains? The apparent world, perhaps? Certainly not! By getting rid of the true world, we have also done away with the world of appearances!

(Noon; the time of the shortest shadows; the end of the longest mistake; the height of humanity. Thus Spoke Zarathustra begins.)

Chapter 5

Morality as The Enemy of Nature

There is a time when all passions are destructive, dragging people down with their reckless force. But there comes a much later time when passions merge with the spirit and refine themselves—they become "spiritualized." In the past, because of the inherent foolishness of passion, people waged war against it. They committed themselves to eradicating it. All ancient moralists agreed on this point: "Il faut tuer les passions"—passions must be killed. The most famous version of this idea is found in the New Testament, in the Sermon on the Mount, where, let's be clear, things are hardly viewed from an elevated perspective. It says there, for example, about sexuality: "If your eye offends you, pluck it out." Thankfully, no Christian truly follows this advice.

Destroying passions and desires simply because of their foolishness or to avoid the unpleasant outcomes of their excess now seems to us like an even greater form of foolishness. We no longer admire dentists who pull teeth just so they won't ache again. On the other hand, it's fair to say that the soil from which Christianity grew could never have allowed for the idea of "spiritualizing passion" to take root. Everyone knows the early Church waged war on intelligence in favor of the "poor in spirit." Under those conditions, how could passions have been fought intelligently? The Church combats passion through methods of removal and suppression. Its solution, its "remedy," is castration. It never asks, "How can desire be refined, elevated, or even sanctified?"

Throughout history, the Church's discipline has always focused on eradicating passions entirely—on destroying sensuality, pride, the thirst for power, the desire for wealth, and even the urge for revenge. But attacking passions at their roots is the same as attacking life at its source. The Church's approach is fundamentally hostile to life itself.

The same methods—castration and eradication—are instinctively chosen to battle passions by those who are too weak-willed or degenerate to impose some form of moderation. These are the kinds of people who, metaphorically (or even literally), need La Trappe or some extreme declaration of war against their desires, a vast gulf separating them from temptation. Only degenerates need such drastic methods. A weak will—or, more precisely, an inability to resist reacting to stimuli—is itself a form of degeneration.

A radical and absolute hatred of sensuality is always a suspicious sign. It gives good reason to doubt the overall health of the person who takes such an extreme stance. Moreover, this hatred reaches its peak only when such people no longer have the strength of character to commit to the ultimate remedy—to renounce their inner "Satan."

Consider the history of priests, philosophers, and even artists. The most venomous attacks on the senses have not come from those who are impotent or naturally ascetic, but from those who found it necessary to become ascetics. These were people whose inner struggles forced them into extreme positions, and their attacks on sensuality reflect their personal battles more than any genuine wisdom.

The spiritualization of sensuality is called love: this represents a great victory over Christianity. Another triumph is the spiritualization of hostility. This means we are beginning to deeply understand the value of having enemies. In short, we now act and think in the exact opposite way from how we once did. Throughout history, the Church sought to destroy its enemies. But we, the immoralists and Antichrists, see an advantage in the Church's survival. Even in politics, hostility has become more refined—more cautious, thoughtful, and restrained. Nearly every political party now sees its self-interest in ensuring its opposition doesn't collapse. The same is true in global politics.

A new creation—such as the new Empire—needs enemies more than friends. It only becomes necessary as a contrast to what opposes it; it defines itself through opposition. We approach our inner conflicts in much the same way. Here too, we have spiritualized enmity and come to understand its value. A person is productive only when they are rich in opposing instincts; they stay youthful only so long as their soul resists comfort and rejects the yearning for peace.

The "peace of the soul," which Christianity holds as its highest goal, has become entirely foreign to us. Nothing could make us less envious than the moral complacency and contentment of a clean conscience—the happiness of a "moral cow." A man who renounces conflict also renounces a life of grandeur.

Of course, in many cases, what people call "peace of the soul" is really something else, disguised and unable to name itself honestly. Let me, without hesitation or bias, suggest a few examples.

"Peace of the soul" could be the radiant glow of abundant animal energy within the realm of morality or religion. Or it might be the first sign of fatigue, the shadow cast by the evening, as all evenings cast shadows. Or it could be a signal of humid air and southern winds on the horizon. Perhaps it is an unconscious gratitude for good digestion, sometimes mistaken for "brotherly love." It could also be the calmness of someone recovering from illness, savoring every flavor of life anew and waiting patiently. Or it might follow the satisfaction of a powerful passion, the comfort of an unfamiliar fullness.

"Peace of the soul" might be the weariness of our will, desires, and vices as they grow old. Or it could be laziness, dressed up by vanity in the clothes of morality. Sometimes, it's the relief that follows the end of long periods of uncertainty, even if that end is marked by terrible certainty. It might also be the expression of mastery during a creative effort, the deep, steady breathing of someone who has achieved true freedom of will.

Who knows? Perhaps even The Twilight of the Idols is nothing more than a form of "peace of the soul."

Let me lay down a principle: all natural morality—that is, every healthy morality—is guided by the instinct for life. It fulfills one of life's fundamental laws by creating definite rules like "you shall" or "you shall not," and in doing so, it clears obstacles from the path of life. In contrast, morality that opposes nature—which describes almost every morality that has been taught, praised, and preached so far—is aimed directly against life's instincts. It secretly or openly condemns these very instincts. When it says, "God sees into the heart of man," it denies the deepest and most vital desires of life, turning God into life's enemy. The saint, whom God supposedly favors, is nothing more than an ideal eunuch. Life ends where the "Kingdom of God" begins.

If you understand the wickedness of this rebellion against life, which Christian morality has made almost sacred, you also see its emptiness, its falseness, and its absurdity. For any condemnation of life by a living being is merely a symptom of a specific kind of life. The question of whether such a condemnation is right or wrong doesn't even arise. To even approach the question of life's value, one would need to be outside life itself and yet know it as completely as everyone who has ever lived. This makes the question entirely inaccessible to us.

When we speak of values, we do so under the influence and perspective of life itself. Life urges us to create values; life evaluates through us. This means that even morality that opposes life—one that sees God as the rejection and condemnation of life—is still an evaluation of life. But what kind of life does it reflect? I have already answered: it is the perspective of declining, weakened, exhausted, and doomed life. Morality, as it has been understood up to now—as Schopenhauer put it in his idea of

"The Denial of the Will to Life"—is the instinct of degeneration turned into a command. It says, "Perish!" It is the death sentence pronounced by those already marked for death.

Now, consider how absurdly simple it is for someone to say, "Man should be like this or that!" Reality shows us a wondrous abundance of types, an endless variety of forms and transformations. Yet the first petty moralist who comes along declares, "No! Man should be different!" This self-righteous fool even imagines he knows what man should be like. He draws his own face on the wall and proclaims: "Behold the man!"

Even when the moralist addresses an individual and says, "You should be this way or that way!" he still makes a fool of himself. The individual, with their past and future, is part of fate—a law, a necessity added to the universe. To say to someone, "Change yourself," is the same as demanding that the entire world change, even retroactively. These moralists have been consistent in their madness—they wanted man to be different, to be virtuous, to reflect their own image. In doing so, they denied the world itself. This is no small form of insanity! Nor is it a humble kind of arrogance!

Morality, when it condemns for the sake of condemnation itself—without any regard for life's goals, needs, or motives—is a specific kind of error. It is a degenerative quirk that has caused immeasurable harm, and no one should feel pity for it. We, the immoralists, on the other hand, have opened our hearts to understanding, acceptance, and affirmation. We do not reject life lightly; instead, we take pride in saying "yes" to things.

Our vision has widened to include the economy of life—a system that knows how to use even what priests and moralists reject.

It finds value even in what the sanctimonious or the sickly-minded condemn. It turns the so-called repulsive elements—priests, bigots, and the "virtuous"—to its own advantage. What is that advantage? We, the immoralists, are the living answer to that question.

Chapter 6
The Four Great Errors

The error of confusing cause and effect—there is no more dangerous mistake than mistaking the effect for the cause.

I call this mistake the fundamental perversion of reason. Yet, this error has been one of humanity's oldest habits, and one that persists even today. In some parts of the world, it has even been elevated to sacred status, taking the form of "religion" and "morality." Every principle put forth by religion and morality is built upon this very error. Priests and moral lawgivers have been the most enthusiastic promoters of this distortion of reason.

Take, for example, the famous book by Cornaro, in which he promotes a strict, modest diet as the key to a long, happy, and virtuous life. This book, widely read and still reprinted in large numbers, has likely caused more harm and shortened more lives than almost any other well-intentioned work—except, of course, the Bible. Why? Because it confuses cause and effect. Cornaro believed his longevity was caused by his restricted diet. However, the truth is that his unique physiology, marked by an unusually slow rate of molecular change and low energy expenditure, was the actual cause of his meager diet. His constitution didn't allow him to eat much—if he had eaten more, he would have fallen ill.

For most people, especially those with a different metabolism, such a diet would be disastrous. A modern scholar, for example, whose nervous energy is rapidly consumed, would waste away on Cornaro's diet. Crede exper to— trust someone who knows from experience.

The same confusion of cause and effect lies at the heart of every religion and morality. Their central message is always: "Do this and avoid that, and you will be happy. Otherwise—" This "otherwise" is an unspoken threat. Every moral or religious imperative repeats this same formula. I call this the original sin of reason—immortal unreason.

But in my hands, this principle is turned on its head. This is the first example of my "transvaluation of all values." A well-constituted person, one who is a masterpiece of nature, instinctively performs certain actions and avoids others. Such a person embodies the natural order and harmony their body expresses. Their virtue is not a cause but an effect of their excellent constitution. Their longevity and ability to have many children are not rewards for their virtue; rather, these qualities result from their robust and healthy nature. This is the true basis of what I call Cornarism.

In contrast, the Church and traditional morality assert, "A race or a people perishes because of vice and luxury." My reinstated reason says the opposite: when a people are already in decline, when they are physically degenerating, vice and luxury naturally emerge. These are not the causes of their downfall but symptoms of their exhaustion. Their declining energy leads them to crave stronger and more frequent stimuli, which is typical of all weakened natures.

Consider a young man who becomes pale and sickly. His friends may blame an illness, but I say the illness itself is merely a symptom of his already weakened state, the result of hereditary exhaustion. Similarly, when a political party makes a fatal mistake, the common view is that the mistake leads to its demise. But my superior understanding of politics says: a party capable of making such errors is already in its death throes. It has lost its instinctual certainty.

Every error, in any context, is the consequence of a degeneration of instincts and a disintegration of the will. This is the essence of what we call "evil." Everything truly valuable arises from instinct and is therefore effortless, necessary, and free. Strain and effort are objections to value. The divine is characterized not by struggle but by lightness—the god has light feet, unlike the hero who battles against obstacles.

The error of false causality also runs deep. Throughout history, humans have believed they understood causality. But where did this belief come from? What gave us such confidence in causality? It came from what we call the "inner facts of consciousness." Yet not one of these so-called facts has ever been proven.

We assumed we were the causes of our own actions, that our will was an undeniable proof of causality. We believed that all the motives for our actions could be found in our consciousness, as if they were sitting there waiting to be uncovered. Without these motives, we thought, we wouldn't be free or responsible. Finally, we believed that thoughts themselves were caused by the ego, the "self."

But now, we have come to our senses. Today, we know none of this is true. The "inner world" is a collection of illusions. The will doesn't cause anything; it doesn't explain anything. It merely accompanies processes and sometimes isn't even present. What we call "motive" is another falsehood, a surface ripple that often conceals the deeper causes of action rather than revealing them. As for the ego, it is now nothing more than a myth, a fiction, an empty word.

What's the result of all this? There are no such things as spiritual causes. The entire foundation of popular experience—our belief that the world is built on causes and effects, wills and spirits—has collapsed. Humanity blissfully projected its own inner illusions onto the world, turning it into a vast system of agents and actions. Man imagined his ego as the root of all things and built the concept of "Being" upon this illusion.

Even the concept of the atom, cherished by physicists, still carries remnants of this old psychological error. And the metaphysicians' notion of the "thing-in- itself" is the ultimate example of this confusion—a disgraceful relic of primitive thinking.

The greatest error of all has been to regard the spirit as a cause, to mistake it for reality, and to use it as a measure of the real. This error was even elevated to the status of a deity—it was called God.

The Error of Imaginary Causes

Starting in the realm of dreams, we often ascribe causes to sensations after the fact. Take, for instance, the sound of a distant cannon shot in a dream. We frequently weave a story around such sensations, turning them into little dramas where we ourselves are the central figures. The sensation lingers, echoing and intensifying, until our instinct for causality demands an explanation. But instead of recognizing the sensation as random, we interpret it as something meaningful—a direct result of a fabricated cause. In dreams, this often leads to a reversal of the natural order of events: the sensation, which should be the starting point, is made the result of the imagined cause. The cannon shot is explained as though it were caused by events that supposedly happened earlier in the dream.

What occurs here? Ideas associated with a particular sensory state are misinterpreted as the cause of that state. This same process happens when we are awake. Many of our general sensations— like tension, pressure, obstacles, or explosions in the interplay of our bodily systems, particularly in the sympathetic nervous system— trigger the instinct to search for a cause. We need an explanation for why we feel good or bad, ill or well. It is not enough for us to simply recognize that we feel a certain way. We only become fully conscious of the feeling when we have assigned it a cause.

Memory plays a key role in this process, unconsciously recalling past states that were similar, along with the causal interpretations we previously attached to them. However, memory rarely retrieves the actual causes. Instead, it presents familiar interpretations. The belief that our thoughts or conscious processes are the causes of these sensations stems from the way memory works. This mechanism leads us to accept a fixed interpretation of causes, one that often hinders or entirely blocks us from investigating the real causes of our sensations.

The Psychological Explanation

Why do we trace the unfamiliar back to the familiar? Because doing so brings relief, comfort, and a sense of control. The unfamiliar provokes fear, anxiety, and unease. Our most basic instinct is to eliminate these uncomfortable feelings. Thus, our first principle becomes: any explanation is better than none at all. Since our goal is simply to free ourselves from troubling ideas, we are not overly picky about the explanations we adopt. The first explanation that makes the unfamiliar seem familiar gives us such comfort that we readily accept it as true.

This process relies on the "proof" of happiness or relief to determine truth. In this way, the instinct for causality is closely tied to feelings of fear and the need to alleviate it. Whenever possible, the question "why?" doesn't just seek any cause but rather a particular kind of cause—one that comforts, liberates, and reassures us.

The easiest way to achieve this is by attributing causes to something we already know, something familiar and stored in memory. The new, unfamiliar factor is excluded from consideration as a possible cause. We prefer explanations that remove the sensation of strangeness, novelty, or unpredictability. Over time, a particular way of explaining causes becomes dominant, solidifies into a system, and eventually crowds out alternative explanations.

For example, a banker instinctively attributes everything to business, a Christian sees sin behind every event, and a young woman interprets everything through the lens of her love life.

The Domain of Morality and Religion as Imaginary Causes

The entire realm of morality and religion can be categorized under the heading of "imaginary causes." Consider how unpleasant sensations are explained in these frameworks. Such sensations are often attributed to malevolent external forces, like evil spirits. For example, the hysteria of women in the past was frequently interpreted as possession by witches. Similarly, feelings of guilt or sinfulness are seen as evidence of moral failings, yet they are often just symptoms of physiological imbalances. People have always found reasons to be dissatisfied with themselves, projecting these feelings onto moral or religious explanations.

Religions often go further, interpreting unpleasant sensations as punishment for wrongdoing, as if suffering proves guilt or sinfulness. Schopenhauer took this idea to its extreme, claiming that all great suffering reveals what we deserve, as it could not happen without a reason rooted in guilt. In this way, morality and religion turn life's natural challenges into accusations and condemnations.

Even physiological conditions like exhaustion or illness are interpreted through this lens. The passions and bodily senses are blamed as causes, and their effects are deemed deserved punishments for indulging in sinful behavior. This moralization of suffering twists natural occurrences into a system of guilt and penalty.

Similarly, pleasant sensations are explained through imaginary causes. They are attributed to faith, good deeds, or divine favor. A "good conscience," for instance, may simply be the result of good digestion, yet it is often interpreted as a reward for moral virtue. Even successful outcomes of endeavors are misattributed; a hypochondriac or someone like Pascal, for example, would not feel general happiness simply because of a fortunate result.

Religious virtues like faith, love, and hope are also misinterpretations. The feelings of strength and abundance that underpin these states are mistaken for their causes. A person trusts in God because they feel strong and peaceful, not the other way around.

Morality and Religion as Psychology of Error

At their core, morality and religion belong to the psychology of error. They consistently confuse cause and effect. They mistake feelings of pleasure or pain for their supposed causes and interpret them through a lens of moral or religious belief. They turn subjective states of consciousness into explanations, obscuring the true causes behind these sensations.

In every case, morality and religion invert the relationship between cause and effect, making them systems of misinterpretation. Truth is conflated with the effects of what is believed to be true, and the underlying processes that produce sensations are hidden behind a false dialect of moral and religious explanations. These systems are not rooted in reality but are deeply embedded in the errors of human psychology.

The Error of Free Will

Today, we have no patience for the concept of "free will." We know too well what it really is: the most audacious theological trick ever devised to make humanity "responsible" in a theological sense—that is, to make humanity dependent on theologians. Let me explain the psychology behind how this sense of responsibility is instilled.

Whenever people assign responsibility to someone, it is driven by the instinct for punishment and judgment. The innocence of Becoming—the natural unfolding of events—is destroyed the moment any state of affairs is attributed to a will, intentions, or deliberate actions. The doctrine of the will was invented primarily as a tool for punishment, specifically to assign guilt.

The entire foundation of ancient psychology, or the psychology of the will, arose because its creators—the priests who ruled early societies—sought to justify their power to punish. They wanted to grant themselves, or their gods, the right to judge and condemn. To make this possible, humanity had to be considered "free," so that individuals could be judged and held guilty. Consequently, every action was framed as voluntary, and the origin of every action was imagined to lie in conscious choice. This fraud became the foundation of psychology: the deliberate falsification of human nature to serve the interests of power and control.

Now, we are moving in the opposite direction. We immoralists are working tirelessly to eliminate the concepts of guilt and punishment from the world. We aim to cleanse psychology, history, nature, and all social customs and institutions of these poisonous ideas. Our most determined adversaries in this effort are the theologians, who still cling to the notion of a "moral order of things." They continue to pollute the innocence of Becoming with the concepts of punishment and guilt. Christianity, in this regard, is nothing more than the metaphysics of the executioner.

What, then, can our teaching be? It is this: No one gives a person their qualities—not God, not society, not parents, not ancestors, and certainly not the person themselves. This nonsensical notion, which has been perpetuated for centuries, was called "intelligible freedom" by Kant and perhaps even earlier by Plato. But it is utterly refuted here.

No one is responsible for their existence, for being the way they are, or for the circumstances in which they find themselves. A person's existence is inextricably linked to the entire chain of events that has been and will be. It is not the product of an intention, a will, or an aim. There is no striving for some "ideal man," "ideal happiness," or "ideal morality." To think otherwise is absurd.

The concept of "purpose" is something we invented—it does not exist in reality. There is no purpose driving existence. Each individual is a necessary part of the whole, a fragment of fate, inseparably bound to the totality of existence. No one can judge, measure, or condemn an individual's existence because to do so would mean judging, measuring, and condemning the entirety of existence. But there is nothing outside the whole to serve as a basis for such judgment.

The liberation we offer is this: no one can be made responsible. Existence cannot be traced to a causa prima—a first cause. The world is not an entity driven by a central consciousness, a divine spirit, or a purpose. This realization restores the innocence of Becoming. It frees the world from the burden of guilt and condemnation.

The concept of "God" has been the greatest obstacle to accepting existence as it is. For centuries, God has been used to justify the idea of ultimate responsibility, judgment, and guilt. But we deny God. We deny responsibility in God. Only by doing so can we truly save the world. This denial restores the innocence of existence and frees us from the chains of metaphysical guilt. This is the great liberation.

Chapter 7

The "Improvers" Of Mankind

You are familiar with my demand upon philosophers: that they rise above the notions of Good and Evil, leaving behind the illusion of moral judgment. This demand arises from a perspective I was the first to articulate—that there are no moral facts. Moral judgment, like religious judgment, believes in unrealities, in things that do not exist. Morality is merely an interpretation of certain phenomena—or, more accurately, a misinterpretation.

Moral judgment belongs to a stage of ignorance, a time when the very idea of reality, the distinction between what is real and imagined, had not yet emerged. At this stage, "truth" was applied to a multitude of things we now consider imaginary. For this reason, moral judgment should never be taken literally. On its own, it is nonsense. However, as a system of signs, it is invaluable to those who understand it. It offers insight into the cultural and psychological conditions of societies that lacked the knowledge to understand themselves. Morality, in essence, is a kind of language, a symptomatology. To make use of it, one must already grasp what it signifies.

Let me offer a preliminary example. Throughout history, certain individuals have sought to "improve" humanity—a goal that has always been closely tied to morality. But beneath this single word, vastly different tendencies are concealed. The "improvement" of humanity has sometimes meant the taming of the wild animal in man, while at other times it has meant the cultivation of a specific type of human being. These two approaches are fundamentally distinct, though both are described as moral.

Take the taming of an animal as an example. To call this process an "improvement" seems almost laughable to modern ears. Anyone who has observed a menagerie knows that animals are not improved there—they are weakened. Their natural power and danger are subdued through fear, pain, and deprivation, transforming them into sick, broken creatures. The same holds true for humanity under the influence of the priestly "improvers."

Consider the Middle Ages, when the Church acted as a menagerie for humanity. The Church hunted down the most vital and noble individuals—the "blond beasts," such as the Germans—and set about "improving" them. But what did this "improved" person look like after the process? He became a shadow of himself, a distorted caricature of humanity. Lured into monasteries, stripped of his instincts, and imprisoned behind oppressive concepts of sin and guilt, he was rendered sick and wretched, filled with self- hatred and suspicion of all that is strong and joyful in life. In short, he became a Christian.

From a physiological standpoint, this "improvement" was no different than what one does to an animal: weakening it by making it sick. The Church understood this strategy well. It ruined man, drained his strength, and then claimed to have made him better.

Now, let us consider a very different example of morality: the deliberate cultivation of a particular type of humanity. The most striking example of this is found in Indian morality as laid out in the Law of Manu. This text describes the structured breeding of four distinct castes: priests, warriors, merchants and farmers, and finally servants (the Sudras). Here, we are no longer dealing with the taming of wild animals. To conceive of such a system presupposes a level of mildness and rationality far beyond that of the lion-tamer.

Emerging from the Christian atmosphere of prisons and hospitals, one can breathe more freely in the world of Manu. Here, the goal is not to break humanity but to cultivate it. The vision is vast, orderly, and noble. By comparison, the New Testament reeks of pettiness and decay. Yet even this grand system had to confront challenges, particularly from those who did not fit into its carefully crafted structure—the "non-caste" people, the Chandala.

For the Chandala, the morality of Manu was as harsh as the Church's morality was to the strong. Unable to assimilate these "mixed" people into the system, Indian morality sought to render them weak and harmless by making them sick. This was a struggle against the sheer numbers of the Chandala, whose very existence threatened the structure of the caste system.

Some of the measures taken against the Chandala are repugnant to modern sensibilities. For instance, the Avadana- Sastra decrees that their diet should consist solely of garlic and onions; they were forbidden access to grains, clean water, or fire. Their drinking water had to be drawn from ditches and animal tracks, and they were prohibited from washing themselves or their clothing. Chandala women were barred from assisting one another during childbirth, and Sudra women were forbidden from helping them as well.

Such sanitary regulations had predictable results: deadly epidemics and venereal diseases ravaged the Chandala population. In response, the Law of the K nife—circumcision for males and genital mutilation for females—was introduced. Manu himself described the Chandala as the offspring of adultery, incest, and crime. Their clothing was to be made from rags taken from corpses, their utensils from broken pottery, and their jewelry from old iron. They were to worship malevolent spirits, wander endlessly, and were even forbidden to write using their right hand or in the direction reserved for virtuous people.

This is the logical outcome of a morality focused on breeding: the deliberate dehumanization of those who threaten the system. The Chandala were treated as the living embodiment of chaos, their suffering justified as the necessary cost of order.

The stark contrast between these two examples—the Christian taming of man and the Indian cultivation of castes—reveals the true diversity hidden within the concept of morality. While both systems aimed to "improve" humanity, their methods and goals were fundamentally different. The Christian moralist sought to weaken and break the strong, while the Indian lawgiver aimed to build a structured and lasting society. Yet both relied on the same principle: to make the undesirable elements weak and subservient, even at the cost of their health and humanity.

These regulations are profoundly revealing: they offer a glimpse into the primal and unfiltered humanity of the Aryans. From them, we see that the concept of "pure blood" is far from innocent—it carries with it a profound and often ruthless seriousness. At the same time, these regulations help us identify the people in whom a deep-seated hatred of this Aryan humanity—the Chandala hatred—has been immortalized. Among these people, this hatred was transformed into both religion and genius.

From this perspective, the gospels are invaluable historical documents, and the Book of Enoch is even more significant.

Christianity, having sprung from Jewish roots and comprehensible only in the context of this heritage, represents the exact opposite of the morality of breeding, race, and privilege. Christianity is, at its core, an anti-Aryan religion. It is the transvaluation of all Aryan values— a complete reversal. It is the triumph of Chandala values, the gospel of the poor, the lowly, and the oppressed.

Christianity embodies the general uprising of the downtrodden— the miserable, the failed, and the broken—against the concept of "race." It is the eternal revenge of the Chandala, disguised as the "religion of love."

When comparing the morality of breeding to the morality of taming, we see that the methods employed by each are equally ruthless. Both rely on a deep commitment to immorality in order to enforce their respective visions of morality. One could even propose a principle: to create morality, one must possess an absolute will to immorality.

This paradoxical principle forms the basis of a profound and perplexing problem that I have studied for years: the psychology of those who claim to "improve" humanity. This problem first presented itself to me in the form of a seemingly trivial yet deeply significant phenomenon known as the pia fraus— the "pious fraud." This concept, the shared legacy of all philosophers and priests who have sought to improve mankind, opened the door to my exploration of this issue.

Figures like Manu, Plato, Confucius, and the teachers of Judaism and Christianity have all relied on the pia fraus. None of them ever doubted their right to deceive. Moreover, they never questioned their right to many other tools of manipulation and control.

To summarize this idea in a formula: every method ever used to make humanity "moral" has been, at its core, thoroughly immoral.

Chapter 8
Things the Germans Lack

Among Germans today, it is not enough to simply possess intellect; one must actively claim it, assert it, even lay hold of it.

Perhaps I know the Germans well enough to tell them a few uncomfortable truths. Modern Germany possesses a vast reserve of inherited and cultivated abilities, so vast that it could afford to spend this accumulated wealth liberally for some time. However, what has emerged in modern Germany is not a superior culture, nor refined taste, nor noble instincts for beauty. Instead, it is a set of virtues—admirable, yes, but also heavily pragmatic—more robust and "manly" than those of other European nations.

Germany still demonstrates a remarkable level of good spirits and self- respect, along with strength in human relationships and a reliable sense of mutual obligations. There is an abundance of industriousness and perseverance, paired with an inherited sobriety that seems to require stimulation rather than restraint. It is worth noting that Germans still know how to obey without feeling that obedience diminishes them, and they maintain respect for their opponents rather than despising them.

You can see that I wish to be fair to the Germans; it is my intention not to betray my commitment to balance, even when critiquing them. But fairness requires me to voice my objections as well. Achieving a position of power comes at a cost, for power inevitably stultifies.

Once upon a time, the Germans were known as a nation of thinkers. But do they truly think anymore? Today, Germans seem bored by intellect, mistrustful of it. Politics has consumed the seriousness once reserved for intellectual pursuits. The rallying cry, "Ger many, Ger many above all," seems to have delivered a fatal blow to German philosophy. Abroad, people ask me, "Are there still

German philosophers? Are there still German poets? Are there any good German books?" I feel ashamed, though I muster the courage to answer, even in my moments of despair, "Yes, Bismarck!"

But could I dare to reveal what books are actually being read in Germany today? The curse of mediocrity dominates.

What could German intellect have become? Who has not lamented this question! For nearly a thousand years, this nation has deliberately dulled its own edge. Nowhere else have Europe's two great narcotics—alcohol and Christianity—been so excessively and destructively consumed as in Germany. To these, a third opiate has been added, one that could alone have sufficed to extinguish the spark of intellectual daring: music. German music—ponderous, bloated, and stifling—has completed the paralysis of German thought. How much sluggishness, heaviness, dampness, lethargy, and beer-fueled languor are entangled in German intellect!

How can it be that young men who dedicate their lives to intellectual pursuits lack the most basic instinct for intellectual self-preservation and drink beer? The alcoholism of academic youth doesn't prevent them from becoming scholars—after all, one can be a great scholar without being truly intelligent. But in every other respect, this is a disaster. What kind of intellectual softness, what kind of dull degeneration, comes from beer?

I once pointed out an infamous example of this kind of intellectual degeneration: the decline of David Strauss, once a leading German free spirit, who devolved into the author of a pedestrian gospel and a "New Faith." His intellect succumbed not just to mediocrity but to the very spirit he himself had celebrated—"the dear old brown liquor," to which he remained faithful to the end.

This kind of degeneration—soft, indulgent, and self-defeating—offers a troubling reflection of the broader intellectual culture in Germany, one that undermines the potential for brilliance with a relentless embrace of comfort, conformity, and the narcotics of religion, alcohol, and art.

I have spoken about the state of German intellect, noting that it has become coarser and shallower. But is that enough? In truth, what concerns me far more is the steady and alarming decline of German seriousness, depth, and passion in intellectual matters. It is not just intellect that has diminished; even the emotional force—what we might call the pathos—behind intellectual pursuits has been transformed.

When I occasionally encounter German universities, I am struck by the atmosphere that prevails there. What barrenness! What smug, tepid intellectuality! These institutions have grown content with mediocrity, and the once-earnest German intellectual spirit now feels lukewarm, drained of vitality.

Some might point to German science as a counterargument to my observations. Such a claim would only prove they have misunderstood me and failed to grasp even a single page of my writings. For seventeen years, I have devoted myself to exposing the dehumanizing and de-intellectualizing effects of modern scientific pursuits. The rigid, mechanical labor demanded by the vast scope of modern sciences has left individuals shackled, unable to cultivate the fuller, richer, and deeper natures that once thrived in intellectual endeavors.

Our age suffers from an overabundance of shallow dilettantes and fragmented personalities—half-formed individuals who flit aimlessly through life. The universities, though unintentionally, have become factories for producing this kind of intellectual decay, training people whose instincts for genuine intellectuality have withered. And this problem is not confined to Germany. All of Europe is beginning to recognize this trend. Large-scale politics, the realm in which Germany has invested so much, fools no one. Germany is becoming, ever more clearly, the flatland of Europe, a place devoid of the peaks of culture and thought.

I am still searching for a German with whom I could engage in the kind of seriousness that defines my way of thinking. And even more elusive is a German with whom I could share genuine cheerfulness. The Twilight of the Idols— what man today could grasp the kind of seriousness from which a philosopher recovers in such a work? Of all things, our cheerfulness is the most misunderstood.

Now let us shift our focus slightly. It is not just that German culture is visibly in decline; there are also clear reasons behind this fall. No one, whether an individual or a nation, can expend more energy than they possess. If your resources of reason, seriousness, will, and self-discipline are poured entirely into pursuits such as political power, economics, large-scale commerce, parliamentary systems, or military ambitions, then you cannot also spend them on culture.

Culture and the state are fundamentally opposed to one another. Let no one be misled: the idea of a "culture-state" is a modern illusion. One thrives at the expense of the other. Throughout history, every great period of culture coincided with political decline. That which is culturally great is always unpolitical, even anti-political.

Consider Goethe. His heart swelled with hope at the rise of Napoleon, a figure of cultural vitality, but it closed at the thought of the "Wars of Liberation," which signaled Germany's move toward becoming a political power. Similarly, when Germany emerged as a dominant force in global politics, France rose anew as a cultural powerhouse. Even now, much of Europe's intellectual seriousness and passion have migrated to Paris. Questions of pessimism, the works of Wagner, and other psychological and artistic debates are approached in France with a level of subtlety and depth that Germany seems incapable of matching.

In matters that truly define culture—those that demand intellectual and artistic earnestness—the Germans are no longer relevant. This shift marks a profound displacement of Europe's intellectual center of gravity. In the history of European culture, the rise of the German Empire signifies not progress but a retreat from cultural significance.

I challenge you to name a single German thinker today who can stand alongside the great figures of Europe's intellectual past. Where is the modern equivalent of Goethe, Hegel, Heinrich Heine, or Schopenhauer? The absence of any contemporary German philosopher worthy of comparison with such minds is an ever-growing marvel—and a deeply troubling one.

The entire higher educational system in Germany has lost sight of everything that truly matters—both the ultimate goals and the means to achieve them. People seem to have forgotten that education itself is the goal, the process of cultivation an end in itself—not "the Empire" or any other external objective. They forget that education demands true educators, not merely public-school teachers or university scholars. What is needed are educators who are themselves cultivated, superior, and noble minds—individuals who can demonstrate their worth at every moment of their lives through their words and their actions. These are individuals who are ripe and refined products of culture.

Instead, Germany is plagued by an abundance of learned louts—"superior wet-nurses"—foisted upon its youth by public schools and universities. These are not educators in the true sense, but mere functionaries. What Germany lacks, with few exceptions, is the very foundation of education: genuine educators. And without educators, there can be no culture. This deficit has led to the decline of German culture.

One of those rare exceptions, and a man I deeply respect, is my friend Jacob Burckhardt of Bâle. It is to him, above all, that Bâle owes its position as a center of true human culture. He stands as a shining example of what an educator should be.

What, then, do Germany's higher schools actually achieve? They ruthlessly and rapidly train vast numbers of young men to become useful and exploitable servants of the state. This process prioritizes utility over cultivation, treating education as a means to an end rather than an end in itself. The very concept of "higher education" contradicts the idea of catering to the masses. True higher education can only concern the exceptional few; it is a privilege reserved for those capable of appreciating and embodying it.

Great and beautiful things cannot belong to the masses. As the Latin phrase goes, pulchrum est paucorum hominum—the beautiful is for the few. This democratization of education— this attempt to make cultivation "general" and common—is one of the root causes of Germany's cultural decline. When higher education is treated as a universal right rather than a privilege, it inevitably deteriorates in quality.

Another factor undermining German education is the influence of the military profession. The privileges associated with military careers drive far too many people into the higher schools, flooding the system and degrading its standards. In modern Germany, no parent has the freedom to provide their children with a noble education. The teachers, curricula, and goals of the higher schools are all built on a fundamentally mediocre foundation.

Everywhere one looks, haste reigns supreme. It is as if something vital would be lost if a young man were not "finished" by the age of twenty-three, or if he were unable to answer the all-important question: "What career should I choose?" But the superior individual, the one truly capable of higher culture, does not think in terms of "careers." Such a person feels called to something higher and cannot simply conform to the idea of a "calling" imposed by society.

The superior individual takes their time—they must take their time. For such a person, the idea of being "finished" is absurd. In the realm of higher culture, a man of thirty is still a beginner, still a child.

Meanwhile, our overcrowded public schools and the mass production of mediocre teachers are nothing short of a scandal. While some may present serious motives for defending this state of affairs—like the professors at Heidelberg recently did—there can be no legitimate reasons to support it. The rush to "complete" education and the focus on quantity over quality are destroying the very foundation of culture.

Germany's educational system is not cultivating exceptional individuals; it is churning out uniform, functional tools for the state. This is a betrayal of what education should be and a clear indication of the decline of German intellectual and cultural life.

To remain true to my affirmative nature—a nature that deals with contradictions and criticism only reluctantly and as a secondary matter—I will begin by stating the three essential goals for which we require educators. People must learn to see, they must learn to think, and they must learn to speak and write. These three abilities are the foundation of a noble culture.

To learn to see means to train the eye in calmness, patience, and the ability to let things present themselves. It involves postponing judgment and approaching every individual case from all possible angles. This is the first and most essential preparation for intellectual development. One must not react immediately to stimuli; one must cultivate the instincts of restraint and isolation. To learn to see, as I understand it, is closely related to what is popularly referred to as "strength of will." Its core is the ability not to want to see immediately, to defer decisions, and to resist impulses.

All lack of intellectuality and all vulgarity stem from the inability to resist stimuli. Such people feel compelled to respond to every impulse and indulge every reaction. In many cases, this immediate response is a sign of decline, a symptom of exhaustion or morbidity. Most of what common language calls "vices" is simply the physiological inability to refrain from reacting.

To illustrate what it means to have learned to see, consider a person who has undergone this training. As a learner, this individual will likely become cautious, slow, and resistant. With a calm and almost hostile skepticism, they will allow strange and unfamiliar things to approach them but will refrain from immediately engaging or forming judgments. They will withdraw their hand, metaphorically speaking, as the new comes near, watching and observing instead.

In contrast, to be perpetually open, to have the "doors of one's soul" flung wide for every trivial fact, to constantly lie in submission before the flood of external impressions—this is what modern people call "objectivity." But such objectivity is in poor taste; it is vulgar and cheap. It is the intellectual equivalent of being at the mercy of every passing whim, ready to leap into others' souls and experiences without discernment or control.

As for learning to think—our schools have long since abandoned any understanding of this process. Even at the universities, among scholars of philosophy, the discipline of logic is withering away, both as a theory and as a practical skill. Look into any German book, and you will find no trace of the understanding that thinking has a technique, a structure, and a discipline. There is no recognition that thinking must be learned, much like dancing must be learned. Thinking, like dancing, demands practice and a will to mastery.

Who among the Germans today knows, from experience, the subtle joy— the delicate shudder—that comes when intellectual movements are as graceful as light footfalls? Instead, intellectual clumsiness abounds. Awkward postures of the mind and a heavy-handed approach to grasping ideas are so distinctly German that outside of Germany, they are mistakenly equated with the German spirit itself. The German mind has no "fingers" for fine nuances.

The Germans' tolerance for their philosophers, particularly for Kant—the most malformed and crippled figure in the realm of ideas—speaks volumes about their lack of elegance. Kant is a testament to their coarse intellectual habits and their inability to recognize intellectual grace.

In truth, no noble education can exclude dancing in all its forms. This includes dancing with one's feet, but also with ideas, with words, and, above all, with the pen. Writing is, in its highest form, a kind of intellectual dance, requiring rhythm, precision, and lightness. Yet at this point, I must acknowledge that these thoughts will likely remain utterly incomprehensible to most German readers.

Chapter 9

Skirmishes in A War with The Age

My Impossible People.—Seneca, the showman of virtue, performing like a bullfighter in the ring of morals. Rousseau, the preacher of returning to nature, lost in his own unpolished, raw state. Schiller, the trumpet of morality, blasting his tunes from Säckingen with little depth behind the noise. Dante, the scavenger who writes poetry over the graves he haunts. Kant, whose moral preaching is nothing more than a cleverly disguised form of empty rhetoric. Victor Hugo, a beacon on the vast sea of nonsense, shining brightly but without direction. Liszt, master of chasing not only after musical greatness but also after women. George Sand, overflowing with creativity, like a cow with an endless supply of beautiful milk. Michelet, all fire and passion, but dressed casually in the everyday garb of enthusiasm. Carlyle, the voice of pessimism, but one born of a poorly digested meal rather than deep reflection. John Stuart Mill, whose clarity is so sharp it feels almost offensive. The brothers Goncourt, two literary warriors battling Homer with their pens, their drama set to Offenbach's music.

Zola, who finds inspiration in the repulsive and thrives in the stench of decay.

Renan. Theology personified, corrupted by the original sin of Christianity. His thoughts are tainted with the contradictions of faith. Even when Renan dares to take a stance, to say "yes" or "no" on a major issue, he almost always misses the point entirely. He tries to combine science with nobility, seemingly unaware that science is inherently democratic and cannot be aligned with his aristocratic ideals. He dreams of an intellectual aristocracy, yet at the same time, he bows down to the gospel of humility and grovels before it. What good is his modern free-spiritedness, his wit, his irony, and his intellectual acrobatics, if deep inside he remains tied to the faith of a Christian, a Catholic, and even a priest?

Renan's strength, much like that of a Jesuit or a confessor, lies in his ability to seduce. His intellect has the same unctuous, self-satisfied tone as a parson. Like all priests, he becomes dangerous when he loves, because his love distorts the truth. He has a rare talent for worshipping dangerous ideas in such a way that they appear benign. But his intellect, rather than invigorating, weakens and softens. For France, already suffering from a broken will and diminishing strength, Renan is one more calamity—a soothing voice at a time when sharp clarity and decisiveness are needed.

Sainte-Beuve. There is nothing manly about him. He is filled with petty malice toward all strong and noble spirits. He drifts aimlessly, subtle yet spiteful, always restless and curious. He listens at keyholes, gathering whispers, but never facing things head-on. At heart, he is more like a woman, full of revenge and sensuality. As a psychologist, he is a genius of slander, endlessly creative in his ability to add a touch of poison even to his praise. His instincts are plebeian, closely aligned with the resentful spirit of Rousseau. This makes him a Romanticist, for beneath all Romanticism lies Rousseau's vengeful nature, grumbling and restless.

Sainte-Beuve is a restrained revolutionary, his actions kept in check by fear. He flinches before strength, whether it comes in the form of public opinion, the Academy, the court, or even the cloistered thinkers of Port Royal. He is filled with bitterness toward all that is great, toward everything that has confidence in itself. He is enough of a poet, enough of a sensualist, to recognize power when he sees it, but he writhes under its weight like a worm being trodden upon.

As a critic, Sainte-Beuve lacks a foundation—no standard of judgment, no clear principles, no backbone. While he speaks with the versatility of a worldly libertine, chattering endlessly about countless subjects, he lacks the courage to own his own libertinism. As a historian, he has no philosophical depth, no ability to see history as a coherent whole. This lack of vision leads him to avoid making judgments, opting instead for a mask of "objectivity" in matters of importance.

Yet when it comes to things that demand subtlety and refined taste, Sainte- Beuve finds his footing. Here, he dares to embrace his true nature, enjoying his own personality and even achieving mastery. In this sense, he is a precursor to Baudelaire, though without Baudelaire's courage to push boundaries.

"The Imitation of Christ." This is a book I cannot even touch without feeling physically repulsed. It reeks of the "eternally feminine," a cloying sweetness that can only appeal to French sensibilities or to Wagnerites. Its saintly musings on love are delivered in a tone so saccharine that even the most worldly Parisian women might find themselves intrigued.

I have been told that Auguste Comte, the clever Jesuit disguised as a man of science, took inspiration from this book in his attempt to lead his countrymen back to Rome by way of science. I can believe it. This is the essence of the "religion of the heart"—a sentimental, deceptive path back to the old faith, cloaked in modern rhetoric. It is as much a symbol of decline as it is of misplaced devotion.

G. Eliot.—They have let go of the Christian God, yet they cling even harder to Christian morality. This is a very English way of thinking, and while it might seem strange, one can hardly blame moral women like George Eliot for following it. In England, even the smallest step away from theology must be balanced by an extreme embrace of morality. It's their way of making amends, their form of penance. Anyone who begins to stray from religious belief feels compelled to prove their virtue by becoming a moral fanatic.

We, however, are different. When we abandon Christian faith, we also give up any claim to Christian morality. This connection might not be obvious to everyone, but it must be emphasized repeatedly, especially to counter the shallow thinkers so common in England. Christianity is not a loose collection of values; it is a complete system, a worldview where every part supports the whole. If you remove its central pillar—the belief in God—the entire structure collapses. What remains is empty, lifeless, and without meaning.

Christianity assumes that humans cannot know what is good or bad for themselves. It teaches that only God knows these things. Christian morality, therefore, is not a product of human reasoning but a divine command. It is immune to criticism because it rests entirely on the belief that God is the ultimate truth. Without God, Christian morality loses its foundation and cannot stand on its own.

The English, however, seem to believe otherwise. They think they can intuitively know what is good or evil without needing Christianity to guide them. But this belief only shows how deeply Christian values still shape their thinking. Their moral standards remain rooted in Christian teachings, even when they deny the religion itself. This is not evidence of independence; it is proof of how strong Christianity's influence remains. The English no longer recognize the origins of their morality, nor do they realize how fragile it is without its theological base. For them, morality is not a question to be examined—it is simply assumed, a problem they have yet to confront.

George Sand.—I recently read the first Lettres d'un Voyageur, and like everything influenced by Rousseau, it felt artificial, exaggerated, and insincere. The style reminded me of cheap wallpaper—bright, decorative, but ultimately shallow. The writing seems overly concerned with appearing noble and generous, yet lacks any genuine depth. What struck me most was Sand's affected masculinity, which came across as forced and unconvincing, like the awkward swagger of a poorly mannered schoolboy.

And how cold she must have been beneath this performance! She seemed like a machine, wound up and ready to produce her work, writing not out of passion but out of routine. This coldness is not unique to her; it is the hallmark of Romanticists like Hugo and Balzac, whose writing often feels detached from true feeling. Sand's self-satisfaction is evident in her prolific output, as if she took pride in her ability to churn out words endlessly. There was something undeniably German in her style—not in the good sense, but in the clumsy, heavy-handed way that marks the decline of true French taste. And yet Renan adores her!

A Moral for Psychologists.—Never engage in psychology just for the sake of observing. Observing for its own sake leads to a distorted view of things, to exaggeration, and to a forced perspective. Experiencing something intentionally, with the purpose of analyzing it, is not helpful. When in the middle of an experience, a person should not turn their attention inward to observe themselves. In such moments, even the clearest vision becomes clouded—it turns into the "evil eye." A true psychologist avoids observing for the sake of observation. The same is true for a true artist. A born painter, for instance, does not work directly "from nature." Instead, they rely on their instinct, their internal lens, to filter and shape their perception of reality. For them, only the general idea, the final impression, reaches conscious thought. They do not bother with the painstaking process of building conclusions from small, particular details.

But what happens when someone approaches this differently? Take, for example, the Parisian novelists who practice "note- book psychology," recording every detail, large or small, that catches their attention. Such people are constantly spying on life, collecting observations like trinkets to carry home at the end of each day. The result? A chaotic mess, at best resembling a mosaic of unrelated fragments. Their work is restless and garish, more like a patchwork quilt than a coherent picture. The Goncourts are the worst offenders in this regard. They cannot write three sentences without causing pain to anyone with an eye for psychology or aesthetics.

From an artistic perspective, nature is no model to imitate. Nature exaggerates, distorts, and leaves gaps—it is full of accidents. To study "from nature" is, in my view, a bad sign. It shows submission, weakness, and a kind of fatalism. This slavish worship of trivial facts is beneath a true artist. The ability to see "what is" belongs to a different kind of intellect altogether—one that is practical and matter-of-fact, not artistic. An artist must know who they are and what their purpose is, rather than bowing before the randomness of nature.

To make art possible—that is, to create an aesthetic way of acting and seeing—a certain physiological state must come first: ecstasy. Without this heightened state of being, art simply cannot exist. Ecstasy heightens the sensitivity of the whole body and mind, making them more receptive and powerful. Many kinds of ecstasy can lead to art, no matter how they arise. Sexual excitement, for example, is the oldest and most fundamental form of ecstasy. Similarly, ecstasy can come from powerful desires, intense passions, the energy of celebration, the thrill of a battle, the bravery of a daring act, the joy of victory, or the rush of destruction. Even seasonal changes, such as the vibrancy of spring, or the use of drugs can trigger this state. Another form of ecstasy arises from a strong surge of willpower, when one feels driven and overflowing with determination.

At its core, ecstasy creates a feeling of increased strength and abundance. In this state, a person projects their inner wealth onto the world around them. They impose their energy onto things, forcing them to reflect their own richness and power. This act of projecting oneself onto the world is called idealizing. Contrary to popular belief, idealizing does not mean removing details or simplifying things. Instead, it emphasizes the main characteristics so powerfully that lesser details fade away.

In this state of abundance, a person enriches everything they encounter. Whatever they see or desire appears to them as larger, stronger, and more alive. They transform objects and ideas until these reflect their own strength and perfection. This drive to transform things into something beautiful is what we call art. Through art, a person celebrates themselves as a reflection of perfection, even in things they are not.

It is also possible to imagine the opposite of this artistic state—an anti- artistic condition. In such a state, a person drains energy from everything around them. Instead of enriching and enhancing, they weaken and impoverish. These individuals lack vitality and draw from others to sustain themselves. History is full of such anti-artists—individuals like Pascal, whose Christian faith exemplifies this draining tendency. A true Christian, by nature, cannot also be an artist. Even suggesting otherwise by pointing to figures like Raphael misses the point entirely. Raphael affirmed life, celebrated beauty, and said "yes" to the world, which means he was not a Christian in the true sense.

The terms Apollonian and Dionysian, which I introduced to aesthetics, represent two opposing forms of ecstasy. Apollonian ecstasy sharpens vision, giving the eye a heightened ability to see and understand. This type of ecstasy inspires painters, sculptors, and epic poets, who are fundamentally visionaries. On the other hand, Dionysian ecstasy awakens the entire system of passions, intensifying them and causing them to pour out in a flood of expression. This state drives transformation and imitation, releasing all forms of mimicry and artistic display at once. The Dionysian artist is incredibly sensitive to every emotion and suggestion. They instinctively grasp and communicate emotions, transforming themselves into whatever role or passion they encounter. Music, as we understand it today, is a surviving fragment of this broader Dionysian expression—a remnant of a once richer form of emotional discharge. For music to become its own art form, many other senses, such as the sense of touch and movement, had to be partially suppressed. Rhythm, however, still appeals to our physical senses to some extent, linking music to its Dionysian roots.

Actors, mimes, dancers, musicians, and lyricists all share a common foundation in their instincts. Over time, however, they have specialized, developing their own distinct fields of art, even to the point of becoming opposites. Among these, lyricists remained closely connected to musicians for the longest period, while actors were similarly linked to dancers. Architects, however, represent something different. Their art is born not from

Dionysian or Apollonian ecstasy but from the overwhelming will to create. Architecture expresses human pride, triumph over nature, and the will to power in physical form. Great men have always inspired architects, who in turn translate this power into structures that symbolize strength and security. Architecture becomes a language of power, speaking through form. It can persuade, command, or simply exist with quiet confidence. True grandeur in architecture reflects power that is self-assured, needing no validation, unconcerned with opposition, and relying only on itself.

Recently, I read about Thomas Carlyle's life, a mix of unintended comedy and moral posturing. Carlyle was a man of dramatic words and gestures, forever in search of a strong faith that he could not find. This unfulfilled longing makes him a quintessential Romantic. The desire for strong faith, however, is not a sign of having it but rather the opposite. A person with true faith can afford the luxury of doubt and skepticism because their foundation is firm. Carlyle's loud proclamations of reverence for those with strong faith, combined with his anger at those who lacked it, reveal his inner turmoil. He needed noise—both literal and figurative—to distract himself from his doubts.

Carlyle's defining trait was his persistent dishonesty with himself. This quality makes him fascinating, though it also explains why he was so admired in England. Honesty, as the English understand it, often overlaps with hypocrisy, and Carlyle fits this mold perfectly. At heart, he was an atheist who stubbornly refused to admit it, making his struggle with faith all the more dramatic and emblematic of the English spirit.

Emerson is far more enlightened, versatile, and refined than Carlyle, and most importantly, he is happier. He lives instinctively, enjoying the best parts of life while discarding what he finds unpleasant. Compared to Carlyle, Emerson has better taste and a lighter, more joyous intellectuality. Carlyle, who admired him greatly, complained that Emerson "does not give us enough to chew." While this criticism may be true, it hardly counts as a flaw—it is simply a reflection of Emerson's different approach. Emerson's cheerfulness shields him from the heaviness of life. He does not burden himself with excessive seriousness, and he approaches existence with a kind of perpetual youthfulness, blissfully unaware of his age or the weight of time. He might have described himself, in Lope de Vega's words, as someone who constantly succeeds himself, always renewing and reimagining his life. His mind naturally seeks reasons to be content, even grateful, and he often approaches a carefree joyfulness akin to the bourgeois simplicity of a man returning from a romantic escapade, satisfied with life's fleeting pleasures.

The "struggle for existence," a centerpiece of Darwinian thought, strikes me as more of an assumption than an established fact. It does happen, but it is the exception, not the rule. Life's general state is not one of scarcity and competition but one of abundance, extravagance, and even absurd excess. Where struggle does occur, it is more often a struggle for power than for mere survival. The idea of nature as fundamentally Malthusian is misleading. Even if the struggle for existence does take place, its outcomes are often the opposite of what Darwin and his followers might hope. Instead of favoring the strong, the exceptional, and the privileged, it often benefits the weak, simply because they are the majority and frequently more cunning. Darwin overlooked the role of intellect—an oversight that seems distinctly English. The weak are often more intelligent, driven by necessity to develop cleverness and adaptability. By contrast, the strong, having less need for such traits, may grow complacent and neglect their intellect, letting it atrophy. Intellect, after all, demands caution, patience, and subtlety—qualities the powerful may disdain in favor of brute strength.

Those who study humanity deeply often have ulterior motives. A politician, for instance, uses his understanding of people to gain power or advantage. But what of the so-called disinterested observer, the one who claims to seek no personal benefit? A closer look often reveals a darker purpose: the desire to feel superior, to distance oneself from humanity, to no longer belong. This kind of person despises mankind, even if they claim objectivity and fairness. By contrast, the more "self-serving" politician may actually be more humane, for at least he sees himself as part of the same world as those he studies.

The German approach to intellect and psychology leaves much to be desired, as evidenced by certain cultural missteps. Consider, for example, the pairing of names like Goethe and Schiller, or worse, Schiller and Goethe, as if they were equals. Has no one yet recognized the vast gulf between them? And then there are other egregious pairings, such as Schopenhauer and Hartmann. Such thoughtless associations reflect a lack of discernment and an inability to appreciate true intellectual refinement.

The most intelligent and courageous individuals often endure the greatest tragedies because they confront life's most daunting challenges. Yet, paradoxically, these struggles lead them to honor life all the more, for it forces them to grapple with its fiercest adversaries. In this way, their suffering becomes a testament to their strength and their profound engagement with existence.

In today's world, genuine hypocrisy has become increasingly rare. Hypocrisy requires a strong belief, a faith so deeply held that one is willing to outwardly adopt another, contradictory stance while maintaining one's inner conviction. Such duality thrives only in an era of fervent faith, where abandoning one's belief is unthinkable. Modern culture, however, allows for a multiplicity of beliefs, making hypocrisy almost obsolete. People no longer feel the need to maintain a façade; instead, they adopt multiple convictions and live comfortably with them, ensuring these beliefs never truly conflict or demand consistency.

This tolerance for contradictions is both a sign of our age and a symptom of its weaknesses. Modern individuals avoid compromising themselves by avoiding consistency. They cultivate convenience rather than conviction, preferring a life free of challenges or demands on their integrity. Even vices, once expressions of strong will, have degenerated into virtues in this climate of comfort and ease. The few hypocrites I've encountered are mere imitations of the real thing, like actors playing a role. They lack the depth and complexity of true hypocrisy, reduced instead to shallow performances in a world that no longer requires or even understands the profound struggles of belief and deceit.

Beautiful and Ugly:—Our sense of the beautiful is deeply relative, tightly bound to the limitations of human perception and context. To try and separate beauty from the joy humans derive from their surroundings, especially other humans, would be to sever it from its grounding altogether. "Beauty in itself" is nothing more than an abstract phrase, a hollow idea without true substance or universal agreement. In perceiving beauty, humans essentially declare themselves as the measure of perfection. At times, in exceptional circumstances, they even idolize themselves as that ultimate standard. This impulse stems from the most basic instinct of survival and self-preservation. Even the loftiest ideas of beauty are, at their core, expressions of humanity's need to affirm and expand itself.

Man views the world as brimming with beauty, failing to recognize that he is the source of this projection. The beauty he perceives is merely a reflection of himself, a human imprint upon the world. Alas, it is not a universal beauty, but rather one that is all-too-human. In truth, man mirrors himself in everything he beholds, deeming things beautiful because they resonate with his own image.

The judgment of beauty is thus the vanity of the human species, an echo of its own self-love. A skeptic might wonder, "Is the world genuinely beautiful because man finds it so?" Perhaps not. Perhaps all man has done is to humanize the world, to imprint it with his desires and perceptions. Yet, there is no definitive proof that man is the ultimate standard of beauty. What if, in the eyes of a more refined judge of taste, mankind appeared peculiar, comical, or arbitrary? Imagine Dionysus teasing Ariadne about her ears during a philosophical conversation, playfully suggesting, "Why are they not a little longer?" The joke may contain a deeper truth.

From this perspective, nothing in itself is beautiful; it is man alone who declares beauty. Aesthetic sensibility begins with this innocent assumption, the first axiom of aesthetics. Alongside it stands a second principle: nothing is truly ugly except the degenerate man. Together, these principles define the bounds of aesthetic judgment. From a physiological standpoint, ugliness weakens and demoralizes. It reminds humanity of fragility, decay, and the loss of vitality. In the presence of ugliness, man's strength diminishes, as if the sight itself drains him of energy. This reaction, measurable even by a dynamometer, reveals a deep instinctual response: ugliness signals something threatening, something that disrupts the will to power.

When a man feels a sudden drop in confidence or courage, it often stems from encountering something that he perceives as ugly. This reaction emerges from deep within his instincts, stored with countless associations between appearances and their inferred meanings. Ugliness is perceived as a symptom of decline and degeneration. Anything that even faintly suggests a deterioration of the human type—be it physical exhaustion, aging, stiffness, or the crudeness of decomposition—is judged as ugly. Colors, smells, and forms associated with decay, even when abstracted into mere symbols, provoke the same visceral rejection.

This response is not simply distaste; it is hatred, a primal and profound aversion. What is it that man hates in ugliness? He hates the signs of decline in his own kind. This hatred is rooted in the deepest instincts of survival, resonating with the need to preserve the strength and vitality of his type. It is a hatred tinged with horror and caution, expressing a far-sighted instinct for the preservation of life. This reaction is not shallow; it is the most profound hatred man possesses, one that is etched into the very fabric of his being.

It is this hatred of decline, this refusal to accept degeneration, that gives art its depth. Art draws from the profound tension between man's yearning for beauty and his rejection of what threatens his sense of vitality and perfection. In this way, art is more than an expression of the beautiful; it is an affirmation of life, shaped by man's most primal fears and desires.

Schopenhauer, the last German thinker of significance, stands alongside figures like Goethe, Hegel, and Heinrich Heine as a European, not merely a national, event. For a psychologist, he is a fascinating case of the highest order. His work represents a cunning and skillful effort to turn the most life-affirming aspects of human existence—such as art, heroism, genius, beauty, deep compassion, the pursuit of truth, and even the grandeur of tragedy—into arguments for a nihilistic rejection of life. In this, Schopenhauer engages in what could be called one of history's greatest intellectual forgeries, rivaled only by Christianity. He reinterpreted all the noble affirmations of life as if they were but expressions of the denial of the "will to live" or as steps leading inevitably toward that denial.

When scrutinized more closely, Schopenhauer appears as an inheritor of the Christian worldview, repackaged for a secular age. Unlike Christianity, which outright rejects many aspects of human culture, Schopenhauer found a way to nihilistically "approve" of them. To him, these elements of culture—art, beauty, and even human striving—were not ends in themselves but tools to draw the soul toward "salvation," mere appetizers to stimulate a hunger for deliverance from life itself.

Take, for example, his view of beauty. Schopenhauer speaks of beauty with a sorrowful intensity, valuing it as a bridge to something beyond, a fleeting liberation from the burdens of the "will to live." He sees beauty as a temporary escape, particularly from the "burning core" of the will—sexuality. To him, beauty negates the reproductive instinct, offering a glimpse of salvation. Singular saint, indeed! But someone challenges this notion— Nature herself. Why does Nature create beauty in sound, color, fragrance, and rhythm if not to affirm life and reproduction? Why does beauty compel and captivate? Schopenhauer's own idol, Plato, offers a striking contradiction to his thesis.

Plato, whom Schopenhauer venerates as a divine authority, takes an entirely different view. For Plato, beauty is not a denial of life; it is an irresistible lure toward creation and procreation. Beauty inspires both the lowest sensual desires and the highest intellectual pursuits. With a Greek innocence utterly foreign to the Christian mindset, Plato claims that without the beauty of young men in Athens, there would have been no Platonic philosophy. It was their radiance that stirred the philosopher's soul, igniting a passion that refused to rest until it had planted the seeds of great ideas in such captivating soil. Plato himself, then, was a singular saint of a different kind—one for whom the aesthetic and the erotic were deeply intertwined.

This reveals a starkly different approach to philosophy in Athens, where it was pursued openly, even playfully. Unlike the cloistered, abstract cogitations of later thinkers such as Spinoza with his intellectual love of God, Platonic philosophy was an extension of the Greek tradition of competitive games, agon, infused with an erotic dimension. Plato's philosophy was, in many ways, an elevated and spiritualized form of the Greek gymnastic competitions, with dialectics becoming a new art form born of this philosophic eroticism.

In defense of Plato and against Schopenhauer's austere view, it is worth noting that much of the higher culture and literature of classical France also flourished on the fertile ground of sexual interests. Whether in gallantry, the passions, sexual rivalry, or the role of women, these themes pervade French culture and cannot be overlooked. The sensual and the intellectual intertwined seamlessly, revealing that higher culture, far from denying life, often springs from its most vibrant and primal energies.

The idea of l'ar t pour l'ar t—art for art's sake—has often been interpreted as a rebellion against the notion that art must serve a moral purpose or improve humanity. This phrase essentially declares, "Let morality go to hell!" Yet, even in this rejection, we see how deeply entrenched the moral bias remains. The act of opposing morality in art still acknowledges its overwhelming influence. If art is stripped of its role as a preacher of morals or a tool for human betterment, this does not mean it is left entirely without purpose or meaning. To say that art has no purpose, no point, no sense—this is what l'art pour l'art suggests. It is like a snake biting its own tail: a pure passion insisting, "No purpose at all is better than a moral purpose."

But a psychologist must question this: What does art actually do? Does it not praise? Does it not elevate certain ideas while diminishing others? Does it not highlight and amplify? In doing so, art reinforces or diminishes certain values. Can this be dismissed as an incidental outcome or a mere accident, independent of the artist's intentions? Or is it, rather, a fundamental instinct of the artist to shape and serve life through art? Is the artist's true drive concerned with art itself, or does it instead lie in the aim of art—to enrich and enhance life, to advocate for a specific way of living? Art is a tremendous stimulus to life; how, then, can it be seen as pointless or purposeless? It is not simply l'art pour l'art.

And what of the dark and unsettling aspects that art sometimes reveals? When art exposes what is ugly, harsh, or deeply troubling, does it not risk making life unbearable? Some philosophers have thought so. For example, Schopenhauer argued that the purpose of art, especially tragedy, was to free us from the relentless desires of the will and to lead us toward resignation. Tragedy, for him, was valuable because it made us more willing to renounce life. But this view reflects a pessimistic perspective—a deeply negative outlook. To understand art, we must consult the artist, not the pessimist. What does the tragic artist convey to us? Surely it is not resignation but rather a fearless embrace of life's terrors and uncertainties. The artist shows us how to face profound suffering with courage and strength. This attitude is a triumph in itself, and those who have experienced it know it is something to be revered. The artist must share this perspective. A true artist and a genius in communication cannot help but share it.

The tragic artist exalts a heroic spirit, one that confronts overwhelming challenges, sublime catastrophes, and terrifying mysteries with dignity and resolve. This spirit celebrates itself in tragedy, finding joy even in suffering. The tragic artist extends this "cup of sweetest cruelty" to those who are attuned to hardship, who seek it out and embrace it as a defining aspect of life. Tragedy is not about giving up; it is about finding meaning and affirmation in struggle.

A related notion is the idea of hospitality in one's soul. To welcome anyone and everyone into one's inner world may seem generous, but it lacks discernment. A truly noble heart holds its finest chambers in reserve, waiting for worthy guests—guests who are not merely anybody but rather individuals of real substance. Such hearts are rich in depth, with shutters closed and windows veiled, not out of fear or selfishness, but in anticipation of those who merit their best.

Too often, we undervalue ourselves when we attempt to articulate the deepest contents of our souls. Our most profound experiences are not verbose; they are beyond words and would resist even the most earnest attempts at expression. The very act of finding words for something suggests that it has already been overcome or rendered less significant. Speech itself diminishes, for in speaking, we simplify and vulgarize. Words are the currency of the average, the mundane, the communicable. To speak is to betray the depth of what one truly feels, revealing instead only a shadow of the truth. This recognition might well serve as a moral guide for philosophers and others who value the unspoken.

And what of those who strive for objectivity, who pride themselves on their detached and impartial perspectives? Their wisdom, patience, and tolerance may seem impressive, even virtuous, but it often comes at the cost of passion and genuine self-control. Such individuals, drenched in their indulgence and sympathy, should occasionally permit themselves a dose of raw emotion, even a small emotional vice. It may feel uncomfortable, even ridiculous, to them, but it serves as a form of self-discipline—a kind of asceticism for those who have mastered detachment but risk losing touch with their own humanity.

In becoming personal, the so-called "objective" individuals reveal their own virtues, for objectivity often masks a deeper desire:

the need to feel above the fray, detached from the common lot. Yet true nobility lies not in keeping oneself apart but in knowing when and how to connect with others authentically. The virtues of objectivity are limited without the courage to embrace and engage with life's messy, subjective truths.

Excerpt from a doctor's exam paper: "What is the ultimate goal of all advanced education?" To transform a human being into a machine. "What methods are employed to achieve this?" Teaching the individual how to endure boredom. "And how is this boredom instilled?" Through the concept of duty. "What model of duty is presented to the student?" The philologist, who embodies the art of relentless, uninspired diligence. "Who, then, is the ideal human being?" The government official. "And which philosophy provides the definitive framework for this ideal?" Kant's philosophy: envisioning the government official as the ultimate abstraction—the thing- in- itself— presiding over his worldly role as mere appearance.

The Right to Stupidity: Picture the exhausted worker, his breath measured, his demeanor mild, his actions guided by inertia rather than intent. This archetype, a product of our era of relentless labor (and "Empire"), now inhabits every class. This weary figure seeks escape and leisure, claiming even Art for himself—books,

newspapers, and, most notably, beautiful landscapes like Italy. This man of the evening, with his "wild instincts lulled," as Faust might say, requires his summer holidays, his coastal retreats, his alpine glaciers, and his pilgrimage to Bayreuth. In times like these, Art gains the right to be utterly frivolous—a playful retreat for wit, spirit, and emotion. Wagner, of course, understood this well. Pure silliness becomes a form of refreshment, a tonic for the fatigued.

A Further Question of Discipline: Consider the methods Julius Caesar used to safeguard himself against illness and headaches: grueling marches, a life stripped to its simplest essentials, constant exposure to the elements, and enduring hardships without respite. These strategies represent the necessary defenses and survival tactics for those intricate, high-performing organisms called geniuses. Such lives, always teetering at the edge of their capacity, demand such rigorous measures to maintain their vitality.

The Immoralist Speaks: Nothing is more repugnant to true philosophers than observing man in the act of wishing. When they see man purely in his actions—this most fearless, cunning, and resilient of animals, navigating life's calamities with remarkable ingenuity—he earns their admiration. They may even encourage him. Yet the moment man begins to wish or pursue "ideals," he becomes contemptible in their eyes. They reject not only the man of desires but also the very concept of "desirability" and all the ideals and aspirations that humans project upon the world.

Were a true philosopher inclined to nihilism, it would not be because of the absence of meaning but because every human ideal reveals not grandeur but something base: futility, absurdity, frailty, cowardice, fatigue, and the residue left over from life's excesses. Why is it that man, so admirable in his tangible existence, becomes unworthy of respect the moment he begins to desire? Is it some kind of cosmic balancing act? Must the heights of his reality be counterbalanced by the lowliness of his imagination and aspirations? Humanity's history of desires has always been its most shameful chapter; one would be wise not to delve too deeply into it.

What redeems mankind is not its dreams or ideals but its tangible reality. This reality justifies humanity—now and forever. A real man, living and acting in the world, is infinitely more valuable than the mere shadow of a man shaped by desires, fantasies, and delusions. Any ideal man, no matter how elevated he may seem, pales in comparison to the flesh-and-blood individual who embodies the truth of existence. And it is precisely the "ideal man"—the product of abstractions, longings, and lies—that a philosopher finds most insufferable.

The Natural Value of Egoism: The worth of selfishness depends entirely on the inherent value of the individual who practices it. This value may be immense, or it may be insignificant and even contemptible. Every person can be evaluated based on whether they represent the ascending or descending trajectory of life. Once this determination is made, it becomes possible to measure the value of their egoism. If a person embodies the upward movement of life—its growth, strength, and vitality—then their worth is extraordinary. For the collective progress of humanity, which advances through such individuals, it is essential to focus on ensuring their well-being and creating the optimal conditions for them to thrive. These individuals are not isolated entities, mere atoms, or passive inheritors of history; instead, they represent the entire trajectory of humanity culminating in their existence.

Conversely, if an individual represents decline, degeneration, or chronic decay, their value diminishes significantly. Sickness, for instance, is often the result, rather than the cause, of such decline. In such cases, it would be most equitable if these individuals took as little as possible from those who are nature's fortunate creations. These declining individuals become parasitic, drawing from the vitality of others without contributing to life's upward momentum.

The Christian and the Anarchist: When the anarchist, as the voice of the decaying elements in society, cries out for "rights," "justice," or "equality," it is not an enlightened demand but a symptom of their deeper ignorance. They do not understand the true source of their suffering: a poverty not of material possessions but of life itself. An instinct for finding blame is at work here; someone must bear responsibility for their discomfort and unease. Their anger, their dramatic indignation, serves as a fleeting relief—a kind of temporary intoxication that offers them a sense of power, however small. To complain, to bewail one's condition, even to hurl accusations, is a twisted consolation. It allows them to endure their existence by adding a layer of satisfaction to their misery.

There is always an element of revenge in lamentation. In every complaint lies the unspoken accusation: "Because I suffer, you ought to suffer too." This logic, though bitter, is the foundation of revolutions. To grumble about one's plight, however, is always degrading. It stems from weakness, whether one blames others or oneself for one's suffering. The socialist blames society; the Christian, by contrast, blames themselves. But both share a common flaw—the need to identify a scapegoat for their pain. This shared instinct, ignoble in both cases, is driven by the desire to alleviate suffering with the sweet, temporary balm of revenge.

The targets of this vengeful instinct are often incidental, chosen simply because they offer a convenient outlet. The Christian turns their blame inward, condemning their own sinfulness, while the anarchist directs their anger outward, railing against society and its perceived injustices. Yet, both are products of decline, symptoms of decadence. Even the Christian, in their acts of condemnation, slander, and defamation, mirrors the same instinct that drives the socialist worker to vilify society. The ultimate Christian fantasy—the Last Judgment—is nothing more than a dramatic extension of this need for vengeance, a cosmic reckoning that satisfies their desire to see wrongs avenged on the grandest scale.

In this way, the Christian's idea of the "Beyond" serves as nothing more than a tool to defame the "Here." It is not born out of a genuine belief in transcendence but from the need to disparage and denigrate this world. Similarly, the anarchist's dream of revolution is merely a more immediate expression of the same instinct—a wish for upheaval to punish those they blame for their suffering. Whether through the promise of an apocalyptic reckoning or the hope for societal collapse, both use these fantasies to lash out at life, unable to embrace its reality or its challenges.

An "altruistic" morality, one that causes selfishness to weaken and fade away, is always a troubling sign. This holds true not only for individuals but especially for nations. When selfishness starts to diminish, it signals the absence of the best and strongest qualities. To instinctively choose what harms oneself or to be drawn to so-called "selfless" motives is nearly a definition of decadence. The idea of "not prioritizing one's own interests" is nothing more than a moral disguise for a deeper problem, a physiological one: the person no longer knows what truly benefits them. This is the collapse of instincts, the breakdown of life's natural guidance system. A person who becomes overly altruistic is on a dangerous path. Instead of admitting honestly, "I am no longer any good," the lie that decadents tell themselves through morality is, "Nothing is any good— life itself is worthless."

This kind of judgment is deeply harmful, as it can spread like a poison, infecting others. On the polluted soil of society, such ideas grow wildly and take root, appearing now as religion, like Christianity, or as philosophy, like Schopenhauer's worldview. In some cases, even the faintest trace of such toxic ideas, sprouting as they do from the decay of life itself, can harm humanity for thousands of years.

The sick man, in this context, becomes a parasite to society. There are times when continuing to live becomes indecent. When life's meaning and one's right to live have been lost, clinging to existence through doctors and treatments should be viewed with disdain. Doctors themselves should be the ones to instill this sense of contempt; instead of prolonging such lives with prescriptions, they should daily serve their patients a dose of disgust. A new duty should fall upon the doctor—to mercilessly prevent and eliminate degenerate life in cases where the higher interests of life demand it. This would include defending the right to be born, the right to live, and even the right to procreate. One should embrace death proudly when living proudly is no longer possible. Death should be a conscious choice, welcomed at the right time, with clarity and joy, and shared with loved ones in a way that allows a proper farewell. A person should remain fully themselves, able to reflect on their achievements and measure the value of life itself before departing.

This vision is the complete opposite of the grotesque drama that Christianity has turned the moment of death into. Christianity has abused the vulnerability of dying people, violating their conscience and exploiting their final moments as a way of judging them and their lives. For this, Christianity deserves no forgiveness. It is our duty to restore the dignity of death, reclaiming it as a natural, physiological process, even though "natural death" is often nothing more than a euphemism for suicide. No one perishes because of someone else; one dies only because of their own nature. Yet the kind of death that happens by chance, at the wrong time, or under cowardly circumstances, is the most disgraceful. Out of love for life itself, one should strive for a death that is deliberate and free, neither accidental nor unexpected.

Let me offer some advice to the pessimists and other decadents among us. We cannot undo the fact of our birth—that mistake, if it was one—but we can choose to correct it if we wish. The act of taking one's own life can be the most honorable deed. In fact, the person who ends their life almost earns the right to live for having had the strength to do so. Such an act benefits society—and life itself—far more than a life wasted in weakness, self-denial, or other so-called virtues. At the very least, the one who takes their own life spares others the burden of their existence and removes one more objection to the value of life.

Pure pessimism can only truly be proven by the actions of pessimists themselves. They must go further in their logic. To merely deny life in theory, as Schopenhauer did in The World as Will and Idea, is not enough; the next step is to deny Schopenhauer himself. Incidentally, pessimism, no matter how contagious it might appear, does not actually increase the decay of an era or a species. It merely reflects the decay that already exists. Like cholera, it only afflicts those who are already susceptible. Pessimism does not add a single person to the ranks of the world's degenerates. Let me remind you of an important fact: during years when cholera rages, the overall number of deaths does not exceed those of other years.

Have we really become more moral? Many insist that we have, yet I find this belief itself to be grounds for skepticism. In Germany, for instance, the entire force of moral indignation—the kind that passes for morality—was directed against my idea of "Beyond Good and Evil." People argued passionately that modern moral sentiment demonstrates our progress, claiming that compared to us, a figure like Cæsar Borgia could not be seen as a "higher man" or the kind of "superman" I described him to be. One editor even congratulated me for my boldness while accusing me of aiming to abolish all decency. A curious compliment indeed! But I pose this question in return: Have we truly become more moral?

We modern people like to imagine our heightened sensitivity and mutual consideration as evidence of moral advancement. This collective sense of care and support, this avoidance of harm or offense, seems to us a significant step forward—proof that we surpass the brutal and daring men of the Renaissance. Yet every era believes itself superior in such ways; it is inevitable.

One thing is certain: we could not survive the raw reality of the Renaissance, nor could we imagine enduring its conditions. Our nerves and constitutions are simply too frail. But this does not signify progress. It only reflects the weakened, more delicate nature of our current state, a kind of physiological aging that has given rise to a morality of tenderness and caution.

If we strip away this frailty and delicateness, our so-called morality of "humanization" loses all meaning. In such a context, it might even appear contemptible. Let us also consider how our humanitarian virtues would have seemed to Renaissance men—those accustomed to a richer, bolder, and more overflowing vitality. They would have laughed themselves to death at our modern notions of virtue. Unwittingly, we have become laughable. Our supposed "progress" in reducing suspicion and hostility is simply a byproduct of our dwindling vitality. Living in such dependency and fragility requires endless caution and cooperation. In this environment, we become a society of mutual invalids and caregivers, calling this arrangement "virtue."

To men of a fuller, more daring era, our lifestyle might be seen as cowardice, weakness, or the morality of the old and infirm. What I call our softening of morals is not progress but evidence of decline. By contrast, a harder, fiercer moral code often arises in times of surplus vitality. When life overflows with energy, people take risks, embrace challenges, and even waste their strength freely. What once added zest to life might now poison us. Even indifference—a form of strength—is beyond our reach because we are too sensitive, too frail. Our morality of pity, which I was the first to criticize, reflects the hyper- irritability that marks all decadence. Attempts to give this morality a scientific foundation, as Schopenhauer's morality of pity sought to do, are fundamentally decadent and closely aligned with Christian ethics.

Strong ages and noble cultures regarded pity, neighborly love, and self- denial as contemptible traits. They measured their worth by their positive forces, their creative tension, and their ability to stand apart. By this measure, the Renaissance stands as the last great age, while we moderns—obsessed with self- preservation, neighborly love, and cautious virtues like industry and equity—represent a weak one. Our virtues arise from our frailty. The modern idea of "equality" and the process of leveling everyone to the same standard are hallmarks of a declining culture. Strong ages celebrated the differences between people, the "pathos of distance," the instinct to distinguish oneself, and the courage to embrace hierarchy. These qualities are eroding. The gap between extremes is closing, and society is flattening into sameness.

All our political theories, including the structure of "The German Empire," reflect this decline. Even the ideals of modern science are unconsciously shaped by the forces of decadence. My critique of English and French sociology remains the same: it takes the symptoms of societal decline—its frailty and leveling instincts—

and mistakes them for universal norms. Sociology today idealizes descending life, the decay of all organizing power, and the erosion of rank and distinction. This is what our socialists champion as progress. But it is not only socialists who are guilty of this error. Herbert Spencer, with his vision of altruism's triumph, was equally a decadent. To him, and to many others, this collapse of vitality appeared as an ideal to be pursued.

My Concept of Freedom.—The value of something is not always found in what it helps us achieve but often in what it demands from us—the price we must pay. Liberal institutions, for example, lose their essence of freedom the moment they become securely established. Once they are no longer contested, they turn into oppressive forces that stifle true freedom. These institutions undermine the Will to Power, promoting mediocrity as a virtue. They encourage conformity, making people timid, complacent, and fixated on comfort. Under them, the herd instinct triumphs, and humanity is reduced to a collective of obedient cattle. Liberalism, stripped of its idealism, becomes nothing more than the domestication of mankind.

However, the same liberal institutions, when fought for and not yet fully realized, can inspire the very opposite. Struggle for their creation and survival fosters freedom because it involves conflict. And it is war—war for freedom— that preserves the untamed, illiberal instincts essential for liberty. War trains individuals to be free. So, what is freedom? Freedom is the will to take responsibility for oneself. It is the capacity to maintain the distance that distinguishes you from others, to embrace hardship, endure privation, and remain indifferent even to life itself when necessary. It is the willingness to sacrifice, not only others but also yourself, for a cause you believe in. Freedom is the triumph of warrior instincts—those that revel in challenge and victory— over the instincts that crave mere comfort and happiness.

The truly free man despises the shallow comfort idolized by merchants, Christians, cattle, women, Englishmen, and democrats. For him, comfort is contemptible. The free man is a warrior. The measure of freedom, whether in individuals or nations, is determined by the resistance they have to overcome and the effort it takes to stay above it all. True freedom is greatest where the challenge is fiercest—just steps away from tyranny, on the threshold of being overpowered. Psychologically, tyranny represents the inner, powerful instincts that demand the utmost discipline to subdue. Julius Caesar is the finest example of such a free spirit, a man who mastered his instincts with an iron will. Politically, the same holds true: history shows that nations worth admiring were never formed under liberal institutions. It was great danger that shaped them into something worthy of reverence. Danger reveals our hidden strengths, awakens our virtues, and compels us to innovate and defend ourselves. It forces us to become resourceful and discover our inner genius.

The first principle of freedom is this: strength is born of necessity. Without the need to be strong, no one becomes strong. The greatest incubators of strength, the strongest individuals and societies to ever exist, emerged from aristocratic communities like Rome and Venice. These societies understood freedom as I do—not as a given, but as something that must be seized, something you either have or do not have, something you will for yourself and take by force.

A Criticism of Modernity.—We all agree on one thing: our institutions are failing. Yet the fault does not lie with these institutions themselves but with us. We no longer possess the instincts that once gave rise to institutions and sustained them. Without those instincts, the institutions themselves are crumbling and disappearing because we are no longer capable of upholding them. Democracy has always marked the decline of organizational power. I pointed this out as early as "Human,

All Too Human," where I described modern democracy, along with its half-measures like the "German Empire," as forms of a decaying State.

For institutions to exist and thrive, a particular kind of will is necessary—a will that is instinctive, commanding, and even harshly anti-liberal. This will demands allegiance to tradition, authority, and a responsibility that spans generations, stretching infinitely backward and forward in time. When such a will is present, empires with lasting power emerge, like the imperium Romanum or, in our era, Russia. Russia is the only nation today that demonstrates the endurance, strength, and patience required for genuine stability, a nation that can afford to wait, that can still promise a future. Russia stands as the antithesis of the petty- statism, fragility, and nervous exhaustion that plague Europe, particularly brought to the forefront by the foundation of the German Empire.

The modern Western world no longer harbors the instincts that produce institutions or the future. These instincts are fundamentally at odds with what is called the "modern spirit." People live recklessly in the moment, at breakneck speed, with little thought for long-term responsibility. And yet, this is celebrated and called "freedom." But all the qualities that make institutions enduring and meaningful are now despised, ridiculed, and rejected. Even the faintest whisper of authority sends people into a panic about a potential new slavery. In our politics and political parties, the instinct to value and preserve what is solid has decayed so deeply that people instinctively prefer what dissolves, what speeds up the collapse of everything.

Take modern marriage as an example. Its original rationality has vanished completely, but this is not a criticism of marriage itself—it is a criticism of modernity. Marriage once had a clear, rational foundation. It rested on the exclusive legal responsibility of the husband, which acted as a stabilizing force within the union. This stability gave marriage a weight and seriousness that countered the fleeting impulses of sentiment, passion, or momentary desires.

Marriage also relied on the absolute indissolubility of the bond, which instilled it with permanence, regardless of the accidents of emotion. Additionally, the responsibility of choosing marriage partners fell to the family, which ensured a certain strategic and long-term coherence in these unions.

The increasing preference for love marriages, however, has undermined the very foundation of matrimony. No institution can ever be built upon a fleeting idiosyncrasy such as "love." Love is too transitory, too unstable to bear the weight of a lasting structure. Marriage can be based on more enduring forces: sexual desire, the instinct of property (with the wife and children seen as possessions), or the instinct of dominion. The latter is particularly vital, as it drives the creation of the smallest yet enduring unit of governance—the family. The family requires children and heirs to carry forward its acquired power, wealth, and influence, ensuring a continuity of purpose and solidarity in instincts from one generation to the next.

Marriage, as an institution, assumes a commitment to the greatest and most enduring forms of organization. It presupposes that society as a whole is willing to secure its own continuity into the distant future. Without this shared commitment, marriage loses its meaning. And this is exactly what has happened to modern marriage: it has lost its meaning, and as a result, it is gradually being abolished.

The question of the working man arises from a combination of foolishness and the underlying degenerate instincts that fuel the intellectual confusion of modern times. There are matters so basic and essential to the order of things that they should never even be questioned. This principle, rooted in instinct, serves as the foundation for survival and continuity. Yet here we are, asking what we should do about the European working class, having transformed their existence into a "question." What is expected now? These workers have been made too aware of their position, their situation framed as an issue, and their sense of entitlement has grown. They question more and more, with increasing boldness, and why wouldn't they? They know they have the numbers on their side.

There's no chance now of cultivating a humble, contented worker like the kind found in China—a course that would have been both reasonable and necessary. Instead, thoughtless and shortsighted decisions have destroyed the very instincts required for the existence of a functional and stable working class. By declaring the working man fit for military service, granting him the right to unionize, and giving him a vote, society has made his discontent inevitable. What did people expect? These concessions have led him to see his position not as a fact of life but as a moral outrage, as an injustice. And yet I ask again, what is the goal here? If people desire a certain outcome, they must also desire the means to achieve it. If society wants workers, it is madness to educate them into believing they are masters.

The kind of freedom being clamored for today is not the kind I mean when I speak of freedom. In our era, leaving individuals to their instincts only leads to chaos. These instincts often contradict and destroy one another, tearing individuals apart from within. Modern life itself can be described as a state of physiological self-contradiction. A rational system of education would seek to suppress some instincts with rigorous discipline, allowing others to grow strong and dominant. This pruning would make individuals coherent and capable. Instead, what we see today is the opposite. The loudest calls for independence, for unchecked development, and for "letting go" come from those who most desperately need restraint. This phenomenon extends to politics and even art. It is a sign of decline, another proof of our instincts faltering. The modern understanding of "freedom" is not a triumph; it is evidence of our degeneration.

When faith becomes necessary, honesty among moralists and saints becomes exceedingly rare. They may claim to value honesty; they may even believe they practice it. But when belief is more effective, more convincing, and ultimately more useful than deliberate hypocrisy, instinct makes that hypocrisy innocent. This principle is key to understanding the behavior of great saints. The same can be said for philosophers, who are their own kind of saint. Their role requires them to uphold certain truths, truths that bolster their craft and grant it public approval. To borrow from Kant, these are the truths of "practical reason." Philosophers know what they must prove. This is their pragmatism, their trade secret. They recognize one another by their shared adherence to these "essential truths." The commandment "Thou shalt not lie" is, for the philosopher, merely a warning: Do not dare, dear philosopher, to speak the entire truth.

A quiet reminder to conservatives: What we have learned—or should have learned—is that regression is impossible. Reverting to a previous state, whether biologically, culturally, or morally, is a fantasy. As physiologists, we know this for a fact. Yet priests and moralists have always believed otherwise. They have tried to bend and force humanity back into older molds of virtue, imposing the rigid standards of morality as if humanity could fit back into them. Even modern politicians mimic these moralists. Today, some political movements aim to force the world into a backward march, longing for an imagined past where everything supposedly worked. But not everyone is suited to move backward like a crab.

The truth is, humanity must move forward, even if this means deeper descent into decadence. This is how I define modern "progress": each step forward is another step further into decay. We cannot halt this trajectory entirely. At best, we might delay it, creating bottlenecks of degeneration that will only result in more violent and catastrophic outbursts later on. But we cannot turn back the tide. Progress, as we conceive of it today, is no more than the managed advance of decline.

My concept of genius begins with the idea that great men and great eras are like explosive forces, holding within them a tremendous amount of stored energy. Their very existence depends on both historical and physiological conditions. They arise only when energy has been conserved, hoarded, and preserved over long periods without any premature release. Once the tension has built to an extreme, even the slightest trigger can ignite the force, giving rise to genius, extraordinary deeds, and monumental changes in the world.

What, then, is the significance of external factors like environment, historical periods, or the so-called "spirit of the age"? Consider Napoleon as an example. Revolutionary France, and even more so the years preceding the Revolution, cultivated values and produced types of people entirely contrary to what Napoleon represented. Yet Napoleon emerged not as a product of that age, but as a legacy of a stronger, older, and more enduring civilization—a civilization whose vitality France was busy dismantling. Precisely because he was different, because he drew from a deeper reservoir of power and tradition, Napoleon became the uncontested master of his time. His strength surpassed that of his contemporaries, allowing him to dominate them.

Great individuals are essential, yet the era in which they appear is largely a matter of chance. Their near-inevitable mastery of their time stems from their greater strength, maturity, and the longer duration for which power has been stored within them. The relationship between genius and its era is like that between strength and weakness, or maturity and immaturity. A genius always towers above his age, which is comparatively youthful, feeble, indecisive, and naive.

Today, however, many people hold a different view, especially in France, where the idea that the "environment" or "zeitgeist" shapes genius has gained almost scientific credibility, even among physiologists. This belief—a sort of nervous disorder disguised as intellectual insight—is a troubling and disheartening sign. England, too, subscribes to this view, but this is hardly surprising. The English tend to interpret genius in only two ways: either through a democratic lens, as exemplified by Buckle, or through a religious perspective, as Carlyle does.

Great individuals and great ages bring with them immense danger. They exhaust what came before and often leave sterility in their wake. A great man signifies an ending, just as a great age—take the Renaissance, for instance— marks the conclusion of a long buildup of energy. Genius, in both action and creation, is inherently extravagant. Its greatness lies in its uncontainable outpouring of energy. The instinct for self-preservation is overridden in such figures; their overwhelming energy compels them to give and expend themselves completely, without restraint. This process is not calculated or deliberate—it is as inevitable as a river bursting through its dams.

People often misinterpret this self-expenditure, labeling it "self-sacrifice" or admiring it as "heroism." They speak of the genius's disregard for personal well- being, their unwavering dedication to an idea, a cause, or a nation. But these are misconceptions. A genius does not act out of deliberate self-sacrifice; they overflow naturally, consuming themselves in the process. They cannot help but give everything—they are compelled by their very nature to do so, just as a river must flow.

Humanity, having reaped countless benefits from such explosive forces, has responded with a peculiar kind of gratitude. It has attributed to these figures a higher morality, seeing in them ideals of selflessness and devotion. Yet this, too, is a misunderstanding. It is not morality that drives the genius; it is the sheer necessity of their nature. Humanity thanks its benefactors in the only way it knows—by misinterpreting them.

The criminal and those like him represent the strong man placed in conditions that do not suit him—a strong nature forced into sickness. He is a man who thrives in wild and untamed environments, where freedom and danger shape life, where the instincts of strength—his shield and sword—find their rightful place. But within society, these very virtues are outlawed. His natural instincts are immediately entangled with emotions like fear, suspicion, and shame. Such a conflict is nearly a formula for physical and psychological decline. When a person must carry out what he is best at—what he most loves—not openly but in secrecy, with constant caution, restraint, and craftiness, it saps his vitality. The repeated necessity of paying for his instincts through danger, persecution, or punishment causes him to turn against those very instincts. He comes to see them as his curse.

This process unfolds most severely in our society, which is tame, average, and emasculated. A natural man, one unshaped by civilization, coming from the mountains or the open seas, is almost certain to decay into a criminal in such an environment. Yet, not always: there are cases where the natural man is stronger than society itself. Napoleon, the Corsican, stands as the most famous example of this triumph.

To explore this further, we can turn to Dostoevsky, a witness of singular importance on this issue. Dostoevsky—incidentally the only psychologist from whom I have learned anything—was among the great discoveries of my life, even more rewarding than Stendhal. This deeply insightful man, who had every reason to hold the shallow Germans in contempt, found among the Siberian convicts he lived with for years—those utterly hopeless criminals with no chance of returning to society—a type of humanity very different from what he had anticipated. These convicts were made of the hardest and most valuable material to be found in Russian society, carved from a superior stock.

Now let us generalize the case of the criminal. Let us think of all individuals who, for whatever reason, fail to gain society's approval. These are people who know they are not seen as beneficial or respectable. They exist with the feelings of outcasts, akin to the Chandala, aware that they are not treated as equals but as untouchables, proscribed, or polluted. Their thoughts and actions are shaped by this awareness, marked by a certain shadowy, subterranean quality. Their inner world becomes dimmed compared to those who live in the sunlight of public favor.

Interestingly, many of the figures we now admire and respect once lived under such conditions. The scientist, the artist, the genius, the independent thinker, the actor, the entrepreneur, and the great adventurer—all of these lived lives that were once disdained. As long as the priest stood as the highest type of man, all others of value were diminished, seen as less worthy. However, the time is coming—this I assert with certainty—when the priest will be regarded as the lowest type of man, as our Chandala, the most dishonest and disreputable among us.

Even now, under the most lenient and humane customs ever known in Europe, any life that stands apart, that is prolonged in obscurity or strangeness, begins to resemble the criminal type. All pioneers of the spirit bear for a time the grim and fateful mark of the Chandala. It is not because they are directly seen as such by others, but because they themselves feel the enormous gulf that separates them from what is accepted and honored in tradition. Nearly every genius experiences this phase of the "Catilinarian life"—a stage filled with hatred, revenge, and rebellion against everything stagnant and established. Catiline—the early form of every future Caesar.

Here the outlook is free. When a philosopher chooses silence, it can signify the greatness of his soul; when he contradicts himself, it might stem from love; and when he lies, it may well be the courtesy of a knight of knowledge. As someone aptly remarked, "It is unworthy of great hearts to spread the turmoil they feel." Yet, it is equally true that there can be greatness in not avoiding what seems undignified. A woman in love may sacrifice her honor, a knight of knowledge who "loves" may sacrifice his humanity, and a god who loved became a Jew.

Beauty is no accident. Even the beauty of a race or family, the grace and perfection of all its movements, does not come easily. Like genius, it is the culmination of generations of effort. Great sacrifices have always been made on the altar of good taste, and much has been deliberately left undone. The 17th century in France serves as a prime example of this, a time when both action and restraint worked hand in hand to elevate aesthetics. A principle of selection was applied to everything—company, environment, clothing, and even the expression of sexual desire. Beauty was prioritized over profit, habit, public opinion, and laziness. The first rule was simple: no one should "let themselves go," not even in private.

Good things are exceedingly expensive. This is true not only in monetary terms but in the discipline required to acquire them.

Whoever possesses beauty or refinement is different from someone still striving for it. Everything good is an inheritance, something passed down and refined over time. What isn't inherited is incomplete; it is only a beginning. In ancient Athens, during Cicero's time, men and boys were more beautiful than women. But this was the result of centuries of rigorous effort and self-discipline devoted to male beauty. Let us not be deceived: refining feelings and thoughts alone is insufficient. This is the great failing of German culture, which emphasizes abstract ideals but neglects the body.

The body must be persuaded first. Maintaining a refined and tasteful demeanor, associating only with others who do the same, shapes one's entire being over a few generations. The destiny of a people or humanity is determined by where they begin their cultural efforts. The starting point must be the body, behavior, diet, and physiology—not the "soul," as priests and moralists insist. The Greeks understood this foundational truth and acted upon it, which is why they remain the first true creators of culture. Christianity, with its disdain for the body, has been the greatest misfortune to ever befall humanity.

Progress, as I see it, is not about returning to a primal state but ascending into a more profound and untamed naturalness. It is about reaching a height where one can grapple with grand challenges, even play with them. Take Napoleon as an example of what I mean by a "return to nature." In his tactics and strategy, he exemplified this ascent. But Rousseau? Where did he wish to return? Rousseau, that first modern man, was both an idealist and a scoundrel. Needing moral dignity to endure his own reflection, he was a creature of vanity and self-loathing. He camped on the threshold of modernity, calling for a "return to nature." But what kind of nature did he envision? I detest Rousseau even in the Revolution. The Revolution's bloody spectacle does not disturb me as much as its Rousseau-inspired morality. It was the morality of mediocrity masquerading as justice.

The doctrine of equality is the deadliest poison of all, for it pretends to speak in the name of justice while veiling true justice. Justice would say, "To equals, equality; to unequals, inequality." Never should unequal things be made equal. The horrors and bloodshed associated with this doctrine have granted it an undeserved aura of sanctity. The Revolution, as a drama, has deceived even noble minds. Only Goethe, as far as I can see, viewed it as it should be seen— with utter disdain.

Goethe was not merely a German figure but a European one. He was a bold attempt to overcome the 18th century by reclaiming the naturalness of the Renaissance. In Goethe, the instincts of his century—its sentimentality, its idolization of nature, and its anti-historical spirit—were transformed. He was a realist who embraced life rather than shrinking from it. Goethe sought wholeness, uniting reason, feeling, sensuality, and will, in opposition to the fragmented doctrines of Kant. He disciplined himself into a harmonious whole and became a master of himself.

Goethe dreamed of a complete human being: cultured, physically skilled, self-respecting, and capable of indulging in life's richness without being destroyed by it. He was tolerant not from weakness but from strength, turning adversity to his advantage.

He embodied a cheerful fatalism, embracing the universe with confidence. Such faith, the highest of all, is what I have called Dionysian—a celebration of life that affirms all existence.

In some ways, the 19th century aspired to Goethe's ideals: broad understanding, bold realism, and reverence for life's facts. Yet, the result was chaos, fatigue, and a retreat into the sentimental mediocrity of the 18th century—romanticism, socialism, and altruism. This century, especially in its later years, became an intensified version of its predecessor: a period of decline. Goethe, despite his greatness, was merely an episode—a magnificent but futile effort.

Great men should not be judged by their immediate utility. Humanity often misunderstands its benefactors, attributing to them motives they never had. Goethe is the last German I respect. He understood the cross, as I understand it, and shared my disdain for what it symbolizes. People often ask why I write in German when I am so little read in Germany. My aim is not immediate recognition but to create works that time itself cannot erode. Both in form and content, I strive for a degree of immortality. The aphorism and the concise sentence, forms in which I am a master, are eternal. My ambition is to say in ten sentences what others cannot say in a whole book.

With Thus Spoke Zarathustra, I have given humanity its deepest book.

Soon, I will give it its most independent one.

Chapter 10
Things I owe to The Ancients

In conclusion, I want to say a few words about that world to which I have sought new ways of access and for which I may have discovered a new passage—the ancient world. My taste, which is perhaps the opposite of tolerant, does not wholeheartedly embrace even this world. In general, I am not eager to say Yes to things. I would rather say No, or, better yet, say nothing at all. This is true of entire cultures; it is true of books; and it is true of places and landscapes.

To be honest, there are very few ancient books that hold a special place in my life, and the most famous ones are not included among them.

My sense of style, particularly for the epigram as a form of expression, seemed to awaken almost instantly when I first encountered Sallust. I still recall the astonishment of my respected teacher Corssen when he was compelled to give his worst Latin student the highest marks. Suddenly, and all at once, I understood everything there was to learn. The condensed and austere language, packed with meaning and with an almost mischievous indifference to "beautiful words" and "beautiful feelings"—in these I found my own inclination. In my writings leading up to Thus Spoke Zarathustra, you will notice a serious effort to achieve a Roman style—a style that aspires to the permanence of "more enduring than bronze."

The same thing occurred when I first read Horace. No poet, even to this day, has given me the same intense artistic pleasure as an ode by Horace did from the very beginning. In some languages, it would be ridiculous to even attempt what Horace achieves. His writing is like a mosaic where every word radiates its influence both to the left and the right. Its placement, sound, and meaning all work together to create an extraordinary effect. This economy of words—

where the least amount of signs produces the maximum energy—is distinctly Roman. And, if you trust my judgment, it is the very definition of noble excellence. Compared to this, all other poetry seems almost crude, like meaningless, sentimental rambling.

I cannot say that I owe the Greeks anything resembling the profound impressions I have received from the Romans. To be frank, the Greeks can never hold the same significance for us as the Romans do. The Greeks are not teachers in the same way. Their style is too peculiar, too fluid, to impose itself as a model or to attain the weight of a true classic. Who has ever truly learned how to write from a Greek? It is impossible to imagine anyone mastering writing without the Romans. They are our true instructors. And do not suggest Plato to me—I remain fundamentally skeptical of him. I have never been able to align myself with the tradition among scholars of admiring Plato as an artist.

Even in antiquity, the most refined critics of taste were not taken by Plato as we are led to believe. To my mind, Plato jumbles all the forms of style into a chaotic mix. In this sense, he is one of the earliest examples of stylistic decadence. He shares this fault with the Cynics, who created the satura Menippea. The Platonic dialogue—a smug, almost juvenile form of dialectics—could only charm someone who has never read good French writers, such as Fontenelle. Plato, I must confess, bores me. At heart, my distrust of him is fundamental. I see him as profoundly removed from the essential instincts of the Hellenes, steeped in moral prejudices, and, in some respects, as a precursor to Christianity. For Plato, the idea of "good" is already the supreme value—a concept that foreshadows the Christian morality to come. If I had to give Plato's philosophy a blunt name, I might call it "lofty nonsense," or, if preferred, "idealism."

Humanity has paid a high price for this Athenian's education among the Egyptians—or perhaps among the Jews in Egypt? Plato, with his double-edged charm—the so-called "ideal"— became the bridge by which the nobler spirits of antiquity were led to misunderstand themselves and cross into the ideology that culminated in the Christian cross. And even now, how much Plato remains entrenched in the concepts of the "church," in its architecture, its system, and its practices!

For me, the cure, the antidote, and the reprieve from all this Platonism has always been Thucydides. His work represents my ideal of clarity and realism.

Perhaps Machiavelli's The Prince is his closest relative in spirit. Both refuse to delude themselves. They seek reason in reality, not in abstract rationality or morality. Thucydides is the antithesis of the sugary, romanticised vision of the Greeks that modern "classical education" instills in young minds. His writings should be read with great care, each line scrutinised, and his unspoken ideas considered just as seriously as his explicit words. Few thinkers possess so much depth in what they leave unsaid.

Thucydides is the consummate expression of the Sophist tradition, that movement grounded in realism which resisted the idealistic pretensions and moral posturing of Socratic thought as it spread in all directions. For me, Greek philosophy represents the decline of Greek instincts, whereas Thucydides encapsulates the unflinching, rigorous realism of the ancient Hellene.

The distinction between Thucydides and Plato is ultimately one of courage versus fear. Thucydides confronts reality with bravery and clarity, while Plato shrinks from it, retreating into the comforting arms of ideals. Thucydides is a master of his own mind and therefore a master of life. Plato, on the other hand, flees from life into the shadows of abstract ideals. This makes Thucydides not just a historian, but a thinker of unyielding power and strength, unmatched in his affirmation of reality.

To unearth examples of "beautiful souls," "golden means," or other supposed perfections among the Greeks, to admire their serene grandeur, their so-called ideal attitudes, or their exalted simplicity—this "exalted simplicity," which in truth is nothing more than a piece of German naivety, was something from which my inner psychologist always saved me. What I saw instead was their most powerful instinct: the relentless Will to Power. I saw them driven by the fierce and untamed force of this will, trembling with its violence. I recognized that their institutions were not built on harmony but on strategies of containment, created to protect every individual from the volatile, explosive energy simmering within their neighbor.

This immense internal tension found its outlet in violent and ruthless aggression directed outward, toward other states. Their cities tore at one another in brutal conflict, each striving to maintain peace within by externalizing the chaos. Strength became an absolute necessity in this environment, for danger was constant and ever-present, lurking at every corner. The extraordinary grace and flexibility of their bodies, the bold realism, and even the characteristic amorality of the Hellenes—these were not innate attributes but rather survival mechanisms. These traits were forged under the pressures of their circumstances, not gifts they were born with.

Even their festivals and artistic achievements were not mere expressions of joy or creativity but instruments of self-assertion and self-glorification. These were deliberate efforts to heighten their sense of superiority, to project it outward, and sometimes to inspire terror in those who observed them. Imagine judging the Greeks through a lens shaped by German interpretations—seeing them through the narrow focus of their philosophers. Worse yet, imagine using the staid, suburban respectability of the Socratic schools as the key to understanding the essence of what is truly Hellenic!

The truth is that the philosophers were the decadent offshoots of Hellas, a counter-movement that ran against the grain of their original and noble values. They opposed the agonal instinct, the competitive drive that defined the Hellenic spirit; they rejected the spirit of the polis, the pride in racial excellence, and the authority of deep-rooted traditions. Socratic virtues were only preached to the Greeks because the Greeks had already begun to lose their virtue. Irritable, cowardly, unsteady, and increasingly prone to theatricality, they were a people in decline, desperate for the moral sermons directed at them.

But these moral prescriptions did not save them. They could not. Instead, these grand gestures and lofty words were little more than adornments for a society in decay. Decadents are always drawn to such displays, for they cling to the illusion of greatness even as it slips further from their grasp. Morality, as the Greeks came to know it through their philosophers, was not a cure but a symptom—a symptom of a people who had already lost their way.

I was the first to take the phenomenon of Dionysus seriously in order to understand the ancient, vibrant, and abundantly rich Hellenic instinct. This phenomenon, remarkable in its essence, can only be interpreted as an expression of overflowing energy. Whoever has studied the Greeks as profoundly as Jakob Burckhardt of Basel, one of the finest connoisseurs of their culture, would immediately recognize that this interpretation opened a new path of understanding. In his Cultur der Griechen, Burckhardt even dedicated a special chapter to this subject, acknowledging its significance. On the other hand, consider the almost laughable deficiency of instinct displayed by German philologists when they approach the question of Dionysus. The famous Lobeck, for example, burrowed into this mysterious realm with the assuredness of a dried-up bookworm, convinced he was being scientific when, in truth, his approach was painfully superficial and immature.

With all the pomp of erudition, Lobeck reduced the mysteries to trivialities, suggesting that the orgies merely taught participants banal facts like how wine stirs desire or that plants bloom and fade with the seasons. He explained away the immense wealth of rites, symbols, and myths rooted in these rituals—which permeate the entirety of antiquity—with the dismissive notion that the Greeks merely invented festivals and myths as idle diversions. His conclusion, that celebratory behaviors like laughing, weeping, and dancing formed the basis of elaborate traditions, is nothing short of absurd. This reductionist nonsense, presented as scholarship, deserves no serious consideration.

Contrast this with the more profound vision of the Greeks as seen by figures like Winckelmann and Goethe. Yet even they misunderstood something essential. Their idealized image of the Greeks—one of calm grandeur, rational simplicity, and harmonious beauty—could not accommodate the Dionysian essence. Goethe, for instance, likely dismissed the ecstatic fervor of Dionysian rites, failing to recognize that these mysteries revealed the core of the Greek soul. This core was their "will to life," expressed most powerfully in the Dionysian state. Through these mysteries, the Greeks secured for themselves a profound connection to life eternal, embracing its cyclical nature and celebrating the continuity of existence through procreation and renewal.

To the Greeks, the mysteries of sexuality symbolized the sacred foundation of life itself. Every aspect of birth, creation, and renewal was steeped in reverence and seen as divine. Even pain, particularly the pain of childbirth, was sanctified, as it was inseparable from creation and growth. This sanctification of pain carried a deeper message: to ensure the endless joy of creation, the "pains of childbirth" must be eternal. Such is the symbolism of Dionysus, the affirmation of life in all its fullness, including its suffering, its ecstasy, and its inexhaustible capacity for renewal.

Christianity later distorted this profound connection, branding sexuality as impure and casting filth upon the very foundation of existence. In doing so, it severed humanity from the instinctual reverence for life that the Greeks held sacred. Yet it was the psychology of orgiasm—this experience of overwhelming vitality, where even pain becomes a stimulant—that gave me the key to understanding the concept of tragic feeling. Aristotle and the pessimists misunderstood tragedy entirely. Far from being an expression of Greek pessimism, as Schopenhauer claimed, tragedy represents the ultimate rejection of such a worldview. It is a triumphant affirmation of life, embracing even its most perplexing and terrifying aspects.

The essence of tragedy lies in its exultation of life's inexhaustible energy, even in the sacrifice of its highest forms. This is the Dionysian spirit, the bridge to the psychology of the tragic poet. It does not aim to escape terror and pity or to purge dangerous passions through catharsis, as Aristotle supposed. Instead, it transcends terror and pity, rejoicing in the eternal cycle of creation and destruction, the endless becoming that is life itself. This lust for life, which includes a love for destruction as part of creation, is at the heart of the Dionysian worldview.

With this understanding, I return to the foundation of my philosophy, to the starting point of my intellectual journey. The Birth of Tragedy was my first attempt to reevaluate all values, and here, once again, I stand upon the same ground from which my will and power originate. I am the last disciple of the philosopher Dionysus, the prophet of eternal recurrence.

The End

The Birth of Tragedy

Friedrich Nietzsche

Prologue

Frederick Nietzsche was born in Röcken, near Lützen, in the Prussian province of Saxony, on October 15, 1844, at 10 a.m. This day happened to coincide with the birthday of Frederick William IV, the King of Prussia at the time. By a fortunate coincidence, the local church bells, which were ringing to mark the king's birthday, also welcomed my brother as he entered the world.

In 1841, while our father was serving as a tutor to the Altenburg princesses—Theresa of Saxe-Altenburg, Elizabeth, Grand Duchess of Oldenburg, and Alexandra, Grand Duchess Constantine of Russia—he had the honor of meeting his sovereign, the witty and devout King Frederick William IV. The meeting left a favorable impression on both sides. Shortly afterward, our father was appointed to his position as pastor in Röcken, by the king's direct order. It is easy to imagine the joy he felt when, on his esteemed patron's birthday, he welcomed the birth of his first son. At the christening ceremony, our father expressed his feelings with the following words:

"Blessed month of October! For many years, the most significant events of my life have unfolded during these thirty-one days.

Today, I celebrate the greatest and most wonderful event of all by baptizing my little boy! What a joyful moment! What a sacred duty! In the name of the Lord, I bless this day! With all my heart, I offer this prayer: Bring me my beloved child, that I may dedicate him to the Lord. My son, Frederick William, this shall be your name on earth, in honor of my royal benefactor on whose birthday you were born!"

Our father was thirty-one years old, and our mother not yet nineteen, when my brother was born. Our mother, the daughter of a clergyman, was a healthy and attractive woman. She came from a very large family with many brothers and sisters. Our paternal grandparents, the Reverend Oehler and his wife, who lived in Pobles, were known for their robust health, strong constitutions, and cheerful temperaments. They had lively personalities and an optimistic outlook on life, qualities that everyone admired in them.

Our grandfather Oehler was an intelligent and spirited man, very much the image of the old-fashioned, well-to-do country pastor who saw no sin in enjoying activities like hunting. He was remarkably healthy, rarely ill, and might have lived well past seventy if his carefree attitude toward his health had not led to a severe cold that ultimately proved fatal. Our grandmother Oehler, on the other hand, lived to the age of eighty-two, and if all German women had enjoyed her level of health, it is said that the German nation would surpass all others in vitality.

She had eleven children with our grandfather, breastfeeding each of them for nearly their entire first year, and she successfully raised them all. Visitors often marveled at the sight of these eleven children, ranging in age from nineteen years to one month. They were described as robust, with rosy cheeks, bright eyes, and thick curly hair—a sight that filled people with admiration. Yet, despite their excellent health, life in such a large family was not without its challenges. Each child was full of energy, strong-willed, and stubborn, making it no small task to maintain discipline. Although they always showed great respect and obedience to their parents, even as adults, conflicts and disagreements among the siblings were frequent.

Our Oehler grandparents were financially well-off. Our grandmother came from an old and distinguished family that had owned large estates near Zeitz for many generations. Her father owned the baronial estate of Wehlitz and a grand residence near Zeitz in Pacht. When she married, her father provided her with a remarkable dowry that included carriages, horses, a coachman, a cook, and a kitchenmaid—an exceptionally generous gift for the wife of a German minister, both then and now. However, the family's fortunes were significantly reduced during the wars of the early nineteenth century, when our great-grandfather lost much of his property.

Our father's family was also relatively well-off and quite large. Our grandfather, Dr. Nietzsche (Doctor of Divinity and Superintendent), was married twice and had twelve children, though three of them died young. I never met him, but he was said to have been a distinguished, dignified, very learned, and somewhat reserved man. His second wife, our dear grandmother, was known for her sharp mind, intelligence, and exceptionally kind nature.

The entire family on our father's side, whom I only got to know in their later years, was remarkable for their great self-discipline, lively interest in intellectual matters, and a strong sense of family unity. This unity was evident in their willingness to help one another and their consistently good relationships. Our father, the youngest son, was especially beloved due to his exceptionally kind and lovable nature. His other talents became more apparent as he grew older, making him the favorite of the family. He was said to have been in excellent health, a claim supported by those who knew him during his time at the convent school in Rossleben, at university, or later at the ducal court of Altenburg. He was tall, slender, and gifted in poetry, with real musical talent. He was also deeply sensitive, considerate of his family, and distinguished in his manners.

My brother often spoke of our Polish ancestry and even undertook research to confirm it later in his life, with partial success. Unfortunately, I know little about these investigations, as many important documents were destroyed after his breakdown in Turin. According to family tradition, a Polish nobleman named Nicki (pronounced Nietzky) had earned the favor of Augustus the Strong, King of Poland, who granted him the title of Earl. However, when Stanisław Leszczyński, a Polish king, came to power, this ancestor was said to have joined a conspiracy in support of the Saxons and

Protestants. He was sentenced to death but managed to escape. The records suggest he was later helped by an Earl of Brühl, who gave him a minor post in a remote provincial town. Occasionally, our elderly aunts would mention our great-grandfather Nietzsche, who was said to have lived to the impressive age of ninety-one. They often struggled to describe his handsome appearance, refined manners, and vitality.

Both sides of our family, the Nietzsches and the Oehlers, were known for their longevity. Among our four pairs of great-grandparents, one great- grandfather lived to ninety, while five great-grandparents reached ages between eighty-two and eighty- six. Only two died before turning seventy.

The greatest sorrow in our branch of the family was the death of our father at the age of thirty-eight, the result of a terrible accident. One night, after walking some friends home, he returned to the vicarage and was greeted by our little dog. It seems the dog got underfoot, causing him to stumble and fall backward down seven stone steps onto the paved courtyard below. The fall resulted in a severe concussion, and after a long illness lasting eleven months, he passed away on July 30, 1849. His untimely death cast a shadow over our entire childhood.

In 1850, our mother moved with us to Naumburg on the Saale, where we lived with our widowed grandmother Nietzsche. There, our mother raised us with a strictness and simplicity that reflected the values of the time and the norms of her family. However, our grandmother helped temper her discipline, and our Oehler grandparents, who were gentler with us than they had been with their own children, also had a moderating influence. It was our grandfather Oehler who first recognized the exceptional talents of his eldest grandchild.

From a very young age, my brother was strong and healthy. He often said that during his childhood and teenage years, people must have thought he was a farmer's boy because he was so plump, suntanned, and rosy-cheeked. His thick, fair hair, which fell in soft waves over his shoulders, softened his otherwise sturdy appearance. Yet, it was his strikingly beautiful, large, and expressive eyes, coupled with his courteous and dignified manner, that set him apart. Without these qualities, his teachers and relatives might never have noticed anything unusual about him, as he was naturally modest and reserved.

He began his education at a preparatory school and then continued at a grammar school in Naumburg. In the autumn of 1858, at the age of fourteen, he was admitted to the prestigious Pforta school, which was renowned for producing excellent scholars. The discipline there was strict, and the students were pushed hard to develop both their mental and physical strength. This rigorous training, free from indulgence or sentimentality, left a lasting impression on my brother. When he later emphasized the value of such discipline, it was clear he spoke from personal experience. At Pforta, he followed the standard curriculum and didn't begin university studies until the relatively late age of twenty. His remarkable abilities were most evident in his private studies and creative pursuits.

Even as a boy, his musical talent was so apparent that he and others who were knowledgeable in the field wondered whether he should dedicate himself entirely to music. However, it's worth noting that whatever he worked on later—whether it was in Latin, Greek, or German—showed an extraordinary level of skill, though naturally within the limits of his age and experience. His abilities seemed to emerge suddenly, after being nurtured quietly for a long time. His first significant work in philology, completed while he was a student under the renowned philologist Ritschl, is a good example of this. The work was so exceptional that it was chosen for publication in the Rheinische Museum. This decision was met with much astonishment and skepticism, as Dr. Ritschl often pointed out that it was unheard of for a student in only his third term to produce such an impressive piece of scholarship.

My brother was also an enthusiastic lover of outdoor activities such as swimming, skating, and walking, which helped him develop into a strong and athletic young man. His friend Rohde described him as a student with a healthy complexion, a sense of both physical and inner cleanliness, a disciplined sense of chastity, and a solemn demeanor. This description aligns with Adalbert Stifter's portrayal of an ideal, wholesome youth.

Although he was a rather serious child, as a teenager and an adult, he always had a keen sense of humor and enjoyed seeing the lighter side of life. His entire personality, along with everything he did or said, was marked by an extraordinary sense of balance and harmony. He was one of the rare individuals who could manage a bad mood and keep it hidden from those around him. His friends universally praised him for his steady temper, his warm and genuine behavior, and his hearty laugh, which seemed to come straight from his affectionate and kind-hearted nature. It could truly be said that nature had created in him a person of rare harmony, both physically and mentally: his exceptional intellect was matched by his equally remarkable physical strength.

The only unusual thing about my brother, something we both inherited from our father, was nearsightedness. In his case, it became much worse during his early school years because of his insatiable desire to learn, which always set him apart. When hearing stories from his friends and classmates, one cannot help but be amazed by the sheer variety of subjects he studied, even as a schoolboy.

In the autumn of 1864, he began his university studies in Bonn, focusing on philology and theology. However, after only six months, he gave up theology and, in the autumn of 1865, followed his renowned teacher, Ritschl, to the University of Leipzig. There, he became deeply committed to philology and worked tirelessly to master the subject. It is important to note, though, that his previous education at the Pforta school had already prepared him exceptionally well for philological studies. Pforta had a team of outstanding teachers, scholars who could have excelled in any university, and it provided students with the opportunity to explore their specific interests in ancient history. One of my brother's last significant works at Pforta was a Latin thesis on the Megarian poet Theognis. On January 18, 1866, he presented his findings on Theognis, discussing the poet as a moralist and aristocrat, before the philological society he co-founded in Leipzig. This marked his first public lecture. The paper revealed my brother's early fascination with the aristocratic ideal, which held a deep significance for him throughout his life. Interestingly, this same work led to Ritschl's recognition of and affection for him.

My brother's time in Leipzig was immensely significant for his intellectual growth. He found himself surrounded by a flood of intellectual influences, and his fiery enthusiasm made him highly receptive to them. However, he did not simply absorb everything without question; he examined and critiqued these ideas, adopting only those that resonated with him. It is essential to understand which influences shaped him during this period and when his more mature thinking allowed him to break free from these influences and forge his own path.

The main forces that influenced him during this time can be grouped into three categories: Hellenism, Schopenhauer, and Wagner. His love for Hellenism had drawn him to philology, but what he truly sought was a broad understanding of the world. For him, philology was a means to that end. His disciplined methods and thorough approach were tools he used to pursue this greater goal.

Hellenism, which first captivated him at Pforta, was his earliest significant influence. However, during the winter of 1865–66, he encountered something entirely new and transformative—Schopenhauer's philosophy. When he arrived in Leipzig in the autumn of 1865, he was deeply disheartened by his experiences during his first year at Bonn. He had tried to adapt to his surroundings in Bonn, hoping to elevate them to his high ideals, but both efforts failed. Determined to chart his own course, he came to Leipzig. It is easy to imagine the profound impact Schopenhauer's The World as Will and Idea had on him at this vulnerable time. He later wrote, "Here I saw a mirror where the world, life, and my own nature were reflected with terrifying grandeur." Having lost his father early in life, he had always felt the absence of a guiding figure. Schopenhauer became that figure for him, inspiring both filial love and respect. Yet, his admiration for Schopenhauer was not blind; from the beginning, he recognized flaws in Schopenhauer's system. Evidence of this can be found in an essay he wrote in the autumn of 1867, where he offered a critique of Schopenhauer's philosophy.

In the autumn of 1865, a third powerful influence entered his life: Richard Wagner. This influence would become the strongest of all. He was introduced to Wagner by the composer's sister, Frau Professor Brockhaus. His account of their first meeting, written in a letter to Erwin Rohde, is deeply moving. For years, since hearing Hans von Bülow's arrangement of Tristan and Isolde for piano, he had been a devoted admirer of Wagner's music. Meeting Wagner in person, with his commanding presence and forceful will, profoundly affected him. My brother felt that Wagner was the modern figure whose character most resembled his own.

As with Schopenhauer, my brother placed great emphasis on Wagner's personality, seeing his works as an extension of the artist's being. At the time, he did not fully understand all of Wagner's creations, but his admiration remained steadfast. My brother was one of the first to passionately champion both Schopenhauer and Wagner, paving the way for a larger group of young followers who later united these names under their banner. Whether Schopenhauer and Wagner truly lived up to the idealized versions my brother created in his letters and writings is a question we cannot definitively answer. Perhaps he saw in them what he himself aspired to become.

The sheer amount of work my brother accomplished during his student years is almost unbelievable. His productivity from 1865 to 1867 seems more like the result of four years of effort rather than just two. During this time, he often said he had the constitution of a bear, knowing neither headaches nor digestive troubles. Despite his nearsightedness, his eyes endured intense strain without issue. Thus, when the opportunity arose for him to become a soldier in the autumn of 1867, he eagerly embraced it. He was excited to find a way to channel his physical strength without interrupting his academic pursuits.

He carried out his duties as a soldier with great energy and enthusiasm, standing out as the best rider among the recruits of his year. He truly enjoyed his time in service, and it was a deep disappointment when an accident forced him to leave the military before completing his term. This incident marked the beginning of his first serious illness.

One day, while mounting a particularly restless horse, the animal reared suddenly, causing him to slam his chest against the saddle pommel before throwing him to the ground. Determined not to be defeated, he tried again and managed to mount the horse successfully, despite having sprained and torn two chest muscles and bruised the ribs around them. He endured the pain for an entire day, refusing to acknowledge the severity of the injury, until he eventually collapsed. The trauma led to a severe inflammation of the injured tissues. He was ultimately treated by the renowned specialist, Professor Volkmann, in Halle, who managed to restore his health.

In October 1868, my brother returned to Leipzig to resume his studies with renewed vigor and joy. He had grand plans: to earn his doctorate quickly, travel extensively through Paris, Italy, and Greece, and then settle in Leipzig as a private lecturer. However, these ambitions were unexpectedly disrupted by an offer from the University of Basel, which invited him to take up the role of professor. Some of the philological essays he had written as a student, which were published in the Rheinische

Museum, had caught the attention of Basel's Educational Board. Wilhelm Vischer, representing this board, sought more information from Ritschl, my brother's former teacher. Ritschl, who had long recognized his extraordinary abilities, wrote a glowing recommendation, stating, "Nietzsche is a genius: he can accomplish anything he sets his mind to." This endorsement was so emphatic that one cautious board member remarked, "If he truly is a genius, it might not be wise to hire him. He won't stay long at a small university like Basel."

Despite the reservations, my brother accepted the position. In recognition of his published academic work, the University of Leipzig granted him his doctorate without requiring the usual dissertation. At just twenty-four years and six months old, he assumed his professorship in Basel. Although he felt the weight of this responsibility and the end of what he called "the golden period of unrestrained freedom," he was motivated by a deep sense of purpose. He wished to instill in his students the seriousness and passion inspired by Schopenhauer, writing, "I do not want to merely train capable philologists. I dream of influencing the current generation of teachers and guiding the education of the young. If we must live, let us do so in a way that others may one day bless our lives once we are peacefully freed from its burdens."

Reflecting on that May of 1869, I wonder, as do his friends, what the world saw in this young professor. At first glance, he appeared to be one of Ritschl's finest pupils, an exceptionally skilled scholar of classical antiquity with a promising career ahead. He was also a devoted admirer of Wagner and Schopenhauer. Yet few, if any, understood the depth of his independent thinking or his unique approach to his field. Even he may have misunderstood himself, presenting himself as a "disciple" who fully embraced his mentor's ideas, though this was far from the truth.

On May 28, 1869, he delivered his inaugural lecture at the University of Basel. The topic, "Homer and Classical Philology," deeply impressed his audience. The distinguished professors and council members, returning home afterward, were absorbed in thought. What had they just witnessed? A young scholar questioning the very foundation of his discipline with a calm and philosophical rigor, while also presenting it with such artistic flair that philology, once seen as a dry and tedious study, now appeared to them as an almost divine messenger. He described philology as a comfort to humanity, offering a vision of a "beautiful, radiant, godlike figure of a distant, happy fairyland" to a world steeped in sorrow.

One professor remarked to a colleague, "We've found a rare bird in Herr Nietzsche." The other, who had championed his appointment, enthusiastically agreed. Even back in Leipzig, word spread about Jacob Burckhardt's comment that "Nietzsche is as much an artist as he is a scholar." Privy-Councillor Ritschl himself shared this anecdote with me, adding with a smile, "I always said so. He can make his academic lectures as captivating as a French novelist's stories."

"Homer and Classical Philology," my brother's inaugural address at the University of Basel, was far from his first foray into literary work. As previously noted, he had already contributed essays to the Rheinische Museum. However, this particular address holds a special significance, as it effectively laid out the foundation for much of his future writing. It is essential to clarify here that neither "Homer and Classical Philology" nor The Birth of Tragedy marks the true starting point of my brother's intellectual journey. Remarkably, he had already begun wrestling with the profound questions that would define his life's work long before these milestones. If one were to pinpoint the beginning of his intellectual evolution, it would have to be in the years 1865 to 1867, during his time in Leipzig.

The Birth of Tragedy, his first full-length book, completed as he entered his twenty-eighth year, was not the starting point of his thought but rather the culmination of years of development. It was the first major fruit of an intellectual process that had been ripening for a long time. Nietzsche's nature was uniquely polyphonic, a harmonious blend of seemingly contradictory talents and interests. Philosophy, art, and science—embodied at the time in philology—each claimed a part of him. Yet the extraordinary, and perhaps quintessentially Nietzschean, aspect of his character was that these diverse elements coexisted without conflict. Rather than battling for dominance, these facets of his nature enriched and stimulated one another.

Even when Nietzsche decided to forgo a career in music to focus intensely on philology, he did not abandon his other passions. He continued to compose music, find joy in it, and even study counterpoint with some dedication. During his years in Leipzig, as he threw himself into philological research, he simultaneously delved deeply into Schopenhauer's philosophy. This immersion not only broadened his intellectual horizon but also solidified philosophy as an enduring cornerstone of his thought. Nietzsche's mind welcomed all these influences, allowing them to coexist and interact, and the result was not fragmentation but a remarkable synthesis. Far from being at odds, these elements fertilized each other, creating a fertile intellectual ground where ideas flourished.

Readers of the first volume of his biography will notice how seamlessly these disparate impulses eventually converged, forming a powerful and unified current driving toward a singular aim. Science, art, and philosophy evolved together in him, becoming increasingly interwoven until they reached their first grand expression in The Birth of Tragedy. This work was akin to a "centaur"—a product that could only emerge from someone whose mind united diverse and seemingly incompatible talents. A person solely gifted in one discipline could not have produced such a unique creation. The ability to harmonize multiple talents, allowing them to sing together in a bold and intricate symphony, was not just the hallmark of Nietzsche's early years but a defining feature of his entire intellectual journey.

This distinctive polyphony continued to characterize his work throughout his life. Even after years of wandering, reevaluating his ideas, and undergoing profound transformations, Nietzsche— the artist, philosopher, and scientist— would unite these aspects of himself once more. Together, they produced an even greater centaur of the highest rank: Zarathustra. This achievement, arising from the interplay of his multifaceted genius, stands as a testament to the extraordinary harmony that defined his life's work.

The Birth of Tragedy requires some explanation, especially since we no longer use the Schopenhauerian or Wagnerian terms in which it was originally framed. Five years after its publication, my brother wrote an introduction in which he candidly expressed his doubts about the views and presentation of the work. While he never renounced the core ideas, he regretted having diluted the grand problem of Hellenism with elements borrowed from modern ideas. Over time, he felt a growing need to clarify the profound meaning of the book and express its essence more precisely. Among his notes from 1886, we find an explanation of its aims that was never published but sheds light on his evolving thoughts:

"The Birth of Tragedy is a book that emerges from experiences of aesthetic pleasure and pain, set against a metaphysical and artistic backdrop. It is also the confession of a romantic spirit—a sufferer yearning deeply for beauty and, through that yearning, creating it. Ultimately, it is a youthful work, filled with the courage and melancholy of youth.

"The term 'Apollonian' represents a state of serene contemplation before a visionary world, a world of beautiful appearances designed as an escape from the chaotic flux of becoming. In contrast, 'Dionysian' stands for a self-aware, dynamic becoming—a fervent, creative energy paired with the destructive rage of the creator who delights in the act of transformation.

"These two forces are fundamentally opposed. The Apollonian strives to eternalize its vision, offering peace, harmony, and reconciliation with existence. The Dionysian, on the other hand, pursues the ecstasy of creation and destruction, embodying an overflowing energy that seeks constant change. Creation, as an instinct, is born from dissatisfaction and abundance, from a divine force that overcomes the sorrows of existence through endless transformation. Appearance becomes a fleeting salvation, while the world itself is seen as a series of divine visions and temporary deliverances.

"This perspective counters Schopenhauer's view of art, which values it from the spectator's standpoint as a form of deliverance from the suffering of existence. Schopenhauer emphasizes salvation through the joy of illusion, while my view recognizes the artist's torment and the Dionysian drive to create. Tragic art reconciles these two attitudes. It celebrates appearance as vital, even as it denies and transcends it. This directly challenges Schopenhauer's concept of resignation as the ultimate tragic response to life.

"The book also opposes Wagner's theory, which subordinates music to drama, asserting instead that music has an independent, primordial significance. It expresses a longing for a tragic myth—a spiritual framework in which certain profound aspects of life can flourish.

"The work distrusts the fleeting optimism of science and critiques the 'serenity' of theoretical reason. It holds a deep antagonism toward Christianity, which it blames for the decline of the Germanic spirit. Ultimately, it argues that the only justification for existence is aesthetic. Morality itself is part of the illusory world. Happiness can only come from appearance, as 'being' is a fiction created by those who suffer from the chaos of becoming. The Dionysian view finds joy even in the annihilation of the real and the dissolution of illusions, reaching its highest fulfillment when the most beautiful appearances are destroyed in the ecstasy of transformation."

The Birth of Tragedy is, in essence, a fragment of a much larger work on Hellenism that Nietzsche had envisioned since his student years. Even this fragment was initially conceived on a grander scale, but his desire to support Wagner led him to narrow its scope. In April 1871, while visiting Wagner at Tribschen, Nietzsche found the composer in a despondent state regarding his life's mission. Wishing to help, Nietzsche decided to set aside his broader plans for a comprehensive work on Hellenism and focus on its tragic aspect. He connected Wagner's music with the Dionysian concept, thereby aligning his work with Wagner's artistic vision.

The book, as we now know it, was written between the autumn of 1869 and November 1871, a period when Nietzsche was deeply immersed in aesthetic questions and ideas. It was first published in January 1872 by E. W. Fritsch in Leipzig, under the title The Birth of Tragedy out of the Spirit of Music. Later, the title was revised to The Birth of Tragedy, or Hellenism and Pessimism, reflecting the evolving focus of Nietzsche's thought. The work stands as a testimony to the dynamic interplay of art, philosophy, and science in his mind, a synthesis that would continue to define his intellectual journey.

An Attempt at Self-Criticism.

Whatever lies at the heart of this perplexing and enigmatic book must surely be a question of the utmost significance and fascination. It is, moreover, a profoundly personal question— this is evident from the circumstances under which the book came into being. It emerged during the turbulent and momentous period of the Franco-German war of 1870-71, a time when many would have been swept up in the tide of patriotic fervor or military action. Yet, against this dramatic backdrop, the thinker and lover of mysteries, who was destined to be the author of this work, retreated to a secluded corner of the Alps. There, immersed in contemplation and consumed by riddles, he seemed both deeply absorbed in and strangely indifferent to the world's upheavals. It was in such a setting that he began to record his reflections on the Greeks—the foundation of this peculiar, dense, and almost impenetrable book, to which this delayed prologue (or perhaps epilogue) seeks to provide some insight.

Only a few weeks later, he found himself standing under the walls of Metz, still wrestling with the profound questions he had raised about the so-called "cheerfulness" of the Greeks and the nature of Greek art. His thoughts refused to let him rest. Even amid the noise of war, they persisted, pressing him to grapple with their implications. And then came the tense month in which the fate of peace was being debated at Versailles. It was during this period of waiting, so heavy with uncertainty, that he, too, reached a form of resolution within himself. Slowly recovering from an illness he had contracted in the field, he finally made up his mind about the Birth of Tragedy from the Spirit of Music.

From music? Music and tragedy? What connection could exist between these two, and why should they lead us back to the Greeks? Greeks and tragic music? Greeks and the pessimistic art- work? These were the questions that loomed largest in his mind. Here was a race of people renowned for their beauty, their vigor, and their joy—a race envied and admired as the very embodiment of life and inspiration. Yet, these same Greeks, so seemingly complete in their vitality, had felt the need for tragedy? They had turned to art—not as mere ornamentation, but as a necessity? What, then, was the reason behind Greek art? Why did such a radiant and life-affirming culture embrace something as dark and profound as tragedy?

These are the questions that run through this work like a hidden current, questions that lend it both its complexity and its allure. They are not easily answered, and perhaps they never can be fully resolved. But the attempt to grapple with them—to illuminate even a fragment of their mystery—is what makes this book, for all its difficulties, a pursuit of truth that remains as compelling as the enigmas it seeks to uncover.

We can begin to surmise where the profound and unsettling question about the value of existence was first raised. Is pessimism always and inevitably a sign of decline, of decay, of a failure in vitality, of instincts grown weary and frail? Was this true of the Indians, as history seems to suggest, or as it appears to be true of us modern individuals, we Europeans, in our restless era? Or might there exist another kind of pessimism, one born not from weakness but from strength? Could there be an intellectual preference, an eager attraction to what is harsh, dreadful, and troubling in life, arising not from despair but from a sense of abundance, from overflowing health, from the very fullness of existence itself? Could it be that even overabundance has its own peculiar form of suffering? Might there be a bold resilience, sharpened and emboldened by an insatiable yearning for the terrifying, the formidable, the adversary worthy of its mettle—a rival from whom it might learn, through confrontation, what it truly means to feel fear?

What, then, did tragic myth signify for the Greeks during their noblest, most vigorous, and courageous age? What are we to make of the extraordinary phenomenon of the Dionysian spirit, and the art it gave rise to—tragedy? And further, what are we to think of that which led to the eventual death of tragedy: the Socratism of morality, the rise of dialectical reasoning, the satisfaction and optimism of the theoretical man? Could it be that this very Socratism, often celebrated as the hallmark of enlightenment, was in fact a symptom of decline, of fatigue, of a life undermined by anarchic and dissolving instincts? Was the so- called "Hellenic cheerfulness" of later Hellenism nothing more than the fading light of a setting sun? Was Epicureanism, with its defiant opposition to pessimism, merely a strategy for the sufferer, a way to manage pain and stave off despair?

And what of science itself, our modern science—if we consider it not as a detached pursuit but as a phenomenon of life, as a symptom of our collective condition? What does it truly signify? Where is it leading us? More troubling still, from what depths did it arise? Could it be that science, far from being a straightforward quest for knowledge, is instead a subtle and complex strategy to avoid confronting pessimism directly? Might it even serve as a means of evading truth itself? In moral terms, could it represent a kind of falsehood, a manifestation of cowardice? And if we step beyond morality, might it reveal itself as an intricate artifice, an ingenious mechanism designed to shield us from the stark realities we dread to face?

Oh Socrates, enigmatic and elusive figure, might this have been your secret? Was this your irony, that you masked a deeper unease beneath your relentless pursuit of reason? Were you, the consummate ironist, harboring an understanding far more disquieting than your serene dialectic revealed? Were you perhaps the first to craft a philosophy that taught humanity how to endure its own anxieties by cloaking them in the guise of logic and virtue? If so, what are we to learn from your legacy, from the questions that linger, unresolved, in the shadow of your great irony?

What I tackled back then was something immense and unsettling—a problem with horns, not necessarily a bull but certainly a formidable, unfamiliar challenge. Today, I would call it the problem of science itself: science questioned and scrutinized, seen for the first time as something problematic, as a riddle to be solved. The book that emerged from this youthful enthusiasm and skepticism, however, is almost unbearably flawed to me now. It was born out of premature, half-formed experiences—insights that had barely crossed the threshold of being shareable—and was constructed on the foundation of art. After all, the essence of the problem of science could not be grasped from within the confines of science alone.

This book, then, was perhaps meant for artists, though not just any artists— only those with a rare analytical and reflective capacity. It was for a kind of artist so unique that one hardly expects to find them or even bothers to look. The work was brimming with psychological novelties and hidden truths of the artist's world, framed by an underlying metaphysics of art. It was a book of youth, full of its boldness and melancholy, independent and defiant, even when it appeared to lean on authority or indulge in self-importance. It bore all the marks of a first attempt, in both the good and the bad sense of the phrase. Despite the aged problem it grappled with, it was riddled with youthful excess: its verbosity, its emotional turbulence, and its "storm and stress."

And yet, for its time, the book succeeded, particularly with the great artist to whom it was indirectly addressed—Richard Wagner. In that sense, it justified its existence. For this reason alone, perhaps, it deserves some patience and understanding. Yet I must admit that when I revisit it now, after sixteen years, it feels utterly alien to me. It stands before my more seasoned and discerning eye as something heavy, clumsy, and overwrought. My perspective has grown far more critical, though my passion for the question it sought to answer—the problem of viewing science through the lens of art and art through the lens of life—remains undiminished.

Today, however, the book seems impossible to me. I find it poorly written, laborious, sentimental to the point of indulgence, and overly reliant on tangled and overwrought imagery. Its tempo is inconsistent, its logic lacks clarity, and it seems unconcerned with the need for proof. It was written as though meant for initiates only—like a piece of music meant for those already attuned to its harmonies, united by shared experiences in art. It reads like a countersign for kindred spirits in artistic matters: lofty, eccentric, and deliberately alienating to the "cultured" masses while also distancing itself from the general populace.

Nevertheless, as its impact revealed and continues to reveal, the book had a way of finding like-minded souls, drawing them toward unexplored paths and secret realms of artistic exploration. At the time, it was recognized—both with fascination and unease— that here was a voice unlike any other. This was the disciple of an unknown god, cloaked in the garb of a scholar, carrying the gravity of a German thinker and the rawness of a Wagnerian zealot. It was a mind teeming with questions, obscure memories, and strange longings, all gathered under the enigmatic banner of Dionysos. Listeners found themselves murmuring with unease: was this a mystic's voice, perhaps even one veering toward the ecstatic, undecided whether to reveal or conceal itself? It spoke with effort and hesitation, as if wrestling with an unfamiliar language.

In truth, this new soul should have sung rather than spoken. What a shame that I didn't express myself as a poet then! Perhaps I could have done so. Or at the very least, I could have approached the task as a philologist, for even now, the realm I sought to explore remains largely untouched by scholarly hands. Above all, the true question remains unresolved: what is Dionysian? Without an answer to this, the Greeks remain as much a mystery to us now as they ever were, their essence as elusive and unfathomable as before.

What is Dionysian? In this book lies an attempt at an answer, voiced by one who claimed knowledge, a devoted follower and disciple of the god himself. Perhaps I should now approach this complex psychological question—the origins of tragedy among the Greeks—with greater caution and less rhetorical flourish. One of the central questions concerns the relationship of the Greek to pain and their sensitivity to it. Did this relationship remain consistent over time, or did it change? Was their ever-growing desire for beauty, festivals, celebrations, and new rituals born out of deprivation, sorrow, melancholy, or suffering? Pericles, or perhaps Thucydides, hints at this in the famous Funeral Speech. But if this were the case, where did the opposite yearning come from—the earlier longing for the grim and terrible, for pessimism, for tragic myths, for depictions of the dark, destructive, and fateful aspects of existence? What was the source of tragedy? Could it have sprung not from despair, but from joy, strength, exuberant health, and an overflow of vitality?

Physiologically speaking, what does the madness signify that gave rise to both comic and tragic art—the Dionysian madness? Could madness, rather than being a sign of degeneration or decay, represent something else entirely? Could it be a kind of neurosis of health, an expression of youthful vitality, as alienists might ponder? What does the synthesis of god and goat in the Satyr reveal? What kind of experience or tension led the Greeks to envision the Dionysian reveler and the primitive man as a Satyr?

As for the origins of the tragic chorus, might it have been rooted in collective ecstasies during periods when Greek bodies flourished and Greek souls brimmed with life? Could these have been times when communities, entire assemblies devoted to cult practices, were gripped by shared visions and hallucinations?

What if the Greeks, in the height of their youthful vigor, had a will to embrace tragedy, to be pessimists? What if, as Plato suggested, it was madness itself that brought the greatest blessings to Hellas? Conversely, what if, during their decline and weakening, the Greeks grew increasingly optimistic, superficial, theatrical, and enamored with logic and its application to the world? What if this shift coincided with a growing cheerfulness and a burgeoning scientific outlook? Might the triumph of optimism—of practical and theoretical utilitarianism—mark a decline in vitality, a symptom of aging, of physiological exhaustion? Could it be that pessimism, not optimism, is the mark of strength? Epicurus, an optimist, was also a sufferer—was his optimism a response to his pain?

This book carries a heavy burden of such questions, and among them lies perhaps the weightiest of all: through the lens of life itself, what is the meaning of morality?

Even in the foreword addressed to Richard Wagner, art—not morality— was identified as humanity's true metaphysical activity.

Within the book itself, the provocative proposition appears repeatedly: the existence of the world is justified only as an aesthetic phenomenon. The entire work is steeped in an artistic perspective, portraying the world as the creation of an artist—a god, if you will, but a thoughtless, amoral god. This god, in both creation and destruction, in both good and evil, seeks only to experience the joy and glory of his existence. In crafting worlds, he frees himself from the torment of overabundance and contradiction. The world, in this view, becomes the god's perpetual redemption, achieved moment by moment as ever- changing visions of the most painful, contradictory being who redeems himself through appearances alone.

This artist-metaphysics, while it may seem arbitrary, idle, or fanciful, hints at a spirit determined to confront the moral interpretation of life head-on. Here, for the first time, a pessimism "beyond good and evil" emerges—a philosophy daring to place morality itself within the realm of appearances, treating it not as truth but as illusion, semblance, error, and artistic interpretation. This perspective even regards morality as a form of artifice, a necessary but deceptive lens through which life is viewed.

The depth of this anti-moral tendency can perhaps be measured by the book's deliberate and guarded silence on Christianity. Christianity, with its absolute moral framework, represents the antithesis of the aesthetic worldview this book espouses. Christianity disowns and condemns art as falsehood, elevating moral truth as the ultimate standard. From the very start, I sensed in this moral absolutism a hostility to life itself, a vengeful opposition to the nature of existence. Life, after all, thrives on illusion, art, and perspective; it depends on error and appearance to endure.

Christianity, in essence, is a profound rejection of life, a disdain for its passions, its beauty, and its sensuality. It invents another world to denigrate this one, masking a deep longing for rest, for nothingness, for an end to existence. This will to define life solely by moral standards reflects a will to perish, a symptom of exhaustion and despair, of life impoverished and weary. Under the judgment of morality, especially the unyielding morality of Christianity, life is perpetually condemned. It is seen as unworthy of desire, a burden to be shed.

Is morality itself, then, a will to deny life? Could it be an instinct for annihilation, a principle of decay, slander, and retreat—a harbinger of the end? If so, then morality may be the greatest threat of all.

It was against this morality that my instinct rebelled in this book, seeking to establish a counter-valuation of life. This counter-perspective was purely artistic, wholly anti-Christian. What should I call it? As a philologist and a lover of language, I chose a name—though not without some poetic liberty. For the Antichrist's proper name, who could be certain? I called it Dionysian.

Do you see the question I dared to approach in this early work? How much I now regret not having had the boldness—or perhaps the audacity—to employ an entirely individual language for such deeply personal reflections and intellectual experiments. Instead, I worked within the frameworks of Kantian and Schopenhauerian formulations to express ideas and evaluations that, at their core, ran counter to the very spirit and sensibilities of Kant and Schopenhauer. What, after all, were Schopenhauer's thoughts on tragedy? He wrote in The World as Will and Representation, Volume II, page 495: "What lends tragedy its unique sense of elevation is the realization that the world, that life itself, cannot satisfy us, and is therefore unworthy of our attachment. This is the essence of the tragic spirit, which ultimately leads to resignation."

But how differently did Dionysos speak to me! How distant from my thoughts, even then, was this entire notion of resignation! And yet, there is something far worse in this book—something I regret more deeply than merely clouding and compromising the Dionysian vision with Schopenhauerian formulas. It is this: that I tainted the great Hellenic question, the profound problem as it unfolded before me, by introducing elements drawn from the modern world. I allowed myself to hope where no hope should have been entertained, where all signs pointed unambiguously to an approaching collapse. I dreamed that, based on the foundations of contemporary German music, the so-called "spirit of Teutonism" might rediscover itself, might find its way back to some forgotten origin.

But what folly that was! I indulged in such fantasies precisely at a time when the German spirit, which not long before had aspired to dominion over Europe—had possessed the strength to guide and lead Europe—was resigning itself, definitively and irrevocably, to mediocrity, democracy, and the shallow waters of "modern ideas." All this under the grandiose pretense of empire- building, a façade for its surrender to the leveling forces of the age. Since then, I have come to view this "spirit of Teutonism" with despair, as something that warrants neither hope nor indulgence but rather unsparing critique. I see it now as inseparable from the condition of German music as it stands today— Romantic through and through, utterly alien to the Greek sensibility, and, moreover, a profound destroyer of the nerves. This music, with its intoxicating and numbing effects, is doubly dangerous to a people prone to drink and prone to venerate vagueness as though it were a virtue. German music, in its dual role as both a stimulant and a narcotic, undermines clarity and fortitude.

Of course, setting aside the premature hopes and the flawed applications to modern concerns with which I marred my first book, the great Dionysian question it posed remains standing. That central interrogation endures, even as it pertains to music. What should we envision as a form of music no longer born from Romanticism, as German music is, but from the spirit of Dionysos? What would such music be, if it could exist at all?

—But, my dear sir, if your book does not belong to Romanticism, then what possibly could? Can disdain for the present, for "reality" and for "modern ideas," be taken further than it is in your artist- metaphysics? Is this not a philosophy that would sooner embrace Nothingness, or even the devil, than accept the "Now" as valid? Is there not a deep, throbbing undercurrent of rage and destructive delight running beneath the beautiful structure of your argument, beneath the enticing charm of your rhetoric? Is it not a vehement defiance of everything that "is," a willful rejection that edges dangerously close to nihilism, whispering: "Better that nothing be true than that you should be proven right, than that your truth should prevail!"

Let us listen closely, my dear pessimist and art-worshipper, with ears open wide, to just one carefully chosen excerpt from your book. This passage, eloquent yet insidious, rings with the call of a dragon-slayer—words that might seduce impressionable minds and young, tender hearts. Is this not, in truth, the Romantic confession of the 1830s, cloaked in the pessimism of the 1850s? And does it not, as always with Romanticism, lead to the same finale—rupture, collapse, and a retreat into the arms of an old faith, of the old God? What else could your pessimistic work be but a piece of anti-Hellenism wrapped in Romanticism—a narcotic, intoxicating and clouding the mind? Is it not, after all, a work of music, unmistakably German music? But listen to your own words:

Let us picture a new generation, bold and fearless in their vision, driven by a heroic yearning for the colossal. Imagine the dragon-slaying courage with which they abandon the effeminate creeds of optimism, choosing instead to live fully, embracing the totality of existence. Would it not be inevitable that these tragic figures, disciplined to face both terror and solemnity, would crave a new kind of art—an art of metaphysical solace? Would not tragedy itself become their Helena, their longed-for companion, leading them to cry out, as Faust did:

"Und sollt' ich nicht, sehnsüchtigster Gewalt, In's Leben ziehn die einzigste Gestalt?"

Would this not be necessary? No! A thousand times no! Young Romanticists, it is not necessary. But, alas, it seems likely that things will end this way for you—that you will end this way: "comforted," as Romanticists inevitably are, in spite of all your sternness and confrontation with terror. Metaphysically consoled, as is always the case, you will find yourselves ending as Christians, retreating into the familiar comforts of faith.

No! Before anything else, you must first learn the art of earthly comfort. You must learn how to laugh, my young friends, especially if you insist on holding onto your pessimism. For if you do, you may one day, through laughter, banish all forms of metaphysical consolation—including metaphysics itself—to the devil! And perhaps you will take inspiration from the words of that Dionysian trickster, Zarathustra:

"Lift up your hearts, my brethren, higher! Even higher! And do not forget your legs! Lift those too, you good dancers—better still, stand on your heads!

"This crown of laughter, this garland of roses—I placed it upon my head myself. I blessed my own laughter, for no one else could bear it today.

"Zarathustra, the dancer; Zarathustra, the light-hearted one, beckoning with his wings, ready to soar, inviting all the birds, full of joy and lightness—this is Zarathustra.

"Zarathustra, the prophet who laughs, the seer who smiles, patient and unyielding, delighting in leaps and sidesteps. I consecrated my own laughter.

"This crown of laughter, this garland of roses—to you, my brethren, I throw this crown! Laughing, I consecrated it: you higher men, learn, I implore you— learn how to laugh!"

Thus spoke Zarathustra, and in his words lies a lesson for you, should you choose to hear it. Learn to laugh, and perhaps you will find a path not to consolation, but to true freedom.

Foreword To Richard Wagner

To avoid any unnecessary doubts, confusions, or misinterpretations that the thoughts collected in this essay might provoke—particularly given the peculiarities of the aesthetic discourse of our time—and to ensure that I may write these introductory remarks with the same contemplative joy that marks every page of this work, I imagine the moment when you, my esteemed and honoured friend, will first hold this essay in your hands. Perhaps it will be after one of your evening walks through the crisp winter snow. You will see the unbound Prometheus gracing the title page, read my name beneath it, and immediately know that whatever content lies within these pages, the author has approached his subject with both gravity and sincerity. You will sense that, throughout his reflections, he conversed with you as if you were present, addressing only what was worthy of your attention and presence.

You will remember, too, that this essay was conceived at the same time your magnificent dissertation on Beethoven was taking shape—both born amidst the horrors and sublime upheavals of the war that had just begun. But it would be a mistake to interpret this collection of thoughts as a mere contrast between patriotic fervour and aesthetic indulgence, between the seriousness of duty

and the playfulness of art. Those who read deeply will instead find themselves unexpectedly confronted by the profound weight of the German problem I explore here. This problem, far from being an isolated issue, stands at the very centre of German aspirations, serving as both a vortex and a turning point for our nation's hopes.

Some readers may recoil at the seriousness with which I approach what they see as merely an aesthetic problem, especially if they regard art as no more than a light-hearted amusement, a dispensable court jester to the so-called "earnestness of life." To those who think this way—as if no one truly understands the deeper meaning of confronting life's "earnestness"—let me say this: I am convinced that art represents the highest calling, the most profound task, and the truly metaphysical activity of our existence. It is the very foundation of how life is to be understood.

To you, my sublime guide along this path, my honoured protagonist in these contemplations, I dedicate this essay.

Basel, at the close of the year 1871.

The Birth of Tragedy

We will have made a significant advancement in the field of aesthetics when we come to understand—not merely through logical reasoning, but with the intuitive clarity of direct perception—that the continuous evolution of art is inextricably linked to the dual nature of the Apollonian and the Dionysian. This relationship is akin to the interdependence of the sexes in procreation, marked by constant tensions and conflicts with only occasional moments of harmony. The terms we use here, borrowed from the Greeks, provide profound insight into their conception of art. The Greeks, through the striking clarity of their mythological figures, reveal the mysteries of their artistic worldview—not through abstract concepts, but through the vivid imagery of their pantheon.

In examining the Greek deities Apollo and Dionysus, the twin patrons of the arts, we uncover a deep-seated opposition within the Greek world. This opposition is both one of origin and purpose, dividing the Apollonian art of form and visual creation from the Dionysian art of music, which resists the boundaries of the visual and physical. These two contrasting artistic impulses often move in parallel, openly clashing and yet inspiring each other toward ever greater creative achievements. In this way, their perpetual strife is perpetuated within the domain of art itself, even as the shared term "Art" seems to suggest a unity that is only superficial. Eventually, through what can only be described as a metaphysical act of the Hellenic spirit, these two forces are brought into a profound partnership. This union ultimately gave birth to the unique and extraordinary fusion of Apollonian and Dionysian elements in the tragic art of Attic drama.

To better understand these two contrasting tendencies, we might first envision them as distinct worlds: the realm of dreams and the state of drunkenness. These two physiological conditions, so different in nature, present an analogy to the opposition between the Apollonian and the Dionysian. In dreams, as the Roman poet Lucretius suggests, humanity first encountered divine figures. It was in this realm of dreams that the great artist envisioned the radiant and idealized forms of superhuman beings. For the ancient Hellenic poet, the inspiration for creative work could also be explained through the mysteries of dreams. Indeed, if asked to articulate the origins of poetic insight, a Greek poet might have responded in much the same way as Hans Sachs does in Die Meister singer :

"My friend, it is the poet's task

To interpret and under stand his dreams.

Believe me, man's truest delusions

Are revealed to him in dreams.

All poetry and creative art

Is nothing more than the interpretation of true dreams."

Through this lens, the Apollonian and the Dionysian emerge as profound, contrasting sources of human creativity, each reflecting a fundamental aspect of our existence and illuminating the deepest mysteries of artistic inspiration.

The beautiful world of dreams, where every individual becomes an instinctive artist, serves as the foundation for all visual art and, as we will see, for a significant portion of poetry as well. Within this realm, we take immense pleasure in the direct perception of forms—every shape communicates with us, every detail carries meaning, and nothing feels extraneous or unnecessary. Yet, alongside the vivid intensity of this dream-reality, we often experience a faint awareness of its illusory nature. This phenomenon, at least for me, feels frequent and even natural, and I could provide countless examples as well as references from poets to support this observation. For those inclined toward philosophy, there is often a profound sense that beneath the reality we inhabit lies another, wholly different reality, suggesting that what we perceive is itself an appearance. Schopenhauer, in fact, identified the ability to occasionally see life as a collection of mere phantoms and dream-images as a hallmark of philosophical insight.

In much the same way, the person sensitive to art stands in relation to the dream-world as the philosopher does to the reality of existence. They are both keen and willing observers, extracting meaning from these ephemeral visions and using the experiences to prepare for life. Yet, it is not only the pleasant and harmonious aspects of dreams that the artist understands so completely. They also grasp the somber, the disquieting, the sorrowful, the ominous—the entire "Divine Comedy" of existence, including its infernos. These are not merely scenes to be observed as if projected onto a distant wall; the artist lives and suffers through these episodes. And yet, even in the midst of such turmoil, there persists a fleeting recognition of their illusory nature. Many, like myself, may recall moments in the depths of a troubling dream where we found the clarity and courage to declare, "This is a dream! I will continue dreaming!" Some individuals have even reported extending the continuity of a single dream across multiple nights, experiencing its causality and narrative as if it were a continuous reality. These instances suggest that, deep within us, our shared core—the universal foundation of human experience—finds profound joy and acceptance in our dreams.

This serene acceptance of dream-experiences is reflected in the Greek conception of Apollo. As the god of all creative energies, Apollo is also the deity of prophecy and foresight. His name, derived from the idea of "light" or "brightness," aligns him as the master of the radiant, inner world of imagination. This elevated truth and perfection of dream states, which stand in stark contrast to the fragmented and often chaotic reality of daily life, symbolize a profound awareness of nature's healing and restorative powers. This alignment of dreams with the prophetic and artistic reveals how such experiences make life not only bearable but profoundly worthwhile. Yet Apollo is not merely a representation of unrestrained imagination. He embodies the delicate balance that dream- pictures must maintain, a boundary they dare not cross lest they lose their transformative power and devolve into delusions indistinguishable from harsh reality. This measured discipline, this calm detachment from the wilder storms of emotion, defines Apollo's essence as the serene sculptor-god. Even in moments of anger or dissatisfaction, his radiance and beauty remain unshaken, underscoring his divine origin.

We might compare Apollo's nature to Schopenhauer's description of the individual cloaked in the veil of Mâyâ, as described in The World as Will and Representation. Schopenhauer writes: "Just as in the midst of a turbulent sea, infinite in its horizons and heaving with mountainous waves, a sailor sits calmly in his frail boat, trusting in its stability, so too does the individual, surrounded by a world of sorrows, find solace and security in their principium individuationis." Similarly, Apollo embodies an unyielding confidence in this principle of individuality, standing as its most sublime expression. He represents the quiet, assured figure whose gestures and presence communicate all the joy, wisdom, and beauty of existence as it manifests in appearance. Apollo, in this light, becomes the divine image of individuation, radiating the splendor and harmony that transform the illusory into the profoundly meaningful.

In The World as Will and Representation, Schopenhauer describes the overwhelming awe that grips a person when they suddenly find themselves unable to account for the familiar cognitive frameworks that structure their experience. This happens when the principle of reason, in one of its manifestations, seems to falter or allow for an exception. To this awe, we can add the profound ecstasy that wells up from the innermost depths of human nature when the boundaries of individuality—the principium individuationis—begin to dissolve. This ecstatic collapse is perhaps best understood by analogy with the intoxication of drunkenness. Whether brought about by the effects of a narcotic draught, so often celebrated in the hymns of ancient peoples, or by the joyous, all-encompassing resurgence of life in spring, this Dionysian state awakens emotions that sweep away the individual self, immersing one in total self-forgetfulness.

Historical parallels to this phenomenon abound. In the German Middle Ages, crowds of singing and dancing people, driven by the same Dionysian force, would travel from place to place in ecstatic waves. These "dancers of St. John" or "St. Vitus's dancers" bear a striking resemblance to the Bacchic choruses of ancient Greece, whose roots extend back through Asia Minor to Babylon and the orgiastic festivals of the Sacæa. Some observers, lacking understanding or sensitivity, might dismiss such displays as mere "folk diseases," regarding them with a mixture of pity and disdain, smug in their own supposed "health." Yet this self-proclaimed health pales into insignificance when set against the vibrant, fiery vitality of the Dionysian revelers, whose overwhelming energy reveals the lifelessness of those who look down upon them.

The Dionysian experience not only rekindles the bond between humans but also reconciles humanity with the estranged and often hostile natural world.

Under this spell, the earth offers its gifts freely, and even wild beasts, the predators of desert and mountain, come forth in peace. Dionysus rides in a chariot adorned with flowers and garlands, with panthers and tigers harnessed to his cause. One might imagine Beethoven's jubilant Ode to Joy transformed into a painting: awestruck masses bowing to the ground as a transcendent harmony binds all things together. In such moments, the barriers of rank, necessity, whim, and societal convention—all the rigid walls separating human beings—collapse. The proclamation of a cosmic harmony unites everyone in a shared experience of oneness, as though the veil of illusion, the Mâyâ, were torn apart, its remnants fluttering feebly before the underlying unity of existence.

Through song and dance, individuals become part of a higher communal whole. They forget the mechanics of walking and speaking as they ascend into a state that feels almost airborne, their gestures charged with an otherworldly enchantment. Like the animals that suddenly speak, or the earth that yields milk and honey, something supernatural emanates from these individuals. They feel transformed into gods, moving among mortals as the divine figures they once glimpsed in their dreams. Here, man ceases to be an artist; he becomes a work of art. The creative force of nature itself manifests through the intoxication of the Dionysian state, achieving the ultimate fulfillment of the primordial unity's desire. Humanity—the finest clay, the most exquisite marble— is shaped and sculpted by the strokes of the Dionysian world- artist. These creative acts are accompanied by the cries of the Eleusinian Mysteries: "Do you bow down, millions? Do you sense the Creator, world?"

Thus far, we have examined the Apollonian and Dionysian as primal artistic forces emanating directly from nature, unmediated by human artistry. These forces fulfill nature's creative impulses in the most immediate and profound ways. The Apollonian manifests as the vivid world of dreams, whose perfection exists independently of an individual's intellectual capacity or artistic training. The Dionysian, on the other hand, emerges as a drunken reality that disregards and even seeks to dissolve the individual, offering redemption through a mystical sense of oneness. Faced with these elemental states, every artist becomes either an imitator of one or the other—or, as in the case of Greek tragedy, an artist of both dream and ecstasy. We might envision such an artist standing apart from the reveling Dionysian chorus, overcome by mystical self-abnegation. In his drunken isolation, he sinks into the depths of Dionysian abandon, and from this state, through the clarity of Apollonian dream-inspiration, he perceives his unity with the primal source of existence. This profound oneness reveals itself to him as a symbolic dream-image, capturing the essence of the universe in a moment of artistic vision.

After laying these general foundations and contrasts, let us now turn our attention to the Greeks to examine the extent and heights to which these primal artistic impulses of nature were cultivated within their culture. This approach will enable us to better understand and appreciate the unique relationship between the Greek artist and the archetypes he sought to imitate, or, as Aristotle described it, their "imitation of nature." While we can only speculate about the dreams of the Greeks, despite their extensive dream literature and anecdotes, there are compelling reasons to believe they possessed a remarkable clarity and precision in their dream imagery. Considering the extraordinary visual acuity of their eyes, their deep appreciation for form, and their delight in vivid colors, it seems plausible that their dreams mirrored the perfection of their best artistic reliefs. In comparison, their dreams might have been as cohesive and artistically structured as Homer's epics, making Homer, in a deeper sense, a dreamer among Greeks and the Greeks themselves dreamers akin to Homer. This is a level of artistic coherence far surpassing the modern comparisons people often make between their dreams and the works of Shakespeare.

On the other hand, when examining the Dionysian aspect of Greek culture, we find a much clearer distinction when comparing it to the Dionysian festivals of other ancient civilizations.

Throughout the ancient world, from Rome to Babylon, we find evidence of Dionysian-like festivals, but these pale in comparison to the Greek celebrations. These foreign festivals, typified by grotesque and unrestrained excess, often centered on unbridled sexual licentiousness, which eroded familial and societal bonds, unleashing a dangerous cocktail of cruelty and lust. This primal mix, reminiscent of a "witches' draught," highlights the untamed nature of these rituals. For a time, the Greeks seemed insulated from such chaotic influences, which infiltrated their world via land and sea. The figure of Apollo, embodying clarity and order, rose as a symbol of resistance, standing against the uncouth Dionysian forces like a guardian wielding the Gorgon's head.

This opposition between Apollo and Dionysus found its enduring expression in Doric art, where Apollo's majestic and forbidding stance rejected the wildness of Dionysian impulses. However, as time passed, similar instincts began to arise organically within the Greeks themselves, breaking through the boundaries imposed by Apollo. This led to a profound reconciliation, where Apollo, rather than attempting to eradicate Dionysus, chose to disarm his formidable rival through compromise. This moment of reconciliation marked a turning point in Greek religious and cultural history. The outcome was not the obliteration of the boundary between these forces but the establishment of a delicate balance, wherein each preserved its distinct identity while occasionally exchanging acknowledgments of mutual respect.

Under this accord, the Dionysian spirit underwent a transformation. Greek Dionysian festivals, when contrasted with the debauched celebrations of Babylon, took on the character of redemptive and transfigurative events. These were not merely orgiastic displays but artistic celebrations where the dissolution of individual identity—the collapse of the principium individuationis— became an aesthetic experience. The violent excesses of foreign festivals were absent, replaced by a profound blend of emotions, where joy and sorrow intertwined. In the midst of their exuberance, Dionysian revelers would experience a bittersweet awareness, a lament for the fragmentation of existence into individual forms. Their songs and pantomimes reflected this duality, as waves of joy gave way to cries of anguish or yearning.

Dionysian music, in particular, stood apart from the Apollonian traditions of the Greeks. Apollo's music, characterized by the measured tones of the cithara, was rooted in rhythm and form, reflecting his association with harmony and structure. Dionysian music, however, introduced a wholly different element: the hypnotic power of melody, the continuous flow of tone, and the dynamic interplay of harmonies. These elements, essential to music as we understand it today, were alien to the Apollonian aesthetic but became the lifeblood of Dionysian art.

The dithyramb, the quintessential expression of Dionysian worship, inspired an unprecedented outpouring of symbolic creativity. The barriers separating individual and universal consciousness dissolved, and humanity's unity with nature emerged as a profound revelation. The symbolism of the body became central: not just the expressions of the face and voice but the entire language of rhythmic, ecstatic movement. Every gesture, every dance step, became an expression of the primal essence of nature. This collective artistic eruption reached its zenith in the synchronization of all symbolic faculties— dance, music, and rhythm—creating an experience of transcendence and unity with the cosmos.

To understand the dithyrambic devotee of Dionysus requires a rare sensitivity and a willingness to relinquish the constraints of individuality. For the Apollonian Greek, observing these Dionysian rituals must have been a profoundly disorienting experience. On the one hand, they were astonished and perhaps even horrified by the fervor and abandon of the Dionysian revelers. On the other hand, they could not escape the unsettling realization that this seemingly foreign world was not entirely alien to them. Beneath the veil of

Apollonian order lay the same Dionysian currents, dormant but always present, waiting to be acknowledged.

To fully grasp this concept, we must meticulously dismantle the artistic edifice of Apollonian culture, piece by piece, until we uncover the foundational stones upon which it stands. When we do so, the first striking feature we encounter is the radiant assembly of Olympian gods. These magnificent figures rise like statues atop the pediments of this cultural structure, their grand deeds rendered in shining reliefs that decorate its friezes. Though Apollo is one among these deities, standing as an individual alongside his divine peers and claiming no explicit supremacy in rank, we must not be misled by this arrangement. The same creative impulse that found its expression in Apollo was the driving force behind the entire Olympian pantheon. In this sense, Apollo may be seen as the progenitor of this illustrious assembly, the central thread from which the entire tapestry was woven.

But what profound necessity could have brought forth such a vibrant and majestic collection of deities? What yearning of the human soul demanded their creation? To understand, we must first approach these gods with the right expectations. Whoever approaches the Olympians with the lens of another religion or moral framework, searching among them for spiritual transcendence, saintly purity, or compassionate love, will quickly be confounded. Here, there is no whisper of ascetic renunciation, no call to spiritual abstraction, no moralistic commandments. Instead, we encounter a boundless celebration of life itself—a life so exuberant and triumphant that it consecrates everything it touches, whether virtuous or wicked, noble or base. This unapologetic deification of existence speaks in a language unfamiliar to those conditioned to seek moral austerity or self- denial.

A modern observer, accustomed to the moral frameworks of other traditions, might find himself overwhelmed by this vibrant affirmation of life. He may gaze at these gods in their exuberant glory and wonder what intoxicating elixir these joy-filled Greeks could have consumed, enabling them to find such beauty and delight wherever they turned their eyes. To him, even Helena, the embodiment of their ideal, might seem to radiate a serene and sensual charm that defies conventional notions of spirituality. Such a bewildered observer might be tempted to retreat, puzzled by what seems an almost reckless indulgence in life's pleasures.

To this retreating figure, we must call out: "Do not turn away yet! Stay a moment longer, and listen to the wisdom of the Greeks—the same Greeks who celebrated this life with such inexplicable joy. Hear what their ancient traditions say about the very existence they appear to exalt." There is a tale, an old and profound myth, that tells of King Midas, who roamed the forests in a long and fruitless quest to capture Silenus, the wise and enigmatic companion of Dionysus. When at last Silenus was caught, Midas asked him a question of great significance: "What is the best and most desirable thing for man?" At first, Silenus remained silent, steadfast and unmoving, as if unwilling to answer. When pressed, however, he finally burst into a piercing, sardonic laugh and spoke these fateful words: "Oh, miserable race of a day, children of chance and suffering, why do you force me to reveal what would be best for you not to hear? The best of all is utterly beyond your reach: never to have been born, never to have existed, to be nothing. The next best, however, is to die swiftly."

This grim declaration strikes like a bolt of lightning, illuminating the deep undercurrent of despair that runs beneath the Greeks' apparent cheerfulness. The Olympian gods, for all their radiant glory, are not disconnected from this wisdom. Rather, they arise in response to it. The world of the Olympian deities is not a denial of Silenus's dark truth but a radiant vision conjured by those who endure its weight. It is akin to the ecstatic hallucination of a tormented martyr, who, in the depths of his suffering, imagines a world of transcendence and beauty as a way to bear his pain. In this way, the Olympian world is not an escape from the grim realities of life but a luminous counterbalance to them, a testament to humanity's ability to transform its deepest sorrows into enduring visions of splendor and meaning.

The Olympian "magic mountain" now unveils itself before our gaze, revealing its deep and hidden roots. The Greeks, perhaps more acutely than any other people, were intimately aware of the terrors and agonies that existence could bring. To endure life at all, they found it necessary to place between themselves and these horrors the radiant dreamscape of the Olympian gods. The overpowering fear of the immense, untamed forces of nature, the unyielding and merciless Moira that ruled over all things, the eternal torment of Prometheus bound beneath the eagle's claws, the tragic doom of Oedipus, and the cursed lineage of the House of Atreus—these myths of inexorable suffering could easily have led them to despair, as they did for the melancholy Etruscans. Time and again, however, the Greeks transcended such grim visions, wrapping them in the artistic brilliance of the Olympian world, obscuring or even dissolving them in its dazzling light.

To live at all, the Greeks felt compelled to bring these gods into being—an act born of necessity, yet executed with astonishing creative power. We might imagine this process as a gradual evolution, where the original titanic pantheon of dread transformed into the joyous and resplendent Olympians, shaped by the Apollonian drive toward beauty, much like roses emerge from thorny bushes. How else could such a sensitive, intensely emotional people, uniquely attuned to both desire and suffering, have borne the weight of existence without these gods who mirrored their world back to them, adorned in transcendent splendor? It was the same impulse that calls art into being—the desire to complete and glorify life, to seduce humanity into its continuation—that gave birth to the Olympian pantheon. In their gods, the Greeks found a reflection of themselves that transfigured and justified their existence. This was, for them, the only true and satisfying theodicy: life became bearable, even desirable, because the gods themselves embraced it and lived it fully.

Under the radiant sun of these gods, life was celebrated as an end in itself. The deepest sorrow of the Homeric Greeks was not life's challenges but its brevity—the inevitable parting from existence, especially if it came too soon. To them, it was not Silenus's wisdom of "not being born" that resonated but its reversal: "To die early is worst of all, and to die at all is the second greatest sorrow." Achilles, the short-lived hero, grieves not for his suffering but for the fleeting nature of life itself. Even the heroic age, destined to fade into history, laments its own impermanence. Homeric lamentations are thus not cries of despair but, paradoxically, songs of praise for existence. In their mourning, the Greeks reveal how profoundly they cherished life, even as they sang of its fleetingness.

It is essential to recognize, however, that this harmony between man and nature, which modern observers often admire in the Greeks, was not a simple or inevitable state. Schiller, with his term "naïve," described this condition, but it is misleading to see it as some natural paradise inherent to all cultures. Such an assumption could only arise in an age romanticizing figures like Rousseau's Émile, imagining Homer as an artist nurtured by nature itself. Yet true naïveté in art is not a primal state but the highest achievement of Apollonian culture— a hard-won triumph. Before reaching this harmony, the Greeks had to overcome the forces of chaos and terror, embodied in their Titanic myths and monstrous adversaries.

Through the dazzling illusions and captivating representations of the Apollonian spirit, they conquered the abyss of profound contemplation and their acute susceptibility to suffering.

The rarity of this achievement makes it all the more sublime. Homer stands as its ultimate symbol—a figure who, as an individual artist, mirrors the entire Apollonian culture of his people, much as a dream-artist reflects the dream- capacity of humanity and nature itself. The "naïveté" of Homer is not simplicity but the ultimate triumph of the Apollonian illusion. It is a feat akin to the deceptions of nature itself, which veils its true purposes with alluring phantasms, guiding humanity toward unseen goals. The Greeks, through their Apollonian genius, created a world of beauty in which they could see themselves glorified. To feel worthy of such glory, they had to imagine themselves as part of this transcendent realm—a realm free from reproach or moral imperatives.

This mirrored beauty, represented by the Olympians, became the Greeks' way of confronting their dual talent for art and suffering. Their artistic triumph over the profound wisdom of suffering finds its eternal monument in Homer, the archetype of the naïve artist. Homer's works stand as a testament to the Greeks' victory over despair, their ability to transform the raw material of suffering into a luminous celebration of life's beauty and potential.

To better understand the essence of the naïve artist, we can turn to the analogy of dreams, which sheds light on their nature and creative process. Picture the dreamer, immersed in the vivid illusion of the dream-world, yet fully aware of its nature, calling out to himself: "This is a dream, and I will continue to dream."

This moment reveals a profound inner joy in the contemplation of the dream. However, to dream with such unbridled delight, the individual must have entirely forgotten the waking world and its relentless intrusions. Under the guidance of the dream- interpreting god Apollo, we can begin to make sense of these phenomena, interpreting them as symbols of a deeper reality.

Despite the fact that waking life, with all its significance and intensity, generally appears to us as the primary and most essential form of existence, we may arrive at a paradoxical conclusion when we consider the deeper metaphysical truths underpinning our existence. When viewed from the perspective of the mysterious source of being, of which we are but fleeting manifestations, dream life might reveal itself as holding a greater value. This becomes evident as we contemplate nature's powerful artistic impulses, which express a yearning for appearance, a craving for redemption through illusion. The more closely we examine these impulses, the more we are drawn to the notion that the ultimate, primordial reality—eternally suffering and self- conflicted—requires the ecstatic vision and joyous appearance of dreams to sustain itself. This appearance, though entirely illusory, is the vehicle of salvation.

From this standpoint, our empirical existence, including the physical world we inhabit, can be understood as a continual expression of this primordial unity. It unfolds moment by moment, manifesting as an illusory representation, an "appearance of reality" shaped by time, space, and causality. If we step away from the assumption of our own concrete reality and instead see our existence as a perpetual projection of the primordial essence, we can view dreams as an even more refined layer of illusion—an "appearance of appearance." In this sense, dreams fulfill a deeper longing for form and transcendence, providing an even greater satisfaction of the primordial drive toward beauty and illusion.

It is for this reason that the core of nature responds with profound joy to the work of the naïve artist. This type of artist, like the dreamer, embodies this process of creating layers of appearances. Raphael, one of the immortal naïve artists, captured this very dynamic in his masterpiece Transfiguration. In the lower half of the painting, we see the anguished scene of the possessed boy, the despairing attendants, and the frightened disciples—a reflection of the eternal pain that lies at the foundation of existence. Here, "appearance" itself becomes the visible form of eternal contradiction, the underlying reality from which all things emerge.

Above this scene, however, arises a luminous vision—a radiant world of pure beauty and bliss, untouched by the torment below. This higher realm of appearances seems to float above, detached and serene, embodying the Apollonian ideal of transcendent beauty and contemplative joy. It is as if the wisdom of Silenus, with all its terror, has been transmuted into a glowing symbol of artistic triumph. Through Raphael's symbolic representation, we perceive the necessary interdependence of these two realms: the terrible truth of existence as the substratum of the Apollonian world of beauty.

In this context, Apollo reveals himself once more as the divine embodiment of the principium individuationis, the principle that affirms the boundaries and distinctions of individuality. Through Apollo, the primordial unity achieves its redemption by manifesting as ordered, comprehensible forms. He teaches us that the torment and chaos of existence are not in vain; they drive the individual toward the creation of redemptive visions. Within these visions, the individual can sit, as if in a fragile boat, calmly afloat amidst the stormy seas of life.

This apotheosis of individuality, if conceived as a guiding principle, establishes a singular law: the reverence for the individual and the strict observance of boundaries. Apollo, as the god of measure and ethical balance, demands self-knowledge and restraint from his followers. Hence, the Delphic maxims "Know thyself" and "Nothing in excess" emerge as essential tenets of the Apollonian ethos. Arrogance, excess, and the breaking of boundaries are condemned as the hallmarks of the pre-Apollonian age, the era of the Titans, or of the non-Apollonian world of barbarism.

The Greek myths illustrate the consequences of violating these principles. Prometheus, for his titanic love of humanity, is condemned to unending torment, devoured by vultures. Oedipus, whose unparalleled wisdom unraveled the riddle of the Sphinx, is cast into a whirlwind of horrifying crimes and curses. Through these cautionary tales, Apollo offered the Greeks an interpretation of their past—a past marked by suffering and hubris but ultimately redeemed through the wisdom of balance and beauty.

The effects brought forth by the Dionysian spirit appeared wild, untamed, even "titanic" and "barbaric" to the Apollonian Greek. Yet, despite this perception, the Apollonian could not fully disown these primal forces; instead, he recognized a deep, intrinsic connection to the very Titans and heroes that Dionysian energy celebrated and overthrew. More profoundly, the Apollonian

Greek understood that his existence, with all its beauty, order, and restraint, rested upon a concealed foundation of suffering and deeper, more primal knowledge—truths that the Dionysian unveiled. This realization led to a paradoxical dependence: Apollo could not exist without Dionysus. The so- called "titanic" and "barbaric" elements were not extraneous; they were as essential as the serene and measured beauty of the Apollonian ideal.

Now let us imagine the compelling strains of Dionysian ecstasy breaking into the meticulously crafted and orderly world of Apollonian appearances. These sounds—wild, intoxicating, filled with unrestrained emotion—spoke a language of raw truth, one that pierced through the serene harp-music of Apollo with its primal force. The Dionysian art, born of intoxication and boundless expression, seemed to mock the carefully constructed illusions of the Apollonian. The wisdom of Silenus—crying "Woe! Woe!"—stood in stark contrast to the cheerful, luminous Olympians. Under the sway of Dionysian fervor, the individual dissolved, losing their sense of boundaries and proportions in the all-consuming ecstasy of self-forgetfulness. Here, pain and joy merged into a singular experience, and nature's profound contradictions were laid bare. The bliss born from suffering—the dual truths of agony and rapture—became inescapable.

Wherever Dionysus held sway, the Apollonian vision was challenged, even annihilated. Yet, when the Dionysian onslaught was resisted, Apollo emerged with heightened authority, his dominion more rigid and resolute than ever before. This fierce opposition can explain the austere and disciplined nature of Doric culture and art. The Doric state became a fortress for the Apollonian spirit, maintaining its ideals against the untamed chaos of the Dionysian. In its unyielding defiance, Doric art surrounded itself with walls of discipline, its rigorous training and relentless order creating a bastion of Apollonian clarity.

Up to this point, we have traced the interplay of these two powerful artistic forces—Dionysian and Apollonian—through the evolution of Hellenic culture. From the "bronze age" with its titanic struggles and austere folk philosophies, the Apollonian impulse emerged, fostering the radiant beauty of the Homeric world. Yet this idyllic vision was overwhelmed by the return of the Dionysian torrent, which, in turn, provoked a resurgence of Apollonian resolve in the majesty of Doric art and its worldview. If this historical narrative can be divided into four major periods, culminating in the Doric age, we must now ask whether Doric art represented the ultimate aim of these developments—or whether it was merely a prelude to something even greater.

This greater culmination reveals itself in the sublime creation of Attic tragedy and the dramatic dithyramb—a synthesis of the Dionysian and Apollonian that united their opposing energies into a single, transcendent art form. It is here, in this miraculous union, that we find the child of both impulses: a creation that embodies the complexity of figures such as Antigone and Cassandra.

To fully grasp this fusion, we must trace its origins in the Hellenic world. The ancients themselves offer symbolic guidance, often depicting Homer and Archilochus side by side as the progenitors of Greek poetry. Homer, the serene dreamer and archetype of Apollonian artistry, is contrasted with Archilochus, the impassioned and tumultuous genius of Dionysian lyricism. Modern aesthetics has interpreted this pairing as the meeting of the "objective" artist (Homer) with the first "subjective" artist (Archilochus). Yet this interpretation is inadequate, for true artistry requires the transcendence of subjectivity. The highest forms of art demand a liberation from personal ego and individual desires, achieving pure, disinterested contemplation. How, then, do we reconcile the existence of the "lyrist"—the one who sings of their own passions and desires—with the nature of art?

Archilochus, with his searing cries of hatred and drunken raptures, may seem the very antithesis of artistry. And yet, he was venerated as a poet, even receiving profound recognition from the Delphic oracle, the very heart of Apollonian objectivity. This paradox forces us to reconsider the role of the subjective in art and the mysterious interplay of Dionysian intensity with Apollonian form. It is through such contradictions that we begin to approach the profound mysteries of Greek creativity and the dynamic union of these two divine impulses.

Schiller offers us a remarkable glimpse into his poetic process through an observation that, while psychologically profound, even he found mysterious. He confesses that, in preparing to write poetry, he did not begin with a clear series of connected images or thoughts. Instead, he described experiencing a "musical mood," an emotional state without definite content, which later gave rise to poetic ideas. He writes, "The perception with me is at first without a clear and definite object; this forms itself later. A certain musical mood of mind precedes, and only after this does the poetical idea follow with me." This insight leads us to reflect on the ancient Greek lyric tradition, where the union of the poet and musician was seen as natural, even inevitable—a unity that is absent in much of modern lyric poetry, which can seem like a statue of a god, beautiful yet decapitated.

Building on this understanding, and within the framework of the metaphysics of aesthetics, we may interpret the lyrist's role as follows. As a Dionysian artist, the lyrist is first absorbed into the Primordial Unity, experiencing its pain and contradiction. This profound connection to the essence of existence is expressed as music, which has been aptly described as a recasting of the world's fundamental nature. Under the influence of Apollonian inspiration, this music is transformed into a symbolic dream- image—a concrete representation of the abstract pain and redemption that music embodies. Thus, the artist transcends personal subjectivity in the Dionysian experience, and what emerges is not a personal vision but a universal one. The lyrical "I" of the poet, rather than representing the individual, speaks from the very depths of being itself. What appears as subjective expression is, in fact, a manifestation of eternal truths.

Consider Archilochus, the first great Greek lyrist. When he writes of his intense love and searing contempt for the daughters of Lycambes, it is not his personal feelings that take center stage. Instead, these passions are transfigured into a universal drama. What we witness is not the man Archilochus in a frenzy of personal emotions, but rather Dionysus and the Mænads in their divine ecstasy. Euripides offers a vivid depiction of this state in The Bacchæ, where the exhausted, intoxicated reveller collapses into a deep, symbolic sleep on a sunlit alpine meadow. In this vision, Apollo appears, gently bestowing his touch with the laurel branch. From this divine interplay emerges not merely the personal utterances of a man, but lyrical works of art—poems that evolve into the grander forms of tragedy and the dramatic dithyramb.

The plastic artist and the epic poet, who share a kinship in their art forms, are immersed in the contemplation of images. The Dionysian musician, by contrast, is not concerned with visual forms but embodies the raw essence of primordial pain and its resonant echoes. The lyric genius, standing at the intersection of these realms, perceives a world of symbols and imagery arising from a state of mystical self-abandonment and unity with the Primordial Unity. This symbolic vision is distinct from the static, detailed focus of the epic poet or sculptor. While the latter revels in each image's intricacies with joyful detachment, the lyrist's images are deeply personal—they are projections of his very essence. The lyrical "I" thus serves as the moving center of this symbolic world, though it is not the "I" of the everyday, empirical individual but that of an eternal self that underpins all existence.

Imagine the lyrist perceiving himself within these images, not as an artist but as a subject—a man driven by desires and passions directed toward an external reality. If this projection gives the illusion that the lyric genius and the subjective individual are one and the same, it is a misconception. The lyrist is not the subjective poet, as was often assumed. Instead, Archilochus, with all his tumultuous passions, becomes a symbolic figure through whom the lyrical genius expresses primordial pain and joy. Archilochus the individual is a vision conjured by the world-spanning genius; the man as a subjective, willing entity cannot, in and of himself, be a poet.

The genius of the lyrist transcends mere personal expression, as demonstrated by tragedy, which expands the scope of the visionary world far beyond the individual figure. Tragedy reveals how the lyric artist's vision, rooted in the universal and eternal, can reach beyond the personal and subjective to encompass a broader and more profound symbolic truth. It is through this dynamic interplay of Dionysian and Apollonian forces that lyric poetry attains its unique and transformative power.

Schopenhauer, while recognizing the unique challenge that lyric poetry poses to the philosophical contemplation of art, offered an explanation that I find difficult to follow fully, though he alone, with his profound metaphysics of music, held the key to resolving this issue. Here, I have sought to address it in a manner that honors his spirit and his contributions. In The World as Will and Representation (I. 295), Schopenhauer describes the nature of song as follows:

"It is the subject of the will, namely, the singer's own volition, which fills his consciousness—often as unrestrained and satisfied desire, such as joy, but more frequently as restricted desire, like grief—always presenting itself as an emotion, passion, or agitated state of mind. Alongside this emotional turbulence, and in contrast to it, the singer becomes aware of himself as a subject of pure, will-less knowledge, drawn to the serene peace that this detachment offers. This contrast, this back-and-forth between the two states, defines the lyrical condition. In this mode, pure knowledge seems to rescue us momentarily from the clutches of desire, but only briefly, as we are soon pulled back into the tumult of our personal aims and emotions. Yet, again and again, the beauty of the world around us beckons us back into contemplation. Thus, in song and in the lyrical mood, the striving of desire and the calm of pure observation mingle. The subjective emotions of the will color the external world we perceive, and, conversely, the world's beauty casts its reflection onto the inner life of the will.

True song captures the entire spectrum of this fragmented and divided state of being."

While poetic, Schopenhauer's characterization ultimately presents lyric poetry as a partially realized art form—a hybrid where the aesthetic and non- aesthetic are intertwined. This view implicitly diminishes the lyric's artistic status, casting it as a semi-art form that struggles, leaping sporadically, to achieve its full potential. However, I believe this critique arises from the very antithesis— subjective versus objective—that Schopenhauer employs as his evaluative framework for the arts.

We contend that this opposition has no rightful place in aesthetics. The subjective, understood as the desiring and self-centered individual, is not the source of art but its antithesis. The artist, as an instrument of creation, transcends their individual will, becoming a medium through which the universal Subject—the primordial unity—expresses itself and achieves redemption in the realm of appearances. The true marvel of art lies not in its capacity for moral improvement or human enlightenment but in its role as an aesthetic phenomenon that justifies existence itself.

For us, the "I" of the lyric poet is not an expression of the empirical, individual self but rather a voice from the eternal, universal essence. In the act of creation, the artist briefly merges with the primal creator of the cosmos, catching a glimpse of that eternal essence. At this moment, the artist becomes simultaneously subject and object, poet and actor, creator and spectator—like a mystical figure in a fable that gazes upon itself with wonder and understanding.

The historical figure of Archilochus exemplifies this union of universal and personal dimensions. Critically acclaimed as the one who brought the folk song into the literary canon, Archilochus stands in Greek tradition as a peer to Homer. But the folk song, in contrast to the Apollonian epic, carries the unmistakable traces of the Dionysian spirit. This enduring form, found across cultures and ages, is a testament to the interplay of these artistic impulses. The folk song, born of collective experience and often linked to moments of communal ecstasy, reveals the power of the Apollonian and Dionysian in tandem.

Indeed, history shows that periods of rich folk-song production often coincide with the stirring of Dionysian energies within a culture. These songs are not mere artistic artifacts but living echoes of a profound duality. They capture the rhythms and ecstasies of a people, embodying the perpetual dance between structured beauty and chaotic vitality. Thus, Archilochus, as the harbinger of this union in Greek literature, represents the lyric poet as both a vessel for timeless truths and a voice for the eternal resonance of art's double impulse.

First, we must approach the popular song as a profound and primal phenomenon—a musical reflection of the world itself, the original melody that seeks to embody its essence in a parallel dream-image, expressed through poetry. This perspective elevates melody to a primary and universal force, one that inherently precedes and surpasses the text. Melody is not merely an accompaniment to words; rather, it gives rise to the poem, birthing it repeatedly in an enduring process of creation. In the eyes of the people, melody assumes a role of paramount importance, standing as the indispensable and generative force in this artistic relationship.

From this understanding, we can appreciate how the strophic form of the popular song reflects this creative dynamic. This form—a repeated musical phrase generating verses of text—has always seemed a source of wonder, revealing a deeply intuitive connection between music and poetry. Only after reflecting upon this phenomenon was I able to grasp its true significance. Anyone who examines collections of folk songs, such as Des Knaben Wunderhorn, through this lens will encounter countless examples of melody functioning as a fountain of inspiration, scattering vibrant, fleeting images in every direction. These "picture sparks," bursting with variety, abrupt transitions, and a wild, even chaotic energy, exhibit a power far removed from the measured continuity of epic poetry.

Indeed, from the perspective of the epic tradition, this irregular, fragmented world of lyric poetry may seem unruly and even offensive. The epic's steady and dignified flow stands in stark contrast to the sudden, unpredictable movements of the lyric. It is not difficult to imagine how the solemn rhapsodists of the Apollonian festivals—those devoted to the stately and ordered forms of Homeric tradition during the age of Terpander—would have dismissed such lyricism. They would have regarded the folk song's unstructured nature as incompatible with the principles of harmony and proportion that governed their craft.

Yet, the very qualities that the epic might condemn in the popular song— its unevenness, its irregular rhythm, its bursts of imagery— are precisely what mark its distinct genius. These qualities reveal the song's Dionysian roots, its deep connection to the primordial forces of nature, emotion, and collective expression. Where the epic strives for a complete and unified narrative, the popular song thrives on moments of intense feeling and symbolic resonance. Its melody, perpetually fertile and dynamic, evokes a sense of immediacy and raw vitality that the polished, deliberate artistry of the epic cannot replicate.

Thus, the popular song, with its musical foundation and lyrical spontaneity, embodies an artistic impulse that challenges and enriches the traditions of its time. It stands as a testament to the creative power of melody to conjure worlds, evoke emotions, and inspire poetic visions that transcend the boundaries of structured narrative. Its energy may seem anarchic to the Apollonian artist, but to those attuned to the interplay of the Dionysian and the Apollonian, it represents an essential and irrepressible dimension of human creativity.

In the creation of popular songs, we observe a profound and unique phenomenon: language stretches itself to its very limits in an effort to emulate music. This effort marks the beginning of a new realm of poetry, fundamentally distinct from the Homeric tradition, and most vividly embodied in the works of Archilochus. With this, we touch upon the only truly possible relationship between poetry and music, between word and tone. Here, words, images, and concepts strive to parallel the expressive power of music and, in doing so, come to experience the transformative essence of music within themselves.

To comprehend this, we can identify two primary trajectories in the development of the Greek language: one that seeks to emulate the visible, phenomenal world of images, and another that seeks to echo the ineffable, abstract realm of music. The linguistic differences between Homer and Pindar illustrate this vividly. By examining their use of color, syntax, and vocabulary, we perceive how, during the period separating these two poets, the ecstatic, intoxicating flute melodies of Olympus must have resonated through the cultural landscape. These melodies, even in Aristotle's era—when music had reached far greater levels of sophistication—could still inspire a state of ecstatic enthusiasm. In their earliest appearances, these Dionysian musical influences likely incited every form of poetic expression in their contemporaries to mimic and adapt themselves to this newfound force.

A parallel phenomenon is familiar in our own time, even though traditional aesthetics often dismisses it. Again and again, we see how a Beethoven symphony, for example, drives listeners to respond with figurative language, attempting to articulate in visual or conceptual terms the impressions evoked by the music. The images conjured by different individuals listening to the same piece of music may vary wildly in their specifics, even contradicting one another, yet they share a common origin: the compulsion to translate the emotional and symbolic depth of music into some tangible form.

Despite the objections of certain aesthetic schools, this phenomenon warrants deeper exploration. Even the composer himself may offer visual or thematic associations to accompany his work, such as Beethoven naming one of his symphonies the "Pastoral" or identifying sections of it with scenes like "By the Brook" or "The Merry Gathering of Rustics." However, such descriptions are not attempts to capture the true essence of the music's Dionysian power. They are merely symbolic interpretations—representations birthed by music but not actual imitations of music. These images, no matter how vivid, remain secondary to the music's ineffable essence and hold no intrinsic value above other symbolic interpretations.

To grasp the origins of the strophic popular song and its relation to this principle of imitation, we must imagine a linguistically fertile and imaginative culture encountering the Dionysian power of music for the first time. The music would provoke an outpouring of poetic creativity, inspiring language itself to transform in response to this new principle. Words would flow like musical phrases, mirroring the emotional and symbolic depth of the melodies. The rhythm, harmony, and dynamic shifts of music would find their echoes in the strophic forms of song, while language, animated by this principle, would gain new expressive dimensions.

This transformative interaction between music and language offers insight into the deep roots of poetic inspiration and the dynamic ways in which art forms evolve through their dialogue with one another. By tracing this process to its earliest expressions in the popular songs of a culture, we glimpse how profoundly the Dionysian spirit can influence human creativity, reshaping not only the forms of art but also the very tools—words and tones— with which we express our deepest truths.

If we are to regard lyric poetry as the radiant outflow of music, expressed through images and concepts, we can now delve deeper into the question: "How does music manifest when reflected through the lens of symbolism and conception?" Music appears as will, employing the term in the Schopenhauerian sense, which positions will as the opposite of the aesthetic, purely contemplative, and passive state of mind. However, we must carefully distinguish between the concepts of essence and appearance in this context. Music, in its essence, cannot be equated with will, for if it were, it would have to be entirely excluded from the realm of art—will itself being inherently unaesthetic. Yet music appears as will, and herein lies the complexity.

To express the phenomenon of music in pictorial terms, the lyric poet must draw upon the full range of emotional experience, from the tender stirrings of nascent desire to the tempestuous roar of unrestrained madness. Driven to articulate music in the Apollonian language of symbols, the poet perceives all of nature, including himself, as an eternal cycle of wanting, yearning, and striving. Yet, paradoxically, while interpreting music through these images of will, the poet himself rests in the serene clarity of Apollonian contemplation. Around him, the world he perceives through the medium of music seems to whirl in chaotic motion, yet he remains detached, an observer freed from the clutches of desire. Even as the poet reflects upon his own image within this musical lens, he sees himself imbued with longing, striving, and lamenting. These become the symbols through which he deciphers music. Thus, the lyric poet, as an Apollonian genius, translates the intangible essence of music into imagery tied to the will, while he himself, liberated from the urgency of desire, embodies the tranquil and unclouded vision of the pure Apollonian eye.

The essence of our discussion emphasizes that lyric poetry is fundamentally dependent on the spirit of music. Music, in its sovereign universality, does not require imagery or conceptual language, tolerating them only as accompanying elements. The poet's verses can express nothing that has not already existed in the vast, encompassing universality of the music that compels him to give it voice through metaphor. Language, bound as it is to the world of phenomena, is inherently incapable of fully rendering the cosmic symbolism inherent in music. Music transcends appearance and phenomena, standing as a symbol of the primordial contradiction and pain at the heart of the Primordial Unity. In comparison to music, all phenomena— including language—are mere symbols. Thus, language, as a tool for representing phenomena, can at best touch music's surface, imitating its rhythm or tone. It cannot, however, bring us any closer to music's profound essence. The deepest significance of music remains ineffable, beyond the reach of even the most eloquent lyric poetry.

With these principles of art as our foundation, we now approach the intricate puzzle of the origins of Greek tragedy. It is no exaggeration to claim that the question of tragedy's genesis has yet to be thoroughly posed, let alone resolved, despite numerous attempts to reconstruct its origins by patching together fragments of ancient tradition. According to this tradition, tragedy emerged from the tragic chorus and was, in its earliest form, entirely chorus—a communal, choral experience without distinct dramatic elements. To understand tragedy's roots, we must explore the heart of the tragic chorus itself, recognizing it as the original proto- drama. We cannot content ourselves with superficial explanations that frame the chorus as merely an idealized spectator or as a representation of the people in opposition to the regal figures on stage.

The latter interpretation—that the chorus symbolized the immutable moral law upheld by democratic Athens, triumphing over the passionate excesses of kings—has often been bolstered by Aristotle's observations and may appeal to modern political sensibilities. However, such a notion is irrelevant to the true origins of tragedy, which lie far removed from the socio-political dichotomies of king and people. The initial formation of tragedy emerged from deeply religious beginnings, entirely disconnected from political or social structures. To retroactively impose notions of "constitutional representation of the people" onto the classical chorus of Æschylus and Sophocles would not only be anachronistic but also, in some sense, sacrilegious. Ancient Greek governance had no concept of constitutional representation in practice, and we can only hope that they did not imagine it within their tragedies either. Tragedy's origins reside not in political representation but in a profound and sacred artistic communion born of the chorus itself.

Far more renowned than the political interpretation of the chorus is the perspective offered by A. W. Schlegel, who encouraged us to see the tragic chorus as, in some sense, the distilled essence or extract of the audience itself— as the "ideal spectator." This perspective, when placed alongside the historical record asserting that tragedy began as nothing more than the chorus, reveals itself to be a bold, imaginative, but fundamentally unscientific claim. Its appeal lies not in its fidelity to historical accuracy but rather in the rhetorical brilliance of its phrasing, its grounding in the German Romantic inclination toward the "ideal," and the momentary astonishment it elicits. Indeed, we are taken aback when we compare the familiar modern theatrical audience with the Greek chorus and consider whether it is even conceivable to elevate such an audience to the idealized form Schlegel proposes.

Instinctively, we deny the possibility, and this denial leads us to marvel not only at Schlegel's audacity but also at the profoundly different nature of Greek spectatorship. For we have long assumed that a true spectator, in any era, must remain aware of the artifice before them—that they are witnessing a crafted work of art, not an empirical reality. Yet the Greek tragic chorus, as tradition tells us, did not share this sensibility. The Oceanides, for example, genuinely believed they stood in the presence of Prometheus, the suffering Titan. To them, the figures on stage were not characters in a performance but living beings, as real as the gods themselves.

Are we, then, to believe that the ideal spectator is one who, like the Oceanides, accepts the figures on stage as corporeally and materially present? Is it a hallmark of ideal spectatorship to leap onto the stage and attempt to free Prometheus from his torment? This notion runs counter to the very foundation of modern aesthetic theory, which holds that the best audience is one capable of perceiving art as art, appreciating its crafted illusion rather than mistaking it for reality. Schlegel's assertion, then, seems to suggest that the highest form of spectatorship is entirely divorced from aesthetic contemplation and grounded instead in a visceral, empirical response. Oh, those Greeks! we might exclaim, as we recognize how thoroughly their approach challenges the assumptions of our modern aesthetics. Yet once acclimated to Schlegel's perspective, we have found ourselves repeating his formulation whenever the topic of the chorus arises, even if it unsettles us.

However, the explicit historical tradition does not support Schlegel's interpretation. The chorus, in its primordial form, existed without a stage; tragedy began as chorus alone. This foundational fact cannot be reconciled with the notion of the chorus as "ideal spectators." What kind of art, one might ask, could originate from the concept of the spectator? What would it mean to view the spectator as the primary form of art itself? The idea of the spectator existing independently of a dramatic performance is, quite simply, absurd. Thus, we must conclude that the origins of tragedy cannot be explained by appeals to the moral intelligence of the audience or by the abstract concept of a spectator detached from the performance. These approaches are too superficial to even approach the profound depth of the problem.

A far more insightful understanding of the chorus's role was offered by Schiller in the famous preface to his Bride of Messina. There, Schiller envisions the chorus as a "living wall," a protective barrier that tragedy constructs around itself to maintain its separation from mundane reality. This wall shields tragedy's ideal and poetic domain, preserving its freedom from the encroachments of the ordinary world. Schiller's conception allows us to see the chorus not as a mere audience proxy or as the embodiment of collective judgment but as a vital, living element of the tragic art form itself.

This "living wall" preserves the sanctity and autonomy of the tragic experience, allowing the drama to unfold in a realm untouched by the contingencies of daily life. It secures the aesthetic distance necessary for tragedy to operate as a form of sublime art, enabling the audience to engage not as participants in empirical reality but as witnesses to a higher, idealized expression of existence. In Schiller's formulation, the chorus becomes not merely a component of the performance but a guardian of its metaphysical and artistic integrity, ensuring that the tragic stage remains a space of pure imagination and transcendence. This interpretation aligns far more closely with the historical essence and artistic purpose of the tragic chorus than Schlegel's concept of the "ideal spectator" ever could.

Schiller wields this concept as his most potent weapon to combat the conventional understanding of the "natural" in dramatic poetry, as well as the demand for illusion as its foundation. He argues that while it is true that the daylight on stage is artificial, the architecture purely symbolic, and the metrical dialogue wholly ideal in its nature, a fundamental misunderstanding persists. This misunderstanding lies in the assumption that these elements are mere concessions to poetic license when, in fact, they represent the very essence of all poetry. Schiller contends that the introduction of the chorus into tragedy marks a bold and unambiguous declaration of war against naturalism in art, asserting the supremacy of idealism.

Our own era, with its supposed sophistication, has often dismissed this perspective with the pejorative label of "pseudo-idealism." Yet, in doing so, we may have betrayed a deeper misunderstanding. While proudly rejecting the ideals championed by Schiller, we have embraced an extreme veneration of the "natural" and "real," descending into an aesthetic quagmire exemplified by wax museums and superficial imitations of reality. Such art, though present in contemporary novels and other media, cannot be compared to the higher ideals of Schiller and Goethe. It is art in form but not in spirit, and to claim that it has surpassed the idealism of the classical tradition is a gross exaggeration.

Schiller recognized that the Greek satyric chorus, the precursor of tragedy, inhabited an "ideal" realm far removed from the mundane world of human experience. This chorus existed in a space elevated above the ordinary, constructed on the scaffolding of a fictitious natural state populated by beings of pure imagination. Upon this foundation, Greek tragedy arose, liberating itself from any obligation to replicate reality with painful exactitude. However, this world of the chorus was not a mere fantasy suspended between heaven and earth; it possessed a reality as credible to the Greek mind as Olympus and its divine inhabitants.

The satyr, the Dionysian chorist, was deeply embedded within a religiously affirmed reality underpinned by myth and cult. The fact that tragedy begins with the satyr and that its Dionysian wisdom speaks through this figure is a phenomenon as striking to us as the broader truth that tragedy itself originates in the chorus. To understand this profound connection, we might start with a proposition: the satyr, this fictitious natural being, stands in relation to the cultivated man of Greek culture as Dionysian music does to the sophisticated structures of civilization. Richard Wagner insightfully observes that Dionysian music neutralizes civilization as daylight overwhelms lamplight. Similarly, the cultivated Greek, in the presence of the satyric chorus, felt himself eclipsed, stripped of the artificial distinctions of culture and status.

This transformative power of Dionysian tragedy erases the barriers between individuals, dissolving societal structures and uniting all participants in an overwhelming sense of oneness. It transports them back to the primordial heart of nature, where distinctions between state and society, self and other, are obliterated. At its core lies the metaphysical comfort that all true tragedy imparts: despite the relentless flux of phenomena, life remains fundamentally indestructible, eternally potent, and inherently joyous. This comfort is rendered tangible and vivid in the form of the satyric chorus—a chorus of elemental, natural beings who endure eternally beneath the ever-changing veneer of civilization. These beings are symbols of the timeless, the unyielding essence of life, persisting through the rise and fall of generations and nations.

For the profound and introspective Greek, whose sensitivity made him uniquely capable of both profound joy and excruciating suffering, the satyric chorus offered solace. This was a people who had gazed unflinchingly into the abyss of universal history's violent processes and nature's relentless cruelty. Such exposure left them vulnerable to a yearning for the nihilistic negation of will, akin to the teachings of Buddhism. Yet, through the Dionysian chorus, art became their salvation. It was art that reconciled them with existence, transforming despair into affirmation. Through this sublime aesthetic vision, life, in turn, preserved itself—not as an illusion, but as a triumphant, unassailable truth. Art, for the Greek, was not a mere distraction from suffering; it was the very means by which life justified and redeemed itself.

In the rapturous state of Dionysian ecstasy, where the boundaries of ordinary existence dissolve, a powerful element of forgetting arises. This lethargic state immerses the individual in an oblivion so profound that the personal experiences and burdens of the past are momentarily erased. It is this chasm of forgetfulness that separates the mundane, everyday reality from the heightened reality of Dionysian existence. Yet, as soon as the individual emerges from this Dionysian immersion and becomes conscious again of the everyday world, the contrast is deeply unsettling. This reawakening to the ordinary fills the individual with a profound sense of nausea and disillusionment, often inducing an ascetic state of paralysis in the will. Such a condition aligns the Dionysian individual with Hamlet, both of whom have glimpsed the true nature of existence.

For both Hamlet and the Dionysian man, the revelation of truth renders action futile. They understand the immutable essence of reality, seeing any attempt to "set things right" as either absurd or disgraceful. Hamlet teaches us not the lesson of indecisive overthinking, as superficial interpretations might suggest, but a deeper and more troubling insight: that genuine knowledge— the piercing understanding of existence's core—undermines all motivation for action. Action, they recognize, requires the protective veil of illusion. Once that veil is lifted, as it is for the Dionysian man, all drives to engage with the world seem trivial. The longing of such a person transcends not only the gods but the very idea of existence itself, as even the glimmers of divine or afterlife comfort lose their appeal. In the stark light of truth, existence appears either grotesque in its absurdity or crushing in its horror.

It is in this extreme crisis of the will, when loathing for existence becomes overpowering, that art intervenes as a savior. Art emerges as a healing force, a magical enchantress capable of transforming the dreadful insights into something bearable. Through art, the horrifying and absurd aspects of existence are transfigured into the representations of the sublime—the artistic mastery of terror—and the comic, which releases us from the nausea of absurdity. Greek art achieved this redemption through the satyric chorus of the dithyramb, where the raw energies and agonies of the Dionysian state found a cathartic outlet.

The figure of the satyr encapsulates this transformative power. While the modern idyllic shepherd might symbolize a sentimental and romanticized connection to nature, the satyr represents something far more profound and primal. Unlike the gentle, flute-playing shepherd of modern imagination, the satyr is a bold and fearless embodiment of untamed nature. The Greeks embraced this figure with a reverence that contrasts sharply with modern society's timid idealizations. To them, the satyr was no mere wild beast or caricature but the archetype of humanity in its most unfiltered and potent form. He was the ecstatic reveler, intoxicated by the presence of the divine; the suffering companion, whose shared agony mirrored that of the god; the voice of nature's deep wisdom; and the symbol of unbridled sexual vitality. The satyr embodied the elemental forces of life, forces that inspired awe rather than shame.

To the weary eyes of the Dionysian man, who had seen through the illusions of culture, the satyr was a sublime and godlike figure. In contrast, the sanitized, artificial shepherd of modernity would have seemed a grotesque mockery. The satyr revealed the unspoiled, majestic truth of human nature, stripping away the false veneers of culture to unveil humanity's raw, authentic self.

Before the satyr's primal power, the cultured man—laden with his pretense of civility— shrank into insignificance, exposed as a hollow facade.

Schiller's insight into the origins of tragic art aptly captures this dynamic. He regarded the chorus, particularly the satyric chorus, as a protective barrier shielding tragedy from the encroachments of mundane reality. The chorus did not merely provide a fantastical escape but offered a more profound truth than the so- called realism of the cultured world. The satyric chorus depicted existence not as a polished product of human artifice but as an unvarnished expression of life's fundamental truths. In doing so, it revealed the great lie at the heart of culture, which masquerades as reality. The poetry of the satyric chorus was not an escape into fantasy; it was an immersion into a deeper reality that laid bare the stark truths of existence.

The contrast between this raw truth of nature and the falsehoods of culture is akin to the relationship between the eternal essence of things—the "thing in itself"—and the fleeting world of appearances. Just as tragedy points to the indestructible core of life beneath the endless cycle of destruction, the symbolism of the satyric chorus expresses the relationship between ultimate reality and transient phenomena. The idyllic shepherd of modernity reflects culture's self-deception, while the Dionysian Greek sought the truth in its most potent, unfiltered form. Through the satyr, he became one with nature, not in its gentle illusions but in its raw and overwhelming power.

The revelry of the Dionysian throng reaches such ecstatic heights that it transforms its participants before their very eyes. In this state, they no longer perceive themselves as mere individuals but as embodiments of nature's primal spirits, as satyrs reborn into a higher unity with the world. This transformation is no idle imagination but a deeply felt metamorphosis that dissolves the boundaries of self, a phenomenon that forms the natural foundation upon which the tragic chorus is later built. The artistic representation of this natural event—the formation of the chorus in Attic tragedy—requires a crucial distinction between the Dionysian revelers and those observing them. Yet, it is vital to recognize that the audience of Greek tragedy did not exist as a detached assembly of spectators in the way modern audiences do. Instead, the audience rediscovered itself in the satyric chorus, erasing the division between watcher and participant. All those present formed, in essence, one vast and exalted chorus, united in song and dance, either as satyrs themselves or as ones represented by them.

This understanding offers a profound reinterpretation of Schlegel's assertion that the chorus is the "ideal spectator." In its most profound sense, the chorus does not merely observe; it is the sole beholder of the visionary spectacle. Unlike the detached audiences we are accustomed to, the Greek theater, with its ascending tiers encircling the stage, provided each individual with an immersive view, allowing them to perceive themselves as integral to the collective experience. In this way, the tragic chorus served as a reflection of the Dionysian man's self-transformation. It was as if the chorus mirrored the visions that arose from the rapture of Dionysian ecstasy, making visible the spiritual essence of the throng's communal experience.

For the gifted poet, this process of transformation was not an abstraction but an immediate reality. The poet sees the forms of his imagination as living entities surrounding him, acting and breathing with an intensity that defies ordinary perception. In modern times, our tendency to analyze artistic creation as an intellectual construct often blinds us to this primal artistic phenomenon. For the true poet, metaphor is no mere rhetorical device but a tangible image replacing abstract thought. The characters envisioned by the poet are not mere aggregates of traits; they are vivid, living beings, animated by a continuous inner life that demands to be expressed. Homer stands as a prime example, creating figures of unparalleled vitality because he truly sees them, not as static objects but as entities alive with action and purpose. The modern inclination to speak abstractly about art stems, perhaps, from a collective inability to access this profound immediacy of vision.

In the Dionysian state, however, this artistic faculty is not limited to individual poets; it spreads like wildfire, enveloping entire communities. Under its spell, individuals are endowed with the capacity to see themselves surrounded by spirits and to feel an unshakable unity with them. This communal vision lies at the heart of the tragic chorus, marking it as the primal dramatic phenomenon. In this state, individuals see themselves transformed, as though they have stepped into another body, another identity. Unlike the rhapsodist, who remains an external observer of his tales, the Dionysian participant merges completely with the character they embody, abandoning their personal identity. This surrender to transformation is not a solitary act but a collective experience, spreading through the throng like an epidemic. The dithyrambic chorus, in this sense, represents a community of beings entirely dissolved into their divine service, their individual pasts and social roles obliterated in favor of their timeless unity with the god.

This quality distinguishes the dithyramb from other forms of Greek choral performance. For instance, the virgins who approach Apollo's temple with laurel branches and solemn hymns remain rooted in their identities; their actions are enhancements of their individual roles within a civic framework. In contrast, the dithyrambic chorus transcends individuality entirely. It becomes a collective of unconscious actors who no longer perceive themselves as separate from one another. This transformative power imbues the dithyramb with a uniqueness that sets it apart from all other choral forms. Where other choral songs amplify the singular voice of the Apollonian singer, the dithyramb dissolves the self into a shared, ecstatic unity. The individuals in the dithyrambic chorus are no longer citizens of a polis; they are the timeless servants of Dionysus, united in their shared metamorphosis.

Thus, the dithyramb represents not just a heightened form of choral song but a profound departure from the Apollonian tradition. It embodies the Dionysian ideal of transformation, where the boundaries between self and other, human and divine, dissolve into a single, pulsating life force. The tragic chorus, as an extension of this phenomenon, serves not merely as an audience or observer but as an active participant in the metaphysical truths revealed through Dionysian art. It is through this chorus that the Greek theater transcends the mundane and touches the eternal, presenting not a reflection of reality but a glimpse into the essence of existence itself.

This enchantment of transformation is the very foundation of all dramatic art, as it emerges from the Dionysian reveler's ecstatic vision of himself as a satyr, a being closer to nature and the divine.

In this state, the satyr looks outward and perceives the god—an Apollonian manifestation that serves as the ultimate realization of his transformed condition. Within this duality of vision and state, the drama finds its completion, an artistic cycle that bridges the raw energy of Dionysian experience with the structured beauty of Apollonian imagery.

When we approach Greek tragedy through this lens, we see it as an evolving expression of the Dionysian chorus, which continuously gives birth to an Apollonian world of images. The chorus itself is not just an element of tragedy but its generative core, the fertile origin of the entire dramatic world. The so- called dialogue of the drama, the action we associate with the stage, is but a manifestation that arises from the primordial energy of the chorus. It is through successive outpourings of this energy that the drama emerges, a series of dreamlike visions that maintain an epic character. Yet, unlike the epic tradition, the drama transcends individualism, offering instead the dissolution of the self and a reunification with primordial existence. In this way, drama becomes an Apollonian embodiment of Dionysian truths, fundamentally distinct from the epic by an immeasurable chasm.

The Greek tragic chorus, representing the collective body of humanity stirred by Dionysian rapture, thus finds its full explanation in this framework. Modern audiences, accustomed to the marginal role of the operatic chorus or similar conventions, struggle to comprehend why the tragic chorus of the Greeks held a position of such primal importance—greater, even, than the staged action itself, as tradition insists. How can such a central, almost sacred function be reconciled with the seemingly lowly origins of the chorus, composed initially of humble figures such as satyrs, creatures of the natural world? Furthermore, the placement of the orchestra before the stage remains enigmatic until we understand that the action of the scene was conceived fundamentally as a vision, an ephemeral projection of the chorus's collective consciousness. The chorus was not merely a backdrop or an observer—it was the wellspring of the drama, creating and narrating the vision through the unifying mediums of dance, music, and speech.

Within this vision, the chorus sees its god, Dionysus, the central figure of their reverence and ecstasy. The chorus does not act in the traditional sense; it exists to serve, reflect, and magnify the divine. This service is the highest calling of nature's Dionysian aspect, and through this role, the chorus gains a voice of wisdom, offering oracles and profound truths born from its union with the god. This unique combination of fervor and insight gives rise to the figure of the satyr—a being that embodies nature's raw, untamed power yet also serves as its wise and artistic herald. The satyr becomes a complex symbol: musician, poet, dancer, visionary, and the ultimate expression of natural impulses transformed into art.

In the earliest forms of tragedy, Dionysus himself did not appear on stage but was instead evoked through the chorus. In this primal stage of tragedy, there was no distinct "drama" as we now understand it, only the chorus as the sole medium of expression. Over time, the theatrical art evolved, striving to present the divine figure of Dionysus as a physical presence, along with the luminous aura of his imagined world. This marks the emergence of the drama proper, where the chorus's function expanded to induce a state of Dionysian frenzy among the audience. In this heightened state, the appearance of the tragic hero on stage was perceived not as a mere actor but as the manifestation of a divine being, conjured from the depths of the spectators' collective ecstasy.

Imagine, for example, the plight of Admetes mourning his lost wife, Alcestis. Engulfed in grief, he meditates deeply on her image until a veiled figure resembling her is led toward him. The trembling uncertainty and emotional intensity of his recognition parallel the experience of the Greek audience as they beheld the masked actor on stage. For the audience, their Dionysian rapture transformed this masked figure into the living god, an epiphany born of their own ecstatic vision. The material reality of the stage dissolved, replaced by an Apollonian dream-world where the mundane was veiled and a clearer, more luminous reality emerged, a world in constant flux yet more vivid and immediate than ordinary life.

In tragedy, this dynamic creates a stylistic duality: the Dionysian lyricism of the chorus stands in stark contrast to the Apollonian clarity and structure of the staged dialogue. While the chorus expresses the unbridled, pulsating essence of Dionysian music—a sea of emotions, forces, and rhythms—the staged action crystallizes these forces into clear, epic forms. Dionysus, no longer a formless presence sensed through music, steps forward as a character, speaking almost as if he belonged to Homer's epics. Thus, tragedy becomes a synthesis of two powerful artistic impulses, creating a work that embodies both the eternal flux of Dionysian reality and the radiant beauty of Apollonian vision.

The dialogue within the Apollonian realm of Greek tragedy rises to the surface with an elegance that appears simple, transparent, and strikingly beautiful. It mirrors the essence of the Hellene, whose nature finds expression most authentically in the dance. In this art form, immense energy lies latent, yet it reveals itself through movements that are fluid, vibrant, and alive. The language employed by Sophocles' heroes, for example, amazes us with its precision and clarity, which is quintessentially Apollonian. It feels as though we are granted direct access to the depths of their innermost being, and we marvel at how brief and unimpeded the path to these depths seems to be.

However, this impression is deceptive. What we encounter in the hero's character is but a surface reflection—a luminous projection cast onto a dark and inscrutable wall. This figure is nothing more than an appearance, an illusion carefully constructed within the Apollonian framework. To truly engage with the myth underpinning these glowing, superficial images is to embark on a much more profound and disquieting journey. Here, a phenomenon unfolds that is the inverse of a familiar optical experience. When we strain our gaze directly at the sun, we are left with dark spots dancing before our eyes, a restorative effect that shields us from further harm. Yet, in Greek tragedy, the radiant figures of the Sophoclean hero—their clarity, beauty, and Apollonian poise—serve as analogous spots of light. They are the necessary salves that soothe and shield our vision after it has been scorched by glimpses into the dark and unfathomable truths of nature.

It is through this lens that we may begin to comprehend the profound and complex notion of "Greek cheerfulness." This cheerfulness, often misunderstood, does not spring from a state of naive contentment or uninterrupted comfort. It is not the shallow, carefree happiness that modern interpretations so frequently attribute to the ancient Greeks. Instead, it is the luminous result of a delicate balance, a response to the terrifying realities that lie beneath existence. The Apollonian light-picture, the hero as a glowing vision of order and beauty, emerges as a necessary counterpart to the Dionysian darkness, a way of momentarily averting the gaze from the abyss.

This "Greek cheerfulness" is thus deeply serious and significant. It arises not in denial of suffering, but as a cultivated ability to endure it through the transformative power of art. The Greeks' capacity for this kind of cheerfulness speaks to their mastery in creating a world of appearances—one that offers redemption and healing even as it acknowledges the inexorable truths that underpin life. In contrast, contemporary interpretations often strip this cheerfulness of its gravity, misrepresenting it as the result of an untroubled existence. This misunderstanding underscores the chasm between the nuanced, artistic worldview of the Greeks and the shallow comforts sought by much of the modern age.

The tragic figure of Œdipus, one of the most sorrowful characters to grace the Greek stage, was interpreted by Sophocles as the embodiment of a noble individual whose wisdom could not shield him from error and suffering. Despite the grievous misfortunes that define his life, Œdipus exerts a profound, almost magical, and redemptive influence on those around him—a power that extends far beyond his mortal existence. Sophocles portrays this deeply complex character not as a sinner, but as a noble man whose actions, though they might disrupt the natural and moral order, ultimately serve as the catalyst for the creation of a higher, more harmonious realm.

The poet's narrative is imbued with the perspective of a religious thinker. As such, Sophocles presents Œdipus's journey as one of paradoxical redemption. Through his immense suffering, a new cosmic balance is forged on the ruins of the old, overthrown order. To convey this, the poet constructs a profoundly intricate and legalistic drama, where every twist and turn of the narrative gradually unravels the tangled threads of destiny. This dialectical untying of the knot—though devastating for Œdipus—offers the Greek audience an intense intellectual and emotional delight. The Hellenic spirit, with its appreciation for reason and structure, finds joy even in the somber unraveling of fate's mysteries. This peculiar cheerfulness tempers the otherwise horrifying events of the play, giving rise to an air of solemn celebration amidst the tragedy.

In Œdipus at Colonus, this unique cheerfulness evolves into something transcendent, offering a vision of sublime transformation. The aged Œdipus, crushed by years of unrelenting suffering and reduced to a passive victim of fate, paradoxically reaches the pinnacle of his influence and power in this state of helplessness. His earlier endeavors, marked by active thought and striving, had only led to his downfall and stagnation. Yet in his surrender to suffering and his passive endurance of destiny, he achieves a divine agency. His legacy and impact reverberate far beyond his earthly life. Through this interplay of suffering and redemption, the myth unfolds the divine artistry of dialectics—a process that offers profound human joy by unraveling what appears to be an insoluble tangle of fate.

If we attribute such an interpretation to Sophocles, we must ask whether it encompasses the full depth of the myth's meaning. Here, we encounter the realization that Sophocles' artistic vision is but the radiant, healing image presented by nature after she has granted us a fleeting, harrowing glance into the abyss. For the myth of Œdipus delves into terrors far deeper than what appears on the surface. The triad of his destiny—father-murder, mother- marriage, and the solving of the Sphinx's riddle—is steeped in symbolic significance.

This triad hints at an ancient and primordial belief, one particularly vivid in Persian traditions, that wisdom—especially the profound, magical kind—can only arise through acts that defy natural law. According to this belief, incest, as a symbolic transgression of the most sacred boundaries, becomes the precondition for the emergence of extraordinary insight. In the case of Œdipus, his union with his mother and the murder of his father symbolize the violent and unnatural rupture of nature's laws. Such acts are necessary, according to the myth, for the unveiling of nature's deepest secrets. By opposing and violating nature, he forces her to relinquish her mysteries, embodying the ultimate tension between human striving and natural order.

In this sense, Œdipus, as the solver of the Sphinx's riddle—the enigma of existence—becomes the figure who must embody and endure the consequences of his insight. The myth whispers to us a sobering truth: that wisdom, especially the profound, Dionysian kind, is an affront to nature. The one who dares to unravel her mysteries, the one who ventures to dissolve her illusions, must also experience her collapse within himself. Wisdom, then, is shown as a double- edged sword, a sharp and dangerous gift that ultimately turns back upon its bearer. The myth's stark message resounds: "The sharpness of wisdom turns round upon the sage; wisdom is a crime against nature." In this view, Œdipus's fate is not merely tragic but cosmically instructive—a cautionary tale of the perilous intersection of knowledge and existence.

Yet, despite the myth's somber warnings, Sophocles, with the radiant touch of his poetic genius, transforms these grim truths into something transcendent. He approaches the myth as one would approach a forbidding statue—a statue that, under the sunlight, begins to sing. The awful depths of the myth are transfigured by his art, softened into melodies that, while acknowledging the abyss, uplift the spirit. It is through this transformation that Greek tragedy attains its highest purpose: not to deny the darkness of existence, but to illuminate it, rendering it bearable through beauty and meaning.

I contrast the pride of passive endurance with the pride of active creation, which shines through Æschylus's depiction of Prometheus. What Æschylus wanted to express as a philosopher but only hinted at through his poetic symbolism, the young Goethe revealed boldly in the words of his Prometheus:

"Here I sit, shaping humanity

In my own image,

A race to be like me:

To suffer, to weep,

The Birth of Tragedy

To enjoy, and to rejoice,

And to disregard you, As I do!"

Humanity, raising itself to the level of the Titans, builds its culture through its own efforts and forces the gods into collaboration. In its self-reliant wisdom, it holds the existence and limits of these divine beings within its grasp. What is most remarkable about the figure of Prometheus, who embodies a hymn to defiance, is Æschylus's profound longing for justice. On one side, there is the immense suffering of the solitary and defiant figure, while on the other, the divine realm itself feels a gnawing need, haunted by the premonition of its twilight. These two worlds of suffering, human and divine, press toward reconciliation and unity. This suggests Æschylus's central worldview: Moira, eternal justice, reigns above both gods and mortals.

Æschylus, with astonishing audacity, weighs the Olympian gods on the scales of justice. Yet, this boldness is rooted in the Greek mind's firm metaphysical foundation, derived from its mysteries. The skepticism of the Greek spirit could be directed at the Olympians without threatening the deeper structure of belief. For the Greek artist, there existed an unspoken recognition of mutual dependence with these deities—a dynamic captured in Prometheus. The artist, with a Titan's audacity, believed he could create humanity and even challenge the Olympian gods through his superior wisdom. Yet, for this boldness, Prometheus suffers eternal torment. This "can-ing" spirit, this creative and defiant energy, lies at the heart of Æschylean poetry. It is the stern pride of the artist, for whom even eternal suffering is not too high a price for creative genius. While Sophocles, in Œdipus, celebrates the triumph of saintliness, Æschylus revels in the glorious struggle of the artist.

However, Æschylus's interpretation of the Prometheus myth, despite its boldness, does not fully capture its terrifying depths. Beneath the joy of artistic creation lies a dark, tragic sea. The myth of Prometheus is a shared inheritance of the Aryan races, reflecting their profound capacity for tragedy. It is likely as central to them as the myth of humanity's fall is to the Semitic peoples. These myths might be seen as sibling tales, deeply intertwined. For the Aryans, the Prometheus myth centers on fire, the sacred gift seen as essential to cultural progress. Yet, to claim this fire as humanity's own, rather than as a divine gift, was viewed as a crime—an affront to the gods. This act of theft set humanity at odds with divinity, establishing a rift at the very gates of culture.

This myth suggests that humanity's greatest achievements come through defiance, through acts deemed criminal. But these gains are accompanied by suffering, a punishment from the offended gods.

This tragic reflection, which ennobles crime through its association with progress, stands in stark contrast to the Semitic myth of humanity's fall. Where the Aryan myth honors active transgression as a Promethean virtue, the Semitic myth links humanity's downfall to curiosity and seduction—qualities often gendered as feminine. The Aryan myth's focus on active sin forms the ethical foundation for tragic pessimism, suggesting that human guilt and the suffering it brings are justified by their deeper cosmic significance.

TheAryan understanding of existence acknowledges a fundamental conflict within reality itself—a clash between different realms, such as the divine and the human. Both realms are justified in their existence, yet their individuality causes suffering. When the heroic individual strives to transcend these boundaries, to merge with universal being, they experience the contradiction inherent in existence. In this striving, they commit acts that lead to their own suffering. For the Aryans, crime is associated with men, sin with women—a distinction underscored in the biting irony of the witches' chorus:

"We see no need to be precise:

With a thousand steps, the woman moves;

But in one leap, the man arrives."

The essence of the Prometheus myth lies in the necessity of defiance. The individual, striving titanically, must commit crimes to achieve greatness, and this tragic inevitability is deeply un-Apollonian. Apollo draws boundaries and promotes self-knowledge and balance as the sacred laws of the universe. Yet, to prevent this Apollonian order from becoming static, the Dionysian spirit rises, disrupting rigid structures and infusing life with chaos. The Dionysian tide lifts all individuals, just as Atlas bears the world on his shoulders.

The Promethean and Dionysian share this impulse to carry humanity forward, to bear its burdens and transcend its limits. In this sense, Æschylus's Prometheus is a mask of Dionysus. Yet, the yearning for justice within Æschylus's work reflects an Apollonian heritage. The dual nature of Prometheus—both

Dionysian and Apollonian—captures the paradox of existence: all things are at once just and unjust, and equally justified in their being.

This is your world, and what a world it is!

"Here I sit, shaping mankind

In my own image,

A race that mirrors me—

To grieve and to weep,

To taste and to hold,

To enjoy and to reject you,

Just as I do!"

The rhythm of existence flows through such expressions:

"Woman, with a thousand steps, may reach her end,

But man, with a single leap, arrives there first."

These words resound as we delve into the roots of Greek tragedy, an art form steeped in sacred tradition. It is beyond doubt that in its earliest iterations, Greek tragedy revolved exclusively around the sufferings of Dionysus, the god who embodied both ecstasy and torment. In those primordial performances, Dionysus himself was the sole figure on stage. Yet, even as tragedy evolved, its essence remained unchanged. Not until Euripides did Dionysus relinquish his place as the central figure, and even then, his presence lingered. Indeed, the great figures of Greek drama—

Prometheus, Œdipus, and others—are but veils behind which Dionysus hides. Behind these masks, the god persists, a shadowy presence giving depth to their tragic heroism.

The divine figure concealed within these characters is the source of their otherworldly quality, a kind of ideality that transcends the human. Some have argued that individuality, by its very nature, tends toward the comic, rendering purely human figures unsuited for tragedy. The Greeks themselves seemed to share this sentiment. Their culture, deeply infused with Platonic thought, inherently valued the "idea" over the fleeting "image." Using Plato's language, we might describe the tragic figures of the Greek stage as the manifold reflections of a singular reality. Dionysus, the one true being, appears in countless forms, each a mask portraying a hero caught in the throes of struggle, a figure ensnared by the complexities of individual will.

As these characters speak and act, they resemble erring and suffering individuals, yet their clarity and precision owe much to Apollo. It is through the lens of the Apollonian that the chorus perceives their Dionysian state, rendered as vivid symbolic representations. In truth, these tragic heroes are none other than Dionysus himself—the suffering god of the mysteries. The myths recount his dismemberment at the hands of the Titans, worshipped in this fragmented state as Zagreus. This act of dismemberment is the quintessential Dionysian suffering, an allegory for the fragmentation into the elements—air, water, earth, and fire. It signifies the agony of individuation, the primal source of all suffering and discord.

From the smile of Dionysus, the Olympian gods were born; from his tears, humanity emerged. As the dismembered god, Dionysus embodies a duality: he is both a savage and cruel demon, and a gentle, benevolent ruler. Yet, in the rituals and mysteries, the faithful held onto the hope of his rebirth, a return that would mark the end of individuation. This prophesied renewal of Dionysus inspired the ecstatic hymns of the initiates, whose jubilant cries envisioned a world restored to unity. Only this hope—a world reunited—casts a glimmer of joy onto the fractured and scattered fragments of existence. This vision is poignantly represented in the myth of Demeter, plunged into eternal sorrow. Her joy is rekindled only when she is promised the chance to bring Dionysus into the world again.

Within these myths lies a profound and somber understanding of life, an outlook steeped in pessimism yet charged with transcendent insight. Here, the doctrine of tragedy reveals itself in its full depth. It proclaims the oneness of all existence, the division into individuals as the root of suffering, and art as the radiant hope for liberation from this fragmentation. Art offers the promise of restored unity, a vision that redeems the broken world with the anticipation of harmony reborn.

It has been suggested that the Homeric epic is the anthem of Olympian culture, celebrating its triumph over the fears and chaos of the Titanomachy. However, when tragedy began to dominate the Greek artistic spirit, these Homeric myths were reborn, reflecting a profound transformation in how the Greeks viewed their world. This metamorphosis signals that the Olympian worldview itself had been overtaken by an even deeper understanding of existence. The defiant Titan Prometheus, for instance, foretells to his Olympian tormentor Zeus that his rule will face a dire threat unless he allies with Prometheus. In the works of Æschylus, we see a Zeus who, terrified of his prophesied downfall, forms an alliance with the Titan. Thus, the once-banished era of the Titans emerges once more into the light, challenging the hegemony of the Olympian gods.

This shift reveals a philosophy grounded in the raw and untamed forces of nature, a perspective that exposes the myths of Homer's world to an unflinching gaze of truth. These myths, which once shone brightly in the Homeric imagination, seem to pale and tremble under the scrutinizing glare of this deeper vision—until the Dionysian artist reclaims them. With a powerful hand, the Dionysian spirit transforms these myths into symbols of its wisdom. Whether through public tragedy or the secret rituals of dramatic mysteries, the myths are reborn, adorned in their ancient guise yet charged with new meaning.

It was the transformative power of music, particularly in its Dionysian expression, that freed Prometheus from his torment and imbued myth with renewed significance. In tragedy, music achieves its highest expression, breathing profound meaning into myths that might otherwise have been confined to narrow historical interpretations. Myths, by their nature, tend to harden into the form of supposed historical realities, stripped of their vitality over time. The Greeks themselves were already on the path to recasting their mythical dreams into a pragmatic history, taming their myths with reason and logic. This process mirrors the decline of religions, which often succumb to orthodoxy as their mythical foundations are systematized and treated as rigid historical truths.

In this rigid state, myths lose their life force and are reduced to mere relics, with religion itself becoming grounded in claims of historical legitimacy. However, the genius of Dionysian music rescued these myths from ossification. Under its influence, myths once again blossomed with an unmatched vibrancy, their hues more vivid and their scent awakening a longing for the metaphysical. But this final flourish of life soon gave way to decay; the myths, now withered, became fodder for satirical minds like the scoffing Lucian, who mocked their faded beauty as the remnants scattered into obscurity.

Through tragedy, myth achieved its deepest resonance, its most evocative expression. It rose like a wounded hero, suffused with vitality, its dying moments illuminated by a philosophical calm that burned with fierce brilliance. Yet Euripides, with his tragic innovation, sought to seize this myth in its twilight, attempting to bend it to his will. Under his hand, the myth faltered and perished. What he offered in its place was a counterfeit—a pale imitation adorned in the finery of the past, but hollow at its core. With the death of myth, the spirit of music also faded. Euripides' creations plundered the gardens of music but produced only lifeless imitations. In turning away from Dionysus, he was also forsaken by Apollo. The passions in his plays, though sharpened and polished, were mere shadows, lacking true depth, their music a hollow echo.

Greek tragedy's end differed from the graceful decline of its sister arts. While other art forms faded peacefully, leaving behind vibrant successors, tragedy met its demise through internal conflict, a self-inflicted death befitting its nature. It died tragically, leaving a void that resonated throughout the Hellenic world. Just as Greek sailors once heard the eerie proclamation that "great Pan is dead," so too did a mournful cry spread across Greece: "Tragedy is dead! With her, poetry itself has perished! Begone, pale shadows, mere remnants of greatness. Seek the underworld and feast on the crumbs left by your masters!"

When a new art form finally emerged, revering tragedy as its ancestor, it bore her likeness—but only the haggard features of her prolonged death struggle.

This new art, the New Attic Comedy, was born from the remnants of tragedy's decline. Its existence was a monument to the pain and violence of tragedy's demise, a poignant reminder of the heights Greek art once scaled and the irreparable loss suffered when those heights were abandoned.

This connection helps explain the deep admiration that the poets of the New Comedy had for Euripides, revealing why Philemon, for instance, famously expressed his willingness to die just to meet Euripides in the underworld—provided, of course, that Euripides retained his intellect in death. To understand what united Euripides with playwrights like Menander and Philemon, and what they so passionately imitated, we need only to focus on one crucial aspect: Euripides brought the everyday spectator onto the stage.

The tragic writers who came before Euripides had crafted their heroes from extraordinary material. These characters were larger than life, with bold, heroic traits that were intentionally far removed from everyday reality. Their purpose was not to replicate the mundane truths of the audience's world but to elevate and transform them. Euripides, however, marked a dramatic departure from this tradition. He opened the doors of the stage to the ordinary, to the unexceptional individual sitting among the spectators.

Through Euripides, the stage became a mirror reflecting the minutiae of everyday life with excruciating detail. The grand and heroic expressions of old were replaced with a realism that did not shy away from depicting even the imperfections and incomplete sketches of human nature. Consider Odysseus, once the epitome of the archetypal Hellene in the Old Art. In the works of Euripides and his successors, Odysseus devolved into a lesser figure, embodying the sly but servile Græculus—a figure of cunning domesticity who now stood at the heart of dramatic focus.

Euripides himself boasts about this shift in Aristophanes' Frogs, where he takes credit for reducing what he calls the "pompous corpulency" of tragic art through his more practical and "household" remedies. His heroes were no longer grand demigods or abstract ideals; they were everymen. The spectator found himself reflected on the Euripidean stage, recognizing in the characters his own voice, mannerisms, and reasoning. The thrill for the audience lay not only in seeing themselves so skillfully portrayed but also in learning from Euripides how to speak with the clever sophistication of his characters.

Euripides explicitly prides himself on having taught people the arts of observation, debate, and logical reasoning. In his contest with Æschylus, he highlights this accomplishment, boasting of how his works provided the people with tools for engaging in rhetoric and sophistry. This innovation extended far beyond the stage, effectively paving the way for the New Comedy. Euripides' revolution in language made it no longer a secret how the mundane and commonplace could be effectively expressed in theater.

This shift was monumental. The demigods who once dominated tragedy and the exuberant, drunken satyrs of comedy were supplanted by characters grounded in civic mediocrity. Euripides built his political ideals on this foundation, granting a voice to ordinary citizens and everyday life. He took pride in showcasing familiar interactions and the routine dealings of people—the kind of life everyone could observe and judge for themselves.

In Aristophanes' caricature, Euripides celebrates having brought the commonplace into dramatic focus, claiming credit for making the populace capable of philosophical reasoning, meticulous management of their affairs, and even legal acumen. He gloried in this new intellectual empowerment of the masses, seeing it as a testament to the transformative wisdom he had instilled in the people. With Euripides, the language of the stage became a language the audience could claim as their own, bridging the once vast chasm between the lofty ideals of traditional drama and the relatable realities of everyday life.

The New Comedy emerged to address an audience already shaped and enlightened by the intellectual groundwork laid by Euripides, who functioned almost like a chorus-master for this transition. However, in this case, it was not the traditional theatrical chorus he trained but rather the audience itself, the spectators. Once this audience had been "taught to sing" in the style and tone established by Euripides, the New Comedy arose as a kind of intricate, calculated performance—a theatrical chess game filled with cleverness and trickery as its central themes. The craftiness and wit of this new dramatic form became its crowning achievements, and yet, at its foundation, Euripides was continuously celebrated as the source of this intellectual inheritance. So high was the regard for his contributions that, if it were possible, people might have sacrificed their own lives just to absorb more of his wisdom. Tragically, they were all too aware that both the tragic poets and tragedy itself were long dead, marking the end of an era.

With the demise of tragedy, the Hellenic world also relinquished something far greater: its belief in immortality. Along with its faith in an idealized past, it surrendered the dream of an idealized future. What remained was an exhausted culture, embodying the sentiment reflected in the well-known epitaph, "as an old man, frivolous and capricious." This phrase could just as easily describe the state of late Hellenism. In this twilight of Greek culture, fleeting pleasures, wit, and a lighthearted disregard for deeper matters became its guiding principles. The divine aspirations of the past were exchanged for the immediate gratification of the present moment, with no responsibility for anything enduring or significant. Even the fifth class, the slaves, rose to prominence in spirit if not in social rank. Their perspective—rooted in the immediacy of survival rather than in lofty ideals—came to dominate the cultural ethos.

If we speak of "Greek cheerfulness" in this context, it is no longer the noble joy of a people striving for greatness or grounded in a sense of transcendent purpose. Instead, it is the hollow cheerfulness of the slave, a superficial contentment born of having nothing to take responsibility for, nothing great to pursue, and nothing to hold in higher esteem than the present moment. This hollow joy, masquerading as the essence of Greek life, deeply offended the profound, intense minds of the early Christian centuries. To them, this easygoing, frivolous avoidance of life's weightier truths, this indulgence in fleeting pleasures, seemed not only contemptible but actively opposed to the Christian ethos of earnestness, sacrifice, and moral striving.

It is because of this superficial "Greek cheerfulness" that subsequent generations developed a skewed perception of antiquity. For centuries, the legacy of Greek culture was filtered through a lens that highlighted this lighthearted facade, preserving it with remarkable persistence. The image of a cheerful, carefree Greek world persisted as if the monumental achievements of the Sixth Century BCE had never existed—achievements that had given birth to tragedy, the Mysteries, Pythagorean philosophy, and the profound insights of Heraclitus. This distorted view ignored the art and thought of that remarkable era, which spoke to a vastly different and far deeper understanding of existence. The cultural artifacts of that time, each a testament to profound and complex ideas, stand in stark contrast to the shallow cheerfulness later attributed to Greek life. They point instead to a richer and more somber vision, one rooted in the struggle to reconcile the profound mysteries of existence.

The earlier claim that Euripides brought the spectator onto the stage, making them better able to judge the drama, might suggest that traditional tragic art was fundamentally misaligned with its audience. This interpretation could lead some to praise Euripides' radical efforts to harmonize the relationship between the art and its public as an improvement over Sophocles. However, the term "public" is nebulous—neither uniform nor consistent—and should not be viewed as a definitive or authoritative entity. Why should an artist feel obliged to adapt to a force whose power lies solely in numbers? If the artist, through their talent and vision, perceives themselves as superior to any single member of this crowd, why should they defer to the collective judgment of the multitude, a sum of lesser capacities, over that of the most discerning individual spectator?

Indeed, if any Greek artist treated their audience with a sustained sense of audacity and self-assurance, it was Euripides. Throughout his career, even as the masses at times hailed him with admiration, he openly defied the very tendencies that had secured their favor. With an almost sublime defiance, he attacked the very foundation of his artistic success, demonstrating a striking lack of reverence for public opinion. If Euripides had held the general public in high regard, he would likely have crumbled under the weight of his repeated failures long before reaching the midpoint of his career. These observations make it clear that the idea of Euripides merely seeking to make the audience competent judges of drama is an oversimplification. Instead, a deeper understanding of his artistic drive must be pursued.

In contrast, it is widely known that Æschylus and Sophocles enjoyed the unwavering favor of the people throughout their lives and beyond. Their relationship with their audience was one of harmony, free from the tensions or conflicts that might suggest a misalignment between their works and public sentiment. This raises a pressing question: What led Euripides, a poet of undeniable talent and relentless productivity, to abandon a path graced by the illustrious names of his predecessors and lit by the steady sun of popular acclaim? What peculiar consideration for the spectator drove him to rebel against that same audience? How did he manage to simultaneously revere and defy the public?

The answer to this paradox lies in the unique relationship Euripides had with his audience. As a poet, he undoubtedly considered himself superior to the general masses. Yet, there were two spectators whose judgment he held in the highest esteem. He revered these two individuals as the only truly qualified judges and masters of his art. For their sake, he brought the broader public metaphorically onto the stage, infusing his characters with the full spectrum of emotions, passions, and human experiences that had traditionally been the unspoken chorus seated invisibly among the audience. These two figures influenced Euripides to reshape not only his characters but also the language and tone they employed, crafting an entirely new dramatic style.

To these two spectators alone, Euripides listened intently. Their voices rendered the final verdict on his work and offered him the promise of eventual triumph, even as he faced rejection from the wider public. It was for them, and under their guidance, that he crafted his bold innovations in Greek tragedy, transforming it into something uniquely his own while challenging the conventions cherished by his audience.

Among these two spectators, the first is none other than Euripides himself—not as a poet but as a thinker. One might say of him, as has been said of figures like Lessing, that his extraordinary critical faculty did not so much create as constantly nourish and stimulate a parallel artistic impulse. With this sharp and discerning mind, Euripides sat in the theater, studying the masterpieces of his illustrious predecessors, scrutinizing them as if they were faded paintings, dissecting each feature and line with analytical precision. But as he delved deeper into these works, something both fascinating and troubling became evident—something that anyone familiar with the inner mysteries of Æschylean tragedy would have expected.

Euripides found in these masterpieces a quality that defied his rigorous analysis: an elusive profundity and a deceptive clarity, as though every seemingly well-defined element was accompanied by an infinite and enigmatic background. Even the most sharply drawn characters trailed behind them something akin to the glowing tail of a comet—a hint of mystery, an unresolved depth that invited yet resisted understanding. The structure of the drama itself confounded him, and nowhere more than in the function and essence of the chorus, which seemed both central and incomprehensible to his rationalist mind.

Ethical dilemmas in the plays appeared to him to be treated with a troubling ambivalence. The portrayal of myth felt riddled with uncertainties, while the distribution of happiness and suffering across characters seemed glaringly unequal. Even the language of Old Tragedy presented difficulties: to Euripides, it seemed to contain an excessive grandeur that felt disproportionate to the simplicity of the actions and characters it sought to convey. There was too much splendor for ordinary matters, too many lofty metaphors for humble subjects.

Thus, Euripides sat in restless contemplation, admitting to himself as a spectator that he simply could not fully grasp the art of his predecessors. And because he equated true understanding with the root of all enjoyment and creative power, this lack of comprehension left him discontented. In his search for validation, he looked around to see if others shared his doubts. Yet, when he expressed these reservations, most people—some of them among the finest minds of the time—offered only skeptical smiles. No one could adequately explain why the works of Æschylus and Sophocles deserved their reverence despite his objections. Feeling isolated in his frustration, Euripides eventually found an ally, a kindred spectator who also failed to comprehend and thus could not value tragedy as it had been traditionally conceived.

Before identifying this other spectator, let us pause to reflect on our own experience, previously described, of encountering the discordant and seemingly irreconcilable elements of Æschylean tragedy. Recall our astonishment at the chorus, whose role defied modern conventions, and at the tragic hero, whose nature challenged both our expectations and the precedents of tradition. Only when we uncovered the duality at the heart of these works—the intertwining of the Apollonian and Dionysian artistic impulses—did we begin to grasp the essence of Greek tragedy.

Euripides, however, sought to sever this primal and powerful Dionysian element from tragedy altogether. His aim was to construct a new, purified form of tragedy based on a different foundation—one rooted in non-Dionysian art, morality, and worldview. It is this underlying ambition that now illuminates his work, helping us understand his revolutionary approach to the art of tragedy.

In the twilight of his life, Euripides crafted a myth that posed a pressing question to his contemporaries about the value and place of the Dionysian in their world. He asked whether the Dionysian should exist at all or whether it ought to be eradicated from Greek culture. The poet himself seemed to admit that while rooting out Dionysus might be desirable, it was far from feasible. Dionysus, as a divine force, was simply too powerful. Even his most intelligent adversaries, like Pentheus in The Bacchæ, inevitably fell under his spell, and this enchantment sealed their doom.

The perspectives of the wise old figures, Cadmus and Tiresias, appear to reflect the view of the aging Euripides. Their cautious counsel suggests that even the wisest minds cannot overthrow ancient traditions or the ever-propagating worship of Dionysus. They hint at the need for a prudent, if not entirely sincere, acknowledgment of such formidable forces. Yet, even this pragmatic diplomacy has its risks. Dionysus may still take offense at lukewarm devotion, just as Cadmus, despite his careful approach, is ultimately transformed into a dragon.

This reflection comes from a poet who had resisted Dionysus with fierce resolve for much of his life, only to conclude his career by glorifying the very god he opposed. His final work, The Bacchæ, stands as a dramatic confession of the futility of his own artistic struggle. The tragedy is not merely a work of recantation but a powerful testament to the inescapable might of Dionysus. It suggests that Euripides, like a figure overcome by vertigo, could no longer bear the strain of his resistance and metaphorically cast himself from a tower.

In The Bacchæ, Euripides seems to protest against the very path he had paved. Yet, by the time he acknowledged his misgivings, his ideas had already triumphed. Dionysus had been driven from the stage, displaced by a new force that spoke not through Dionysus or Apollo, but through a novel, emergent presence: Socrates. It is this new antagonist—the Socratic spirit—that had come to dominate, and it was upon this opposition between the Dionysian and the Socratic that the art of Greek tragedy ultimately foundered.

Even if Euripides' recantation aimed to offer some measure of consolation, it was too late. The temple of Greek tragedy had already crumbled into ruins. The poet's admission of guilt—that he had destroyed the most beautiful of temples—provided no solace. And even the harsh judgment of later critics, who metaphorically transformed Euripides into a dragon as punishment, feels like a hollow reckoning in the face of such a monumental loss.

Turning to the Socratic tendency that Euripides embodied, we must ask ourselves what this movement sought to achieve by severing tragedy from its Dionysian roots. If tragedy was no longer to emerge from the deep, mysterious womb of music and Dionysian ecstasy, what form could drama take? The answer lies in what can be called the dramatized epic, a genre bound to the Apollonian realm, yet inherently incapable of achieving the true tragic effect.

In such dramatized epics, it is not the events themselves that fail to evoke tragedy. Indeed, even Goethe, in his unrealized Nausikaa, would have struggled to make the idyllic heroine's suicide genuinely tragic. This is because the epic, with its Apollonian serenity, transforms even the most horrifying events into beautiful illusions, offering redemption through the joy of appearance. The dramatized epic retains this Apollonian distance, with its poet remaining a detached observer, never fully blending with the images he creates. Like the epic rhapsodist, the dramatized poet embodies a serene contemplation, presenting his characters and events as pictures before his wide, calm gaze.

How, then, does Euripides' drama compare to this ideal of Apollonian art? It is akin to the younger, more impassioned rhapsodist described in Plato's Ion, who says, "When I speak of sorrow, tears fill my eyes; when I speak of terror, my hair stands on end." Euripides' drama, much like this younger rhapsodist, lacks the composed detachment of the true Apollonian artist. Euripides, as a Socratic thinker, designs his plays with cold rationality, yet as an impassioned actor, he executes them with fiery intensity. In neither role is he fully an artist.

Thus, the Euripidean drama is marked by a paradoxical blend of cool intellectualism and raw emotionalism. It fails to achieve the harmonious effect of the Apollonian epic, while simultaneously distancing itself from the ecstatic power of Dionysian art. To sustain itself, it resorts to entirely new stimulants, abandoning the Apollonian and Dionysian impulses that define true artistic creation. Instead of Apollonian visions, it offers sharp, paradoxical ideas; instead of Dionysian ecstasies, it delivers unvarnished passions. These elements, vividly realistic and devoid of the ethereal quality of genuine art, leave Euripides' drama stranded in a realm far removed from the heights of Greek tragedy.

If we understand that Euripides failed to anchor drama purely in the Apollonian ideal and instead veered into a naturalistic, unartistic direction, we can now delve into the essence of aesthetic Socratism. Its core principle could be phrased as: "To be beautiful, everything must be intelligible," a statement akin to Socrates' moral maxim, "Only the knowledgeable are virtuous." With this rule as his guiding light, Euripides dissected every component of tragedy—its language, characters, dramaturgy, and choral music—and reshaped them to align with his ideal of rational clarity. Much of the artistic decline often attributed to Euripides, particularly when compared to Sophocles, stems from this rigorous rationalization and its uncompromising quest for intelligibility.

Consider the Euripidean prologue as a prime example of this methodical approach. Nothing could stand further from modern dramatic techniques than the prologues of Euripides. On today's stage, a single character stepping forward to explain who they are, the events preceding the play, and even what will transpire throughout the drama would be viewed as a blatant violation of suspense, robbing the audience of the mystery essential to dramatic tension. With everything laid bare from the start, where is the incentive to watch events unfold? Moreover, this approach lacks the dreamlike quality of a prophetic vision foreshadowing an eventual reality.

Yet Euripides approached drama differently. For him, the impact of tragedy did not rest on suspense or the tantalizing uncertainty of what might occur. Instead, it was centered on powerful rhetorical and lyrical moments, where the passions and reasonings of the central characters surged forth like a mighty flood. In Euripides' view, everything in tragedy must serve the purpose of pathos— evoking profound emotional intensity. Anything extraneous to this aim was discarded. However, the audience's ability to engage fully with these climactic scenes was hampered by any lingering confusion about the backstory or characters' motivations.

In contrast, the tragedies of Aeschylus and Sophocles carefully wove the necessary background into their early scenes. These playwrights used subtle, artful techniques to unobtrusively provide the audience with the narrative threads needed to understand the unfolding drama. This approach concealed its formal structure behind a veil of apparent spontaneity, demonstrating a masterful artistry. Euripides, however, perceived even this as problematic. He believed that audiences, during these early scenes, were too preoccupied with piecing together the backstory to appreciate the poetic brilliance or emotional intensity of the exposition.

To resolve this, Euripides introduced the prologue as a prelude to the drama, delivered by a trustworthy figure—often a god— who would recount the essential details of the myth and ensure the audience's understanding. This divine narrator guaranteed the story's credibility and anchored the play's events in a mythological reality, much as Descartes appealed to God's truthfulness to validate empirical existence. Similarly, Euripides employed the deus ex machina at the conclusion of his plays, using divine intervention to clarify the future fates of his characters. Between these epic bookends—the explanatory prologue and the resolution by deus ex machina—lay the dramatic-lyric heart of the play, the "drama" proper.

In this way, Euripides' work reflects his intellectual vision of tragedy. He embodied the critical spirit of his age, bringing to life the notion from Anaxagoras: "In the beginning, all things were mixed together; then came understanding and created order." Like Anaxagoras, who introduced reason (νοῦς) as a principle of cosmic organization, Euripides sought to impose order and clarity on the chaotic art of his predecessors. He may have imagined himself as a sober figure amidst drunken poets, compelled to bring lucidity and structure to an art form that had thrived on mystery and excess.

Sophocles once remarked that Aeschylus "did the right thing, though unknowingly." Euripides, however, could not have shared this view. For him, unconscious creation was tantamount to error. His contempt for unreasoned artistry aligned with the philosophy of Plato, who often downplayed the value of poetic inspiration, likening it to the irrational insights of seers and dreamers. Like Plato, Euripides sought to demonstrate the superiority of intelligent, deliberate creativity over the instinctive and unconscious processes that characterized earlier tragedy. His aesthetic creed—"To be beautiful, everything must be understood"—paralleled Socrates' moral dictum, "To be good, everything must be known." Thus, Euripides became the poet of aesthetic Socratism.

It was Socrates, then, who emerged as Euripides' ally and intellectual co- spectator, sharing his distaste for the enigmatic and unrestrained qualities of the old tragedy. Together, they represented a new artistic ethos that opposed the Dionysian spirit. Euripides' alliance with Socrates heralded the destruction of traditional Greek tragedy, a casualty of this rationalist revolution.

In this struggle, Socrates stood as a symbolic antagonist to Dionysus, a new Orpheus rebelling against the god of ecstasy. Like the mythic Orpheus, Socrates sought to tame the overwhelming power of Dionysus with reason and restraint. Yet, just as Orpheus was ultimately torn apart by the Maenads, the forces of ecstatic worship, Socrates' intellectual rebellion could not fully vanquish the primal power of Dionysus. Instead, Dionysus retreated, finding refuge in the mystical undercurrents of secret cults that would quietly spread across the world.

Through Euripides, Socrates became a force that redefined the trajectory of Greek art. Yet, this triumph over the Dionysian marked the end of an era. The grandeur of Greek tragedy, born of the union between Dionysus and Apollo, could not survive the cold, rational gaze of aesthetic Socratism. In its place arose a new artistic order, fundamentally transformed by the very forces that had once sought to destroy it.

That Socrates shared a profound connection with Euripides in the nature of their philosophical and artistic endeavors did not escape the awareness of their contemporaries. This alignment was captured in a popular tale in Athens, which suggested that Socrates often assisted Euripides in his compositions. The two were frequently mentioned together by proponents of the "good old days," who saw them as harbingers of a new intellectual movement they distrusted. These critics lamented what they perceived as a gradual erosion of the robust character—both physical and moral—that had defined the heroic days of Marathon, replaced by a precarious enlightenment that seemed to sap vitality from both body and mind.

This sentiment was vividly echoed in Aristophanic comedy, which often portrayed both figures in a tone that combined indignation and derision. Modern readers are often puzzled by this treatment, especially when Socrates is depicted by Aristophanes not as a revered philosopher but as the archetypal sophist, embodying and epitomizing all sophistical tendencies. While many might readily dismiss Euripides as a polarizing figure, the idea of Socrates as the chief sophist leaves them bewildered. Some have attempted to reconcile this dissonance by framing Aristophanes himself as a scandalous and deceptive Alcibiades of poetry. However, leaving aside the defense of Aristophanes' profound instincts against such accusations, it is worth exploring the prevailing attitudes of the time to understand the intimate relationship between Socrates and Euripides.

It is particularly significant that Socrates, who was known for his criticism of tragic art, rarely attended performances unless the play in question was a new work by Euripides. This selective patronage highlights the philosophical alignment between the two. Even more striking is the juxtaposition of their names in the famous Delphic oracle, which declared Socrates the wisest of men while assigning Euripides the second prize in wisdom. Sophocles was deemed third in this hierarchy—a ranking he might have accepted with pride, given his claim that, unlike Aeschylus, he not only acted rightly but did so knowingly.

This hierarchy illuminates the shared emphasis on knowledge that binds these three figures, each representing a different facet of the pursuit of wisdom in their age. Yet, the most definitive statement of this new veneration for knowledge came from Socrates himself, who famously professed that his wisdom lay in his acknowledgment of his ignorance. As he moved through Athens, engaging with its greatest statesmen, orators, poets, and artists, Socrates uncovered a troubling conceit of knowledge among these figures. To his astonishment, he found that even those most celebrated in their fields lacked true understanding of their own craft, relying instead on instinct.

It is this revelation—"only by instinct"—that captures the essence of Socratism. Socrates regarded instinctual practice, whether in art or ethics, as fundamentally flawed. He saw in it not only a lack of insight but also a dangerous reliance on illusion. To him, this absence of knowledge signified an intrinsic disorder and unworthiness in the existing order of things. Convinced of his mission, Socrates believed it was his calling to correct this flawed existence. With an air of assured superiority, he set out to challenge the prevailing norms of culture, art, and morality, presenting himself as the harbinger of an entirely new paradigm.

In this endeavor, Socrates stood in stark opposition to a world that, for others, represented the pinnacle of human achievement. A world where touching even the hem of its fabric might be counted as the highest form of fulfillment. Yet, Socrates approached this revered world not with reverence but with a resolve to dismantle it, driven by his unwavering belief in the transformative power of knowledge and reason. His critical gaze sought to redefine what it meant to live, create, and act rightly, marking the beginning of a cultural and intellectual revolution that would leave an indelible mark on Western thought.

Here lies the peculiar and persistent unease that arises whenever we contemplate the figure of Socrates, compelling us again and again to question the purpose and significance of this most enigmatic character of antiquity. Who is this man who dares to stand alone in defiance of the Greek spirit—a spirit embodied by the sublime figures of Homer, Pindar, Æschylus, and Phidias; by the lofty achievements of Pericles; by the oracle of Pythia and the ecstasy of Dionysus? This Greek spirit, which encompasses both the profoundest depths and the most exalted heights of human experience, commands our awe and admiration. What strange and powerful force would dare to pour this enchanting elixir of Greek genius upon the ground? What sort of demigod is this, to whom the chorus of humanity's noblest spirits must cry out in despair: "Alas! Alas! You have shattered the beautiful world with your mighty fist; it collapses, it falls apart!"

An essential clue to understanding Socrates lies in the extraordinary phenomenon known as his "daimonion." This mysterious inner voice, described by Socrates himself, would manifest in critical moments when his formidable intellect seemed to waver. It did not encourage or guide him forward but always counseled restraint, dissuading him from specific actions. In this utterly unique personality, instinctive wisdom made its presence known only to obstruct the forward march of conscious thought. Unlike in other creative figures, where instinct acts as a generative and affirming force while consciousness critiques and refines, in Socrates this relationship was reversed. Here, instinct became the critic, and consciousness assumed the role of creator—a complete inversion of the natural order, a true monstrosity arising from an absence, a defectus.

Indeed, this peculiar deficiency extended to Socrates' mystical capabilities, or rather, the lack thereof. He could be aptly described as the quintessential non- mystic, in whom logical reasoning had developed to an extraordinary degree, overshadowing the instinctual wisdom found in mystics. Yet this very "logical instinct" in Socrates operated with an unyielding force, incapable of turning against itself. It moved forward with an unchecked and native power, startling in its intensity and akin only to the most profound instinctive drives. Anyone who has felt even a glimpse of the divine simplicity and certainty in Socratic logic, as presented in Plato's writings, will sense that behind Socrates lies an immense and inexorable machinery of logical thought. It is as though he is but a shadow cast by this vast mechanism, through which it operates and reveals itself.

That Socrates himself had an inkling of this dynamic is evident in the solemnity with which he consistently proclaimed his divine mission, even before his judges. To counter such a claim would have been as futile as to fully accept the profound dissonance of his influence, which fragmented the instincts that underpin human life. When finally brought before the tribunal of the Greek state, this fundamental tension left only one plausible course of action: exile. Socrates might have been sent across the borders, banished as an unfathomable and inscrutable anomaly, and posterity would have had little ground to fault the Athenians for such a decision.

Yet Socrates himself chose a different path. It seems that his death sentence, rather than mere exile, was an outcome Socrates knowingly invited. He approached this fate with perfect understanding and without the ordinary human fear of death. Plato's depiction of Socrates in his final moments portrays a man of serene composure, meeting his end as effortlessly as he might leave a symposium at dawn. Having outlasted the other revelers, he begins a new day while his weary companions lie behind, lost in dreams of the true eroticist—the one who had inspired them.

The image of the dying Socrates became a transformative ideal for Greek youth, an ideal they had never before encountered. In his final act, he embodied a new kind of nobility that transcended the traditional virtues of the Greek world. Most profoundly, it was Plato—the quintessential Hellenic youth—who knelt before this scene with an intensity that reflected the full depth of his visionary spirit. This moment marked the birth of a new ideal in the history of thought, one that would reverberate far beyond the life and death of Socrates, casting a long shadow over the cultural and philosophical heritage of the Greeks.

Woe! Woe!

You have destroyed it, The beautiful world; With a mighty hand,

You have hurled it into ruin!

Now imagine Socrates with his great Cyclopean eye, fixed upon the art of tragedy. This was an eye in which the fiery passion of artistic enthusiasm had never burned—a gaze that could never find joy in the Dionysian depths. What else could such an eye see in what Plato called the "sublime and greatly lauded" art of tragedy? To Socrates, it must have seemed absurd: a chaotic mix of causes that seemed to lead nowhere and effects that appeared to come from nothing. It was all so jumbled and varied that it offended his thoughtful mind. To sensitive and emotional souls, though, it must have been a dangerous temptation.

We know what kind of poetry Socrates did appreciate: the simple and clear Æsopian fable. He likely viewed it with the same approving smile that the gentle poet Gellert gave when he praised poetry in his tale of the bee and the hen:

"You see through me, what it is worth, To one who lacks much sense on earth, To tell the truth through simple scenes."

But even this mild praise seemed too much for tragic art in Socrates' eyes. He thought tragedy didn't even try to "tell the truth," and worse, it appealed to those who, in his view, "had little wit." Therefore, it had no value to the philosopher—a double reason to reject it outright. Like Plato, he classified tragedy among the seductive arts that focus on what is pleasing rather than what is useful. For this reason, Socrates demanded that his followers avoid it entirely and remain strictly separate from such unphilosophical distractions. His influence was so strong that he persuaded the young Plato, who had been a budding tragic poet, to burn his works in order to devote himself fully to philosophy under Socrates' teachings.

However, when innate talent and creative drive were too powerful to be stifled by Socratic teachings, the strength of Socrates' ideas and his overwhelming personal influence still managed to redirect poetry itself into new and previously unexplored forms.

Plato, who rejected tragedy and art as fiercely as his teacher Socrates, was nevertheless compelled by his own artistic instincts to create a form of art that, despite his opposition, closely related to the very art forms he denounced. His chief critique of traditional art—that it was merely an imitation of illusions and therefore belonged to a realm even more illusory than the material world—did not apply to the new form he crafted. Plato sought to go beyond mere appearances and represent the deeper ideas that underlie this perceived reality. Ironically, as a thinker, he arrived at the same place where he had always stood as a poet, the same place from which Sophocles and other great artists had defended their work against such critiques.

Tragedy, which once absorbed all earlier forms of art, found its unusual successor in the Platonic dialogue. This hybrid form, born from a fusion of narrative, lyric, and dramatic styles, straddled the boundaries between prose and poetry, breaking the old rules of unity in language. This movement toward a freer form of expression was later amplified by the Cynic writers, who created works with a chaotic mix of prose and verse, mirroring the eccentric and unpredictable nature of the "raving Socrates" they often depicted in life.

The Platonic dialogue was like a lifeboat, rescuing the fragments of ancient poetry after its shipwreck. Crowded together under the command of Socrates, the remnants of old art embarked on a journey into a new world, one that gazed in wonder at the fantastic spectacle of this innovative creation. Plato thus gave future generations the blueprint for a new kind of art—the novel—an infinitely refined version of the Æsopian fable. In this form, poetry was relegated to the role of a servant to dialectic philosophy, much as philosophy had once served theology for centuries. Plato's work signaled the subjugation of poetry under the intellectual dominance of the Socratic spirit.

In this new order, philosophy overtook art and forced it to cling closely to the framework of dialectical reasoning. The Apollonian impulse became enshrined in strict logical structures, much as Euripides had earlier transformed the Dionysian into raw, naturalistic emotion. Socrates, the logical hero of Platonic drama, bears a striking resemblance to the Euripidean hero, who often defends his actions through arguments and counterarguments, risking the loss of the audience's emotional connection. The optimistic essence of dialectics— rejoicing in every conclusion and thriving on clarity and rationality—gradually consumed the Dionysian elements of tragedy, inevitably driving it toward its own destruction and ultimately transforming it into a more mundane, bourgeois drama.

The consequences of Socratic principles are clear: "Virtue is knowledge; man sins only out of ignorance; and he who is virtuous is happy." These optimistic ideas dealt a fatal blow to tragedy. The heroic figures of old now had to become dialecticians, their virtues tied to their knowledge, and their morality to their beliefs. The deep, transcendental justice of Æschylean tragedy was reduced to the shallow concept of poetic justice, often resolved by the clumsy intervention of a deus ex machina.

The tragic chorus, and the entire Dionysian foundation of tragedy, was reduced to a mere accessory under this Socratic-optimistic worldview. This reduction began with Sophocles, who diminished the chorus's role so much that it became nearly equal to the actors. This shift, which Aristotle later endorsed, marked the beginning of the chorus's decline. In Euripides, Agathon, and the New Comedy, this erosion accelerated until the chorus was effectively annihilated. The optimistic dialectic of Socratism expelled music from tragedy, dismantling its very essence. Tragedy, rooted in Dionysian states and expressed as a visual symbol of music, was drained of its meaning and vitality.

If we accept that an anti-Dionysian tendency existed even before Socrates, culminating in his dramatic impact, we must ask what this phenomenon of Socrates represents. While it's clear that Socratic rationalism led directly to the dissolution of Dionysian tragedy, we must also consider whether there is room for reconciliation between Socratism and art. Could the emergence of an "artistic Socrates" be more than a contradiction, and might it suggest a deeper, more complex relationship between these forces?

The relentless logician, Socrates, was not entirely immune to moments of unease, as if some inner voice were pointing to an unfulfilled duty toward art. He confessed to his friends in prison that a recurring dream had visited him throughout his life, always delivering the same instruction: "Socrates, practice music." This enigmatic command puzzled him, for he had always comforted himself with the belief that his philosophizing was the highest and most refined form of artistic expression. It seemed inconceivable to him that a divine message could be urging him toward the mundane realm of "common, popular music." Yet, in his final days, confined within his prison cell, he chose to heed the dream's persistent call, feeling an almost desperate need to ease his conscience. It was then, in this state of reflection and submission, that he composed a hymn to Apollo and adapted a few of Æsop's fables into verse.

This act of turning to music and poetry so late in life bore a resemblance to the warnings of his daimonion, that inner voice that often dissuaded him from action. Like the daimonion, the dream seemed to highlight the limitations of his logical approach. It was as though Socrates, with all his towering intellect, had failed to grasp the profound significance of the divine image and was in danger of transgressing against a higher power—not out of malice, but ignorance. The recurring vision served as a rare moment of doubt in his otherwise unwavering confidence in logic. "Could it be," Socrates asked himself, "that what I cannot comprehend is not, for that reason alone, unreasonable? Might there be a realm of wisdom where logic has no jurisdiction? Could it be that art, far from being frivolous, is an essential counterpart to science, complementing and completing it?"

The pressing questions raised by this dream hint at a deeper truth about the legacy of Socrates. His influence, which stretches across generations and continues to shape the present day, resembles an ever-lengthening shadow cast by the setting sun. This shadow not only challenges but also compels the periodic renewal of art—a rejuvenation imbued with the broadest and most profound metaphysical significance. The endurance of Socratic thought, with its relentless pursuit of knowledge, seems to ensure the perpetual vitality of art, for it is in art that the limits of reason find their counterpart, their balance, and their transcendence. Thus, the eternity of Socrates' intellectual legacy guarantees the enduring necessity and renewal of art, anchoring both in an unbroken continuity that speaks to their mutual dependence.

Before the profound and undeniable connection between all art and the Greeks—spanning from Homer to Socrates—could be fully understood and acknowledged, humanity first had to endure an uneasy relationship with these Greeks, much like the Athenians did with Socrates himself. Throughout history, nearly every era and cultural movement has, at some point, harbored a deep- seated frustration with the Greeks. Their presence, like a bright and piercing light, has often cast an unflattering shadow on what each age held dear as its own accomplishments. Every achievement thought to be original, admirable, and authentically self-made seemed, under the Greek gaze, to fade into insignificance, appearing as nothing more than a pale imitation—or worse, a clumsy caricature—of something greater.

This recurring discontent has given rise to outbursts of indignation against this "arrogant little nation," which, with audacious self-assurance, dared to label all that was foreign to them as "barbaric." Such disdain invites the inevitable question: who were these people, that they could lay claim to such cultural superiority? What gave them the right to hold themselves above others? After all, their historical splendor, though dazzling, was fleeting. Their political institutions were notably narrow in scope, their social customs open to doubt and critique, and their moral fabric often tarnished by the presence of glaring vices. Yet, in spite of these flaws, the Greeks boldly asserted their unique and exalted standing among nations, a status akin to the position of genius within the multitude of humanity.

This claim to preeminence has incited not only incredulity but also resentment, as if one could wish for a figurative cup of hemlock to resolve the matter swiftly and decisively. And yet, all the poisons brewed from envy, slander, and deep-seated resentment have failed to diminish the Greeks' enduring grandeur. Their self-contained magnificence remains impervious, defying every attempt to reduce or eliminate it. Faced with their brilliance, one feels not only irritation but also a deep sense of inadequacy and unease—unless, that is, one values truth above all else and possesses the courage to admit an uncomfortable reality.

That reality is this: the Greeks are, metaphorically, the charioteers of culture. They hold the reins not only of their own civilization but also of every culture that has followed. Yet, more often than not, the "chariot" and "horses"—the raw materials of these subsequent cultures—prove to be woefully inadequate to match the Greeks' extraordinary skill and vision. Like guides of unparalleled brilliance, the Greeks seem to drive these insufficient teams with ease and daring. And when the journey grows perilous, when the road veers toward the edge of an abyss, it is as though they relish the challenge. With the grace and strength of Achilles, they leap effortlessly over the chasm, leaving the rest of us to marvel—and to struggle to keep up.

To bestow upon Socrates the distinction of occupying such an exalted position in the history of human thought, it suffices to recognize him as the embodiment of an entirely new and unprecedented form of existence: the theoretical man. Understanding the essence and purpose of this archetype is our next undertaking. Much like the artist, the theorist finds profound and endless satisfaction in what exists, in the nature of reality itself. This satisfaction serves as a protective shield, insulating him from the grim practical ethics of pessimism, which perceives the world with piercing clarity, like eyes that only illuminate the darkness.

While the artist gazes with enraptured vision at the mysteries still concealed after every act of revelation, the theorist derives his joy from what has already been unveiled. He takes delight in the discarded veils of mystery and finds ultimate pleasure in the continual act of uncovering truth through his own efforts. It is this process of discovery, rather than its finality, that defines him. Science would not have come into being if its sole purpose were to grasp some singular and definitive truth, some solitary, unattainable ideal. For in such a case, its practitioners would resemble those who dig endlessly toward the earth's core: each one realizing, after a lifetime of toil, that they have penetrated only a small fraction of its depth. Even worse, their progress would soon be erased by the labors of those who follow them, filling in the void with their own endeavors. The next digger, wise to this futility, might choose instead to start afresh, selecting a new spot to excavate, as though the act itself were its own reward.

If someone were to definitively prove that the ultimate destination could never be reached by such direct means, who would then continue to labor in the old depths? Only those who had learned to value the process itself—the discovery of precious stones or the unveiling of natural laws—would persist. This insight was at the heart of Lessing's profound declaration that he valued the search for truth more than truth itself. In this statement, Lessing laid bare the secret of science, a revelation that both astonished and unsettled his contemporaries in the scientific world. Yet alongside this brutally honest perspective stands a sublime illusion, one that first found its fullest expression in Socrates. This illusion is the unshakable belief that through the thread of causality, human thought can reach the very depths of existence. More than that, it suggests that thought not only comprehends being but has the power to correct it.

This towering metaphysical illusion acts as an instinct, one embedded deeply in the foundations of science. Again and again, it drives science to its outermost limits, where it must inevitably transform into art. In fact, this transformation is not just incidental but serves as the ultimate culmination of the scientific endeavor.

Viewing Socrates through this lens reveals him as the first individual who could not only live but also willingly and triumphantly face death under the guidance of this scientific instinct. His life, and even more so his death, exemplifies this principle. The image of Socrates in his final moments, liberated from the fear of death by the power of knowledge and logical argumentation, becomes an enduring symbol. It stands like a coat of arms above the gateway to science, reminding all who pass beneath of its noble mission: to render existence comprehensible and, through this understanding, to justify it.

When reason and argument prove insufficient to achieve this goal, myth must step in as their ally. Myth, then, becomes not just an alternative but an inevitable consequence, even the ultimate aim of science itself. In this way, science, through its very striving, reaches a point where it becomes art, embracing the narratives and symbols that offer meaning and illumination where logic alone cannot suffice.

Whoever truly understands how, after the death of Socrates—the great guide of scientific inquiry—philosophical schools rose and fell in rapid succession like waves crashing upon the shore, will recognize the profound and transformative legacy he left behind. Socrates' influence set into motion an unprecedented thirst for knowledge that permeated the intellectual fabric of the cultured world. This movement became a defining characteristic of highly gifted individuals, propelling science into uncharted waters from which it has never been entirely displaced. Out of this boundless pursuit arose the concept of a shared intellectual framework, a vast net of ideas encompassing the globe and hinting at the promise of universal laws extending even to the dynamics of the solar system.

To comprehend this evolution, alongside the towering edifice of contemporary knowledge it has erected, is to understand Socrates as the pivotal figure in the history of human thought. He is the point of inflection, the vortex through which the trajectory of so-called universal history was irrevocably altered. Imagine for a moment the incalculable energy expended in this collective endeavor toward knowledge being redirected solely toward practical or self-serving ends—toward the narrow goals of individuals and nations. Such a world would likely have been engulfed in endless wars of destruction and relentless migrations of peoples, weakening the instinctive love of life itself. In the face of such devastation, the specter of suicide might rise as the final refuge of duty. The individual, worn down by despair, might find their last sense of obligation fulfilled in acts of horrifying mercy—perhaps strangling a parent, as in the traditions of the Fijian Islands, or taking the life of a close friend, driven by some twisted sense of pity. This grim vision of "practical pessimism" might even give birth to a monstrous ethic—a morality of universal slaughter justified as an act of compassion. Indeed, such a pestilential atmosphere has emerged wherever art, science, or religion has failed to appear as a counterbalance, as a remedy to humanity's darkest impulses.

Against this bleak backdrop, Socrates stands as the ultimate figure of theoretical optimism. His belief in the intelligibility of the universe elevated knowledge and perception to the status of a universal cure. For Socrates, error and evil could be overcome by understanding; the solution to human suffering lay in unraveling the mysteries of existence. To penetrate the depths of reality, to distinguish truth from illusion—this was, for Socrates, not just the highest calling but the defining trait of humanity itself. From his time onward, the mechanisms of logic—concepts, judgments, and inferences—were exalted as humanity's most extraordinary gift and the apex of intellectual achievement.

Socrates and his intellectual descendants did not stop at reconfiguring knowledge; they reinterpreted even the highest moral acts. Acts of compassion, self-sacrifice, heroism, and the serene self-mastery the Apollonian Greeks termed sophrosyne— all were reimagined as products of rational understanding and thus deemed teachable. To those inspired by Socratic reasoning, the joy of discovering and categorizing the world's phenomena became an unparalleled force, one that could justify existence itself. Such individuals found their life's meaning in expanding the reach of knowledge, weaving its intricate web ever tighter and more comprehensive.

To these thinkers, the Socrates of Plato emerges as the herald of a new form of "Greek cheerfulness." Unlike the earlier tragic or Dionysian cheerfulness rooted in an acceptance of life's suffering, this optimism expressed itself through action and influence. It was a joy that sought fulfillment through mentorship, intellectual midwifery, and the cultivation of excellence in others. Socrates' teaching primarily discharged itself in shaping the minds and souls of noble youths, striving toward the ultimate goal of nurturing genius. In this way, Socrates not only redefined the Greek ideal of happiness but also laid the groundwork for an enduring vision of intellectual and moral flourishing.

Science, propelled by its powerful and captivating illusion, moves irresistibly toward its outermost boundaries, where the optimism inherent in logic inevitably collapses. The vast circle of knowledge has an infinite periphery, and as one delves deeper into its limits, the noble and brilliant mind inevitably encounters those enigmatic edges where reason falters and the inexplicable looms large. At these limits, logic, like a serpent, coils upon itself and ultimately bites its own tail, revealing its cyclical and self-consuming nature. Here, at this precipice, a new form of understanding emerges— tragic perception—which, to be endured, requires the protective balm of art as both a safeguard and remedy.

When we look at the highest realms of existence through the lens sharpened by the Greeks, we see the insatiable drive for optimistic knowledge, exemplified by Socrates, transforming into a tragic resignation and an undeniable need for art. Yet, on its lower levels, this relentless hunger for knowledge often manifests as hostility toward art, particularly toward Dionysian tragedy, as seen in Socrates' opposition to the works of Æschylus.

With this perspective, we turn our gaze to the present and the future, questioning whether this transformation might lead to new expressions of genius—perhaps a rebirth of the "music- practicing Socrates"—or whether the fragile web of art stretched over existence will be torn apart by the restless, barbaric energy of what we call the modern age. Standing at this crossroads, we are not merely observers but participants in these monumental struggles and transitions. We are caught in the magnetic pull of these battles, where witnessing them compels us to take part, for the charm of such conflicts lies in their demand for engagement.

Through this historical lens, we have sought to illustrate a profound truth: tragedy cannot endure without the spirit of music, just as it owes its very birth to this spirit. To explore this claim fully and to clarify its deeper meaning, we must now confront the analogous phenomena of our own time. We must immerse ourselves in the ongoing battles between the boundless optimism of scientific understanding and the tragic necessity of art, battles that unfold at the highest levels of our contemporary world. While other opposing forces have long worked against art, especially tragedy—forces that today manifest in the shallow triumph of farce and ballet—I will focus on the most illustrious adversary of the tragic worldview: optimistic science, with Socrates as its founding figure. In this confrontation, I shall also point to the forces that, I believe, hold the promise of a rebirth for tragedy and, perhaps, other great hopes for the German spirit.

Before we venture into these struggles, let us arm ourselves with the insights we have gained so far. Unlike those who derive all art from a single, exclusive principle, I remain fixed on the duality represented by the two artistic deities of the Greeks: Apollo and Dionysus. These figures symbolize two fundamentally different worlds of art, each with its own essence and ultimate aim. Apollo appears as the deity of transfiguration, embodying the pr incipium individuationis, the principle through which redemption is achieved in the form of illusion and beauty. Dionysus, by contrast, represents the breaking of individuation, offering access to the primordial unity at the heart of existence. This profound opposition—between the Apollonian domain of visual and plastic art and the Dionysian domain of music—reveals the deepest truths about Greek tragedy.

Only one great thinker has fully grasped this stark contrast. Schopenhauer recognized that music, unlike all other arts, is not an imitation of phenomena but a direct expression of the will itself. It reflects the metaphysical essence of the physical world, the very "thing-in-itself" behind every appearance. Richard Wagner reaffirmed this profound insight, asserting in his Beethoven that music must be judged by principles distinct from those applied to the visual arts. Music transcends the concept of beauty as understood in plastic art, which has misled aesthetics to demand from music a similar delight in form, neglecting its unique and deeper power.

This realization drew me irresistibly toward the essence of Greek tragedy, the most profound revelation of Hellenic genius. Here, I believed I had discovered a key that allowed me to move beyond the conventional language of aesthetics and grapple directly with the fundamental problem of tragedy. This journey into the heart of Greek tragedy illuminated the character of the Hellenic world in a way that cast doubt on the validity of much of what passes for classical scholarship. It seemed that our proud classical studies, which claim to understand the Greeks, have so far subsisted largely on superficial interpretations and illusions. With this realization, we stand ready to delve deeper into the mysteries of Greek art and its timeless relevance to our age.

To approach this foundational problem, we might ask: what aesthetic impact occurs when the inherently distinct artistic forces, the Apollonian and Dionysian, act simultaneously? Or, to phrase it more concisely: how does music interact with image and concept? Schopenhauer, whose clarity on this subject Richard Wagner praised as unparalleled, provides an in-depth exploration of this question in the following passage from The World as Will and Representation (Book I, p. 309). This passage is worth quoting in full:

"From all this, we can view the phenomenal world—nature—and music as two different expressions of the same essence. This essence serves as the sole medium that allows for the analogy between the two expressions, requiring a knowledge of this medium to understand the analogy itself. Music, when regarded as an expression of the world, becomes the most universal language, akin to how concepts are universal yet distinct from particular things. However, music's universality is not the empty abstraction found in mere concepts; it is a unique kind of universality, inseparably linked to clarity and specificity.

In this way, music is similar to geometrical figures or numbers, which represent universal forms applicable to all possible experiences. These forms are not abstract in the usual sense but are perceptible and distinctly defined. Music captures every possible emotion, impulse, and manifestation of the will— everything that stirs within the human heart and is encompassed by reason under the broad term 'feeling.' Music conveys these in their pure form, as universal expressions without material substance, encapsulating the essence of the will itself rather than its outward phenomena. It reproduces the soul or core of these phenomena, stripped of their physical appearance.

This profound relationship between music and the true essence of all things explains why music played in harmony with a particular scene, event, or setting seems to reveal its most hidden meaning. Music often appears as a perfect commentary on such moments. Similarly, when someone fully immerses themselves in the experience of a symphony, they seem to witness all possible events of life and the world unfolding within them. Yet, upon reflection, they can discern no tangible connection between the music and the thoughts or images that came to mind. This is because music does not imitate external phenomena; it is not a reproduction of the objective world, nor is it an 'adequate objectivity of the will.' Instead, it is a direct manifestation of the will itself. In this way, music represents the metaphysical essence behind all physical existence and the 'thing-in-itself' underlying all phenomena.

For this reason, one could just as accurately call the world 'embodied music' as 'embodied will.' Music gives a heightened significance to every image, scene, or experience, amplifying its meaning when the melody resonates with the inner spirit of the depicted phenomenon. This relationship allows us to set poetry to music in the form of songs, combine music with visual representation in pantomime, or merge both in opera. Yet these representations are not bound to music with strict necessity; they merely serve as chosen examples to illustrate music's universal concepts. In their specificity, they depict what music conveys in pure and universal form.

Melodies, like general concepts, abstract from concrete reality. The actual world, with its particularities, provides the perceptible forms and individual cases for both the universality of concepts and the universality of melodies. Yet these two universalities stand in opposition: concepts capture the external forms abstracted from perception—the outer shell of things, as it were—making them true abstractions. Music, on the other hand, conveys the innermost kernel, the essence that precedes all forms—the heart of existence itself.

To express this in scholastic terms: concepts are univer salia post rem (universals derived from reality), while music represents universalia ante rem (universals preceding reality), and the material world embodies universalia in r e (universals within reality). A relationship between a musical composition and a visual representation is possible because both are expressions of the same inner essence of the world. When such a connection is achieved—when a composer translates the emotional core of an event into the universal language of music—the resulting melody or opera expresses this essence. However, this analogy must stem from the composer's direct, intuitive understanding of the world, one that bypasses reason. If the composition is instead a conscious imitation constructed through rational concepts, it fails to express the true nature of the will and becomes a mere imitation of external phenomena. All deliberately imitative music falls into this trap."

This rich and nuanced passage captures the unique relationship between music and the other arts, positioning music as a direct expression of the metaphysical will, transcending the representational limitations of other forms. It offers profound insights into the nature of music as a universal yet deeply personal art form, one that engages with the very core of existence itself.

Following Schopenhauer's doctrine, we recognize music as the immediate language of the will. It speaks to us with such intensity that it stirs our imagination, urging us to create tangible forms for this otherwise invisible and dynamically active spirit- world. This unseen force moves us to translate it into analogous representations that embody its essence. At the same time, under the influence of music that truly aligns with its deeper purpose, images and concepts gain an elevated significance. Dionysian art, as a result, exerts two profound effects upon the Apollonian art- faculty. First, music inspires a symbolic intuition of Dionysian universality, urging us to perceive and represent its boundless essence. Second, it enhances the symbolic image, bringing it to its fullest expression and meaning.

These observations, though requiring some contemplation, are not beyond the grasp of deeper reflection. From them, I conclude that music possesses the extraordinary capacity to generate myth—and not just any myth, but the most profound and meaningful of all, the tragic myth. Such myths convey the symbolic language of Dionysian understanding, offering a glimpse into its profound wisdom through archetypal imagery. When we consider the phenomenon of the lyric poet, for example, we see how music seeks to reveal its intrinsic nature by manifesting itself through Apollonian symbols. In the lyricist's work, music takes shape, expressing itself through the metaphoric language of images.

If we now ponder music's ability to achieve its fullest symbolic realization, we must entertain the possibility that it can find an equally profound expression for its inherent Dionysian truths. Music in its highest form, embodying its deepest power, must also seek the most profound symbols to articulate its wisdom. Where else, then, should we expect to find this symbolic expression of its Dionysian insight if not in the realm of tragedy, and more broadly, in the entire concept of the tragic?

Here, tragedy emerges not merely as a form of artistic representation but as the ultimate embodiment of music's inner essence. It becomes the symbolic mirror in which Dionysian knowledge finds its most complete and compelling reflection. In this sense, tragedy stands as the highest fulfillment of music's creative drive, a synthesis where its wisdom and universality are transmuted into a visible and deeply moving form. Through this lens, we begin to understand that the tragic is not only an aesthetic category but also a philosophical and existential one, rooted in the interplay of music's Dionysian force and the symbolic power of Apollonian artistry.

From the conventional understanding of art, which is often limited to the categories of appearance and beauty, it is impossible to honestly deduce the essence of the tragic. It is only through the profound influence of the spirit of music that we come to comprehend the strange and paradoxical joy found in the annihilation of the individual. This joy arises because such annihilation, seen in its particular instances, reveals to us the eternal phenomenon of Dionysian art. This art expresses the will in its boundless omnipotence, existing beyond the boundaries of the principium individuationis, beyond the confines of individual existence. It points to an eternal life that persists beyond all appearances, a life that remains undisturbed despite endless cycles of destruction.

The metaphysical delight we find in tragedy is a translation of the instinctive and unconscious wisdom of the Dionysian spirit into the tangible and visual language of the stage. The tragic hero, who represents the highest manifestation of the will, is sacrificed before our eyes—not to invoke despair, but to elicit joy. This joy stems from the realization that the hero, being only a fleeting phenomenon, cannot touch the eternal life of the will that continues undiminished. Tragedy, through its sublime art, cries out: "We believe in eternal life!" And in this expression, music becomes the nearest and most immediate idea of that eternal life.

In contrast, the domain of plastic art, as guided by the Apollonian spirit, offers a completely different objective. Here, Apollo triumphs over the suffering of the individual by transfiguring it into radiant beauty, celebrating the eternity of appearances. Through this process, beauty conquers the anguish embedded in life, and pain is subtly erased from nature's visage. Dionysian art, however, strips away this Apollonian veil and speaks to us with an unadorned and truthful voice, proclaiming: "Be as I am! In the midst of endless transformation, I am the eternally creative primordial mother, driving existence forward and finding satisfaction in the perpetual flux of phenomena."

Dionysian art strives to reveal the eternal joy of existence, but it asks us to seek this joy not in the ephemeral phenomena of the world but beyond them. It compels us to confront the harsh reality that all which comes into being must inevitably face a sorrowful end. We are made to gaze directly into the heart of the terrors that define individual existence. Yet, even in this confrontation, we are not paralyzed or defeated. Instead, a profound metaphysical comfort lifts us out of the chaotic whirl of transforming forms, granting us fleeting moments of transcendence. In these moments, we become, in a sense, the Primordial Being itself, infused with its indomitable will to create and its ecstatic joy in the act of existence.

Through this perspective, the struggle, the suffering, and the destruction of individual forms appear not as tragedies in themselves but as necessary processes. They are rendered meaningful by the overwhelming abundance of existence, the boundless fertility of the universal will, which perpetually generates new life and new forms. In this endless cycle, every pain and loss is counterbalanced by an infinite surplus of being.

In these moments of Dionysian ecstasy, we are pierced by the sharp and maddening sting of existence's pains, but this agony is interwoven with an immense, eternal joy. We are no longer isolated individuals but have merged with the universal life force, the one undivided being whose procreative exuberance flows through all. In this unity, even as we witness fear and pity, we find ourselves as joyful participants in the grand and eternal celebration of existence. It is not as separate beings but as part of the universal whole that we embrace the indestructible and everlasting joy of life itself.

The development of Greek tragedy vividly illustrates that its origins lie in the spirit of music. This understanding, perhaps for the first time, illuminates the original and remarkable significance of the chorus, which has so often been misunderstood or undervalued. Yet, even as we recognize this profound connection, we must also acknowledge that the deeper meanings embodied in tragic myth, as described here, were not always fully transparent to the Greek poets or even their philosophers. The heroes of these dramas often speak in ways that seem shallower than their actions. The spoken word, the dialogue of the play, does not entirely capture or express the myth's deeper truths. Instead, the structure of the scenes and the vivid imagery within the tragedy carry a wisdom that surpasses the poet's conscious articulation in words and concepts.

This phenomenon is not unique to Greek tragedy; it can also be observed in Shakespeare. For example, Hamlet conveys his lesson not directly through his words, which often seem more superficial than his actions, but through a deeper, more holistic understanding that emerges when we contemplate the play as a whole. Similarly, with Greek tragedy, which we primarily encounter today as "word-drama," there is an inherent tension between the profound mythological content and its verbal expression. This incongruity might lead modern observers to underestimate the depth and significance of Greek tragedy. It tempts us to view these works as less impactful or meaningful than they truly were, to the extent that we might assume they produced a more superficial effect than the ancients themselves attest.

It is easy to forget that what the playwrights may have struggled to achieve through their words—namely, the highest level of spiritualization and ideal representation of myth—was often accomplished through the medium of music. This music, inseparable from the original performances of these tragedies, elevated their emotional and symbolic power in ways the spoken word alone could not. To recapture even a fraction of the incomparable solace and profound impact that Greek tragedy offered, we must almost reconstruct the influence of its musical foundation, adopting something akin to a philological method of recovery. But even with such reconstruction, we must admit that the experience of this musical supremacy could never be truly grasped unless we were Greeks ourselves. The music of ancient Greece, as compared to the vastly richer and more developed forms we know today, may strike us as a youthful and tentative expression, a first exploration of the musical genius that we now take for granted.

The Greeks, as the Egyptian priests once remarked, were "eternal children," and this childlike quality extended to their tragic art. They did not seem to fully comprehend the grandeur of the sublime creation they had brought into being or the profound plaything they had devised. And, like children, they also seemed unaware of how quickly and easily they could demolish what they had so masterfully constructed.

The yearning of the musical spirit for symbolic and mythic expression, which began modestly in early lyric poetry and reached its most luxuriant development in Attic tragedy, came to an abrupt halt. It seemed to vanish from the surface of Hellenic art just as it had flourished most richly. Yet the Dionysian worldview, born from this same musical striving, did not disappear entirely. Instead, it continued to live on in the Mysteries, finding expression in strange transformations and even debasements, and it remained a source of fascination for those of earnest disposition.

Might it be that one day this Dionysian vision, submerged in the depths of mysticism, will rise again to the surface as art? Will it reemerge in a new form, reclaiming its rightful place and giving voice once more to the eternal truths it once so powerfully embodied? Such questions linger, as the spirit of music and myth continues to stir within the hidden recesses of the human soul.

Here we are faced with the question of whether the force that once opposed and ultimately caused the downfall of tragedy is powerful enough to forever suppress the revival of both tragic art and the tragic view of life. If ancient tragedy was overthrown by the relentless advance of dialectical reasoning and the optimism of scientific thought, it might suggest that there exists an enduring conflict between the theoretical worldview and the tragic worldview. It would then follow that only when the spirit of science reaches its limits, and its claims to universal validity are dismantled by its inability to transcend those boundaries, could we hope for the rebirth of tragedy. Such a revival might align with the cultural image of the "music-practicing Socrates" we discussed earlier, representing a fusion of intellectual insight and artistic intuition.

In this context, the "spirit of science" refers to the belief that Socrates first personified—the conviction that nature can be fully understood and that knowledge acts as a universal remedy for all human ills. If we consider the immediate consequences of this ever-pressing drive toward scientific understanding, it becomes clear that it led to the destruction of myth. In the wake of this destruction, poetry, detached from its natural and ideal foundation, was left homeless and displaced. If, as we have argued, music has the inherent ability to regenerate myth from within itself, then we must also recognize that the spirit of science actively works to oppose this myth-creating power of music.

This antagonism is particularly evident in the emergence of the New Attic Dithyramb, a form of music that no longer conveyed the inner essence of things—the will itself—but instead attempted to mimic outward appearances through conceptual representation. This shift marked a profound degeneration of music, reducing it to mere imitation. Truly musical individuals instinctively recoiled from this degraded art form, as they did from the art-destroying tendencies embodied by Socrates. Aristophanes, with his sharp instinct for cultural criticism, rightfully grouped Socrates, the tragedy of Euripides, and the music of the New Dithyrambic poets into the same category of cultural decline. He correctly perceived these as symptoms of a deteriorating culture.

In this New Dithyramb, music was outrageously reduced to the role of mimicking external phenomena—imitating battles or storms at sea, for example. By doing so, it was stripped of its capacity to create myth. This approach sought to delight audiences by forcing them to find superficial analogies between natural or human processes and the rhythms or sounds of music. However, this reductive imitation leaves no space for the reception of myth, which demands to be apprehended as a profound, universal truth transcending specific phenomena. True Dionysian music, by contrast, functions as a vast mirror reflecting the universal will. Within this mirror, individual events are refracted and elevated to represent eternal truths, expanding our consciousness to encompass a greater reality.

In stark opposition, the tone-painting of the New Dithyramb deprives events of their mythical essence. Instead of deepening our understanding, it transforms music into a feeble copy of the phenomena it seeks to portray. This imitation impoverishes not only the music itself but also our perception of the phenomena, reducing them to superficial representations. For instance, a musical imitation of a battle may consist solely of marches and signal calls, leaving the imagination stranded in trivialities. Tone- painting, therefore, stands in complete opposition to true music and its myth-creating power. Whereas true Dionysian music expands and enriches phenomena into a cosmic vision, tone- painting trivializes and diminishes them, leaving the listener trapped in a shallow realm of surface details.

The rise of the New Dithyramb marked a decisive victory for the anti- Dionysian spirit, as it severed music from its true essence and subordinated it to the imitation of external appearances. Euripides, who must be regarded—albeit on a higher plane— as fundamentally unmusical in nature, eagerly embraced this degraded form of music. He freely appropriated its flashy techniques and superficial effects, deploying them with the opportunistic flair of a plunderer. In doing so, Euripides aligned himself with the forces that had estranged music from its mythic origins, accelerating the cultural shift away from the Dionysian spirit that once sustained the tragic worldview.

In another dimension, we observe the potent influence of this un- Dionysian, anti-mythic spirit when we consider the rise of character portrayal and psychological complexity that emerged with Sophocles and developed further thereafter. Characters could no longer embody eternal, universal types; instead, they had to manifest unique individuality through detailed artistic nuances and intricate psychological shading. This shift made the audience less conscious of the underlying myth and more absorbed in the individual artistry of the character's representation. The myth, which once enveloped the narrative in universal significance, faded into the background, overtaken by an almost scientific fascination with individual peculiarities and the intricate anatomy of human nature. Here we witness the triumph of the specific over the universal and the elevation of analysis over the symbolic unity of myth.

Sophocles, although still shaping complete, multi-dimensional characters within mythic frameworks, set the stage for Euripides, who shifted focus to fragmented and exaggerated individual traits. These traits found their fullest expression in moments of intense passion or psychological outbursts. By the time we reach the New Attic Comedy, this trend culminates in a world populated by caricatures—stock figures like frivolous old men, cunning slaves, and duped panders endlessly repeated, each reduced to a single defining trait. The mythopoeic spirit of music, the profound creative force that once birthed myths, had now all but vanished. What remained was either excitatory music— a stimulant for weary nerves—or superficial tone-painting that imitated phenomena without capturing their deeper essence. The heroes and choruses of Euripides already displayed this dissolution, and his successors only amplified this trend.

This un-Dionysian spirit reveals itself most starkly in the resolutions—or dénouements—of later dramas. In the Old Tragedy, the audience left with a profound sense of metaphysical consolation, a feeling that transcended the suffering portrayed on stage. This consolation, resonating most purely perhaps in Sophocles' Oedipus at Colonus, affirmed the eternal truths underpinning the tragic experience. But with the departure of music's genius from tragedy, this profound metaphysical comfort was lost. In its place, earthly resolutions were introduced. Heroes, after enduring sufficient torment, would be rewarded with material gains—perhaps a splendid marriage or divine approval. The tragic hero was transformed into a mere gladiator, battered and bruised for the entertainment of the audience, and then granted freedom as a reward. Where once the audience encountered the solace of eternal truths, they now faced the artificial contrivance of a deus ex machina, a mechanical resolution imposed upon the narrative.

The tragic worldview was not entirely eradicated by this new anti-Dionysian spirit; rather, it was forced to retreat into hidden realms, surviving in the shadows as a secretive cult or mystical tradition. Yet across the broader Hellenic world, this spirit spread with a devouring fervor, manifesting itself in a shallow form of so-called "Greek cheerfulness." This was a senile and barren cheerfulness, in stark contrast to the earlier, vibrant naïveté of the Greeks. That earlier form of joy—springing from the Apollonian culture's triumph over the abyss of suffering—emerged from a profound mirroring of beauty and life. It was a radiant affirmation of existence despite the pain inherent within it.

By contrast, the cheerfulness of the later Alexandrian culture was symptomatic of a culture in decline. It celebrated the theoretical man, a figure who sought to dissolve the wisdom of Dionysus and the metaphysical comfort of myth. In place of myth, this spirit offered the contrived resolutions of human ingenuity— the god of the machine and the laboratory, the power of human knowledge harnessed to serve egoistic ends. This theoretical worldview clung to the belief that existence could be justified and improved through the accumulation of knowledge, that life could be contained within a manageable framework of solvable problems. It encouraged a shallow love of life, proclaiming: "I embrace you, life, for you are worth knowing."

This phenomenon is not unique; it is eternal. The will to life, in its insatiable craving, perpetually ensnares beings within illusions that compel them to continue existing. Some are drawn onward by the Socratic thirst for knowledge, clinging to the hope that reason can heal the wounds of existence. Others are seduced by the veils of beauty art casts over life, while still others take solace in the metaphysical comfort that existence persists eternally beneath the ceaseless flux of appearances. These illusions are designed for those deeply sensitive individuals who feel the weight of existence most profoundly, offering them exquisite distractions from their existential despair. All culture, in essence, consists of these illusions, and depending on their composition, a culture may lean toward Socratic, artistic, or tragic orientations. Historically, these cultural modes have found expression as Alexandrian, Hellenic, or Buddhistic worldviews.

Our modern age is ensnared by Alexandrian culture, idealizing the theoretical man epitomized by Socrates. Modern education and intellectual life are rooted in this ideal, and other forms of existence struggle to assert themselves against this dominant paradigm. For centuries, the archetype of the cultured individual was synonymous with the scholar, and even our poetic traditions originated from learned imitations rather than organic artistic expression. The very structure of modern poetic forms, such as rhyme, betrays their origins in artificial experiments with borrowed languages.

How alien Faust, the quintessential modern man, must have seemed to the ancient Greeks! Faust, tormented by dissatisfaction, driven through the sciences by an insatiable thirst for knowledge, even aligning himself with the devil in his quest—he stands as a stark contrast to Socrates. Faust symbolizes the modern recognition of the limits of reason and the yearning for a shore in the boundless ocean of knowledge. When Goethe remarked to Eckermann, with a touch of naïve charm, that there is a "productiveness of deeds," he reminded us how incomprehensible the non-theoretical, action-driven existence has become to modern man. It is as though we need Goethe's wisdom to rediscover that such a mode of life is not only conceivable but perhaps even admirable.

We must not shy away from confronting what lies at the core of this Socratic culture: an optimism so unwavering that it deems itself absolute. This is not a modest optimism but one that aspires to dominate every aspect of existence. We must brace ourselves for the eventual harvest of such optimism, a process that may provoke unsettling transformations. As society imbibes this intellectual ferment down to its deepest layers, it begins to vibrate with restless aspirations and unfulfilled cravings. The belief in universal earthly happiness and the feasibility of a universally shared intellectual culture might gradually evolve into a formidable demand for this utopian vision—a demand that invokes, as if out of desperation, a Euripidean deus ex machina to fulfill it.

Let us be clear: Alexandrian culture, in its essence, requires a subordinate class—a class of slaves—to sustain itself over time. Yet, in its idealistic outlook, it denies the necessity of such a class. It cloaks its dependence in seductive affirmations of human dignity and the nobility of labor. But once the comforting allure of these affirmations has faded, society risks veering toward a grim reckoning. There is no calamity greater than an oppressed slave class that has come to view its subjugation as a profound injustice. When such a class awakens to its plight, it prepares not merely for its own revenge but for vengeance on behalf of all generations that have suffered under similar chains.

Faced with the brewing storms of such a reckoning, where can modern society turn for assurance? Our pale, fatigued religions, weakened to the point of mere scholasticism, offer little solace. These systems, built upon myths, now find their mythical roots withered and ineffective. Even in this realm, the optimistic spirit—this very force that has undermined the mythic foundations of religion—has seized control. It has infiltrated and eroded the last vestiges of metaphysical comfort, leaving society vulnerable to the consequences of its unchecked growth.

As the latent dangers of theoretical culture begin to disturb modern humanity, people start combing through their experiences in search of solutions to avert disaster. Yet they do so with little faith in the remedies at their disposal. Meanwhile, some great and profoundly gifted individuals have undertaken the monumental task of using science itself to illuminate the limitations and relativity of human knowledge. In doing so, they have challenged science's pretense of universal validity and ultimate authority. For the first time, they have exposed the illusion at the heart of this claim—that causality can reveal the innermost essence of things.

The extraordinary courage and intellectual rigor of philosophers such as Kant and Schopenhauer have enabled them to achieve the most challenging victory of all: a triumph over the optimism embedded within the essence of logic. This optimism, which had rested on supposedly indisputable eternal truths, believed in the complete intelligibility of the world and the solvability of its mysteries. It elevated concepts like space, time, and causality to the status of unconditioned, universally applicable laws. But Kant demonstrated that these constructs merely serve to elevate appearances—the illusory work of Māyā—to the level of ultimate reality. In doing so, they obscure the deeper truths of existence and render genuine knowledge of the essence of things unattainable. As Schopenhauer aptly remarked, such constructs only lull the dreamer into an even deeper slumber, deluding humanity with the illusion of understanding.

With this realization, a new form of culture emerges, one that I call tragic culture. Its defining feature is the replacement of science with wisdom as the ultimate goal of human aspiration. This wisdom remains unswayed by the dazzling allure of scientific achievements and instead seeks to confront existence as a whole. With an unwavering gaze, it contemplates the eternal suffering at the heart of existence, approaching it with a profound, empathetic love.

Let us imagine a generation arising with this bold vision, armed with a heroic desire to face the immense and the unfathomable.

Picture their fearless stride, their defiant rejection of the soft doctrines of optimism, and their resolute commitment to living fully and deeply. Such a generation, disciplined by an earnest engagement with the terror and beauty of existence, would undoubtedly crave a new form of art. They would yearn for an art that offers metaphysical solace—a tragic art that belongs to them as profoundly as Helen belonged to the Greeks. This art would be their response to life's ultimate questions, and they might echo the words of Faust in longing:

"And should I not, by all my fiercest will,

Draw forth the one true form to life instill?"

Now that the once-dominant Socratic culture finds itself shaken from two sides, its grip on the scepter of infallibility falters. On one hand, it trembles in the face of its own conclusions, which it is beginning to sense with unease. On the other hand, it has lost the naïve confidence it once held in the eternal validity of its foundational principles. The sight of this culture's dance of thought, constantly reaching out for new forms only to recoil in sudden horror, evokes a sad and restless spectacle. Like Mephistopheles with the seductive Lamiae, it flirts with alluring ideas but quickly withdraws, unsure of their value. This oscillation marks the symptom of the deep "breach" so often lamented as the fundamental affliction of modern culture.

The theoretical man, alarmed and dissatisfied with the consequences of his reasoning, no longer dares to surrender himself to the wild, icy current of existence. Instead, he paces nervously along the banks, fearful of the unpredictable forces of life. He no longer seeks to embrace life in its entirety, complete with its natural cruelties and inherent contradictions. His optimism has spoiled him, softening his outlook and making him shrink from the harsher truths of existence. At the same time, he recognizes that a culture founded on the principles of science is doomed if it grows illogical—if it evades the conclusions that its own reasoning demands.

This universal malaise is reflected in modern art. Desperate for solutions, one turns to the imitation of great productive eras and artistic geniuses of the past. One surrounds oneself with the treasures of "world literature," as if their accumulated wisdom could offer solace. One immerses oneself in the art and styles of every age, naming and categorizing them like Adam naming the animals. Yet this effort is in vain. Despite these attempts, the modern individual remains perpetually hungry, forever the critic, drained of joy and vitality. He is the quintessential Alexandrian man—a librarian and proofreader, buried in the dust of books and consumed by trivial corrections. His unfulfilled longing and disconnected existence are pitiable, and he ultimately goes blind from the unending labor of sifting through errors and minutiae.

The essence of Socratic culture can perhaps be most vividly captured by calling it the culture of the opera. It is within this art form that this culture has expressed itself with a remarkable naïveté, revealing its underlying aims and perceptions. This is especially surprising when we contrast the origins and development of opera with the eternal truths embodied in the Apollonian and Dionysian artistic impulses. To understand this, one need only consider the emergence of the stilor appresentativo and the recitative. How is it possible that this entirely externalized operatic music, devoid of true devotion, was greeted with such enthusiastic acclaim as if it were a rebirth of authentic music? How could an age that had recently given rise to the ineffable, sacred music of Palestrina—a towering achievement of the Christian Middle Ages—so readily embrace the shallow artifice of operatic expression?

One might be tempted to attribute the rapid spread of opera to the pleasure- seeking decadence of the Florentine elite or the vanity of their dramatic singers. However, such an explanation seems inadequate to account for the fervor with which opera was embraced. That this passion for a semi-musical form of speech emerged alongside the awe-inspiring harmonies of Palestrina is a paradox that demands deeper scrutiny. This coexistence can only be explained by the presence of an extra-artistic tendency within the essence of the recitative—a tendency that shaped its appeal and directed its rapid ascent. This dynamic reveals a profound shift in the cultural undercurrents of the time, one that replaced the spiritual depth of sacred music with the superficial allure of theatrical representation.

The listener, who desires to clearly hear the words beneath the music, finds his wishes accommodated by the singer, who leans toward speaking rather than fully singing. This approach intensifies the emotional delivery of the words in a kind of half- song, enhancing their pathos and making the meaning more accessible. By heightening the expressive force of the spoken words, the singer helps the audience grasp the narrative while reducing the role of music to a secondary element. Yet, a danger arises: if the singer allows the music to take precedence, the emotional impact of the speech and the clarity of the words risk being overwhelmed. On the other hand, the singer often feels drawn to the musicality of the performance and the opportunity to showcase technical vocal skill.

At this point, the "poet" intervenes, crafting the performance to suit the singer's dual inclinations. He introduces lyrical interjections, repetitions, and dramatic pauses—moments where the singer can immerse fully in the musical aspect without worrying about enunciating every word. This oscillation between expressive, half-sung speech and fully musical interludes defines the stilor appresentativo, a style that alternates rapidly between appealing to the intellect through words and evoking emotion through music. Yet this very alternation, unnatural and fundamentally contradictory to both the Apollonian ideal of clarity and the Dionysian principle of unity, suggests an origin for recitative that lies outside any true artistic instinct.

Recitative can therefore be understood as a blend of epic narrative and lyrical expression—though not a harmonious fusion, for these elements are too disparate to achieve true synthesis. Instead, the result is a superficial patchwork, a mosaic of parts stuck together without precedent in nature or artistic tradition. However, the inventors of recitative, along with the audiences of their time, believed quite differently. They were convinced that in stilor appresentativo, they had rediscovered the secret of ancient music. They imagined that this new style explained the legendary power of Orpheus, Amphion, and even Greek tragedy itself. To them, the recitative represented the revival of the pure and potent music of the Greeks.

This conviction was bolstered by their popular understanding of the Homeric world as the original and ideal human condition. They allowed themselves the illusion of having returned to a paradisiacal time, where music possessed an unmatched purity, strength, and innocence. In their pastoral plays, poets celebrated these qualities as central to their vision of humanity's idyllic beginnings. Within this context, opera emerged as a thoroughly modern yet paradoxical art form, arising not from aesthetic impulses but from the desire to fulfill an entirely non-aesthetic need. It expressed a longing for the idealized innocence of a mythical past and a belief in the inherent goodness of humanity.

Recitative was interpreted as the authentic language of this imagined "primitive man," while opera itself was seen as a return to his idyllic existence. In this vision, primitive man was a naturally good and artistic being who instinctively blended speech with song, breaking into full-throated melodies at the slightest emotional provocation. To the humanists of that era, this image served as a counterpoint to the Church's portrayal of humanity as innately corrupt. Opera thus became the artistic expression of an opposing doctrine: the celebration of humanity's natural goodness. For many intellectuals and artists, it provided solace amidst the uncertainties and upheavals of their time, offering an optimistic affirmation of human dignity and potential.

The deeper appeal—and the origin—of opera lay in its ability to fulfill this unspoken need: the optimistic glorification of humanity and the belief in a naturally good, creative, and artistic "primitive man." Over time, this principle of opera has evolved into something far more potent—a demand that now looms large in contemporary social movements. The image of the "good primitive man," once an aesthetic ideal, has transformed into a call for justice and recognition. Today, we cannot ignore its implications as it echoes through the political and cultural spheres, hinting at paradisiacal visions—but also at the potential upheavals such dreams may entail.

Opera, as a form of art, reflects the optimistic ideals of Alexandrine culture—a culture that prioritizes understanding and theoretical clarity over the instinctive and emotional depths of true artistic creation. It is no coincidence that opera was born from the desires of theoretical minds and critical laymen, rather than from artists themselves. This fact remains one of the most surprising aspects of art history. Opera originated as a response to the demands of those who lacked innate musicality yet insisted on comprehensibility above all else. These audiences dictated that music must serve the text, placing words in a dominant role akin to a master commanding a servant. To them, the word was as superior to the harmonic accompaniment as the soul is to the body.

This unartistic viewpoint shaped the early development of opera in Florence, where poets and singers in prominent intellectual circles sought to create a form of art tailored to their taste. Their work was grounded in a fundamental misunderstanding of art's essence. Unaware of the Dionysian depth of music, they transformed it into a vehicle for rhetorical expression, designed to evoke emotion through the stilor appresentativo. Lacking the ability to behold artistic visions, they turned to machinists and scenic designers to fabricate spectacles. Without grasping the true nature of artistic creation, they conjured an "artistic primitive man"—an idealized figure who sang and recited verses driven solely by passion. This idyllic conception falsely imagined that raw emotion alone could generate art, neglecting the deeper, more complex processes of artistic creation.

The foundation of opera thus rests on a flawed premise: the belief that every sentient person is inherently an artist. This idyllic notion, paired with the cheerful optimism of the theorist, led to a form of art governed by the tastes and demands of laypeople rather than true artistic instincts. If we consider the dual influences behind opera's origins, they converge on what can only be described as an idyllic tendency. Using Schiller's language, this tendency reflects a perspective in which both nature and the ideal are treated as realities, rather than as unattained aspirations or lost perfections.

According to this idyllic belief, there once existed a primitive age of humanity when individuals lived in perfect harmony with nature, embodying the ideal of artistic and moral purity. Opera was seen as a means of returning to this paradisiacal state—a nostalgic journey back to the origins of humanity's artistic expression. Just as Dante turned to Virgil as a guide to paradise, so did the creators of opera turn to Greek tragedy as a model, only to surpass it by restoring humanity's imagined original art world. This effort reflected a charming naivety, rooted in the belief that man, in his essence, was an eternally virtuous and artistic being—a shepherd fluting and singing in harmony with nature.

This cheerful optimism pervaded opera, which did not express the sorrow of an irretrievable loss but instead reveled in the joy of rediscovery. It celebrated an idyllic reality, allowing audiences to believe, however fleetingly, that this vision of harmony and innocence was tangible and attainable. Yet anyone who measured this idyllic opera against the harsh realities of human existence and the raw truths of primitive life would recoil with disdain. It would become clear that this supposed reality was nothing more than a fanciful illusion, a hollow escapism that could not withstand the scrutiny of genuine artistic seriousness.

To dismiss opera as mere illusion, however, is to underestimate its persistence and appeal. It embodies the cheerfulness of Alexandrine culture—a cheerfulness rooted in an idealized view of human nature and artistic creation. But what consequences does this have for art itself? Opera, born of unartistic impulses and sustained by idyllic fantasies, risks reducing art to a trivial pastime. Instead of confronting the profound truths of existence, it seduces audiences with superficial pleasures and escapist fantasies. This diversion undermines art's highest purpose: to provide metaphysical solace and to elevate humanity by confronting and transcending the suffering inherent in life.

The impact of opera extends beyond its own sphere, influencing the broader trajectory of modern music. As it gained prominence, the Dionysian essence of music—the capacity to reflect the cosmic and existential depths of existence— was eroded. Music, under the optimistic influence of opera, was stripped of its profound, universal mission and reduced to a source of formal enjoyment and light entertainment. This transformation parallels the shift from the tragic grandeur of the Æschylean worldview to the shallow optimism of Alexandrine culture. The decline of Dionysian music into the ornamental frivolity of the stilor appresentativo mirrors the broader cultural metamorphosis, in which profound artistic truths were replaced by superficial pleasures and theoretical ideals.

If, as we have outlined, the decline of the Dionysian spirit coincided with a profound transformation and decline in the character of the Hellene, then how much greater must be our hope when we perceive signs of a revival of that same Dionysian essence in our modern world. This awakening is not merely a faint echo of the past but a reversal of that earlier decline—a resurgence of the spirit that shaped the most profound expressions of art and life. The power of Herakles, bound and subdued in servitude to Omphale, cannot languish forever. The primordial energy of the Dionysian has already begun to manifest anew, particularly in the form of German music—a phenomenon utterly alien to the foundations of Socratic culture. Indeed, German music stands as a force inexplicable and antagonistic to the optimistic, knowledge- driven ideals of that tradition.

This music, which stretches its vast arc from Bach to Beethoven and from Beethoven to Wagner, emerges as a demon from unfathomable depths, defying all attempts by modern rationalism to capture or categorize it. No operatic melody, however intricate, nor the arithmetical rigor of counterpoint and fugue, can impose order upon this elemental force or compel it to yield its secrets. It resists the very frameworks of logic and beauty that Socratism holds dear. Witness the aesthetes who pursue this genius of music, clutching at it with their frail nets of "beauty," only to find themselves bewildered by its incomprehensible vitality. Their cries of "beauty! beauty!" betray not genuine reverence but a thinly veiled attempt to disguise their own inability to grasp the profound truths embodied in this music.

Consider these self-styled arbiters of taste more closely. Are they truly the favored children of nature, nurtured in the lap of the beautiful? Or do they seek in their aesthetic judgments a pretense to mask their own dullness and lack of emotional depth? One need only think of figures like Otto Jahn to see this hypocrisy laid bare. But let such impostors beware of German music, for it stands as a pure and purifying force—one that burns away falsehood and reveals the truth at the heart of existence. This music, like the fire-spirit described by Heraclitus, moves all things in a double orbit, consuming and creating anew. Everything we call culture, education, and civilization must one day stand before Dionysus, the unerring judge, to be measured and weighed.

Let us also recall the contributions of Kant and Schopenhauer, whose philosophical insights arose from the same Germanic sources and delivered a devastating critique of Socratic optimism. By defining the limits of knowledge, they undermined the complacent delight in existence that characterized scientific Socratism. In doing so, they opened the door to a deeper and more profound understanding of ethics and art—an understanding we might justly call Dionysian wisdom expressed through conceptual thought. This convergence of German music and philosophy points unmistakably to the emergence of a new form of existence, one whose substance we can only begin to glimpse through analogy with the Hellenic world.

For us, who stand on the boundary between two modes of existence, the Hellenic prototype offers an invaluable guide. It serves as a classical mirror reflecting the struggles and transitions that we now experience in reverse. Where the Greeks moved from the age of tragedy to the Alexandrine era, we seem to be journeying back from the Alexandrine age toward a new tragic epoch. In this sense, the rebirth of tragedy represents not an innovation but a return—a rediscovery of the German spirit's authentic self after a long period of external influence and cultural servitude. Having endured the distortions imposed by Romanic civilization, this spirit now finds itself prepared to walk confidently and independently among the nations, provided it is willing to learn from the Greeks—the greatest teachers humanity has ever known.

At no time have we needed these teachers more than now, when we stand on the threshold of a new tragic age. This moment of rebirth brings both opportunity and danger: the opportunity to reconnect with the profound truths embodied in tragedy, and the danger of misunderstanding its origins and failing to recognize its ultimate purpose. To comprehend where this rebirth comes from and to discern where it is leading, we must turn once again to the Greeks, whose wisdom remains the beacon guiding us through the uncharted waters of our own cultural transformation.

It is worth pondering when and in whom the German spirit has most ardently sought to learn from the Greeks. If we confidently assign this distinction to the intellectual achievements of Goethe, Schiller, and Winkelmann, we must also confront an unsettling reality: since their time, and following the immediate influence of their works, the pursuit of Greek ideals and culture has inexplicably waned. This decline cannot but give pause to those who cherish the German spirit. Might it not suggest that even these cultural luminaries, for all their efforts, fell short of penetrating the very essence of Hellenic nature? Could it be that they failed to establish a lasting alliance between Greek and German culture? If so, an unspoken awareness of this limitation might well have sown seeds of doubt in those who came after, leaving them uncertain whether further progress along this path was even possible—or whether the ultimate goal was attainable at all.

As a result, attitudes toward the Greek contribution to culture have deteriorated alarmingly. The once-reverent tone has given way to a blend of indifference and condescension. We now hear expressions of patronizing superiority from various intellectual and non-intellectual quarters alike, while elsewhere, empty rhetoric toys with phrases like "Greek harmony," "Greek beauty," and "Greek cheerfulness," drained of their original depth. Even within those institutions most entrusted with fostering German culture through the Greek legacy—the higher educational establishments—a disheartening compromise has emerged. Many educators have come to terms with the Greeks in ways that dilute or distort their value, often abandoning the Hellenic ideal altogether. Antiquarian studies have devolved into exercises in skepticism or aimless pedantry, reducing Greek culture to historical curiosity rather than a living source of inspiration.

In these academic circles, those who resist being confined to correcting ancient texts or dissecting linguistic minutiae often approach Greek antiquity through a "historical" lens, lumping it together with other eras and treating it with the detached air of modern historiography. As a result, the intrinsic effectiveness of higher education has perhaps never been weaker. Meanwhile, the "journalist," that servant of the moment, has overtaken the academic as the arbiter of culture, leaving the latter scrambling to adopt the breezy, superficial tone of popular media. The academic teacher, now a mere shadow of their former stature, flutters about as a lightweight cultural commentator, adapting to the ephemeral style of the journalist. Against this backdrop, one can scarcely imagine the bewilderment of those attuned to culture when confronted with a phenomenon as profound and enigmatic as the reawakening of the Dionysian spirit and the rebirth of tragedy.

This tension between so-called culture and genuine art has perhaps never been greater than in the present era. It is clear why a feeble culture harbors an instinctive hatred for true art— it fears annihilation at its hands. But must not the very domain of Socratic-Alexandrine culture, having stretched itself to the utmost, be nearing exhaustion? What else could be expected when such a culture has culminated in the fragile, precarious refinement of our own time? If even towering figures like Goethe and Schiller could not breach the enchanted gates of the Hellenic magic mountain—if their boldest efforts left them only with the yearning gaze of Goethe's Iphigenia, casting her longing eyes from barbaric Tauris toward her distant homeland—what can the successors of such heroes possibly hope for?

Yet, perhaps the gate will not yield to the labors of any who seek it through the well-trodden paths of culture as we have known it. Perhaps it will open only unexpectedly, in a wholly different place—one overlooked by all prior cultural endeavors—and amidst the mystical strains of a reawakened tragic music. There, within the resurgent Dionysian spirit, lies the possibility of rediscovering the profound truths that once animated the Hellenic world, truths that now beckon anew to the German spirit to rise from the shadows of its estrangement and reclaim its connection to art and life.

Let no one try to diminish our faith in the coming reawakening of Hellenic antiquity, for it is in this rebirth alone that we place our hopes for the revival and purification of the German spirit through the transformative power of music. Amidst the barrenness and lifelessness of the current cultural landscape, what else offers even the faintest glimmer of expectation for a brighter future? We search in vain for even a single robust, deeply rooted foundation, for the smallest patch of fertile, life-giving soil. All around us lies only dust and sand, stagnation and decay, a landscape where nothing grows, and where all vitality seems to have withered away.

In such desolate conditions, where no promising sign appears on the horizon, a solitary wanderer, resigned to his fate, might find no more fitting emblem of his plight than the image of the Knight with Death and the Devil, as Dürer so vividly captured. Clad in impenetrable armor, this knight bears a face set in grim determination, a countenance that speaks of stoic endurance even as his path is flanked by dreadful companions. Unyielding and undeterred by the specters of doom that accompany him, he rides forward with his loyal steed and hound, his journey defined by isolation and relentless pursuit, despite the hopelessness of the road ahead.

Such a figure is not merely a symbol; it is embodied in the figure of Schopenhauer, who stands as a true Dürerian knight of our age. He walked the path of truth, stripped of illusions and bereft of hope, yet never veering from his purpose. He sought truth with a singular and unyielding intensity, confronting the harsh realities of existence without flinching or faltering. In his stoic resolve and fearless search, he found a kind of nobility that remains unmatched. There is no other like him, and perhaps there never will be again.

How suddenly the desolate and dreary landscape of our weary culture is transformed when touched by the enchantment of Dionysian magic! A tempest erupts, sweeping away all that is decayed, withered, and feeble, hurling the remnants into a swirling crimson whirlwind of dust that spirals upward like a bird of prey taking flight. In the chaos, our eyes strain to find what has been carried off, but instead, they settle upon something entirely new—a realm bathed in golden light, emerging as if from a sunken gloom, vibrant and overflowing with green, teeming with the fullness of life, pulsing with boundless energy and infinite promise.

In the heart of this thriving abundance, tragedy takes her place, a figure both exalted and rapturous, embodying the intertwining of sorrow and joy in sublime harmony. She listens intently to a distant, haunting melody—a lament that whispers of the primordial Mothers of Being, those ancient forces named Delusion, Will, and Woe. This song does not speak of despair, but rather of profound truths that underlie all existence, truths that tragedy herself transforms into a celebration of life in its most profound and unbridled form.

Yes, my friends, join me in believing in this Dionysian life and in the reawakening of tragedy, for it is upon us! The era of the Socratic man, with his dry rationalism and insatiable quest to dissect the mysteries of existence, has come to an end. Let us adorn ourselves with ivy, a symbol of eternal growth, and grasp the thyrsus, the sacred staff of Dionysus. Do not be astonished if wild creatures—tigers, panthers, and other beasts of untamed spirit—approach and lay themselves at your feet, tamed not by fear but by the awe of your newfound power.

Now is the time to embrace your destiny as tragic beings. Let go of your hesitation and step boldly into the revelry of Dionysian life, for in this transformation, you shall find redemption. You are called to join the great Dionysian procession, journeying from the mystic lands of India to the luminous shores of Greece. Arm yourselves for the struggle ahead, for the path will not be without its trials. Yet take heart and place your faith in the miraculous wonders of the god who calls you. It is through him, through this embrace of the tragic and the divine, that you shall rise anew, and the world shall once again be aflame with life's uncontainable beauty and power.

Returning now from these exhortative tones to the reflective mood suited to a contemplative mind, I reiterate: only from the Greeks can we learn what the sudden and miraculous awakening of tragedy signifies for the fundamental essence of a people's life. It was the people steeped in the mysteries of tragedy who fought the battles against the Persians. Equally, it was the people who endured and emerged victorious from such wars who found in tragedy not merely a cultural adornment but an essential healing elixir for their collective soul.

Who could have foreseen that, within this very people—who for generations had been shaken to their core by the violent upheavals of the Dionysian spirit—there still resided such a potent and unified expression of the simplest political loyalties, the most natural domestic instincts, and the primal, unrestrained joy in the struggles of life? Indeed, every significant eruption of the Dionysian forces initially manifests as a loosening from the constraints of individual identity, leading, in many cases, to an indifference or even hostility toward political structures and civic order. Yet, we must also recognize that the Apollonian force—the state-forming genius of the principium individuationis—stands in sharp contrast to this chaos, for it upholds the structures of the state and nurtures the sentiment of personal and domestic stability, which cannot thrive without a firm assertion of individuality.

A people swept up in Dionysian ecstasy ultimately face only one path if such energy remains unchecked: the road toward Indian Buddhism. This path, with its yearning for ultimate nothingness, requires rarefied ecstatic states to make existence bearable, offering a fleeting elevation beyond space, time, and individuality. These states, in turn, necessitate a philosophy capable of softening the profound gloom of the intermediate phases with imaginative flights of thought. Conversely, when a people are dominated by relentless political impulses, they are inexorably driven toward radical secularization, the most magnificent yet most terrifying expression of which is the Roman imperium.

Situated between the ascetic mysticism of India and the brutal pragmatism of Rome, the Greeks succeeded in devising a third way—a form of life marked by classical purity and balance. This way was not meant for long-term private use; rather, it achieved immortality precisely because of its brevity. As the old adage goes, "Those whom the gods love die young," but equally true is the belief that such lives are elevated to eternal communion with the divine. It would be wrong to demand from the noblest forms of existence the rugged durability of coarse materials. The tenacious resilience inherent in the Roman character, for example, is not necessarily a hallmark of ultimate greatness or perfection.

If we inquire how the Greeks, during their most luminous era, managed to avoid both the self-destructive ecstasies of Dionysian contemplation and the soul-draining pursuits of imperial ambition, we are drawn inevitably to the immense power of tragedy. Tragedy acted as a force of excitation, purification, and catharsis, unburdening and rejuvenating the collective life of the Greek people. Its value lies not simply in its artistic beauty but in its unparalleled capacity to harmonize and mediate between the most potent and perilous tendencies of a nation. Tragedy stands as the essence of all healing and prophylactic forces, a divine mediator that reconciles and balances the most fateful elements within a culture. In the Greeks, we see this sublime interplay at its zenith, a reminder that true greatness resides not in rigid durability but in the brief, brilliant radiance of an enduring legacy.

Tragedy, as the ultimate vessel of artistic expression, absorbs the peak of musical ecstasy into its form, achieving an unparalleled perfection of music among the Greeks and, in a different manner, among ourselves. Yet tragedy transcends mere musical fulfillment by placing beside it the tragic myth and the tragic hero—figures that stand like colossal Titans bearing the weight of the entire Dionysian world upon their shoulders, thereby relieving us of its overwhelming burden. Through the figure of the tragic hero, tragedy achieves something even more profound: it liberates us from the consuming desire for this fleeting existence and directs our gaze toward another realm of existence and a higher form of joy. The hero, destroyed rather than victorious, becomes a harbinger of this transcendence, preparing himself and, by extension, the spectator for the promise of something greater.

Tragedy, in its sublime artistry, positions myth as a powerful intermediary between the universal authority of its music and the receptive, Dionysian audience. The result is an enchanting illusion that convinces the spectator that music serves primarily to animate the vivid, plastic world of myth. Under the protection of this noble illusion, tragedy is free to engage in the ecstatic dithyrambic dance, surrendering itself to an unrestrained orgiastic sense of freedom. Such liberation could not be indulged in as pure music alone without this mythic framework to temper and contextualize its power. Myth acts as a safeguard against the overwhelming force of music, while simultaneously granting it the ultimate freedom to communicate its truths. In return, music imbues tragic myth with a metaphysical depth and significance that no combination of words or imagery alone could ever achieve. Through this union, the tragic spectator experiences an almost mystical awareness of a supreme joy that lies beyond destruction and negation, hearing, as it were, the profound whispers of the universe's innermost abyss speaking directly to him.

If, in these observations, I have managed to offer even a preliminary understanding of this complex relationship, it may be accessible only to a select few at first. Yet, I must persist in encouraging my companions in thought to explore this concept further and to prepare themselves by reflecting on a detached example from our shared experiences. I must, however, draw a clear distinction here: I am not addressing those who rely solely on the scenic imagery, the spoken words, or the dramatic emotions of the performers as their primary means of approaching musical understanding. Such individuals, though they may attempt to use these elements as bridges to music, can never move beyond the outskirts of true musical perception; they remain, as it were, outside the sacred temple of music's innermost sanctuaries. Some, like Gervinus, fail even to reach those outskirts.

Instead, I turn to those who are intimately connected with music, for whom it serves as a kind of maternal embrace—a primal language through which they engage with the world on a nearly unconscious level. To these genuine musicians, I pose the question: can you imagine a person capable of listening to the third act of Tristan und Isolde without the aid of words or stagecraft, experiencing it solely as an immense symphonic movement, without feeling as though their very soul might burst apart under the strain of its transcendental force?

Consider a person who, in such a state, has figuratively placed their ear against the very heart of the cosmic will, feeling the furious torrents of desire for existence surge forth as a deafening cascade or a gentle brook into every vein of the universe. Could such a person endure the ceaseless echoes of joy and anguish emanating from the boundless void of cosmic night? Would they not, overwhelmed by the metaphysical symphony of existence, be irresistibly drawn back to their primordial origin, carried away by the pastoral melody of eternal truth? And yet, if such a monumental work can be experienced in its entirety without necessitating the obliteration of individual existence, and if such a creation can come into being without shattering its creator—where, then, are we to find the resolution to this profound contradiction?

Between our deepest musical ecstasy and the music in question, there stand the tragic myth and the tragic hero, symbols that embody the most universal truths—truths which only music can convey directly. If we could fully immerse ourselves as pure Dionysian beings, these symbols, such as myth, would become irrelevant and go unnoticed. They would not obstruct the pure resonance of the universalia ante rem, the eternal truths of existence. Yet, in this moment of near-disintegration, when the individual teeters on the edge of dissolution, the restorative power of the Apollonian bursts forth like a healing balm. It provides a blissful illusion that reconstitutes the self. Suddenly, we no longer hear the primordial cries of existence but instead focus on Tristan, his voice subdued, pondering, "The old tune, why does it wake me?" The immense cosmic ache that once swept through us, like a vast and hollow sigh from the depths of being, now narrows its focus, expressing itself only in the lament: "Waste and void is the sea."

When we had been pushed to the brink, our feelings stretched to their utmost limits, tethered to existence by the thinnest thread, we now see only the hero, mortally wounded yet unable to die, crying out in despair: "Longing! Longing! In dying still longing! For longing, not dying!" Earlier, the overwhelming jubilation of creation and renewal rent our hearts with its excruciating intensity; but now, Kurwenal stands before us, mediating between us and the raw essence of that jubilation, his gaze fixed upon the approaching ship carrying Isolde. The Apollonian influence transforms even our most profound shared suffering, lifting us from the primordial agony of existence. In this way, the mythic image protects us from directly confronting the ultimate cosmic truths, just as thought and language protect us from the untamed flood of the unconscious will. The radiant illusion of the Apollonian makes it seem as if the realm of tones itself takes form as a tangible, sculpted cosmos, and as if the fate of Tristan and Isolde is shaped and molded from the most delicate and responsive material.

Thus, the Apollonian draws us away from Dionysian universality, anchoring us instead in an admiration for individuals. It captivates our emotions, rivets them to the fate of these figures, and satisfies our yearning for beauty by presenting sublime, majestic forms. Through these forms, it encourages contemplation of life's essence, captured in vivid, biographical portrayals. The Apollonian influence lifts us out of our Dionysian self- dissolution, transforming the chaotic, universal process into a comprehensible, distinct representation—a picture of the world, epitomized by Tristan and Isolde. Through music, we believe we are not only seeing this picture but perceiving it with greater clarity and depth. Such is the enchanting magic of Apollo that it can convince us of the illusion that Dionysian forces serve the Apollonian, that music itself becomes a vehicle for expressing an Apollonian reality.

The preordained harmony between a perfect drama and its music elevates the clarity and impact of the drama to a level that mere spoken theater can seldom achieve. The figures on stage, animated in their independent melodic lines, resolve themselves into a harmonious simplicity before our eyes, as distinct and graceful as a flowing catenary curve. Simultaneously, the coexistence of these melodic lines is audibly expressed through harmonic shifts, which resonate with the unfolding action. These harmonic changes reveal the relationships between elements in a tangible and immediate way, allowing us to perceive the essence of each character and melodic line with a directness that transcends abstraction. Music, in this way, compels us to see beyond the surface, to engage with the world of the stage more profoundly. It expands the visible world into a vast, luminous cosmos that unfolds both outwardly and inwardly, illuminating itself from within for our introspective gaze.

The word-poet, by contrast, struggles to achieve anything comparable. The mechanisms of spoken language and conceptual thought are far less refined for achieving the expansive illumination of the stage-world that musical tragedy so effortlessly provides. While musical tragedy also employs words, it roots them in their source, laying bare the foundation from which they emerge. It renders visible the process by which words and meaning unfold outward, allowing us to witness their growth as though from within the very core of existence. In this way, musical tragedy achieves an internal coherence and radiance that transcends what mere language could ever hope to accomplish.

The process described above could still be accurately characterized as a magnificent appearance, an exalted manifestation of the Apollonian illusion. Through this illusion, we are momentarily shielded from the overwhelming force and chaotic exuberance of the Dionysian. Yet, upon closer examination, it becomes evident that the true relationship between music and drama is fundamentally inverted compared to what this Apollonian veil might suggest. Music represents the profound essence, the adequate idea of the world itself, while drama emerges as a reflection, a faint shadow of this idea, a surface emanation that does not directly engage with the deeper reality it seeks to depict.

The supposed congruence between the melodic line and the structural form, or between the harmonic framework and the relational dynamics of the characters, must be understood in a way entirely contrary to the impression created by musical tragedy. No matter how vividly the form is animated or how brightly it is illuminated, it remains tethered to the realm of phenomena. It is an outward manifestation, incapable of bridging the chasm that separates the world of appearances from the core reality, the true heart of existence. Music, by contrast, speaks directly from that core, embodying its essence. Even though countless forms might emerge as expressions of music, none of them can ever exhaust its infinite depth; they are merely surface reflections, externalized echoes of its profound interiority.

The intricate interplay between music and drama defies simple explanation, and it is often obscured by the pervasive yet false dichotomy of soul and body. This crude opposition has become a convenient yet misleading dogma for many aestheticians, who either lack the philosophical insight to recognize the more profound distinction between phenomenon and thing-in-itself or have chosen, perhaps deliberately, to ignore it altogether.

If our analysis has demonstrated that the Apollonian element in tragedy has, through its veiling power, achieved dominance over the primal Dionysian force of music—making music subordinate to the goal of rendering the drama as lucid and articulate as possible—then an important qualification must be made. At the most pivotal moment, this Apollonian illusion does not merely falter; it is dismantled and ultimately negated. The drama, enriched by music and rendered with extraordinary clarity in all its movements and figures, achieves an overall effect that surpasses all purely Apollonian artistic accomplishments.

In the total effect of tragedy, the Dionysian reasserts its supremacy. Tragedy concludes with an impact that transcends the bounds of Apollonian art, producing a resonance that could never originate from its domain. Thus, the Apollonian illusion is revealed for what it is—a careful disguise that momentarily conceals the underlying Dionysian essence of tragedy. Yet this Dionysian power is so overwhelming that it ultimately compels the Apollonian structure to enter a realm where it speaks with the wisdom of Dionysus and even renounces its own clarity and distinctness.

The complex relationship between the Apollonian and Dionysian in tragedy must therefore be understood as a profound synthesis, a fraternal union of these two opposing forces. Dionysus finds expression through the voice of Apollo, while Apollo, in turn, adopts the language of Dionysus. In this harmonious interplay, the highest purpose of tragedy—and of art itself—is fulfilled. Herein lies the sublime achievement of tragedy, where the seemingly disparate forces of creation unite to illuminate the profound truths of existence, offering a vision of unity that transcends both the Apollonian world of form and the Dionysian chaos of the abyss.

Picture the experience of watching a true musical tragedy, drawn simply from your own memories and impressions. I believe I've described this experience in both of its main aspects, so you should now be able to relate it to what you have felt yourself. You may remember that, as the myth unfolded before you, you felt lifted to a state of almost godlike awareness, as if your ability to perceive was no longer limited to the surface of things but had reached deep within. With the help of the music, it seemed as though you could actually see the inner surges of the will, the clash of emotions, and the powerful currents of passion. These inner forces appeared almost as if they were visible, taking the shape of vivid, moving lines and figures. Through this, you found yourself immersed in the deepest secrets of feelings that lie beyond conscious awareness.

As you reached this heightened state, your instinct for recognizing beauty and transformation grew stronger than ever. Yet even so, you may have also noticed something else just as clearly: this series of artistic effects, as wondrous as it was, didn't bring about the serene, detached contemplation that comes from purely Apollonian art, such as sculpture or epic poetry. These Apollonian forms of art allow you to see the world as justified through its distinct shapes and individualities. But with musical tragedy, something different occurs. You witness the world of the stage transformed and glorified, yet you still reject it. You see the tragic hero portrayed with sharp clarity and beauty, yet you find yourself oddly pleased by their destruction. The events of the play unfold with perfect precision, and yet you long to escape into the unknown. You understand the hero's actions as fair and reasonable, yet you feel even greater joy when those actions destroy the hero. You are moved by the suffering that the hero endures, yet this suffering also fills you with a strange and overwhelming sense of joy. It is as if you see more deeply and widely than ever before, yet paradoxically, you desire to close your eyes.

How can we explain this strange contradiction? This collapse of the Apollonian clarity and order seems to arise from the influence of the Dionysian force. While the Dionysian energy heightens and magnifies the effects of Apollonian art, it ultimately bends that Apollonian power to its own purpose. Tragic myth, therefore, serves as a symbol of the wisdom of the Dionysian spirit, expressed through the tools and techniques of Apollonian art. Through myth, the visible world of appearances is led to its limits, where it denies itself and seeks to return to the one true reality. In that moment, myth gives voice to this return, much like Isolde's metaphysical swan song:

"In the billowing surge of the sea of delight, In the fragrant waves of sound, In the wafting breath of the universe— Drown— sink— unconscious—supreme bliss!"

In considering the experiences of the truly aesthetic listener, we begin to grasp the essence of the tragic artist. This artist, like a divine creator of infinite fertility, shapes individual figures— not as mere imitations of nature, but as manifestations of his Apollonian creative impulse. Yet this same artist is also driven by a vast Dionysian force that seeks to embrace the entire world of appearances, only to transcend and annihilate it in pursuit of the primal artistic joy found within the core of existence, the Primordial Unity. Strangely, our aestheticians have little to say about this dynamic interplay between the Apollonian and Dionysian elements or their impact on the listener. Instead, they tirelessly focus on notions such as the hero's struggle with fate, the triumph of moral order, or the cathartic release of emotions through tragedy. These interpretations suggest that such aestheticians may not experience tragedy aesthetically at all, but rather as moral observers.

Since Aristotle, no explanation of tragedy's effect has adequately described its aesthetic impact on the audience as arising from its artistic elements. Some claim that fear and pity are purged through catharsis, offering emotional relief, while others argue that tragedy uplifts us through the victory of noble ideals or the hero's sacrifice for a moral vision of the world. While it's clear that many people experience tragedy in this way, such responses reveal that they, and their interpreting aestheticians, lack an understanding of tragedy as the highest form of art. Aristotle's concept of catharsis, whether understood as medicinal or moral, parallels Goethe's admission: "Without a lively pathological interest, I have never succeeded in developing a tragic situation, and I have often avoided attempting one." Goethe speculated that perhaps the ancients achieved a purely aesthetic form of pathos, while we require the "truth of nature" to create such works. Recent experiences with musical tragedy reveal that the deepest pathos can indeed function as aesthetic play. This insight permits us, for the first time, to approach a clearer understanding of tragedy's primal essence.

Those who persist in discussing tragedy solely in terms of external effects, whether moral or psychological, and who cannot elevate themselves above such interpretations, might despair of their aesthetic capacities. For them, we might recommend studying Shakespeare through the lens of Gervinus or pursuing poetic justice as a harmless substitute. With the rebirth of tragedy, however, the aesthetic listener is also reborn. Replacing the pseudo-aesthetic critics who once occupied the theater are genuine participants in the experience of art. These critics, embodying a curious blend of moralistic and intellectual pretensions, have shaped the theater into a place of artificiality. Performers, playwrights, and composers, caught in the grip of these lifeless audiences, have struggled to engage their creativity with such barren and unresponsive spectators. These critics have long constituted the primary audience, influencing education and social perceptions of art, often to the detriment of authentic engagement.

Artists of nobler inclinations have sought to awaken moral and religious feelings in their audiences, invoking ideals of a moral world order to compensate for the absence of true artistic enchantment. Dramatists have depicted political and social tensions so vividly that audiences, fatigued by criticism, could feel swept away by emotions similar to those evoked by political speeches or moral debates. Yet this diversion of art toward such "tendencies" has led to a rapid deterioration of purpose. For instance, the idea that theater might serve as a means of moral education—a notion taken seriously in Schiller's time—has now become a relic of a bygone culture.

As critics took control of theaters and concert halls, journalists dominated schools, and the press shaped social discourse, art devolved into mere conversational fodder. Aesthetic criticism became the glue holding together a fragmented, self-absorbed, and unoriginal society, much like the porcupines in Schopenhauer's parable, who huddle together for warmth yet prick one another with their quills. In such an environment, talk about art flourished, but genuine respect for it dwindled. Can we still converse meaningfully with someone about Beethoven or Shakespeare?

Let each answer this question honestly. The response will reveal their notion of culture—provided they can even articulate an answer and have not fallen silent in bewilderment.

Some individuals, possessing a more refined and noble nature despite having been shaped into critical barbarians as previously described, might recall an unexpected and entirely inexplicable impact from witnessing a successful performance of Lohengrin, for instance. Such an experience could leave them bewildered, especially if they lacked any guiding hand to help interpret or explain it. This led to a sensation that felt both strikingly unique and utterly unmatched—a feeling so extraordinary that it remained isolated, burning brightly for a fleeting moment before fading away like a mysterious star in the night sky. Yet, in that brief brilliance, they perhaps caught a glimpse of what it means to be a true aesthetic listener.

In the sea of pleasure's Billowing waves,

In the ether's flow, Tolling like chimes,

In the world's breath Moving and whole— To drown, to sink,

Lost in a swoon—the greatest gift!

Anyone who wishes to examine rigorously their own capacity to resonate with the true aesthetic listener—or to determine whether they are instead more aligned with the mindset of the Socrato-critical individual—need only ask themselves how they respond to the element of wonder portrayed on stage. Do they feel their historical sensibilities, rooted in strict psychological causality, affronted by such depictions? Do they instead view the wonder with a sort of indulgent tolerance, as something suitable for a child's understanding but long since abandoned by their own matured intellect? Or do they experience something altogether different, something deeper and more profound? By probing this response, one can gauge their overall ability to comprehend myth— that distilled, concentrated vision of the world which, as a condensed representation of phenomena, must necessarily embrace the marvelous and the extraordinary.

Yet, for most individuals, it is likely that when they examine themselves honestly, they will find they have been so fragmented by the critico-historical spirit of our age that they can only attempt to grasp the past reality of myth through abstract, scholarly reconstructions. Without myth, however, no culture can retain its vital, generative force. It is only within a horizon bounded by myths that a society's movements achieve unity and coherence. Myth alone can channel the energies of imagination and the Apollonian dream, preventing them from wandering aimlessly and losing their potency. The mythical figures must serve as the unseen guardians, ever-present but intangible, whose silent influence nurtures the development of young minds. These figures offer the symbols by which individuals find meaning in their lives and the inspiration to strive and endure. Even the state itself, in its deepest structure, derives its most binding unwritten laws from the mythical foundation that affirms its connection to religion and roots its growth in mythical ideas. Without such grounding, a culture risks becoming aimless, fragmented, and ultimately incapable of renewal.

Let us now consider the abstract man, untethered from myth, navigating a world defined by abstract education, abstract customs, abstract laws, and an abstract state. Imagine the unchecked wandering of artistic imagination unmoored from the guidance of any native myth. Envision a culture without a sacred and stable origin, one doomed to exhaust every possibility while desperately sustaining itself on borrowed fragments of other cultures. This is the condition of the present, the result of Socratism's relentless drive to dismantle myth. In this state, the man deprived of myth becomes a perpetual hungerer, endlessly searching through the remnants of history, sifting through the dust of antiquity in a futile effort to find nourishment. The insatiable appetite for knowledge, the feverish gathering of disparate cultural elements, and the endless pursuit of historical discovery—what does all of this signify if not the profound loss of myth, the loss of a mythical homeland and its life-giving source?

Let us question whether the frantic, almost uncanny energy of modern culture is anything more than the desperate grasping of a famished spirit. What value does this culture hold, a culture that remains insatiable despite devouring everything in its path? Worse still, even the most nourishing and vibrant contributions it consumes are transformed, reduced to lifeless "history and criticism" in its grip. Who would willingly contribute more to a culture that, in its contact, drains vitality and transforms the rich into the sterile?

We might despair for our German spirit if it were entirely enmeshed in this culture or, even more dire, indistinguishable from it. Such an identity, which has for so long given France its cultural dominance, now serves as a cautionary example. For as we observe with growing horror, this complete merging of people and culture in France has led to a hollow civilization. How fortunate we are, by contrast, that this dubious culture has not yet merged with the noble core of the German character. Indeed, our hopes lie in recognizing that beneath the restless and chaotic surface of our so-called civilization, beneath the upheaval of education and society, there resides a profound and inherently healthy primal force. This deep, ancient vitality awakens only in rare, transformative moments before retreating once more into a slumber, waiting for its time to rise again.

It is from this hidden wellspring that the German Reformation emerged, heralded by its chorale hymns. In those hymns resounded the first melodies of what would become German music, imbued with depth, courage, and the breath of the soul. These hymns, overflowing with goodness and tenderness, carried the power of a springtime awakening—a Dionysian call bursting through the dense thickets of winter. This call was answered by the jubilant, spirited procession of Dionysian revelers, to whom we owe the birth of German music. From these same roots, we may yet see the reawakening of German myth, an event that promises to restore the soul of our people.

I now feel compelled to guide the sympathetic and attentive reader to a higher plane of solitary contemplation, a place where the path becomes lonelier and companions fewer. Yet, I urge you to hold steadfast to the radiant guides who have illuminated our way thus far—the Greeks. From them, we have drawn the two divine figures who preside over distinct realms of art, and whose interplay and elevation we have glimpsed most clearly through the phenomenon of Greek tragedy. However, the disruption and eventual severing of these primal artistic forces heralded the demise of Greek tragedy itself—a downfall that was intricately linked to the transformation and eventual decline of the Greek national character. This connection prompts us to reflect deeply on how art and the people, myth and custom, tragedy and the state, are fundamentally interwoven at their very core.

The collapse of tragedy coincided with the collapse of myth. Until that point, the Greeks had lived with an almost instinctive need to anchor every experience to their myths, interpreting life and its events solely through these associations. This unbroken link with myth imbued even the immediate present with a sense of the eternal, allowing the Greeks to view their world through the lens of timelessness. Art and the state, too, were immersed in this current of the eternal, finding in it a sanctuary from the demands and chaos of the fleeting moment. A people—or even an individual—is only as valuable as its ability to inscribe the stamp of eternity upon its experiences, thereby transcending the purely temporal and demonstrating an unconscious recognition of life's metaphysical meaning. It is through this process that the secular veil is lifted, and life reveals its profound and timeless truths.

The reverse occurs when a people begins to understand itself solely through the lens of history, dismantling the mythical structures that once defined and protected it. This shift inevitably leads to a pronounced secularization, severing ties with the unconscious metaphysical foundations of earlier existence and manifesting in profound ethical consequences. Greek art, and particularly Greek tragedy, served as a powerful force delaying this destruction of myth. But once myth had been eroded, it became necessary to obliterate art itself to achieve a life detached from the native soil—a life unmoored, wandering aimlessly through the unbridled wilderness of thought, behavior, and action.

Even in such barren conditions, the metaphysical impulse within the human spirit continues to seek expression. In its diminished form, it finds a kind of exaltation in the Socratic pursuit of knowledge and the relentless drive to bring meaning to life through scientific inquiry. On a lesser plane, however, this same impulse degenerates into a frantic, feverish search, which devolves into a chaotic assemblage of myths and superstitions drawn from every corner of the world. Amid this maelstrom, the Greek found himself yearning, lost in heart and soul. To cope, he either masked his turmoil with an affected cheerfulness and superficial levity, or numbed himself entirely through the narcotic embrace of dark and somber Oriental superstitions. Thus, the once-proud Hellene, now a diminished figure, lingered in the ruins of his cultural foundation, yearning for the vitality and transcendence that had been lost.

We have arrived at this state of affairs in an especially vivid way since the revival of Alexandrian and Roman antiquity in the fifteenth century, following a long and complex interlude that defies easy description. On the heights of culture, we now find the same boundless thirst for knowledge, the same intoxicating delight in discovery, and the same profound secularization. Alongside these tendencies, however, there exists a pervasive sense of dislocation, a restless wandering without a true home, a habit of intruding upon foreign cultures and adopting their customs, a careless idolization of the present moment, or a dull and apathetic estrangement from life—all viewed through the fleeting lens of the current age. These symptoms unmistakably point to a common deficiency at the heart of this culture: the destruction of myth. Without myth, a culture loses its anchor, and the vitality that once gave it purpose and coherence begins to wither away.

It is nearly impossible to graft a foreign myth onto the cultural tree with lasting success. Such an attempt often inflicts grave harm upon the original tree. Occasionally, if the tree is strong and resilient enough, it might succeed in expelling the foreign element after a fierce and protracted struggle. More often, however, it languishes in a state of perpetual stunted growth or, conversely, deteriorates into an unnatural and overgrown decadence. We hold a belief in the robust and genuine core of the German spirit, a belief that gives us hope this spirit may possess the strength to purge itself of forcibly implanted foreign elements. Only the German essence, we dare to say, seems capable of this monumental task. We also believe it is within the realm of possibility that the German spirit will eventually return to itself, rediscovering its unique identity and innate vitality.

Some might argue that the German spirit must begin its efforts by confronting and removing the Romanic influences that have embedded themselves deeply within its culture. To these individuals, the recent war—with its displays of bravery and the grim grandeur of its sacrifices—might serve as an external catalyst, a call to action. Yet the true impetus for this transformation must come from within, spurred by the ambition to prove continually worthy of the towering figures who have charted this path before us: Luther, as well as our greatest artists and poets. Let no one believe, however, that such monumental battles can be waged without the support of one's household gods, without the mythical home that serves as both sanctuary and foundation. A "restoration" of all things German must be the bedrock upon which this struggle is undertaken.

If the German people, uncertain and hesitant, find themselves searching for a guide to lead them back to their long-lost home, the paths and landmarks of which have faded into obscurity, let them turn their ears to the beguiling and joyful call of the Dionysian bird. This wondrous creature hovers above, urging them forward, eager to show them the way. Its song carries with it the promise of rediscovery, the return to a life rich with meaning, myth, and the harmonious beauty that only a culture deeply rooted in its own essence can achieve. The Dionysian bird calls not just to remind the German spirit of its origin but to lead it back to the fertile ground from which it once drew its greatest strength.

Among the unique artistic effects of musical tragedy, we must highlight the remarkable Apollonian illusion that serves to shield us from direct and overwhelming unity with the Dionysian essence of music. This illusion allows our heightened musical emotions to find expression and resolution within an Apollonian realm, an interposed visible middle world where these energies can manifest and find release. In this process, it becomes apparent that this very discharge of emotion transforms the middle world of theatrical action—the drama itself—into something not only visible but also deeply comprehensible in a way that surpasses other forms of Apollonian art. Here, where Apollonian artistry is imbued with the spirit of music, its powers are elevated to their zenith. Thus, in the harmonious union of Apollo and Dionysus, we witness the fulfillment of the highest artistic aspirations of both forces.

However, the illuminated Apollonian imagery, intensified through its musical foundation, does not entirely achieve the same effect as the more restrained forms of Apollonian art. The epos, with its grandeur, or the silent perfection of sculpted stone, can command the viewer's eye to rest in serene admiration of the individuated world. Yet, this level of tranquil satisfaction is not fully replicated in the realm of musical tragedy, even with its heightened vibrancy and clarity. In observing the drama, we delve with acute perception into the restless and layered world of its motives. Yet, paradoxically, the drama itself appears less like a concrete reality and more like a symbolic tableau—one whose profound meaning seems tantalizingly close to comprehension, but still shrouded. It is as if this symbolic representation beckons us to peel back the layers and penetrate the mystery it obscures. At the same time, the brilliance and clarity of the scene rivet our gaze, preventing us from fully breaking through to the depths beyond.

Those who have not felt this simultaneous experience—of seeing with vivid clarity while yearning for a view beyond—may struggle to grasp how these two impulses coexist in the contemplation of tragic myth. Yet, to those who have truly immersed themselves as aesthetic spectators, this duality is among tragedy's most striking and defining characteristics. The viewer is both captivated by the spectacle and compelled to seek something more profound, beyond what is immediately presented. This tension between revelation and concealment lies at the heart of the aesthetic experience of tragedy.

Now, let us transpose this phenomenon, observed in the aesthetic spectator, to the creative process of the tragic artist. By doing so, we gain insight into the genesis of tragic myth. Tragic myth emerges from a synthesis of Apollonian and Dionysian impulses. On one hand, it shares with Apollonian art the pure joy of appearance and contemplation. On the other hand, it transcends and even denies this joy, finding a deeper, almost paradoxical satisfaction in the obliteration of the visible world of appearances. The essence of tragic myth lies in its epic portrayal of heroic struggle and exaltation. Yet, it is precisely here that we encounter its most enigmatic and compelling feature: the persistent and deliberate representation of suffering, harrowing defeats, agonizing inner conflicts, and the most wrenching dilemmas of human existence.

What drives this fascination with the painful wisdom of Silenus, the embodiment of the Ugly and Discordant, rendered over and over in myriad forms? Why is this dark and challenging subject matter so beloved, particularly in the most vibrant and flourishing periods of a people's history? Surely, it must arise from a profound and paradoxical delight—a higher form of joy found in confronting and embracing these tragic truths.

The fact that events unfold in such a tragic manner does not, in itself, explain the origin of a form of art like tragedy. Art, after all, is not a mere replication of the natural world's reality; rather, it stands as a metaphysical complement to that reality, existing alongside it as a force that seeks to transcend and even conquer it. Tragic myth, as a legitimate part of art, shares in this transformative, metaphysical purpose inherent in all art. But what, precisely, does it transform when it presents the phenomenal world to us in the image of a suffering hero? Certainly not the "reality" of this phenomenal world itself, for it seems to say to us: "Behold! Look closely! This is your life; this is the ticking of the clock marking your existence!"

Yet, if myth lays bare this life, is it meant to elevate and transfigure it for us? If not, how else can we explain the aesthetic pleasure we derive from watching these tragic images unfold before us? I am specifically addressing the kind of aesthetic pleasure that arises from tragedy, fully aware that such representations may, at times, provoke moral responses—such as a sense of pity or a feeling of moral triumph. But to those who would claim that the impact of tragedy stems entirely from these moral responses, as has so often been asserted in aesthetics, I must insist that such interpretations do not truly serve Art. Art, above all, demands purity within its realm. To properly understand tragic myth, we must begin by acknowledging that its defining pleasure resides purely within the aesthetic domain. It does not encroach upon the territories of pity, fear, or moral exaltation. The central question remains: how is it that the ugly and the discordant—the core elements of tragic myth—can evoke aesthetic pleasure?

To answer this, we must take a bold leap into the metaphysical realm of Art. I reiterate my earlier proposition: it is only when existence and the world are viewed as aesthetic phenomena that they become justified. Tragic myth functions within this framework to demonstrate that even what is ugly and discordant is an artistic game—an expression of the will's boundless joy, playing with itself in an eternal dance. Though this foundational aspect of Dionysian Art may seem difficult to grasp at first, its meaning becomes vividly clear when we consider the profound nature of musical dissonance. In fact, music, more than any other medium, offers us a glimpse of what it means for the world to be justified as an aesthetic phenomenon. The unique joy that tragic myth inspires arises from the same source as the pleasure we find in musical dissonance. Both draw from the Dionysian wellspring, where primal joy is found even in pain.

By comparing tragic myth to the musical experience of dissonance, might we not bring clarity to the elusive question of tragedy's emotional effect? Now, we understand what it means to view tragedy while simultaneously longing for something beyond the viewing. This state of mind mirrors the response to dissonance in music, which compels us to listen while evoking an equally strong yearning for something beyond the act of hearing. This striving for the infinite—the fluttering wings of longing that accompany our greatest pleasure in vivid reality—makes clear that both responses are fundamentally Dionysian phenomena. They repeatedly reveal to us the playfulness underlying creation and destruction, the building up and tearing down of the individual world, as an outpouring of primordial joy.

Heraclitus, the enigmatic philosopher, offers a striking analogy that enriches this insight. He likens the creative force of the world to a child at play—a child arranging stones or forming sandhills, only to scatter and dismantle them again. This image beautifully captures the essence of the Dionysian process, reminding us that all forms, even those most deeply felt, are ultimately fleeting. The tragic hero's suffering, like the dissonance in music, serves not to bind us to despair but to awaken in us a profound awareness of the infinite, a realization of the joyful transience that underlies existence.

To truly evaluate the Dionysian capacity of a people, it is essential to consider not only their music but also their tragic myth, as both stand as profound witnesses to this capacity. The deep connection between music and myth suggests that a decline in one inevitably signals a deterioration in the other. If the weakening of myth indicates a diminishing Dionysian spirit, then we must confront this truth with unflinching honesty. Observing the course of German culture should leave no doubt: whether in the abstract nature of our myth-less existence or in the descent of art to mere entertainment, the life-consuming, inartistic essence of Socratic optimism has revealed itself in all its starkness. Yet, amidst this apparent desolation, there are whispers of hope—hints that somewhere, in an unreachable depth, the German spirit remains alive, dreaming in its profound, untarnished health and Dionysian strength, like a dormant knight waiting for his awakening. From this mysterious abyss, the song of Dionysus rises, reminding us that the German spirit still dreams of its primal Dionysian myth in radiant, earnest visions.

Let none assume that the German spirit has permanently severed ties with its mythical home. How could this be, when it still understands so intimately the voices of the birds that sing of that home? One day, the German spirit will awaken, refreshed from its deep sleep, to destroy the dragons, vanquish the malignant dwarfs, and awaken Brünnhilde. Even the mighty spear of Wotan will be powerless to halt its path. Friends, those of you who believe in the power of Dionysian music, you also understand the meaning of tragedy for us. In tragedy, we find the rebirth of myth, emerging anew from the depths of music. In this renewal lies the promise of endless possibilities and the power to forget what is most disheartening. And what troubles us most deeply, perhaps, is the prolonged estrangement of the German spirit, forced to serve malevolent forces far from its true home. Yet, as you understand my allusions, so too will you grasp the hopes I share with you.

Music and tragic myth are not merely connected; they are two expressions of the same Dionysian force and cannot exist independently. Both emerge from a realm beyond the purely Apollonian, transfiguring the world with harmonies that make even dissonance fade into beauty. Both play with the sting of pain and suffering, trusting their profound magic to justify even the most tragic aspects of existence. Here, the Dionysian force stands revealed as the primal artistic drive, the source of all phenomena, creating a world of appearances where individuation blossoms. If we imagine dissonance incarnate—and what is man, if not this?—then life's continuation requires a glorious illusion, veiling its harsh nature with beauty. This is the true role of Apollo as the god of art: embodying the countless manifestations of illusion that make life worth living and inspire us to anticipate the next moment with eager joy.

Simultaneously, only as much of the Dionysian essence of existence enters human consciousness as can be counterbalanced by Apollonian transfiguration. These two artistic drives operate in strict harmony, adhering to an eternal balance of justice. In times like ours, when Dionysian energies rise with extraordinary intensity, it is clear that Apollo, veiled and unseen, has descended among us. A future generation will likely witness Apollo's grandest beautifying works, ensuring equilibrium is restored.

One cannot doubt this necessity, especially when transported, even in dreams, to the existence of ancient Greece. Picture yourself walking beneath towering Ionic columns, gazing out at a horizon of perfect, noble lines, with reflections of your form mirrored in radiant marble. Around you, solemn figures move in rhythmic harmony, their voices blending in a serene, melodic balance. Amid such constant influxes of beauty, one would surely raise their hands to Apollo and exclaim: "Blessed are the Hellenes! How magnificent Dionysus must be among you, if the god of Delos must bestow such beauty to temper your dithyrambic fervor!"

In this state of awe, perhaps an elderly Athenian, with the sublime gaze of Æschylus, would approach and reply: "Curious stranger, say also this: what profound sufferings must this people have endured to achieve such beauty! But come now, follow me to witness a tragic play and offer sacrifice at the temple of these two mighty deities."

Appendix

To understand The Birth of Tragedy (1872) properly, one must set aside a few things. The book had an impact—it even captivated readers in ways it fell short, especially in how it tied itself to Wagnerism, as though Wagnerism symbolized a cultural ascent or revival. Because of this association, the book became significant in Wagner's life. From that moment onward, great hopes were pinned on Wagner's name, hopes stemming directly from this work. Even today, during discussions about Parsifal, people often remind me that I, of all people, am responsible for elevating the perception of Wagner's movement as having high cultural value.

On more than one occasion, I've heard the book referred to as The Rebirth of Tragedy out of the Spirit of Music. People focused solely on the idea of a new formula to describe Wagner's art, its purpose, and its mission, missing entirely what was truly valuable in the book. A more accurate title would have been Hellenism and Pessimism. It would have more clearly communicated the book's core message: a lesson in how the Greeks triumphed over pessimism and the methods they used to overcome it.

Greek tragedy itself proves that the Greeks were not pessimists. Schopenhauer was mistaken on this point, as he was on many others.

When viewed without bias, The Birth of Tragedy feels out of step with its time. It might surprise readers to learn it was conceived during the turmoil of the Battle of Wörth. I pondered these ideas deeply during the cold nights of September before the walls of Metz, while nursing the sick. In fact, the book might seem like it was written fifty years earlier. It is politically neutral—some might call it un-German by today's standards. In places, it has a distinctly Hegelian tone, though only a few of its ideas carry the somber fragrance of Schopenhauer's philosophy.

At its heart lies the concept of the opposition between the Dionysian and Apollonian forces, which is then elevated to the level of metaphysics. History itself is interpreted as the unfolding of this tension. In tragedy, these two opposing forces dissolve into unity. Through this lens, unlikely connections emerge, as though they had always been destined to illuminate each other. For instance, it draws parallels between opera and revolution.

The book introduces two key innovations. First, it offers a deep understanding of the Dionysian phenomenon in Greek culture. It provides the first psychological exploration of this concept, recognizing it as the singular root of all Greek art. Second, it delivers a critical examination of Socratism. Socrates is revealed for the first time as a tool of Greek decay, a symbol of decline. He embodies the battle between rationality and instinct. Rationality pursued at any cost is exposed as dangerous, a force that undermines life itself.

Throughout the book, there is a notable and deliberate silence on Christianity. Christianity is portrayed as neither Apollonian nor Dionysian. Instead, it negates all aesthetic values—the only values that The Birth of Tragedy acknowledges. Christianity is framed as nihilistic in the broadest sense, standing in stark contrast to the Dionysian, which reaches the furthest heights of affirmation. Only in passing does the book refer to Christian priests, describing them as "a malicious breed of dwarfs" or as "subterranean beings."

This beginning is unique beyond words. I had discovered, through my own deepest experiences, the one symbol and counterpart to history: the phenomenon of the Dionysian. In understanding this, I became the first to grasp its true nature. Moreover, by identifying Socrates as a decadent, I provided undeniable proof that my psychological insight was not compromised by any moralistic bias. To see morality itself as a symptom of decadence is a revolutionary idea, a groundbreaking innovation in the history of knowledge. With this, I leaped far beyond the shallow debates about optimism and pessimism.

I was the first to uncover the essential opposition: on one side, the decaying instinct that turns against life with a bitter, hidden resentment—this includes Christianity, Schopenhauer's philosophy, and to some extent even Plato's ideas and other idealistic systems. On the other side is a formula of ultimate affirmation: a complete and unreserved acceptance of suffering, guilt, and all that is strange and questionable in existence. This ecstatic and joyful "Yes" to life, which embraces even its darkest aspects, is not just the highest insight—it is also the deepest. It is upheld by truth and science as well. Nothing in existence can be excluded or considered unnecessary. In fact, the very aspects of life rejected by Christians and other nihilists hold infinitely greater value in the hierarchy of existence than what the instincts of decadence allow or dare to acknowledge.

To understand this requires immense courage and, even more importantly, an abundance of strength. The farther one's courage reaches, the stronger one's will, the closer one comes to the truth. For the strong, perception—saying "Yes" to reality—is a necessity, just as avoidance, fear, and retreat into ideals are for the weak. The weak cannot afford to perceive the truth; they require lies for their survival—it is essential for them. Anyone who not only understands the concept of the Dionysian but also feels its resonance within themselves does not need Plato, Christianity, or Schopenhauer to be refuted. They can sense the decay in these ideas.

Through this understanding, I uncovered the true meaning of "tragedy" and the key to its psychology. As I recently explained, the affirmation of life—even when it involves its harshest and most difficult challenges—is the essence of the Dionysian. It is the will to life, celebrating its boundless creativity even as it sacrifices its finest forms. This is what I call the Dionysian, and it serves as the bridge to understanding the psychology of the tragic poet. Tragedy is not meant to rid us of fear and pity or to purge dangerous emotions through their release, as Aristotle misunderstood it. Instead, it leads us beyond terror and pity, allowing us to experience the eternal joy of becoming—a joy that even includes the ecstasy of destruction.

In this sense, I claim the title of the first truly tragic philosopher, standing as the complete opposite of a pessimistic philosopher. Before me, there was no integration of the Dionysian into philosophical thought, no tragic wisdom. I have searched in vain for traces of such wisdom, even among the great Greek philosophers of the two centuries before Socrates. One lingering doubt I have concerns Heraclitus, in whose company I often feel a warmth and clarity that I find nowhere else. Heraclitus's affirmation of impermanence and destruction— the core of Dionysian philosophy—his willingness to embrace conflict, transformation, and becoming while rejecting the static concept of "being," comes closest to my own thinking.

The doctrine of eternal recurrence, the unending cycle of all things repeating infinitely, might have already been hinted at by Heraclitus. At the very least, the Stoics, who inherited many of their fundamental ideas from him, reveal traces of this concept in their philosophy.

The End

Thank You for Reading

Dear Reader,

We hope this timeless classic has sparked your imagination and enriched your literary journey. Now that you've turned the final page, we want to share a vision for the future of reading—one where every classic you've ever wanted to explore is at your fingertips, in a format that best suits your life.

We'd like to invite you to gain immediate, unlimited digital & audiobook access to hundreds of the most treasured literary classics ever written—along with the option to secure deluxe paperback, hardcover & box set editions at printing cost. Together, we can spark a new global literary renaissance alongside our small, independent publishing house called "The Library of Alexandria."

Thousands of years ago, the Library of Alexandria stood as a beacon of knowledge—until it was lost to history. We aim to reignite that spirit of preservation and discovery right now, in the modern age—only this time, it's accessible to all, in every language and every format.

Picture a world where every timeless classic, novel, poem, or philosophical treatise is not only available to read but also updated for today's readers—modernized, translated into any language or dialect, and ready to enjoy in any format you choose, whether that is in an eBook, audiobook, paperback, or deluxe hardcover & box set version a printing cost.

By joining our movement to rebuild the modern Library of Alexandria, you become part of an unprecedented mission to offer:

- **Unlimited Audiobook & eBook Access to the Greatest Classics of All Time**

  Instantly explore thousands of legendary works, from Plato and Shakespeare to Jane Austen and Leo Tolstoy. All are instantly ready to read or listen to, giving you a complete literary universe at your fingertips.

- **Paperback & Deluxe Editions at Printing Costs:**

  Purchase any title in a paperback, deluxe hardbound, or deluxe boxset edition at printing costs, shipped right to your doorstep. Curate your personal library of Alexandria with editions worthy of display—crafted to last, designed to captivate, and delivered straight to your door.

- **Modern translations for Contemporary Readers in all languages and dialects**

  Discover a vast selection of classics reimagined in clear, current language—no more struggling with outdated phrases or obscure references. Next to the original versions, we aim to offer translations in as many languages and dialects as possible.

  As we continue our translation efforts and add new languages, readers everywhere can connect with these works as if they were written today. By bridging linguistic divides, you're contributing to ensuring that these timeless stories become more meaningful, accessible, and inspiring for people across the globe.

- **Your Personal Library of Alexandria:**

  Over the months and years, you'll curate a unique physical archive of classics—each volume a testament to your taste, curiosity, and love of knowledge. It's not just about owning books—it's about curating a cultural legacy you'll cherish and pass down for generations to come.

- **Join a Global Literary Renaissance:**

  Your support fuels an ongoing mission: allowing us to reinvest in offering deluxe print editions (including special boxsets) at their true cost, broaden the range of available formats and translations, and extend the reach of these works to new audiences worldwide. By joining today, you're not just preserving a legacy of masterpieces; you set in motion a powerful wave of literary accessibility.

  We are more than a publisher—we're a movement, and we can't do it alone. Your support lets us scale our mission, preserving and reimagining history's greatest works for tomorrow's readers.

Become a Torchbearer of knowledge.

Thank you for picking up this book and allowing us into your literary journey. As you turn the pages, know that you're part of something larger: a global effort to keep these stories alive, share their wisdom across borders and generations, and spark a true cultural revival for the modern era.

If this resonates with you—please consider taking the next step by visiting:

www.libraryofalexandria.com

With gratitude and a shared love of knowledge,

The Modern Library of Alexandria Team

Visit:

www.libraryofalexandria.com

Or scan the code below:

www.ingramcontent.com/pod-product-compliance
Lightning Source LLC
Chambersburg PA
CBHW010748310726
48980CB00003B/367

9781806297153